COMING HOME TO GREENLEIGH

COMING HOME TO GREENLEIGH

MAYA RUSHING WALKER

APOLLO
GRANNUS

First paperback edition March 2020

First large print edition March 2020

First hardcover edition March 2020

Published by Apollo Grannus Books LLC
www.apollogrannus.com

Cover design by Streetlight Graphics, www.streetlightgraphics.com

ISBN 978-1-7325158-7-1 (paperback)

ISBN 978-1-7325158-6-4 (ebook)

ISBN 978-1-7325158-8-8 (large print)

ISBN 978-1-7325158-9-5 (hardcover)

www.mayarushingwalker.net

To all those who struggle for and against the past

JOIN MY NEWSLETTER!

My weekly newsletter keeps my readers updated—almost to the day—with my latest publications, and offers lots of sneak peeks, chunks of works-in-progress, and your feedback will influence my decisions as I write. Join us and I'll send you a deleted scene from *Coming Home to Greenleigh*! (It's an alternate storyline!)

1

From the cozy refuge of her bed, Elisabeth could hear the sounds of the pipes clattering as the ancient boiler struggled to push heat around its network. This was the sound of the real world reminding her that it was time to deal with it.

She rolled over onto her back, squinting up into the sunlight as it filtered down through the leaves of the old oak tree next to her window. It all felt too familiar, this dread of facing whatever had to be faced on a fall day in Greenleigh.

Fall was Elisabeth's favorite time of year. Yes, it was sad. The angle of the New England sun was sad. The bare trees were sad. Even the slow-moving bugs were sad. But it had always seemed to Elisabeth that the brightness and energy of the summer weren't real anyway, and that fall was simply a return to the truth, the way things really were. Kind of like the realization after a night of drunken revelry that the world is a sober, sensible place, and that one had better take it seriously.

Elisabeth had never experienced a night of drunken revelry, but sometimes the joy of summer felt a little too breathless, a little too dizzy. Fall always felt more like the world that she knew. She would be able to see her breath when she went outside this morning, wet leaves would be littering the lawn. It would feel normal.

Her aching muscles were telling her that she must have spent the night scrunched into a stiff, tense ball. It was cold, and the heat wasn't managing to reach the second floor. She swung her legs over the side of the bed and sat up in one fluid motion; the ancient bed frame was so high off the floor, her feet dangled a foot above her slippers. She found herself staring blankly into the mirror over the antique oak dresser in the opposite corner of the room. Her curly brown hair was a tangled mess about her shoulders, and her face was blotched with fatigue. She smoothed her hair with her hands, gazing at the serious woman in the faded pink flowered nightgown.

Oh, my God, she thought. *I look so old. I don't look like I'm thirty.*

She pulled on a robe and made her way downstairs, padding through the kitchen, wincing at the cold. The radiators were hissing, but it was freezing downstairs, too. She swayed a bit as she measured out the coffee, listening to the rhythmic creaking of the wide pine floors, the sound familiar and comforting to her ears. As the coffee dripped, she wandered out of the kitchen and over to her office, a bright, south-facing room with big bay windows and a fireplace.

She peered outside through the wavy old glass. Mrs. McPherson was watering her roses next door, a bent figure in a bright yellow sun hat, wielding an ancient watering can that looked far too heavy for her. In the other direction, Elisabeth could see part of the town common and the red brick town hall, as well as the steeple of the Congregational church.

The office held dusty bookcases that had been in the same spot for at least a hundred years, jammed with an odd mix of fiction and law books, and the maple secretary in the corner was heaped high with papers. Elisabeth tried not to look, but her gaze fell to the stack anyway.

I should save some trees and just do all of that online, she thought. She was still back in the twentieth century, with all of the household bills arriving in the mail just as they had when she was a child, most of them still in her father's name, even though he'd been dead for many years.

She went over to peer at the stack, her hands shoved into the pockets of her robe as if afraid to touch the papers. With a quick, involuntary shudder, she backed away.

I'm going to fix everything, she promised herself. *It'll all be better. After today.*

She poured her coffee, and then by habit, checked the cookie jar, where she stashed the grocery money. Twenty dollars, plus a little change. Her stomach tightened, and she pushed the jar away and headed upstairs.

Her room was the same one she'd had her entire life. She kept all the other rooms shut and rarely went into them. Once in a while, if the wind was coming from the wrong direction, the hallway felt like a giant wind tunnel, and then she would check the windows everywhere just to make sure they were tight and caulked shut. She lived in fear of leaky ceilings and broken windows, and there was one corner pane of glass in her bedroom that she had duct-taped to within an inch of its existence rather than try to get it fixed. It was ugly, and it upset her to see it. But that was what one did in old houses like hers, because replacing windows would cost an obscene amount of money.

She could just about feel a draft under her robe, and it occurred to her that she should check the windows, but she knew what she really needed was to stop all of these depressing thoughts. She hurried into her bedroom, reminding herself that she was going to take action. She was going to stop the downward spiral, if she could just get out the door in order to do the deed.

Elisabeth scanned her closet and pulled out a blue flowered dress with a wide, generous skirt. She held it up to herself. *I won't try to look different from the way I always look,* she thought. Everyone at Mr. Murray's law firm knew her anyway. Everyone in town, for that matter, knew her. If she turned up on the doorstep of Lawson & Lawson wearing anything other than the usual, there would be no end to the gossip.

Better to look as if she were merely paying a friendly call. And anyway, the only business suit she owned was the cheap blue thing she had worn to her graduation from law school, and it had never fit well. She didn't bother with suits for court—what would be the point, since the judge had known her since she was a baby? But after her shower, as she was acknowledging to herself that she hadn't had a haircut in about two years and needed one desperately, the energetic ringing of the doorbell sent all thoughts of grooming out of her head. Panicked, she peered out the window.

She didn't have time to chat with Mrs. McPherson, even if she wanted to pass along some late-season tomatoes or basil plants—and Elisabeth was such a terrible cook, she didn't know what she would do with them anyway—but she saw that there were two women standing stiffly at the front door. The older of the two she recognized as Mrs. Miller, an elderly Greenleigh resident and widow. She was a well-known town busybody, as well as Elisabeth's client. Elisabeth occasionally pestered the social security office for her when her checks were late. The other, a good twenty years younger than Mrs. Miller, was a stranger.

"Darn!" Elisabeth muttered. Mrs. Miller was so difficult to deal with, and this had all the markings of the kind of interaction that she disliked the most: gossip, judgment, and minding someone else's business. She wanted to stay on Mrs. Miller's good side because she did refer clients to her, but she was so pretentious, it was sometimes hard to refrain from making a sarcastic comment in return. And what was worse, this would make her late for her Lawson & Lawson appointment.

For a moment, she wavered, tempted to not answer, but in the end she knew she couldn't afford to turn away business. She didn't know the other woman, so maybe this was a potential client. She didn't have any other clients at the moment, and she needed the work.

"Beth! I thought you weren't home, you took so

long to answer." Mrs. Miller's white hair was care-fully coiffed under a black felt hat, and she wore a heavy black wool coat. Mrs. Miller was one of those old timers who always made the big seasonal clothing switch after Labor Day, no matter what the weather did. She marched confidently into the front hall.

"I was saying to Angela, Beth is always happy to help." Mrs. Miller's companion followed a little awkwardly, murmuring hello as she passed Elisabeth, who stood helplessly holding the door open.

"Good morning, Mrs. Miller," Elisabeth said, trying not to sound desperate. "So nice to see you, but I—"

Mrs. Miller had already led her friend into the office, calling behind her, "Have you been outside yet? Frost! It feels like winter! You need to bring those geraniums in, dear. And don't forget to have that chimney swept, Beth, before you start any fires. Beth still uses her wood stoves, Angela. It's wonderful. She keeps up all these old traditions." She had begun to unbutton her coat, but changed her mind as she realized that the office was cold and that the wood stove wasn't lit.

Elisabeth bit back a retort. She used wood stoves because the central heating worked so poorly, and she couldn't afford to heat up the entire house with oil anyway. She also had a client who dropped off wood in lieu of payment. It had nothing whatsoever to do with tradition.

"Mrs. Miller," she began again, but Mrs. Miller was inviting Angela to have a seat in a wingbacked chair in front of the office fireplace. She hadn't stopped talking.

"Seventeen eighty, I believe. The Burnhams didn't move in until the 1800s, but the house was built in 1780. Of course, these bay windows aren't original—they're Victorian. There were additions with every new owner. Did you see the carriage house out back?"

Elisabeth sat down. She saw Mrs. Miller's friend smiling politely, and felt the flush creeping over her cheeks as she prayed for Mrs. Miller to stop talking.

"It's just a big old house," she tried to say, as Mrs. Miller talked over her.

"I wish everyone in Greenleigh took care of these old houses the way Beth does. People either knock them down or gut them and fill them with giant screen TVs and pool tables." She grimaced in distaste.

Sometimes, Elisabeth thought, *sometimes I wish this house would just burn down.*

"It's been in my family for so long," she said, aiming the comment at Mrs. Miller's friend. "I'm very fond of it."

Her stomach twisted. She hated playing a role in

Mrs. Miller's fantasy, but at this point in her life it was just too hard to fight.

"Exactly," Mrs. Miller beamed.

And if I don't get to that meeting, I'll be the last Burnham in this house. With this reminder, she interrupted Mrs. Miller, who was pointing out the butler's pantry and maid's quarters off the kitchen.

"I'm sorry, Mrs. Miller, but I've got an appointment this morning—"

"Oh! Well. This will just take a minute. This is Angela Stuart."

Angela had taken some lip balm out of her purse and was applying it to her chapped lips. She bobbed her head politely, but Elisabeth saw that her hands were shaking as she replaced the cap and returned it to her handbag.

"I told her, Beth, that you are the best lawyer in town. I would never go to anyone else, right, Angela?" Mrs. Miller put a firm hand on her friend's shoulder and went on without pausing for a reply. "I told her how much you've helped me with those dreadful social security problems and all the things you did after Bertie passed away, God rest his soul —" she raised her eyes heavenwards "—and thanks to you, I've been able to stay in my home."

"It's my pleasure, Mrs. Miller, I—" Elisabeth tried again, speaking a little louder, but Mrs. Miller continued.

"I knew her mother, you know, did I tell you that, Angela? She passed—oh, almost ten years ago, was it, Beth? It's so nice when young people stay in Greenleigh. So many of our best leave us and go to Boston or New York or California—"

Mrs. Miller paused, and Elisabeth saw an almost-imperceptible hesitation in her bony shoulders, a shadow that crossed her face briefly. This, of course, was why she kept reaching out to help Mrs. Miller. Abandoned by her children, all of whom were sick of Greenleigh and sick of their mum talking about Greenleigh, Mrs. Miller lived alone in a small, neat cottage in what used to be a modest, slightly run-down section of town. She was now surrounded by garish, newly-built faux-colonials populated by young families with lots of money and no taste, a daily reminder that the old were dying and the new didn't care about the old. Developers eyed those old parcels of land hungrily, hoping to subdivide and create tracts of identical homes on half-acre lots. There was much money to be made in getting rid of the stale and the old, and bringing in the new.

Elisabeth understood all too well the stubborn stuff that Mrs. Miller was made of, even though she didn't want to, and often feared that she herself was made of the same. Mrs. Miller would never sell. She would never leave. She exasperated her grown children and annoyed her neighbors, but she would only be pried away from Greenleigh by death itself.

"What can I do for you, Ms. Stuart?" Elisabeth took the opportunity to jump into the conversation. "Mrs. Miller and I are old friends. She's known me almost since I was born."

"Angela has a problem," Mrs. Miller announced, lowering her voice dramatically. "Go ahead, Angela. Tell her." She nodded toward Elisabeth.

Suddenly, it was as if the dam had burst. Angela Stuart's face crumpled as she dissolved loudly into heaving sobs.

Elisabeth rose hastily and fetched a box of tissues. She sometimes had distraught clients cry during their meetings, so she always kept the tissues handy, but another glance at the clock confirmed her fears. She was going to be late for her meeting.

"I'm sorry, Ms. Burnham. I thought I would be able to go through with this, but—" Angela choked and pressed a wad of tissues to her mouth.

"She wants a divorce," Mrs. Miller said. She eyed Angela with displeasure. "Come on, Angela. We talked about this. You need to tell Beth your story."

Elisabeth tried to still her racing heart. Divorce? She'd never handled a divorce before.

Angela was now snuffling miserably, head bowed. In spite of her reddened eyes and puffy nose, she was quite pretty in a comfortable, round sort of way. She had dark hair pulled back in a bun, and her skin was very fair. Her cranberry-colored sweater was elegantly styled and clearly hand-knit.

Mrs. Miller was leaning over to squeeze her friend's hand. "Beth is the best person in the world to help you."

"I don't know," Elisabeth stammered. "I—I don't usually handle divorces." She wasn't in any kind of position to turn away business. And she never said no to anyone who begged her for help. She often went out on a limb for people, researching issues and arguing obscure points on things she'd never studied in school. But divorce? She had no idea what one was supposed to do in a divorce case. Wouldn't that involve going deep into people's private lives and personal problems?

Elisabeth thought of the many times she had tried to ignore the angry shouts of her mother floating up through the registers in her bedroom floor. Her father had never raised his voice, but he'd often stayed away for weeks at a time, supposedly "on the road" selling cleaning products. He couldn't be counted on to bring in any kind of steady income, and he mostly just wanted to play cards with his buddies in the back room of the Athena Diner. It drove her mother crazy, especially when he managed to also spend through their tiny income on extravagant presents and fancy treats.

Why don't they just get a divorce, she often thought. But now that she was an adult, she understood perfectly well why adults stayed in bad relationships.

It was called "being stuck" and she knew all about "being stuck." But what right did she, of all people, have to advise someone on how to get unstuck?

She, Elisabeth Burnham, the queen of stuckness. Stuck-dom? Whatever. Stuck in Greenleigh. Stuck in this old house. Stuck in failure.

Angela was saying timidly, "Sarah is right. I'm here to ask about getting a divorce."

"She's staying with me," Mrs. Miller added. "Because she's left him."

"I've left him," Angela whispered. "I've been thinking about this for a long time—this wasn't something I did rashly, I mean. And Sarah said she could help—"

"Beth can help you," Mrs. Miller said. She turned to Elisabeth. "Nearly thirty years of marriage. You can't fix something that broken."

Angela choked, and a fresh sob escaped. This was one occasion where Mrs. Miller's plain-spoken Yankee honesty was definitely not helpful, Elisabeth thought ruefully.

But what if she was right? Was it impossible to fix thirty years of broken?

That's about as long as my life, Elisabeth thought. *I wonder if I'm thirty years of broken.*

What if my flavor of broken is not fixable?

Then she looked up at the clock and nearly jumped out of her skin.

"Oh, ladies. I'm sorry. I'm very late for an appointment. Perhaps we could meet tomorrow?"

Angela was on her feet. "I'm so s-s-sorry," she stuttered. "Of course, don't let us keep you—"

"Don't run away," Mrs. Miller said loudly, rising before Angela could scurry off. She caught her friend's elbow and turned to Elisabeth.

"Angela will never have the courage to come here on her own. Why don't you come over to my house tomorrow? You can discuss everything over a nice cup of tea."

Elisabeth reflected that Angela would never have the courage to say anything in front of Mrs. Miller, either. She would have to get her alone. But she nodded, following both ladies to the door. "Yes, of course. I'll stop by after lunch. Maybe at around three?"

Angela shook hands with her, the grasp tentative, her smile watery and weak. "Thank you."

Elisabeth could hear Mrs. Miller's voice, expounding on the layout of the lawn and the placement of the shrubbery, as she shut the door behind them. She raced to grab her briefcase from the front room before dashing out the door and down the sidewalk in the opposite direction from the two ladies.

First things first, she thought, panting. *Save myself, then save Angela Stuart.*

If I can.

2

"I'm supposed to see Elisabeth Burnham this morning. Do you know her? Beth Burnham."

Richard Murray, Senior was speaking with his mouth full of jelly doughnut, coffee balanced atop a thick stack of documents. He coughed slightly, and Shawn tried not to wince, imagining what would happen if he suddenly choked on jelly doughnut and had to spit it out all over himself, as well as the red oriental carpet below.

"She knew my daughter," Ricky Senior continued, chewing and swallowing, then swiping at his mouth with his shoulder. Shawn tried not to wince again.

"She's a good kid, always liked her. She was supposed to come in this morning but she didn't show —and now she's out front. I've got this brief to get filed by five or this case isn't going to trial and I'm in a lot of hot water. Will you see her for me? Tell her I'm sorry I missed her."

"But—" Shawn stammered, suddenly panicked. Meet Beth Burnham? Now?

He wasn't ready. He'd repressed all thoughts of Beth for years. He hadn't arrived at his new job this morning with even the vaguest idea that Beth would be on his agenda today, or ever.

"She knew my daughter," Ricky Senior added again, unhelpfully. He backed carefully out of the doorway, nearly knocking over a passer-by, and cursed gently as the coffee slopped over the sides of his cup and trickled down onto the stack of papers.

"Tell her I'm sorry," he repeated, his voice echoing down the hall. "Hey, I need someone to run to the courthouse for me," he boomed. The sound of his footsteps quickened, then faded until it disappeared.

"Right," Shawn muttered. He got up and shut the door.

Elisabeth Burnham. Did he know her?

Excellent question, he thought grimly. *Did I ever know her?*

He paced in front of the desk a few steps, stopped, then went to peer out the window. It was a generous corner office, with a separate sitting area some distance away from his desk, surrounded by leather armchairs and oriental rugs. It was the very least that a managing partner of a venerable old New England firm deserved, never mind that it was in tiny Greenleigh.

It was also a sight better than his old office in New York, he acknowledged, turning around to admire the handsome mahogany desk and matching credenza. While he had made the cut for partner in New York, space there was at a premium, and a junior partner in a firm of 150 attorneys was not exactly a candidate for a corner office. The pay here was never going to have the possibilities that practicing in New York offered, but of course life here did not cost what it did in New York. The thought entered his mind regretfully as he contemplated the evenings at the opera and the grand art galleries he had left behind.

He shook his head. No point in being morose about it. His father needed him home, and so he had come.

And of course, the truth was that he was done with New York. He'd run out of Greenleigh as fast as he could, the moment he'd had his diploma in hand, thinking that New York would be the cure for Greenleigh. In the end, it had not been. He had loved its arts, its culture, its status as a welcoming beacon for soul searchers everywhere. But he couldn't fight it any longer. Greenleigh was calling him back, and as much as he wanted to resist it, age had made him honest.

And part of the honesty thing was admitting that he'd never stopped thinking about Elisabeth. Somewhere deep inside of him, in the back of his mind and in the depths of his heart, he had kept thinking about her. He'd wondered about her life, her well-being. He hadn't reached out to her even once since that warm August evening so many years ago. He'd visited his father faithfully every Christmas and occasionally for summer weekends, but he hadn't seen or spoken to Elisabeth. He hadn't run in to her around town, hadn't spoken of her to anyone, hadn't heard a single thing about her.

What he had done was resent her bitterly. He'd almost hated her for what she'd done. But something inside still wondered how she was, where she was.

But never why. That was one question that had never floated into his mind. He had never once wondered why she hadn't left Greenleigh with him. Because he knew the answer. Greenleigh got its claws into you and never let go. Just look at him now—back to stay.

Shawn walked back to his desk and sat down, but on the edge of the chair. It swiveled forward, and he nearly lost his balance because he'd been too tentative. He grabbed the edge of the desk.

Now he would have to see her, to talk to her. It was the last thing he'd expected and possibly the thing he dreaded most. He was angry and bitter, and he was afraid he might say something he unforgivable.

His mother was so fond of Beth, he thought. She'd died with such regret that she wouldn't be alive long enough to see them marry.

The pit in his stomach told him that his walk down memory lane had gone too far, so he wrenched his mind away from thoughts of his mother and the horrible year she'd spent battling leukemia when he was in college. And now, he'd come home to make sure he didn't have any regrets. His father was getting older and starting to fail. No way in hell was he going to make things worse by mooning over Beth, his mother's last months, and past mistakes and the consequences of past mistakes.

He felt a sour taste in his mouth and took a quick swig of the lukewarm coffee on his desk. *I should be ready for this,* he said ruefully to himself. *It's been a long time. And it's been over for a long time.*

He shrugged into his suit jacket, and strode toward the door.

He walked out into the reception area, prepared to greet Elisabeth with icy formality. But no one was there. He checked with the receptionist.

"Ms. Burnham is in conference room A. But I thought she was waiting for Mr. Murray Senior?"

"He couldn't make it, so I'll speak to her instead. Would you pick up my phone for a few minutes? I'm sure I won't be long."

Shawn had no idea where conference room A was. He walked down the hallway, past the mail room, past the library. He could hear a low rumble of conversation coming from one office, a group of laughing voices in another. After a week at his new job, he still wasn't sure of everyone's names, and since he'd taken the aggressive step of banning most pointless meetings, he hadn't yet been in a conference room. But he found it, a few steps away from the kitchen. The door was shut.

Shawn was startled to discover that his palms were sweating. He paused outside the door, wiping them surreptitiously on his pants and adjusting his tie. He knocked softly. There was no answer. He cracked the door open, then went in, closing it quietly behind him.

Her effect on him was instant, and he wondered briefly if it was because he was already nervous, or if she really still had that power over him. He knew her immediately from the angle of her head, the intensity of her concentration on something out the window. She was dressed in a drop-waisted, wide-skirted blue floral print dress, with a bit of lace collar evident. Shiny brown curls, tinged slightly gold in the morning light, were neatly caught up in a ponytail knotted with a dark blue bow. From the back, she still looked like a schoolgirl.

For one brief moment, his heart ached terribly for what might have been. It was as if time had stood still. When he left Greenleigh, she was twenty-two, he was twenty-six. They were both so young. The world was full of options. There was no reason to let Greenleigh hold them back, to let the sadness of the cycle of life and death bring them down. Go, go, his mother would have urged. Go live your life, go do new things, go see the world. Green-leigh will always be here.

He could see now that this last sentence was the nail in the coffin for Beth. *Greenleigh will always be here.* That had been the problem all along.

And he hadn't been enough for her to break through that barrier. Greenleigh was much older, stronger, and wiser than he was.

Almost as quickly as the thoughts had passed through his mind, he felt the searing pain of rejection and disappointment, and the intense emotion in his gut registered in his brain as resentment and contempt. He refused to let her imagine that he had cared beyond that one moment, all those years ago, when he had realized that she was not going to go with him to New York. Damn her, he would not give her the satisfaction of supposing that she had wounded him so profoundly by holding him more cheaply than her nag of a mother and her stupid library clerk job.

"Elisabeth." What the hell? He'd never called her by her full name. She'd always been Beth to him.

When she heard him speak her name, she turned around in surprise. For an instant, she looked shocked, but then her clear, brown-eyed gaze settled on him in dismay.

So she has the grace to be upset, does she, he thought. He evaluated her coldly, as if he were picking over produce at the supermarket, but his chest felt as if it would explode with tension and stress.

She didn't look well. Her color wasn't very good, and there were shadows below her eyes. She was thin, too thin. He felt instinctive fear, the way he had since those days of his mother's illness. He and illness would never have an easy relationship.

Shawn tamped down his fear with ugliness. *She's probably still doing the fetch-and-carry routine for her mom,* he thought sardonically. Working double shifts at that clerk job. Being the model dutiful daughter and throwing her life away. Doing exactly what she had been doing all those years ago. A life she had preferred to a life with him.

He couldn't stop his biting tongue. "You look surprised," he said.

"I am—" she stammered. "I—I didn't expect to see you here."

I'll bet you didn't, he thought. *I'll bet you didn't expect to ever see me again.*

"So sorry to disappoint you," he snapped. "I didn't expect to see you here, either. This isn't any more pleasant for me than I'm sure it is for you."

"I didn't suppose that it was. I must have the wrong room. I'm supposed to be meeting Mr. Murray." There was a frosty edge to Elisabeth's words.

"I'm sorry. But I'm the one you'll be dealing with."

To his surprise, his words caused more distress than he'd expected. Sure, he wasn't eager to have this meeting, and he knew she wouldn't be, either. But he hadn't expected her to look as if she were about to faint.

"What do you mean?" she gasped. Her face had blanched, and the fingers of one hand grasped the edge of the conference table. He moved involuntarily toward her, concerned for a moment that she might actually pass out.

But she did not faint; she merely continued to stare up at him, knuckles whitening as she gripped the table.

"Does Mr. Murray know I'm here?" There was a

choked quality to her words, but her voice was under careful control.

"He does. He said you had an appointment this morning." Elisabeth's cheeks reddened. She had put her briefcase on the shiny conference table, a worn, sad leather thing with a tarnished brass buckle. It looked like it had sat in an attic for fifty years, which Shawn realized it probably had. He knew exactly what her attic looked like, and that it was filled with old Burnham hand-me-downs.

He could see her reflection slanted across the surface of the table, the troubled bent of her head. What was wrong with him? It was as if he was out-side of himself, able to evaluate her every gesture, as if he wasn't the one she had dumped so easily.

"I apologize for being so late," she said. "I had a visit from a client just as I was walking out the door."

Client? Shawn suddenly felt odd, as if the ground beneath him had buckled. Stupid as it was, he couldn't think of Beth as having gone on with her life without him. In his mind, she was still the Beth of so many years ago. Was it possible that she had gone on with her life, had indeed created a new life without him over the past years?

He'd assumed that the problem was with her, that she'd preferred the dullness of her safe, small town existence over the adventures she would have at his side. It had wounded him badly to imagine that her passion for him took second place to being a clerk at the library and running errands for her shrewish mother, but it had also justified his anger, and his dropping all thought of her from his existence.

He hadn't thought at all that perhaps she had altered her own life, that she might have been able to achieve that on her own, without him.

He suddenly realized that she was speaking.

"I'll just call Mr. Murray again for a new appointment. Please tell him how sorry I am for being late." Elisabeth was drawing herself up to leave. She reached for the worn-out briefcase, took a step back from the table.

"Actually, Ricky Senior asked me to speak to you today. About whatever it was you were going to talk to him about." Shawn did not give up his place in front of the door. He watched curiously as she looked up at him in obvious panic.

"What?" she exclaimed.

Shawn shrugged. "He said he had some idea of why you were here, and that you were better off speaking to me about it. Something like that." He itched to pull out his phone to check the time. His impatience was growing. This encounter was both unpleasant and mystifying. *Spit it out, Beth*, he wanted to say. *Is this some kind of stupid errand for your mother?*

"Oh." Elisabeth slowly put her briefcase back down on the table. She looked tentative, as if she were reorganizing her thoughts. Just as Shawn was about to give in to the urge to make an excuse and flee, she spoke.

"Shawn. I—I wonder if we can sit down. If you don't mind."

She spoke quickly, but quietly, and Shawn saw her press her lips together in that brave mannerism that he knew so well. Life had been so hard for her, he thought involuntarily. Damn it, why hadn't she let him just take her away from it all?

She was looking up at him, almost desperately.

He caved. But angrily.

He hadn't asked for this. It wasn't fair. He wasn't a saint. And he didn't want any part of whatever this was. He wanted her to go away and let him get back to his life. The life where he made smart decisions, not dumb ones like hers.

"All right," he replied. "But I haven't got a lot of time. Is this an errand for your mother?"

"My mother died a few years ago," Elisabeth said.

Shawn stood where he was, staring at her and feeling foolish.

"But it's okay. Of course you wouldn't have known that," she continued.

Shawn bit back the automatic words that sprang to his lips. Why had he not known? Dead? He couldn't imagine Beth without that albatross of a family.

So she was alone, then. All alone, presumably in that gigantic old house. He wanted to apologize for his cruelty, but he didn't know how.

Actually, he did know how. He needed to start over. This meeting, thrust upon him unexpectedly, had gone all wrong. He was too busy feeling sorry for himself, and he hadn't been paying attention to what was going on in the actual moment. That was poor behavior on his part, and he knew it. He also knew why he was feeling so angry and so cruel, and he was ashamed. She hadn't loved him enough to escape the Greenleigh trap, and he was humiliated. Well, he could be the bigger person. He could be generous.

They needed to start over. At least right now.

"I'm really sorry, Beth. I didn't know. And yes. Let's sit down. And talk," he agreed.

3

Only the fact of a mere twenty dollars left in the grocery jar and the scary pile of bills on her desk could have persuaded Elisabeth to sit down with Shawn Waterstone for any reason.

She couldn't believe what was happening to her. It was all she could do not to just pick up her briefcase and leave, but Shawn stood between her and the door, preventing any kind of dignified exit. It had taken her a lot of courage to come to this decision at all, and she had been tempted half a dozen times during her walk to the Lawson & Lawson offices to just cut and run, but she'd stuck it out. If she pushed past Shawn and fled, she'd be wasting all that anguish, all that effort.

Shawn looked great. She had to admit it to herself. He even looked like he had a tan, a suggestion of a summer on Cape Cod, his ash-blond hair cut briskly in almost a crew cut to frame the angular lines of his face. Eyes somewhere between gray and hazel and brown glared down at her from way above her own five feet, two inches.

She had no idea what he was doing here in Greenleigh, here at Lawson & Lawson. Was he visiting? No, that couldn't be right. He must work here. But why? He'd been so eager to get the hell out of Greenleigh—so eager, in fact, that he'd argued her into going with him. She had nothing going for her in Greenleigh, he'd said. If she'd just leave Greenleigh, he would take her to New York with him and she could do anything she wanted. She could finish that college degree that was taking her so long to pay for, credit by credit. She could study something interesting, like English or art history, instead of the practical accounting and finance that her mother had pestered her into studying. He could take care of her, and they would be happy.

But when the appointed time came, she'd been watching the old grandfather clock in the front hall, watching the hands tick past, watching her opportunity go by. She could hear her mother coughing upstairs, she could see the bills on the kitchen table, her father's name still on them, the pay stubs from her job and the empty jar of grocery money, and she knew she wasn't going anywhere.

And she knew she should have told Shawn this, but she couldn't explain why she wasn't able to do what was clearly the smart thing to do. Who kept living with their mother at the age of twenty-two? Who turned away an offer of help that was based in love and trust? What kind of person did that?

This kind of person, she thought miserably. *I'm that person.*

And now look at me. She almost laughed. *It's like I've come full circle. I can't run away from it, and poor Shawn can't run away from me.*

She looked up at Shawn and decided to feel sorry for him. He was about to have the most uncomfortable business meeting of his lifetime. She could see his discomfort, and none of this was his fault, unless it lay in his desire to fix other people's problems.

"Ricky Senior didn't tell me what this was about," he was saying. "Can I do something for you?"

"I'm not sure," Elisabeth said. She took a deep breath. "Last year, Mr. Murray said that—" She stopped. Could she say it?

She would have to.

She started again. "Mr. Murray said that if I ever needed help, I shouldn't hesitate to talk to him. I didn't actually think I would need the help, but I think I do."

Another pause. Shawn was visibly perplexed. He leaned back in his chair and motioned for her to go on.

"I need work," she said, finally.

"Work," Shawn said. He frowned in confusion. "You wanted to ask Ricky Senior for work?"

"Yes," Elisabeth said. "I didn't want to ask. But—I need another source of income." Her voice was hoarse, so she cleared her throat. "It's been difficult. Trying to keep that house going."

At that moment, she saw Shawn's expression change, and she wished she hadn't.

The house. Even though she'd never told him why she couldn't go with him to New York, why she couldn't leave Greenleigh, he had to know that her attachment to the Burnham home was at the bottom of it. The house represented everything that the Burnhams had ever worked for, stood for, and been trapped by. To let it go was unthinkable.

It had meant more to her than Shawn did, was the unspoken accusation.

"I'm sure there's enough work around here for an army of assistants," Shawn said. A cool mask had replaced his initial expression of confusion. "But I've only just started working here. I don't know why

Ricky Senior thought I would know anything about hiring you."

"I'll do whatever you need to have done." Elisabeth brought out a notepad from her briefcase, a cheap ballpoint pen clipped neatly to the spiral binding. "Athena Diner," the lettering on the pen read. Elisabeth saw Shawn's gaze drop to the pen for a moment, then go back to her face. Embarrassed, she unhooked the pen from the notebook.

"Maybe you should be talking to his admin assistant," Shawn said. "That's where all the temp clerical help would be—" He stopped, something registering on his face.

Elisabeth had looked up from her notebook. Temp clerical help? She tried to tamp down the little bubble of fury that began to rise in her belly, in her chest. She knew she couldn't blame him. When he'd left Greenleigh, she was a library clerk. She was working her painful way through a bachelor's degree in accounting. There was no reason why he would think that she had changed.

But she was angry. She'd worked so hard to get that degree, and then she'd worked doubly hard to get through law school. She was short, she was plain, she was ordinary—she knew all of this—but she resented it when people assumed she had no education and skills, just because she was a mousy little thing in a flowery dress. Like when those big insurance companies kicked her clients around because they were poor and barely literate, unable to comprehend the fine print on their policies. It made her mad.

She took a deep breath. She was desperate. She needed the work. She'd done the math, looked at the number of hours she had available in a week, and at the bills she had to pay. If he wanted to give her secretarial work, she would take it. At least it was in a law firm, and maybe they would eventually give her something else to do, something that matched her experience and abilities.

"I'll do whatever you need to have done," she repeated. She realized that she had been nervously clicking her pen, so she put it down. "But I'm actually a lawyer. I've been in solo practice here in Greenleigh for a few years. I'm just having a hard time right now."

There were so many other things she could say. She could tell him that she'd inherited the money for law school when her mother died—she discovered her mother's hidden nest egg that she'd inherited from her own family decades back, which made complete sense. Her mother had to have been raiding that fund for years and years, because there couldn't have been enough money from the Burnhams alone to keep the house going. She could tell him that she'd tried to get a job at some of the lower-tier firms in town, but that no one wanted a general practitioner who wasn't going to bring lucrative clients into the practice with her. She could tell him that she was sometimes flooded with business but that her clients often couldn't pay her, and that the local natural foods store sent groceries every week because they were paying off a legal bill from the previous year.

She could tell him that her beloved leather briefcase was her grandfather's, and that Judge Burnham had presided in the old white frame courthouse for over fifty years. But wait, he already knew that. Of course. When you almost marry someone, he knew all of these sorts of things. He just didn't know who she'd become in his absence.

And what I've become, she thought, *is broke and a failure*.

She began again. "I'm sorry I didn't make myself clear. But it's probably a waste to have me doing clerical work. I can do a lot more."

"If you don't mind working at a paralegal's wage, we have all the research work you could want," Shawn said. "I'm sorry that I misunderstood. And we could probably get you on some cases, it's just that it would depend on the individual attorney—"

"I understand," Elisabeth said.

"—and as long as there isn't any conflict of interest, of course. You'll have to check with the attorneys in charge of the projects to make sure you aren't representing anyone at odds with our clients."

"Yes, obviously," Elisabeth said, a little tersely.

"I'm sorry, I had to make that clear," Shawn said. His voice had turned chilly, professional. He was looking distracted, as if his mind were drifting elsewhere.

No, no, thought Elisabeth. *Come back, Shawn. I'm not done with this horrible conversation.*

"I have something else I need to ask," she said. She paused, then said in a rush, "I need to ask for an advance. I'm afraid that things have—things have gotten that bad."

Shawn's gaze snapped back, and his eyes, which had been glazing over, sharpened. For a moment, he looked at her, almost as if he were trying to figure her out. Then he nodded. "All right. Come in later this afternoon. I'll leave a contract with the receptionist, and a check. You can sign the contract when you pick up the check."

"Thank you." Elisabeth rose. Shawn stood up automatically, but his attention was on his phone, which he had pulled out of his pocket. He appeared to be scrolling rapidly through a text chat.

At the door, she stopped for a moment to put on her coat, and turned just in time to see Shawn turn to watch her go. She felt herself flush, just as she saw him avert his eyes. So he hadn't wanted her to know that he was watching her.

"Shawn," she said, then in a rush, "Shawn, why did you come home?"

"My father needed me," he said.

She nodded, twisted the handle, and walked out without another word.

Once outside, Elisabeth felt the resolve that had kept her back up and the tears down dissolve. She felt the blood rush into her face as she recalled the humiliation of having to ask Shawn Waterstone, of all people, for a job. And the humiliation of the moment where he revealed what he thought of her abilities—that she was never going to be anything more than that library clerk he'd once known.

She wondered if her knees would buckle under her. She stopped outside the entrance, steadied herself with one hand against the sun-warmed brick of Lawson & Lawson. She gasped, choking on a painful knot of tears in her throat. She couldn't stay there—it was a busy entrance and she might run into someone she knew—so she hurried blindly down the street toward home.

She went to sit on a bench in the shaded garden of the old Congregational church, not knowing where else to go in a town so small that she had practically walked the entire length of the downtown merely by walking from home to the offices of

Lawson & Lawson. The branches of an ancient black walnut tree dwarfed the tiny courtyard, and it was cold here despite the beautiful warm fall day. The stone of the bench seeped right through her coat and into her bones. The blue sky above seemed to be overlooking another planet entirely.

How on earth had she ended up in this situation?

It was clear that she should have gone with him to New York. If she had, this wouldn't be happening. What could be worse than having to beg Shawn Waterstone for a job? If she had planned it herself, she could not imagine a more devastating turn of events. Obviously, she'd never forgotten him. She'd loved him so much, the only source of sunshine in her colorless life in those days. They'd fallen in love during the summers when he'd come back to Greenleigh from college and borrow stacks of books from the library where she worked as a clerk. He would chat with her as she shelved books, ask her out for coffee and take her out for drives.

She'd often teased him, asking him to tell her why he'd fallen in love with her, because she couldn't believe it. He was handsome, smart, and had so many exciting things to look forward to. She was so ordinary, just a Greenleigh girl from an old Greenleigh family. He told her that he loved her patient goodness and dedication to doing the right thing, and that she reminded him of all the good things about home.

Once he'd said to her that he loved her because his mother loved her, and he always trusted his mother. She hadn't known what to make of that, because she was fairly certain that her own mother did not love her, at least not in that all-encompassing, uncomplicated way. Of course, she couldn't say that, but she often felt he knew it as well as she did.

She'd grown close to his mother, and when the leukemia took her, the hole in her life was vast, and she wasn't sure it could ever be fixed. Certainly, she knew that Shawn would never be the same again. For a long time, he didn't say much, and she didn't ask him to. There were a lot of silent dates that summer.

But he'd changed irreversibly. He couldn't bear to be in Greenleigh anymore, which she found mystifying. His mother had loved Greenleigh, so why wouldn't he stay in Greenleigh? But he was done with small town living, he'd said. Done, and ready to move on. And he argued that it was bad for her, too. They would get out of Greenleigh and that would fix everything that was wrong and bring the light back into their lives.

Unspoken was his opinion that her mother and the old house were bad for her. Elisabeth knew it was true, and she listened eagerly at first. But when the time came to actually leave, she found herself unable to get out the door. It wasn't her head that wouldn't get in the game. It was her body. It just wouldn't go.

He had been right all along. I just couldn't do it, she thought. *And now he'll get to see how right he was to leave Greenleigh, and how mistaken I was to have not gone with him.*

4

Later that afternoon, Elisabeth returned to Lawson & Lawson. She was terrified that she would see Shawn again, but she needn't have worried. The promised packet of paperwork was there, as well as the promised check. In addition, there was a sheaf of documents with a sticky note on it from Richard Murray, Junior. She remembered him from high school, a chubby, red-faced guy with his father's trademark good humor.

"Hey Beth! HELP!" Ricky Junior had scribbled, along with a googly-eyed smiley face.

So Shawn had found her some lawyer work to do after all. Elisabeth thanked him silently, but also felt herself shrink into a ball of shame. This was no way to live, she thought, constantly afraid of small kindnesses.

Elisabeth was at Lawson & Lawson early the next morning, making use of their library and legal databases. Ricky Junior's paralegal obtained a log-on for her and showed her how to get into the computer system. She seemed relieved that Elisabeth would have the authority to handle aspects of Ricky Junior's cases that she herself could not.

"Here," she said, plunking a stack of folders in front of her. "I've been stuck on these for a week, and Ricky Junior doesn't have time get into them. Maybe you can take them off my desk?"

"Sure," Elisabeth said gratefully. She still felt the sting of yesterday's humiliating conversation with Shawn acutely, but this work was going to take care of her past-due electric bill and put some heating oil in the tank. She would be able to pay the Nutley boys for their yard work. She wouldn't be able to think about a new roof or a paint job, but that was something to worry about in the spring. For now, this pile of folders and her willingness to beg would take care of things.

She stopped by Ricky Junior's office to drop off the initial results of her work. She hadn't known him well, but he appeared to remember her in all kinds of surprising detail. In fact, his gaze was admiring as he listened to her explain where she had decided to take the arguments in his case.

"Am I getting this completely wrong?" she asked,

hesitant, when she noticed that his attention appeared to be wandering.

He jumped and turned red. "I'm so sorry, Beth. No, I was just thinking about how both of us are lawyers and we're sitting here in my office discussing a case. Isn't it weird? I remember back when you and my sister were friends at school, but I just never imagined—are you joining the firm? Is that why Shawn hired you?"

Elisabeth didn't know what to say. So Shawn, at least, hadn't said anything to anyone about the truth.

"No," she said. She didn't want to lie, but she also didn't want to sabotage her own private practice reputation by sounding like she was desperate. "I have some space in my calendar, and I wanted to learn some new things. I've never done one of these corporate cases before." She winced inwardly. Actually, her personal calendar right now was empty, but for Angela Stuart.

"I'm glad to see you around here. It would be awesome if you came aboard, but I get it if you like your freedom." Ricky nodded in the direction of his closed door and lowered his voice. "It can get stuffy around here. And stressful."

Elisabeth gathered up her notes, thinking that Ricky Junior had no idea what stress was like. "Is Shawn around this morning?" she asked casually.

"No, he's not," Ricky Junior replied. "He takes a lot of mornings off to manage things at his dad's factory. You know about his dad's heart attack, right?"

"Oh, no. I didn't. That's terrible. Is he all right?" *So that's what he meant by his father needing him home,* she thought.

"He's getting better, but he's not allowed to do anything stressful. I guess that company puts a lot of demands on him," Ricky replied. "Shawn left a really amazing firm on Wall Street to come home and look after the company. At least if he works here, he can step out and do stuff at home." He shook his head. "He's such a good guy. Who would give up that kind of life in order to come back to a boring little town like Greenleigh?"

He stood up and reached for his jacket. "Let me take you to lunch, Beth. We'll celebrate your new job."

"Oh, I can't," Elisabeth objected. She looked at her watch. It was past noon, and she had that three o'clock appointment at Mrs. Miller's to talk to Angela Stuart. She had thought to read up on divorce law in the meantime. However, she was hungry, and Ricky could tell her more about Lawson & Lawson.

"It'll be fun," Ricky Junior said. They walked down the hall together until Ricky remembered that he had promised to pick up his father's car from the repair shop, and went off to get the keys from him.

Elisabeth stood waiting in the reception area, marveling at Ricky Junior's ease of life. How nice to be so stable, so boring, and to have done exactly what one's parents expected. No risk, no turmoil.

"You've had a lot of calls from Stuart Construction." Elisabeth turned around to see the receptionist handing a sheaf of notes to Shawn. He'd apparently just walked into the building and was shaking raindrops off his dark gray trench coat.

"Thanks," he was saying, when he saw Elisabeth. He walked over.

"How are things going?" he asked. His voice was politely neutral.

"Fine, thanks," she said. She saw that his jaw was tight with tension, and his smile did not reach his eyes, which were gray today. *They always turn gray when he's upset,* she thought.

She determined that she would not be the cause of his worries. "Thank you very much for—for yesterday."

"Not at all," he said, his voice cool. "Happy to have you. Have you talked to Ricky Junior yet?"

"Yes, actually—we talked this morning. I did some work on his case, and his assistant helped me get into the computer system."

"Good. I'm sure there are others who would like the help. I'm new, so I don't have a full grasp of everyone's projects yet. But I'm sure there's a lot more where that came from." He looked like he wanted to get away, but Elisabeth was determined to thank him for the advance and get it over with.

She glanced over her shoulder at the receptionist, who was busily transferring calls. She lowered her voice. "I wanted to specifically thank you for the advance."

"Don't worry about it," Shawn said. He hesitated, then asked, "Was it enough?"

Elisabeth felt her neck grow hot. She nodded, not knowing how to respond. On the one hand, she was grateful. On the other hand, this wasn't exactly professional, was it? Did the fact that she had once nearly married the managing partner mean that there was something ethically wrong with her receiving an advance from Lawson & Lawson? There hadn't been any examples like this in her ethics textbook.

She changed the subject. "I heard about your dad. Is he better?"

"Much better, thanks."

Ricky Junior was sauntering into the reception area. "Hey! New managing partner! Come to lunch with us, we're celebrating! And maybe we can convince Beth to join us full time."

Oh, no, Elisabeth thought.

But she needn't have worried. Shawn was declining, saying that he had too much work to do.

As they left the building, Elisabeth couldn't help one last backward glance at Shawn, who was still standing absently in the reception lounge, the stack of phone messages limp in his hand. He was gazing into the middle distance, seemingly lost in thought. She suddenly knew exactly what he was thinking, because their conversation had been almost border-line normal.

But we can't be friends, Elisabeth thought. *Just let it go.*

It was drizzling. As they walked toward the small cluster of eateries on Main Street, Ricky Junior prat-tled cheerfully about his never-ending pile of work, adding that he was not only grateful for Elisabeth's help, but that he was hoping no one else at the firm managed to steal her away.

"Shawn came to me first, because he knows me," he was saying. "But pretty soon the others will hear and then they'll try to nab you. I hope you've got the time."

Elisabeth decided to tell Ricky Junior the truth. "It's really slow right now," she confessed. "Some-times I really have a hard time making a go of it."

"Yeah, it's hard to make it on your own," Ricky Junior agreed. "What helps is that I get to specialize, because I'm part of a practice. If someone needs something that I don't do, I can pass that over to someone who does."

"That actually reminds me," Elisabeth said. "I just picked up a divorce client. And I know nothing about divorce law."

"Yikes," Ricky Junior shuddered. "Are you sure you want a divorce case? You can pass it over to someone who does divorces."

Elisabeth shook her head. "Well, I'm not sure it'll end up as a divorce—yet. The client looked pretty sad when she talked to me. Maybe she can work things out. And to be honest, I can't afford to let go of clients right now. I really need this one."

"Yeah. Well, that's a hard one. Times are tough for small firms right now. You should just come on board. We're so busy all the time, and you must already know everyone in town. I would think you could fit right in."

"Thanks, Ricky," Elisabeth said, smiling. She couldn't possibly explain to him that she didn't think she could ever work for a blue-chip law firm, especially one where Shawn Waterstone was the managing partner. She couldn't even explain to herself why she hadn't tried harder to find a proper law firm job when she'd graduated law school. Somehow, she'd thought that she could just make it work, that she could hang out a shingle, the way her grandfather had when he was a young man, and the way his father had. She had this idea that she could help people, that she would know all her clients personally and hold their hands through difficult times in their lives.

But times were different. People wanted specialists. Computers needed information systems staff to figure them out. There was so much technology involved, it was all that Elisabeth could do to stay functional. Her laptop was ancient. Her internet access was poor. And she'd avoided upgrading her old flip phone because she was afraid of the expense of the data package that was required of all smartphones. Never mind that even her clients complained that she was only intermittently reachable via text—she would chide them with the admonition that they knew exactly where to find her, either at the courthouse or beavering away in her study in the old Burnham manse on Church Street.

Maybe Ricky is right, she thought as he led her into a cute little Italian place on Main Street. *Maybe I should just tell Angela no. Maybe someone at Lawson & Lawson can handle her divorce.*

No, she couldn't afford to turn away business. She could charge several hundred dollars for an uncomplicated divorce, and if there were assets to divide she could charge even more for the time it would take to negotiate. Angela seemed prosperous. A good client would come back for other services, too. She would just have to learn about divorce law as she went along.

When she arrived at Mrs. Miller's home, however, she learned that Angela had canceled their appointment.

"Beth, my dear—" Mrs. Miller sighed deeply. "She is terrified out of her wits. Absolutely terrified. She hasn't ever lived her life alone. She moved straight from her mother's house to his when she got married. She's having such a hard time."

"Can I go in to see her, at least?" Elisabeth asked.

Mrs. Miller shook her head. "She won't come out of her room."

"I see," Elisabeth said, disappointed. "Well. Let her know that I stopped by. And she knows where to find me if she wants to talk." She felt a faint sensation of panic in her stomach. This was her only current lead. At least she could scrape by with Ricky Junior's case. As long as no expensive disasters struck, anyway.

"Will I see you at the baked bean supper on Sunday at church?" Mrs. Miller was saying.

"Um—yes, I imagine so," Elisabeth said. She was sure she looked as guilty as she felt. She hadn't realized there was a dinner on Sunday, and she normally would have volunteered to help.

"Well, good," Mrs. Miller said. "Don't worry about Angela. She'll come around. She's much better off without that man. He's such a big shot with that company of his, he probably hasn't noticed that she's left." She snorted. "I never liked him. He built all these ugly houses." She gestured around her.

"Oh, I didn't know that," Elisabeth said.

"Yes. Horrible. Simply horrible. Well, you take care, Beth. I will keep trying with Angela, but this may take time."

Elisabeth clanged the gate to Mrs. Miller's garden behind her. While the neighborhood around her had grown up into oversized faux-colonial mansions with acres of close-cropped lawn, Mrs. Miller still maintained an old-fashioned messy flower garden, with hollyhocks rising tall and nasturtiums clambering around in rich hues of oranges and reds and yellows over her white picket fence. The frost would get them soon, Elisabeth thought. Pausing to touch a particularly vibrant red blossom, her eye was caught by a movement above her head. Startled, she squinted upwards into the clear afternoon light. Someone was waving from a gabled side window.

It was Angela Stuart.

5

He'd been tempted to accept Ricky Junior's invitation and join them for lunch. Shawn sat in his office, glumly evaluating a soggy tuna sandwich. He had been entirely too tempted. But who was he kidding? He could not put aside his past with Beth, not even for an hour. Not when watching her pretend that there was nothing between them caused his chest to constrict with pain.

He couldn't get the sight of her thin body out of his mind, hovering in a cloud of flowery cotton print, and the fine, weary lines around her eyes.

Her mother was dead, she had said. When had that happened? He allowed his mind to wander back in time, back to the summer before he'd left. Her mother had been ill, off and on. He'd hardly seen her, in fact. But he had never supposed that she was really all that sick. After all, she had seemed to devote an enormous amount of energy nagging away at Beth. Beth was always running around, trying to anticipate her every need, and that woman had hardly had a kind word for her, he mused. Didn't even approve of college, for God's sake. A waste of time, she had said more than once. Implying, of course, that Beth herself was rather a waste of time.

Shawn found himself getting angry. Abruptly, he tossed the sandwich into the trash can and got up to pace about the room. He had always felt that Paula Burnham would not be content with less than ruining her daughter's life, just as she had felt her own life was ruined by her marriage to a pleasant but unfocused man who would never make anything of himself.

He paced restlessly, his anger getting the better of him as he considered the injustice. He should have known, he thought, scowling. She should have called him, emailed him. He would have come back to be with her, to have helped her with the funeral, to have sorted out the inevitable messes that death brings. Maybe this eight-year estrangement would have been a lot shorter. Maybe she would have joined him in New York after all, and they'd have been married by now. They'd have started a family. They'd be happy.

And then of course, his lawyer's brain said sensibly, why hadn't he been the one to reach out to her? It would have been just as easy for him to have called, or indeed to have stopped by. He could have sought out a mutual friend or two in order to ask after her. He'd had plenty of opportunity. It wasn't as if he had turned his back on Greenleigh completely during that time.

But I couldn't, he protested to himself. *How could I, when she's the one who left me standing around waiting? I'm not the one who changed my mind about getting married. Oh, no. I'm just the one who sat up all night in the high school parking lot. I'm just the idiot who couldn't believe that she would really stand me up, after all those promises to each other. How could I be the one to break the ice? When I had nothing to do with putting it there to begin with?*

Eight years spent shoving his feelings away had obviously not amounted to any kind of success at healing his wounded heart. He needed to work through his pain, or he would not be able to survive a new start in Greenleigh.

Shawn sat down at his desk again. He had to get some work done. He had spent the entire morning on the factory floor, trying to direct a repair crew from Wisconsin who had come out to maintain the equipment. His father had not been feeling well, and was spending the day at the hospital, where his doctors were hoping to adjust his heart medication after running a few additional tests. All in all, it seemed that his father was mending, but slowly. Years of overwork and bad diet could not be reversed so quickly. But perhaps he would be able to get back to his former active self, and then perhaps Shawn could leave again, get back to a place where he wouldn't have to spend his days looking at Elisabeth Burnham's work and his nights thinking about Elisabeth Burnham in his arms. Lawson & Lawson could find another managing partner.

He worked late, trying clear his mind of the voices that assailed him, plowing through the mass of paperwork laid upon him by the other partners at the firm, all of them grateful that he and not they would have to deal with the day-to-day responsibility of running a law firm. The housekeeper had prepared dinner that evening, under his strict instructions about cutting back on the salt and fat, and when he called to check up on his father at about six he found that his dad was on his way out to play chess with some friends at the senior center.

"Should you be running around town like that, Dad?" Shawn wished he had called the hospital earlier to confirm his father's discharge instructions.

"Don't be such an old woman," his father retorted. "I'm perfectly fine. I wasted the entire day getting my arm poked and peeing into a cup. I'm going to play chess."

"But you shouldn't drive—"

"I'm not. Joe Peterson is giving me a ride. See, he's honking the horn, he's waiting. Gotta run. Don't work too hard." His father hung up on him before he could reply.

Great, Shawn thought. *I'd better stop by a little later and take him home or he'll try to play chess all night.* He glanced at his watch. Ten o'clock would probably do it. That would give him ample time to clear off part of his desk, and perhaps to take a look at a few cases he was thinking of assigning to himself. He ordered some take-out food, removed his tie, and settled in for the evening. By nine o'clock his mind was wandering and the room was littered with the remains of his dinner and the local sports pages. He decided to give up on doing any more work, cast a disparaging glance over the state of his office, and hoped that the maintenance crew would take care of it the following morning before he arrived. Slinging his jacket over his shoulder and stuffing his tie into a pocket, he locked up and went in search of his father.

The Greenleigh Senior Center was in a residential part of town, in a neighborhood of small, neat cottages and modest frame houses. It was an unremarkable neighborhood, the houses much newer than those closer to the center of town, and in some parts it resembled a suburban housing tract. Many of the owners of these homes were elderly, and they had actively supported the building of a senior center in their neighborhood when it was proposed back in the nineties. *An entirely different constituency from the folks who live in those grand old houses downtown*, Shawn observed as he slowed the car down outside.

The senior center itself was a low brick building next to the middle school, and on any given night it catered to the local contra dancing troupe, the book club, the knitting guild, or any one of a number of active groups managed by the patrons of the center. Tonight there was a film and a speaker in the auditorium on the state of the environment in New England, and it seemed from the occasional bursts of applause wafting into the night that the meeting was well-attended. Shawn parked the car in the lot and made his way over to the entrance.

The building smelled like scorched coffee and floor polish. Shawn was stopped at the door to the multi-purpose room by several old cronies of his father's, warning him that his father's chess match was close to being over and that he would not forgive even his only son for interrupting his concentration.

"Not a chess player, are you?" Joe Peterson, baseball cap perched atop a shock of white hair, jabbed a bony finger at Shawn's chest. Shawn grinned. He thought to himself every time he saw Mr. Peterson that he really wanted to know whether he'd been wearing the same navy blue baseball cap for decades, or if he had more than one.

"No, not me. I'm not that kind of strategic thinker, I'm afraid. A disappointment to my dad."

"No!" A chorus of protest arose, and a short, skinny man in a khaki work uniform shook his head in disapproval. "Your dad does nothing but talk about how proud he is of you."

"Yeah," added another voice, "and he still has hope for your chess game."

Laughter followed. Shawn sat obligingly down on a sofa, noting that his dad was grimly surveying a chessboard in a far corner of the room, his opponent a pleasant-looking gentleman in his early sixties.

"Who's that?" he asked Mr. Peterson. Mr. Peterson glanced in the direction of the chess game.

"That's Bob Stuart. Don't you know him? He's one of the town selectmen. Got a big construction company."

Shawn suddenly recognized the name. "Stuart. Yeah, I think his company is a client."

"He hasn't been around the senior center for long," the man in the khaki uniform interjected. Mr.

Peterson nodded. Shawn cast him a questioning look.

"Wife left him, you see. Been hanging out here since."

Shawn felt embarrassed, rather as if he had been prying. "Oh. That's too bad."

"Yep. Terrible thing. My wife's known Angela for —oh, mebbe these twenty years or more. Nice lady. Never knew there was a problem."

"But that's how it is," Khaki Uniform said in solemn tones. "They up and leave ya, and you're left wondering what hit them all of a sudden."

"Once they leave, it's too late," Mr Peterson said. "Ya gotta take care of 'em before they leave. Ya need to talk about stuff." He nodded in the direction of the chess game, where a burst of laughter heralded the end of the game. Shawn's father, Sam, and Bob Stuart were standing up and shaking hands.

"Bob's a good guy. But Angela's a real sweet lady, and there's no such thing as 'all of a sudden.' If she left him, she's been mad for a long time. Hey there. So who's the champion?" He directed the question toward the two chess players making their way across the room.

"Shawn! You didn't have to come and get me. Joe would've taken me home." Sam sounded annoyed. He was a lean, angular man, balding and wearing wire-rimmed glasses, shorter than his son but with a quick, nervous energy in his step. He wore a red plaid flannel shirt and stained khakis. There was a pencil behind one ear and a steel tape measure clipped to his belt.

Shawn gave Mr. Peterson a knowing glance. "Yeah, right. Only after you two painted the town red."

"This is my son," Sam said to Bob. "The lawyer." He sounded mournful, as if he were announcing bad news.

"Sorry about that introduction," Shawn said, holding out his hand. "That's really not the only way to describe me. I'm not that bad."

Bob laughed, shaking his hand, the clasp firm. "No, no, I have lots of respect for lawyers. They save my butt all the time. I've heard all about you. Are you home from New York permanently?"

"More or less," Shawn said, noting the flicker of discomfort crossing his father's face. "Dad, you look tired."

"Tired? Bob, am I tired?" Sam sounded insulted.

"If that's how you play when you're tired, don't challenge me to any games when you're awake," Bob responded. He nodded at Joe Peterson. "Beat me in no time at all."

"We warned ya," Mr. Peterson said, shaking his head.

"That's not exactly true," Sam said magnanimously. He paused. "But I'm pretty damned good, ain't I?"

"And on that note," Shawn said, grasping his father's arm firmly. "G'night fellas. We're going home to bed." Deaf to his father's protests, he steered him gently in the direction of the door. Once in the hallway, he relaxed his grip.

"I played a really good game," his father was saying. "Bob Stuart is a very good chess player, though. I'll play him again tomorrow."

"Dad, can't you make your chess dates on the weekends? In the daytime?" They emerged from the senior center and walked in the direction of the parking lot. "I don't like you up and about this late at night."

"Don't mother-hen me," Sam said. Shawn sighed, exasperated, as Sam walked slightly ahead toward the car. He noted that his dad seemed to have shrunk in height, in addition to having lost weight since the heart attack. Their faces had never looked particularly alike, with Shawn favoring his mother's fair hair and almost girlish good looks, but in height and build they had been the same, tall and angular. Shawn was a strong, clear physical copy of his dad, down to the way he stood and walked, but now his father seemed wrinkled and faded. Shawn went up to the car, where Sam stood waiting with his jaw set stubbornly.

"I'm not trying to mother-hen you, Dad." He unlocked the doors, observing the parking lot lights shining on Sam's balding pate. He almost asked him why he wasn't wearing a hat, then decided not to annoy him further. "But you've just had a heart attack. And I want you to continue to be able to do all the things you like to do. If you're not careful, you'll have another heart attack and then I'll really mother-hen you. You won't enjoy that at all."

He started up the car, glancing at his father's profile as he did so. The grim lines about his mouth had faded, and he was humming something that sounded like "My Wild Irish Rose," only it wasn't quite right. Shawn knew better than to comment, since it would lead to a protracted discussion about the right melody, and finally to a loud, tuneless concert in the car.

"It's been over ten years," Sam said suddenly. Shawn, who had been thinking vaguely about the mess he had left in his office, was startled. Then he realized what Sam was referring to.

"Yes, it has," he said softly. They stopped for a traffic light. Shawn glanced at his dad, who was drumming away softly on the car door. It sounded like the "1812 Overture."

"It's been a long time," Shawn said.

"I guess you still miss her." Sam cast a sidewise look at his son.

"God, yeah." Shawn smiled, his eyes on the road. "She was my mom. I'll never get used to her being gone. The house still feels weird without her." He stopped abruptly, wondering if he was hurting his dad's feelings.

"I was thinking about her tonight. I'm surprised I could win a chess game, I was so distracted. But I kept thinking about her." Sam shook his head.

"Why tonight?" Shawn hoped that Sam wasn't going to talk about his own death, or about growing old, two subjects that they had successfully avoided after the heart attack. Just contemplating it made Shawn feel sick with apprehension.

"Bob Stuart."

"What?"

"Bob Stuart. His wife left him, you know."

Oh, that, Shawn thought with relief. He made his tone light, glad that they were talking about someone else's problems. "I heard. That's too bad. He seems very nice. I think my firm represents his company."

"He's a good guy. Town selectman, you know. And very successful businessman. He's a good contractor. You can trust him. He started that environmental group that was in the auditorium tonight." There was a silence. Shawn waited. The silence continued, Sam drumming genially on the car door in time to an invisible conductor. Shawn knew his father too well to imagine that the conversation was over.

"Were they married long?"

"What?"

"Bob Stuart. He and his wife." Shawn slowed down for a stop sign, thinking in exasperation that sometimes he wished his dad weren't such a consummate Yankee and would just spit out whatever it was that he wanted to say.

"Dunno. He's younger than me. Maybe thirty years or so."

"That's a long time. Must be hard."

"Mmm." There was another silence. Sam changed the pattern of his drumming.

This time Shawn couldn't pick out the tune. "Don't Cry For Me, Argentina?" Something from "Carmen?" Whatever it was, it definitely sounded like a tango.

"It's like death."

"What?" Shawn jumped. Death? What was like death? He gazed at his dad, worried. He did not want to have a conversation about death.

"Light's green."

"Oh. Right." Shawn pressed on the accelerator again. "What's like death?"

"Divorce. You know. Splitting up. Your family is changed forever."

Shawn was perplexed. He wasn't sure whether to respond. Happily, his father continued.

"Bob Stuart's wife just up and left one day. They'll never be the same again." They were pulling into the driveway of the Waterstone home, a dark red farmhouse toward the edge of town, surrounded by cornfields, which at this time of year were filled with post-harvest debris. Development had not yet come to these fields, and Shawn hoped it never would. It was somewhat out of the way, but it was the last bit of rural New England left in the town of Greenleigh. His grandfather had bought this farmhouse and the land around it back at the turn of the century, and until the interstate had come by in the seventies, it had remained the last isolated corner of Greenleigh. They weren't isolated anymore, but at least there were still ponds and open fields here.

Shawn turned off the engine. He turned to his father, but Sam was opening the door and stepping out of the car. "Maybe they'll both be happier this way. Or maybe they can patch things up," he offered. This was a really depressing subject, and he was ready to ditch it.

"Yeah," Sam said over his shoulder as he trudged in the direction of the house. "I hope they fix it. No one should be alone." He fumbled at the door for a second before the porch was flooded with a pool of light from the lamp overhead.

Shawn sat immobile in his seat. Sometimes he didn't know whether his father was truly a philosopher or perhaps just going slightly senile. But the realization that whatever was wrong in the Stuart household, they still had a shot at happiness, caused him to feel what must have been just the merest taste of his father's loneliness. It must seem incomprehensible to his widowed father that someone would voluntarily part with a thirty-year relationship, unless something truly terrible were happening.

Shawn had gone off to college, gone off to law school, gone off to New York. He'd left his dad behind. It was much better to be the one to leave, than to be the one left behind. That must be why the thought of someone else's divorce didn't affect him in particular. He'd imagined that a divorce meant both people deciding to leave a relationship. He hadn't considered that in some cases, there was a person who walked out on another person.

Actually, he admitted, he'd been the one to walk out on Beth. He'd never considered that before.

It's awful to be alone, he suddenly thought. *I've never been alone.* His thoughts flitted to Elisabeth, who was at this very hour probably sitting alone in her kitchen, staring into a cup of tea. His spine stiffened. No, he had miscalculated once already by imagining that her life had not changed since he left. Perhaps she was sitting in a warm, friendly room, surrounded by friends.

"Hey, Shawn, do something about Martha's cooking, will you?" Sam was shouting back at him, walking into the kitchen, groping for the light switch. "It's gotten bland. If I say something she'll be hurt. But you're a lawyer—think of something tactful to say." The kitchen light went on.

Shawn chuckled. He got out of the car, not bothering to take his keys with him. No need for that in good old Greenleigh. He cast one last look about the darkened fields, the scorched remains of the summer's harvest only faintly evident in shadowy heaps on the ground. The air was chilly, and he could hear the faint hum of the interstate in the distance. Autumn crickets added their song to the night.

He'd been homesick, he realized. He just hadn't known for what exactly—and he still wasn't quite sure.

6

Angela Stuart was peering down from one of Mrs. Miller's upstairs bedroom windows, her face pale and strained with anxiety. She waved at Elisabeth through the billowing folds of crisp white curtains, leaning precariously forward.

"I would like to talk to you," she said in a stage whisper. Elisabeth cupped her hand around her ear, indicating that she could barely hear her. Angela tried again.

"Alone," she mouthed exaggeratedly. "Talk to you alone."

"Of course," Elisabeth mouthed back. Mrs. Miller was so overwhelming. She was probably pressing Angela at every opportunity to file for divorce. She called up softly, "Can you come down?"

"Side door," Angela mouthed.

"How about coffee? Pierre's? I'll go ahead?" Angela nodded and ducked behind the white curtains again.

Pierre's was a little coffee shop opened by a French-Canadian Greenleigh resident back in the seventies. The decor and ambience was still exactly as it had been back in the day, complete with dusty curtains and green walls. It had long since been bought out by a young woman sporting an intimidating collection of body art and piercings, but it would always be the old Pierre's to the denizens of Greenleigh. It had the best coffee—apparently Ms. Tattoo had bought the coffee secrets from the previous owners as well—and one could go in for a coffee and stay all afternoon for the price of a cup. Even in this digital era, the shop was filled with old books, newspapers, and magazines. Elisabeth ordered a coffee and stood, browsing through the comics, until Angela arrived.

Elisabeth recalled again how pretty she was. Today she had taken less care in her appearance, and was wearing a faded yellow blouse and a denim skirt, but she had truly perfect white skin and shiny dark hair. She was breathing hard, as if she had run all the way.

"Oh, I'm so glad I caught you!" she exclaimed.

"So am I," Elisabeth said. "Coffee?"

"Oh, I'll get it," Angela said, heading toward the ancient push-button cash register in the corner, where Ms. Tattoo sat reading Dostoevsky. She said over her shoulder, "I'll get you a refill."

"Thank you."

"Let's leave. Do you mind if we talk while we walk? I just don't want to be overheard. I'm always afraid of running into people," she said ruefully.

"Privacy? In Greenleigh? What's that?" Elisabeth joked, pushing the door open and gesturing for Angela to precede her. They strolled slowly down the street, narrowly avoiding the path of a skateboarder who skipped nimbly off the sidewalk just in time to avoid them. The teenager called out an apology and waved.

"There was a skateboard craze back in the seventies. I remember when even I had one." Angela was sipping slowly, savoring the coffee.

"I think it never left," Elisabeth said. She was used to starting out her meetings with aimless chitchat. People needed to warm up a bit before they could talk about something upsetting. Yankees always had this way of sussing you out, she thought. They put you through the ropes, find out if they liked your style, and then they might confide in you —or they might part with you amiably and never say another word. She wondered if people in other parts of the country did that, too. "You have children, Mrs. Stuart?"

"Angela. Please call me Angela. I have three. They're not children anymore, though. Rob is twenty-seven, Jennie's twenty-five, and Grace is twenty-four. They've all been out of the house for a while now, since leaving for college."

"Boston?" Elisabeth asked. Most of Greenleigh's young people went to Boston, then off to parts unknown from there.

"The older two went off to Boston, but Grace—she's stubborn, wouldn't do what everyone else did. She's in California, studying architecture. Not the kind of architecture her father deals with, obviously," Angela added. "I think she is completely uninterested in old houses. And anyway, they have all kinds of different rules for building out there. You know, earthquakes."

"Oh, of course. But that's wonderful. You must be very proud," Elisabeth said.

"I am," Angela said, her face lighting up. They were coming up on the neighborhood elementary school, and they turned naturally into the empty playground, making themselves comfortable on a bench. The long slanted rays of afternoon sun cast a golden glow about the yard, the jungle gym and the swing set gleaming brightly, almost blindingly.

Elisabeth noticed a sparkle on Angela's right

hand, and tried not to stare, but curiosity got the better of her. Angela noticed her expression. She extended her hand.

"Anniversary present. Twenty-fifth."

"It's lovely." Elisabeth examined the diamond, turning the plump white hand slightly so that the stone's facets caught, winking, in the sunlight. It was of a generous size, classically cut, mounted in a fussy setting of yellow gold and smaller diamonds. Elisabeth released the hand, looking up to see Angela's expression. Angela wore a small smile, but the corner of her mouth quivered slightly.

"I don't usually wear it. I took it with me when I left the house—I thought, well, I thought I was going to give it back." Angela laughed a little, her voice fading as a wave of pain swept over her brow. "Isn't that silly of me? I don't know what I was thinking, but I just—packed my bags and figured I would work it out with him later. And I took the ring."

"Do you want to tell me about it?" Elisabeth watched as Angela examined the ring on her hand, twisting it and turning it this way and that.

Angela looked up. Tears filled her eyes. There was a long pause.

"I just needed to do something. I couldn't stand it anymore. If I didn't do something, anything—I was going to burst. What do you do when you've had it with years of waiting? All I can think about now is all the times when he could have chosen me and he chose something else instead. Usually work." She coughed, reaching into her handbag for a tissue. "It does add up. I'm just tired of it."

Tired relationships and broken promises. It seemed the entire world ran on the fumes of good intentions. If things had finally fallen apart between her parents, Elisabeth mused, her dad would have continued to live in the Burnham home. Her mom's family was in Vermont, and she wasn't on good terms with them. Where would she have gone? She tried to imagine her mother walking out the door, suitcase in hand. Would she have taken Elisabeth with her? She couldn't be sure. Could she, Elisabeth, have lived anywhere else but in the Burnham house? It was something she'd never thought about in all those years when she'd wondered why her mother just didn't leave this man whom she had seemingly misjudged so badly.

She wondered, for the first time, if her mother blamed her for her inability to walk out of that miserable marriage. Maybe that was why she'd been so awful to her, because having a small child made it impossible for her to start over.

Elisabeth sat up a little straighter as the thought occurred to her. Maybe, just maybe—that was why she'd clung to Elisabeth so desperately. Maybe she'd given up on her own happiness because of Elisabeth, so she needed Elisabeth to stay with her, to give her life meaning.

She thought again about the night that she'd promised to meet Shawn in the high school parking lot so they could leave Greenleigh together. She hadn't been able to bring herself to do it, to leave her mother, the house, and Greenleigh. She'd blamed her own weakness. But she'd blamed her mother, too, for preventing her from finding happiness. And she'd been angry. And she was still angry. But maybe her mother wasn't so much selfish and mean, as terrified of being left alone, because she was unable to leave Greenleigh herself.

Angela continued. "He gave me this ring a few years ago. I was thinking of leaving him then, too, but I kept hesitating. Grace was still in school, and she would come home during vacations. I kept thinking how unfair it would be to her if she had nowhere to come home to. And then this—" She held out her hand, turning it so that the ring sparkled. "When I saw it, I thought that he must still love me. He's not the emotional type, the sentimental type. Really a grumpy old New Englander. So when I saw the ring, I just—I thought it meant a lot. I thought that maybe it was an apology, even. But no." She laughed without humor and shook her head.

"Turns out, he had a client who couldn't pay, and

this was part of what he got. The guy was a jewelry dealer. So this was free. He was so pleased!" Angela laughed again, bitterly.

"Oh, dear," Elisabeth said. She felt secret kinship with Bob Stuart. She'd done just the same kind of barter with her clients when they couldn't pay. She got it, she really did—but there was no way to put a good face on this for Angela.

"Bob shares nothing with me. Nothing. I don't know anything about what he does with that company of his. After the kids left, I was bored out of my mind. I thought about getting a job, but I don't think anyone would hire me. I've never had a career. I went to art school in the seventies. I have no idea how designers do their work anymore."

"Could you ask Bob? Maybe someone at the company could mentor you, show you how to use all the new programs. You could go out on your own after that," Elisabeth suggested.

Angela shuddered. "No, I don't want to have anything to do with that company of his. It's like he's really married to the company, not to me. It would be like asking his mistress for help."

"I understand," Elisabeth said.

"I'm really afraid of the day that he finally retires. I don't know if I can be with him all the time. I don't know who he is anymore, and he makes me nervous every time he walks through the door. I can't imagine he likes being with me, either. He's never been very talkative, but I guess after the kids left for college, it really started bothering me. It's like I could suddenly see how irrelevant I was if there weren't any kids around to take care of."

They sat quietly for a moment, watching their shadows elongate as the sun sank lower in the sky.

"There's no other explanation for the fact that hardly a sentence passes between us that we haven't spoken before. So to shake things up, the other day I asked him if he wanted to go to a movie. He looked at me like I was nuts. He said he didn't know I went to movies." Angela pressed her hand to her mouth for a moment, halfway between a sob and giggle, before continuing. "After twenty-eight years he said he didn't know I went to movies! And I could tell you down to the last calorie what his favorite foods are and what kinds of pants he won't wear, but I have not the faintest clue what makes his mind tick nowadays. And I don't think he's interested in what I think, either."

"He's a selectman, I understand," Elisabeth said. "So he's active in town politics."

"Yes, but he had to be persuaded to do it." Angela shrugged. "If you ask me, there was something sketchy about the whole thing. I think it's because of Bob's company. These developers want to take all the open land in Greenleigh and build housing tracts. They all come to Bob—Bob is very, very honest, and he's never had a problem getting permits from the zoning board. They know that. They all want Bob on their projects because they know he'll get it done, and they know that if they run into trouble with environmental regulations, he knows the right people to call. And if he's a selectman, even better. When the vacancy came up a few years back, a squad of those good old boys came over and talked him into it. I thought it was disgusting. When they showed up, I left the house." She gave a bitter laugh. "I went to a movie!"

"But he also started the environmental group that meets over at the senior center every month," Elisabeth countered. "I know a few people who go to those meetings. I can't imagine that he'd be involved in a project that isn't good for Greenleigh. Isn't that the same Bob Stuart?"

"The same," Angela said. "I had no idea that Bob was starting an environmental group in Greenleigh. No idea. But of course, I'm just his wife. No reason at all why he would tell me such a thing. And you're right, people know him as an environmentalist. He's not going to take on a project that will damage the environment or make Greenleigh a wasteland of ugly houses. But I didn't like it that he got support from developers for that selectman's seat." She hesitated. "All right, perhaps I'm being unfair. But as his wife, I didn't like being the last to know. I wish—I wish he'd confided in me. There was some ugly pushback and he lost sleep over it. I lost sleep because he lost sleep." She dabbed her eyes.

She still loved him. Elisabeth could see it, as clear as day. Even with her own dashed hopes and fear that she had become boring and irrelevant, Angela loved him so much, she would lose sleep over anything that pained him. She'd given him a family, a home, and the best years of her life. Her husband was a part of her story. Elisabeth had no doubt that she'd do it all over again.

She stared into space, thinking about how one would go about repairing a broken marriage. Mrs. Miller was wrong. This wasn't thirty years of broken. It was something else. Maybe a missing piece? Maybe a misaligned gear, somewhere? This didn't feel like two people at loggerheads. "Irreconcilable differences," was the term. This didn't fall under that category.

It was more like—a stuck gear. Rust.

She felt like she was just the wrong one to consult about something like this. *I'm biased*, she thought. *No, scratch that. I'm damaged. I can't give a good recommendation because I can't think straight about broken relationships. Especially since I was the one who was left behind.*

But she needed the business. She needed the

money. She would have to muddle through. And if Angela was determined to go through with this, she would need help.

"Angela, your home—could you bear to move? Sell it, even?"

"It'll break my heart," Angela admitted. Her brow wrinkled as she traced the rim of her empty cup with a finger. "Bob built that house for us. That was back when we were young and broke. He asked me what I wanted and I told him. He did everything himself, and I love that house as if it were my child." She laughed. "It sounds so silly. But we made that house together."

"It doesn't sound silly at all," Elisabeth said.

"I don't know what would be worse," Angela said. "To live there alone, with my marriage over, or to not live there." She blew her nose. "Although I want to be upfront with you, Beth. I'm financially independent. I inherited quite a large sum from my parents when they passed. And I also saved a nest egg for myself over the years. Bob told me to do it, because he was worried that if something were to happen to him or the company, he wanted me to have my own money in my own name. So whatever this costs, I can pay for it. And whatever happens afterwards, I can afford it. I'm pretty much set for life. I'm sorry, that sounds so crass, but I wanted to be clear about that. And I'm ready with a check for you."

She opened her purse and removed an envelope. She handed it to Elisabeth, who took it.

"I hope it's enough. But if it's not, I'll write you another check."

"Thank you, Angela." Elisabeth was touched. She appreciated Angela's thoughtfulness, her generosity, and the depth of her devotion to her family. She decided that she would do anything at all possible to help sort this relationship out—whatever that meant. "Go back to Mrs. Miller's and try to relax for a few days. Don't think about it too much. Does your husband have a lawyer?"

Angela got up from the bench, walking over to a trash can, where she deposited her paper cup and several shredded tissues. She stood there for a moment, back turned to Elisabeth.

"I don't know," she said, her voice muffled.

"I'll find out. Don't worry about anything."

Angela returned slowly to the bench, her knuckles whitening as she pressed her handbag hard against her knees. She was, Elisabeth knew, struggling not to burst into tears again.

"I just didn't know what came next, how to face this. It was all so big and—big and messy. And with Sarah nagging me day and night to get my act together—it was just too much. I couldn't think of what to do. Sarah's a good friend," she added hastily, "but she gets a bit over-enthusiastic sometimes."

"Yes, I know Mrs. Miller very well," Elisabeth said, smiling. "I think I mentioned to you that she's known me most of my life. I know how she is." She stood up from the bench, shivering slightly. "Goodness, the wind has turned. Amazing how these days just suddenly turn into fall weather."

LATER THAT EVENING, AFTER A FIGHT WITH THE boiler to heat up the tepid water in the tank, Elisabeth sat in the kitchen with her feet propped up on a chair as she typed up her notes from her conversation with Angela Stuart. Peppermint tea steeped in the cracked mug in front of her, and she watched with interest as an ant, fleeing from the newly chilled garden outside, tugged a leaf across the width of her kitchen table. She could somehow never bring herself to squash the ants that brazenly invaded her kitchen from time to time. Mrs. Miller had said darkly that she knew how to get rid of them, and for good, but Elisabeth reasoned that since they had been around longer than the Burnhams had, it wasn't really fair to vanquish them with technology. They made their appearance each spring and fall, struggling across the old pine kitchen table as they hoarded their booty, and Elisabeth sat and watched them come and go.

She wiggled her toes thoughtfully, watching as another ant struggled up the table leg, this one burdened with a minuscule crumb. Yesterday's toast, Elisabeth realized. She took a sip of tea. The kitchen had such ancient appliances, and the doors and windows weren't sealed up tight, which explained the presence of all those ants. But it was the coziest part of the house to sit in, especially in the winter when she got the woodstove going. Elisabeth had once read in some magazine that woodstoves were popular among young professionals in places like New York. She found that hysterically funny. People in Greenleigh had woodstoves because it was cold in the winter. Full stop.

She stared at the empty corner next to the china cabinet, remembering the bitterly cold winter before her mother's death, when she had lugged a mattress into the kitchen and shoved it into that corner, settling her mother there for what she had realized would be her last months. The old bedrooms were just too drafty and cold, and the boiler too cantankerous, and from her vantage point on the mattress, her mother was able to keep the woodfire stoked during the hours when Elisabeth was away. Proud to the end, her mother insisted that she didn't need help, that she could take care of herself. She was resentful of the set-up at first, accusing Elisabeth of treating her like an old woman. But she eventually acquiesced silently to the fact that she was very ill, and spent her days on the old mattress, waiting to die.

Elisabeth never again wanted to see a mattress in the kitchen, she thought. And because she was wrapped in her old yellow robe and sitting with her herbal tea in the old cracked mug, she allowed herself to shed a tear for her mother. It had been a hard life for a proud young woman accustomed to a leisurely existence. At what point did she realize, Elisabeth wondered, that Ralph Burnham was running through money like water and unlikely to make more? At what point did her feelings of fear and disappointment overtake her youthful love and passion?

Sometimes Elisabeth wondered whether there had even been any youthful love and passion. Her mother had been plain, a tall woman with straight brown hair and strong features. Her father, by contrast, was a short, slight man with golden brown curls, always cheerful, always pleasant. As Elisabeth remembered them from her youth, they had never gotten along. There had always been that worry about money, for one thing, since the money from Grandfather's trust was running out. Paula would scold, Ralph would smile and mutter a non sequitur. Then he would leave, packing up the old Plymouth with his cleaning products, and return ten hours later, having sold nothing, with scarcely a mention as to where he had been, although they all knew that he was at the Athena Diner with his childhood friends, smoking and playing cards. He would pick Elisabeth up, tickle her a bit distractedly, then escape to the front room with his newspaper. Paula didn't like to go in there because it smelled like old Burnham books, she complained, and it gave her the willies.

Her father didn't come home from his sales trip one day; he had been killed in a car accident in a neighboring town, some forty miles away. Elisabeth had wept, sad to lose the playful daddy of her childhood, but Paula had been stony-faced and resentful, as if in death Ralph Burnham had become even more useless than he had been in life. There was life insurance, and Paula was a good and frugal manager of the proceeds. But without her customary target, she focused her sharp tongue instead on her daughter, a slight, pale girl with golden brown curls and a shy smile who looked exactly like her father.

Human relationships, in fact, were Elisabeth's trade, and she knew all too well that they buckled and frayed under pressure. She stood up to put her empty mug in the sink. Was a bad marriage worth saving? Had her parents come to her, Elisabeth

84

Burnham, attorney-at-law, what would she have counseled?

She did not know the answer. All that she did know was that she needed the clients, and that Angela had given her a large check. She was going to try hard to make Angela happy. She thanked her silently and went to bed.

7

When the phone rang, Shawn was tempted not to answer. He was deep in the middle of a pleading that he was trying to compose, and knew that another distraction would make it impossible for him to regain his train of thought. On the other hand, it was his cell phone, and not many people actually called him on that number. He searched until he finally found the phone under a pile of papers on the couch.

"What the heck takes you so long?" His father sounded annoyed.

"Sorry. I couldn't—" He left the sentence dangling, not wanting to admit that he couldn't find the telephone under the mess in his office.

"Listen. I'm at the factory. Bob Stuart just stopped by."

"Your chess buddy?" Shawn's gaze wandered over to the bookcase. One of his books was missing. *Why don't people tell me when they borrow things*, he thought, irritated.

"Right. Well, I'm sending him over to you."

"Me?" His attention focused back on his father. "Why?"

"You know. His problem."

"His problem," Shawn repeated, not understanding.

"You know." His father's voice took on an impatient tone. "Look, I can't stay on because the dye on number six isn't coming out right. I told him you could see him this afternoon."

"Dad, you need to let me know when you send people my way," Shawn said, grumpily pulling his phone away from his ear briefly to check the time. "I'm tied up this afternoon."

"What?" There was a roar of machinery in the background as someone opened the door to his father's office and shouted something.

"Shawn! Hello? Gotta run!" His father hollered briefly at him and hung up without waiting for a reply. Shawn put his phone down, noting with distaste the pizza stains on his desk from the previous night's dinner. He'd gotten into the habit of working late and eating in, and the custodians were clearly too terrified to clean his desk. Shawn swiped at the stains, but only succeeded at smudging them further and adding a small splotch of red to his sleeve. He cursed.

He went over to the bookcase to inspect the space in his New England collection. He remembered his father's comments a couple of weeks ago about Bob Stuart and his wife having marital problems, but he didn't practice family law, so he couldn't conceive of why Bob Stuart would come to see him. Perhaps it was a town selectman thing. Civic duty of one kind or another. Maybe even a charitable function. It was getting into fall, after all, and to the extent that Greenleigh had any social activity at all, it would usually take place in conjunction with the holiday season.

Shawn continued to scowl at the bookcase. He hated it when books were missing. "Why don't people ask," he muttered, stalking over to the door. He flung it open and stormed down the hallway to the men's room, hoping to do something about the tomato stain on his sleeve. A couple of the clerks stopped dead in their tracks in the hallway, gawking, and fled when he turned his sour gaze upon them. *What's your problem*, he thought.

When he returned to his office the door was shut. He was in even worse spirits than before, having succeeded not only in smudging the tomato stain further but in soaking his entire sleeve. He had rolled it up in the bathroom, but it was dripping wet and clung clammily to his arm. He then had to roll the other one up as well in order to prevent the inevitable questions about why he would roll up one and not the other, and why roll up sleeves on such a chilly day anyway? He wondered if he should just wear his jacket all day and forestall the questions. He scowled and pushed the door to his office open, slamming it shut behind him.

At first he wasn't aware that there was anyone else there. He stood just inside his office, examining the rolled-up tomato stain, which was now prominently displayed over his forearm. A movement distracted him, and he looked up, surprised.

"I'm sorry. I thought you had gone out." Elisabeth stood next to his bookcase, the missing volume in her hand, actively in the process of replacing it. He gaped at her for a moment. She was looking a little better than she had over the past couple of weeks, the shadows under her eyes neatly camouflaged with makeup, he realized. Her lipstick matched the pale pink dress she was wearing, the wide skirt cinched in at the waist with a sturdy belt made from the same fabric. He marveled again at how thin she was, the sweetheart neckline of the bodice revealing the bones of her collar and neck, where the skin was almost translucent. The bodice gaped a bit, as if the dress had been purchased for someone else.

Shawn transferred his gaze from her bosom to her face. He glared at her, remembering that he didn't like it when people took his books. What was she doing nosing around his books anyway?

Elisabeth moved away from the bookcase, but did not approach his desk, her hands folded primly in front of her, briefcase dangling limply from her shoulder. *Christ, I'm not going to eat you*, he wanted to say. But he steeled himself and said instead, "How are you getting along with those projects?"

"Very well, thank you. I have enough to keep me busy for a little while."

"Let me know if you run out of things to do." Shawn indicated the pile on his desk. "There's a lot going on here, as you can see."

Elisabeth nodded, taking another step backwards. She was, Shawn realized, trying to slip away.

"Was there something—?" His voice faded. He found himself hoping that she had come to talk to him. About something, anything.

Elisabeth shook her head. "No." She began to head toward the door, but halfway there she paused and turned.

"Actually, I should thank you for the loan of that book."

"Book?" Shawn feigned innocence. He didn't

want to admit that not ten minutes ago he had been ready to boil in oil the silent borrower of his books.

"You weren't here yesterday morning and Ricky Junior and I were settling a bet. He thought you wouldn't mind if we confirmed the winner by checking your books. More reliable than the internet."

"Of course not," Shawn said, trying to sound pleasant. "I hope that it helped." Ricky Junior? She was playing games with Ricky Junior? He felt momentarily jealous that she hadn't turned to him, before he remembered that he was still angry at her for jilting him.

She was on her way to the door again. "Yes," she said over her shoulder, "it was a ring-necked duck, not a mallard that we saw at the common. Thanks." With that she shut the door behind her.

Shawn felt his knees weaken a bit, and he sat down. He shook his head. He laughed. Then he surveyed the mess on his desk.

"Ring-necked duck," he said aloud. So she and Ricky Junior were taking walks down to the common and watching the ducks. "How sweet," he muttered. But he felt anything but sweet. He felt vicious and nasty. Frustrated.

Go after her, he thought. *Go after her. Ask her back in. Ask her to have lunch with you. Dinner. Anything.*

Give her the whole damned lot of books. Drag her out to that confounded duck pond.

Kiss her.

That last thought entered his brain along a line of logic that he realized needed to be sternly banished from his existence. He would not fall in love with Elisabeth Burnham again. And the surest way in which to fail at that promise was to feel her again in his arms, her pulse quickening as he ran his hand along the slim lines of her waist and his lips along the curve of her chin—

Stop that. He tore his mind away from its wretched contemplation of what he would never again possess. *No more*, he told himself, *no more. One rejection is enough. It's more than enough.*

He noticed that she had left a half-empty packet of tissues on the desk. Slowly, and with great reluctance, he picked up the packet. He weighed it in his hand, then quickly, as if someone might be watching, he lifted it to his nose. It smelled of her, of soap, chewing gum, chamomile tea, and the polished leather of her briefcase. The scent reminded him of evenings spent huddled on the worn couch in her front room, stealing kisses as they kept one ear on the door for her mother's footsteps. He opened the top drawer of his desk and tossed the packet into it, shutting it quickly, not wanting to ask himself why he was doing such a silly and sentimental thing.

To work, he muttered. *Damn it all*. With one vigorous gesture, he swept part of the pile on his desk onto the floor, the papers and files landing with a dull thud, and felt better.

He had almost forgotten his father's phone call. The receptionist informed him at exactly two o'clock that Bob Stuart was there to see him, and he was tempted to say he wasn't in. He had a long and boring meeting to go to, and he hadn't gotten very far in getting his desk into any kind of order. But as he hesitated, something made him recall the conversation with his dad in the car that night on the way home from the senior center. He remembered the feeling of isolation that he had gleaned from his father's words.

Bob is the one left behind, he thought. *Like Dad.*

"I'll be right there," he told the receptionist. On his way out he stuck his head into Ricky Junior's office, asking him to go in his stead to his meeting. Ricky Junior seemed delighted and flattered to be asked. This was one of the hidden perks of being managing partner. *Everyone imagines that if it's a meeting that I'm attending, it must be either interesting or important,* he mused as he sauntered down the hall. *Little do they know.*

Bob Stuart awaited him in the reception area, pacing a little nervously. Shawn called out to him in a friendly way.

"Still playing those late-night chess games?" The two men shook hands.

"Playing with your dad is a revelation," Bob said, shaking his head and smiling. "I always learn something."

"He's a stubborn old geezer," Shawn said affectionately. "Best dad in the world. I don't play chess, though, so in that department I'm persona non grata."

"My kids never played chess, either," Bob admitted. "I don't think they even know how." Shawn led the way into his office and shut the door.

"Will you let me get you some coffee? Tea?"

"Oh, no, not for me, thanks. I'm cutting back. All that caffeine."

"I'm sure we've got decaf," Shawn began, but Bob waved this away as well.

"No, really, I'm just fine. I know you're very busy, and I don't want to take up too much of your time." Shawn motioned for him to sit down at the sofa, an offer that Bob accepted hesitantly. He looked down at his hands, as if weighing his words carefully before speaking.

Shawn jumped into the breach. "How are things at town hall?"

Bob furrowed his brow, puzzled. Shawn smiled. "I take it that you're not here to discuss town business."

Bob broke into a rueful grin. He rubbed at his crewcut. He was a pleasant-faced, portly fellow in a navy blue fisherman's sweater and an expensive-looking navy blue wool jacket. He didn't look at all like a man in the construction trades, but perhaps for the large ring of keys at his waist, and the leather phone carrier on his belt. He looked instead like a prosperous grandfather on vacation. "No—no, I'm not. I wish I were, but I'm here on a personal matter." He paused. "Your father told me I could come to you, but I don't want to take up too much time—"

"Don't be ridiculous," Shawn interrupted. "I'm happy to help."

"Thank you," Bob said, looking grateful. He stopped, then continued, his voice firm. "It's about my wife, Angela. She left me several weeks ago. I assume that she probably wants a divorce, and I just need a little guidance before I go ahead and involve myself in all the legal mess that I'm sure a divorce always creates."

"I hope I can help, but I don't do family law," Shawn said. He added, "I can refer you to someone with more experience in these things."

"No, no, I don't really need specific advice—at least, not at the moment." Bob dug a small notebook out of his pants pocket and flipped through it, coming to a page with neatly numbered items on a list. He referred to it briefly before continuing.

"I don't intend to contest anything that Angela says. I want it to be as painless as possible for her. Mainly, though, I want her to be secure—we're both getting on in years, and anything could happen."

"I see," Shawn said. "I suppose you aren't worried about her making any—well, how do I put it?—unreasonable demands?"

Bob smiled. "That's not really her style."

"If I may ask," Shawn said, "what is it exactly that she is saying? The grounds for divorce, I mean."

"I don't know, to be honest."

Shawn sat back in his seat, perplexed. Bob continued, "I haven't spoken to her since she left. I thought that maybe she wanted some time away to think, and I hoped—" Here his voice, until now a rolling, gentle cadence, choked slightly. "I hoped that she would come home after a spell, and we could work things out." A faint smile appeared. "I waited these past weeks, and I heard nothing. Then late last week, I got a phone call from her attorney. It looks like Angela is serious about getting a divorce, and her lawyer wants to see me. I wanted to talk to someone before seeing her lawyer."

"If you've gotten a call from your wife's attorney, you need to hire an attorney yourself," Shawn exclaimed. "You shouldn't be sitting around speculating as to your wife's motives. You need representation."

"I've been putting off meeting with her lawyer—basic dread, I guess. I finally made an appointment, but then I changed it a couple of times. I just couldn't face the whole situation." Bob sighed deeply.

"Listen to me, Bob," Shawn said, rising from his seat. "I urge you to get legal counsel before you talk to your wife's lawyer. I'm sure her attorney will be talking about money and settlements, and you absolutely should not get into those territories without a lawyer to protect your interests."

Bob smiled. "I'm not particularly worried about that, Shawn. I'm prepared to give her everything I have."

"Bob, you can't really mean that. Surely you've got a pension, plus your home and your savings. Not to mention all the assets you've bought over the years. And your company! You need to take a look at your company assets as well." Shawn knew next to nothing about divorce law, but he gave a mental shudder at the thought of the havoc a divorce could wreak on a prosperous business owned by one principal.

"No, I mean it. She can have all of it," Bob said. "I'd like to leave something for the kids, and I'm sure Angela would not object to that. Otherwise, all of it. Me, I don't need a lot to live on, and I can find a small apartment somewhere. But Angela deserves to live well, in the manner to which she's accustomed. In her own home. My God, she built that home, really. It was nothing when we moved in. She told me what to do and I did it—but I was always working, so I never really got to enjoy it. Angela—that's her house. She made it what it is today."

"That's very noble of you, Bob. But you need to think about this. Carefully." Shawn tried not to sound too lawyerly. He felt almost rude giving advice of this sort to a man thirty years his senior, but he felt obliged to express his disapproval of the path Bob seemed determined to take.

"I've put a lot of thought into it, Shawn, and the one thing I want both of us to come away with is dignity. I may have failed at keeping Angela happy, but I don't want us to part on bad terms."

"I see." Shawn sat down on the arm of the nearest easy chair. "All right. But you at least need to have your attorney with you when you speak to her lawyer. Otherwise you'll have a communication problem when you try to tell your lawyer everything that you talk about."

"I suppose I hadn't thought of that," Bob admitted. "I was trying to put off hiring a lawyer until I had settled the money issue with Angela."

"No, no, then it'll be too late. Everyone needs to understand everything that you and Angela decide on. From the beginning."

"Well, it's a good thing that I was able to check with you before heading off to my meeting with Angela's lawyer." Bob paused. "My last question—can you recommend a lawyer for me?"

Shawn felt a rush of emotion. He remembered his father's words, remembered the ache that he had felt thinking about what it meant to be alone, and how wrong it seemed for anyone to be alone. And Angela had left Bob without a word, the way he had left Beth without a word. Bob was making drastic decisions without asking Angela why she'd left, why they couldn't be together. Beth had made drastic decisions in her life, too, because she and Shawn hadn't resolved things. They'd avoided the conversation that Bob needed to have with Angela. He didn't want Bob to suffer the way he, Shawn, had made Beth suffer. He said, the words tumbling out in spite of himself, "I'd be happy to do this for you."

Bob looked surprised. "Oh, no, don't feel like you need to—you're very busy—I know you don't—"

"Please, let me do this," Shawn said quietly. "I really want to help. Really. You play chess with my dad, after all." He struggled to find the right words, words that wouldn't insult the older man. "I want this to be easy for you."

"It can never be easy," Bob said. His voice was

matter-of-fact, as if he were discussing auto repair rather than divorce. But his eyes were sad.

"A relationship of nearly thirty years' endurance is going to be hard to break up," Shawn said. "But let me do this as a friend, Bob."

"If you would, I would be grateful," Bob said. "I don't think I've ever been so terrified in my life, and lawyers tend to terrify me even further. Sorry, Shawn, but that's how most of us ordinary folks react to you guys."

"I know," Shawn said. He got up and went over to his desk, where he was fortunately able to locate his appointment book under a pile of papers. "When are you meeting with your wife's lawyer?"

"Friday morning. Angela is not going to be there, apparently. Not that I blame her." Bob rose from the sofa, tucking his notebook back into his pants pocket.

"Friday morning." Shawn was circling something and arrowing it over to another day. "All right. Done. I'll be there. Where do I go?"

"It's a little home office in one of those mansions on Church Street," Bob said, walking across the room toward the door. Shawn, who had been following, stopped suddenly, standing stock still in the middle of the room. A terrible thought had just entered his brain.

"Church Street?" His voice was strained. Bob turned around at the door, eyeing him curiously.

"Yes, literally several doors down from the Congregational Church. Her name's Elisabeth Burnham. I'm sure you must have heard of her. People in town really like her. She was very nice on the telephone, too, not at all lawyer-like." He laughed as he realized what he had said. "Sorry. You know what I mean."

Shawn hadn't moved. "Elisabeth Burnham." His voice sounded to himself like a stranger's. "Yes, I know her." Hadn't he just had this conversation? Oh, right, Ricky Senior had asked him if he knew Elisabeth. So *did* he know Elisabeth? Here again he was being shown some other Elisabeth Burnham, some woman he could not identify as the woman who had destroyed the Shawn Waterstone he had been so long ago. Had he ever really known her?

He was having trouble remembering who she'd been, back in those days. His Elisabeth had been sweet, generous of spirit. His Elisabeth had needed protection from the world. But this Elisabeth didn't need him to take care of her; she was in the business of looking after others. He definitely didn't know this Elisabeth.

He realized that he ought to say something to Bob, even to renege on his offer, but his throat was tight, and his mind was not responding to the rapid-fire "oughts" piling up in his brain.

"We can meet there," Bob was saying. "If you'd like." He stopped, watching Shawn. Shawn looked at him blankly.

"Where?"

"Church Street. Elisabeth Burnham's office. Do you know where that is?"

"Uh—yeah, yes, I mean, I do. What time?"

"Ten o'clock." He held out his hand to Shawn. "I can't tell you what a relief it is to know that I can turn to you with my questions. Thank you. I don't want to get in your way, so if you ever get too busy—"

"Absolutely not," Shawn said quickly, realizing that his hesitation must be showing on his face. "I'll see you Friday morning, Bob." The door closed.

His head was starting to pound. He went over to his desk and sat down limply. "I'm screwed," he said out loud.

He'd gone through the years feeling angry and abandoned, but actually, he'd been the one to leave. He'd been the one who'd done the abandoning. And, like Angela, he'd left without a word and hadn't bothered to explain. He'd figured that Beth had rejected him, so there was nothing else to say. And like Bob, Beth had soldiered on, probably concluding from his silence that Shawn was the one doing the rejecting, just as Bob was sure that Angela was rejecting him.

This was ridiculous. People needed to talk these things through. It was stupid to go nearly a decade without a word, just suffering alone. He needed to talk to Beth. Right away. Maybe they could be friends. Or maybe they could salvage the remains of that relationship and move forward into something better.

8

Besides having had the very bad luck to run into Shawn Waterstone while she was trying to return the book she had pilfered from his bookshelf, the quarterly water bill had arrived, and Elisabeth had spent the afternoon doing complex calculations concerning her bank account and the various household bills. At least, it had seemed complex. In actuality it had been no more than addition and subtraction—mostly subtraction—but it left her mind dazed and her stomach in knots. No matter how much fancy footwork she tried to come up with, the fact was that there were many bills but little cash.

But of course, when it rains, it pours, Elisabeth thought, banging absently at the water tank with a wrench. She had been operating for weeks now with lukewarm water at best, but this morning it had verged on cold. She'd ended up heating water for a tub bath in a kettle on the woodstove. She viewed the tank with dismay. It was a big old thing, and she'd never paid it the least bit of attention. A new one would break her budget. She had seen that when she'd tried to concoct some way of paying for that water bill. There just was no money to spare for extras—although this wasn't an "extra," Elisabeth thought ruefully.

She twirled the wrench about in her fingers, sitting back on her haunches. She looked about the cellar. It was musty and dark, the single bulb dangling overhead a mere twenty-five watts. She had never wanted to waste the wattage of a more powerful bulb since she never came down here. Her father had not been a very good repairman, and he tended to just turn things off when they stopped working, so he had not spent much time down in the cellar, either.

Elisabeth sighed, pushing back a curl from her face, re-tucking it into her ponytail. How much longer before everything propping up this house just gave up and failed? How much longer before she, Elisabeth Burnham, attorney-at-law, just gave up and failed?

She tossed the useless wrench into the cluttered steel toolbox and slammed the lid shut. She had hoped that Lawson & Lawson would be a temporary solution, a source of income to tide her over during a rough spot. But she knew that her life was much like this house, in dire need of restructuring. Patchwork repairs wouldn't do the job forever. Neither would temporary checks from Lawson & Lawson.

What she needed was clients. Angela Stuart was a gift from the gods at the exact time that she needed one. And yes, it meant she would have to endure Mrs. Miller's gossipy interventions for the foreseeable future. But Angela's check had reminded her that big checks from multiple clients with deep pockets were the only answer to the permanent problem of this run-down old home.

Of course, the problem with Angela was that she clearly did not want a divorce. Elisabeth was sure of this. She thought that she could convince Angela to talk to her husband, to go for counseling, to not give up—so long as her husband wasn't an utter jerk. And she somehow couldn't imagine that the man who'd given Angela the house of her dreams had mysteriously transformed into a jerk.

But a divorce would pay for a new water tank.

Elisabeth stood, giving the tank one last weary look. Apart from a faint hissing sound, she couldn't tell whether it was behaving particularly oddly. She was tempted to give it a small kick, but refrained, just in case it collapsed into pieces.

As she climbed the cellar steps, lugging the toolbox with both hands, she thought she could hear faint tapping. She paused, listening. For a moment all was silent. Then just as she began to move again, the tapping started up. Someone at the door.

"Coming!" she called. She hurried as best as she could, but banged her knee hard with a corner of the toolbox as she arrived at the top of the stairs. Wincing with pain, she dropped the toolbox, causing the lid to flip open with a crash, scattering its contents across the smooth wooden floor of the kitchen. She saw immediately that the hinge on the lid had finally given way, the metal bits bent apart.

"Damn!" she said with force, rubbing her knee. She suspected that it was bleeding underneath the stretchy knit leggings, and in any case it would certainly turn a most unattractive purple in a day or so. She limped out into the hall, grimacing at her reflection in the hall mirror. Grease stains marred her neck, as well as her oversized blue flannel shirt, and wisps of curly hair were escaping from her ponytail. She hobbled over to the door, swiping at her neck with her sleeve. Swinging it open, she uttered a hasty apology for her tardiness. The words died on her lips.

Shawn Waterstone stood uncomfortably on her doorstep. His starched white shirt collar still managed to look crisp and professional after a long day at the office, though he'd removed his tie. He must have left his coat in the car, because he was in his suit jacket, a dark gray wool. An enormous briefcase stood at his feet. Elisabeth stood speechless as she leaned down to rub her knee with one hand.

"Hi," he said. He seemed awkward, almost embarrassed.

"Hi," Elisabeth responded. She could feel the legging fabric beginning to stick to her kneecap. She looked down. There was a small rip and a dark stain.

"What happened to your knee?"

"Nothing," Elisabeth said, straightening. She attempted an air of nonchalance. "Banged it, that's all. What's up?" Her knee was beginning to throb.

"I brought some files by—a project that just came up this afternoon. You weren't around. Just thought I'd drop them off—I'm on my way home."

"Is it urgent?" Her tone was polite, but she eyed him suspiciously. There was something a little odd about his demeanor, but she couldn't put her finger on it. She didn't want him to be so sorry for her that he began to give her work out of pity.

"Sort of. It's a case of Ricky's. Junior, I mean. He's so overloaded that it would be good to get this one out of the way quickly." Silence followed. Elisabeth felt her cheeks warming, the flush rising from her neck to her face, and knew that Shawn saw it, too.

She felt like a bug under a magnifying glass. Exposed.

"You need to take care of that knee." Shawn was frowning at her leg. Elisabeth glanced down. The wet spot was beginning to ooze. She looked back up at Shawn. She knew she had to invite him in but the mental image of them sitting stiffly in the front room, talking about Lawson & Lawson, made her feel sick with dread.

"Why don't you come in?" she said hesitantly.

"Please don't worry about it. I'll just wait right here." Shawn stepped back from the doorway a little, glancing casually over his shoulder into the deepening dusk. A big, unpruned rhododendron bush, its leaves dark and waxy green, dwarfed the veranda leading off the entryway to one side of the house. "You've taken your porch furniture in, I see."

"Actually, I never brought it out." Elisabeth said, a slightly bitter edge to her voice. "I somehow missed summer this year. Mrs. McPherson next door hounded me about bringing out the porch furniture but every time I thought about doing it, something else came up. No one ever sits out here anyway." She caught her breath. "But of course, that's a stupid thing to say, isn't it? Since here you are, looking around for a place to sit." She smiled at him ruefully, and he responded, the hazel eyes lighting up with humor. Her heart ached as she realized how familiar and comforting his silhouette on the porch seemed.

"Come in." She stepped back, gesturing for him to enter.

"No, really, I can just drop these off. I'll wait." His words sounded insincere, and that settled it for her. She turned away from the door.

"I'm going upstairs to do something about my knee," she said over her shoulder, heading toward the stairs. "Shut the door behind you." Halfway up the stairs she heard the door shut quietly and the floor creak as he stepped into the hallway. Something tugged at her heart, a little flicker of excitement, quickly dampened by the reality of her situation.

I won't, she thought. *I won't get all wrought up over a little bit of kindness.*

She winced as she rounded the corner of the staircase, both from the throbbing in her knee and the embarrassing knowledge that he knew how badly she needed the work. Apparently, she needed work so badly that he came to her front door with it. Well, he didn't know everything, thank goodness. She would die of humiliation if he knew just how desperate things had gotten. He probably couldn't imagine anything that bad.

She limped into her bedroom to try to gingerly step into a pair of jeans, but the rough denim caused her to wince and pull her leg out again. At a loss, she pulled on a sweater and a short knit skirt. At least that didn't rub against her knee. She hastily checked her image in the mirror. She'd gotten the grease stains off her neck, but her hair was still a mess. She loosened the elastic that held it up and let the curly brown locks tumble about her shoulders. No, she decided. She didn't want it to look like she was trying to look nice for him. She swept the hair up again and limped out into the hall, where she gingerly negotiated the stairway down.

A noise from the kitchen caused her to limp in that direction. She walked in just as Shawn was re-placing the last wrench in the broken tool box. He stood, picking up the heavy box to put it on the kitchen table.

"I think you need a new tool box." The glimmer of amusement in his voice caused Elisabeth to stiffen. She did not want him to laugh at her sorry efforts to do her own repairs.

"I can probably fix that one," she said, moving to take the toolbox.

"Watch it." Shawn caught it just as she picked it up by the lid, half lifting the body of the box and nearly causing it to overturn onto the floor again. "I'll bet I know how you hurt your knee. What were you trying to fix?"

Elisabeth pushed the box toward the center of

the table, angry that she was so clumsy, angry that anyone had been a witness to her own pathetic circumstances.

"The water tank," she muttered, moving off in the direction of the stove. She turned her back and busied herself with the kettle. "Let me make you some tea."

"What's up with the water tank?" Shawn persisted.

"Well, what else would be up with a water tank?" Elisabeth snapped. "It isn't heating water."

"Would you like me to take a look at it?" Shawn started toward the cellar door.

"No, I would not," Elisabeth retorted, but Shawn was already continuing down the steps. She half-turned, ready to protest, but she could hear him thumping down the creaky old steps, pausing to feel around for the light switch, then letting out a muffled curse. She giggled involuntarily. He must have banged his head on something hanging from the low ceiling.

She went in search of something better than her old cracked mug while he shuffled about in the cellar. As she poured the hot water into the cups, she realized that despite the years of separation, she could still recall how he liked his tea. *All this useless information, stored up in my brain*, she thought. *It would do me good to get rid of the stuff that I don't need anymore. It would make room in my head for something else, something more useful. Something more lucrative.*

She heard his footsteps coming up the stairs. Shawn was saying something as he came into the kitchen. "—be something wrong with the coil."

"What does that mean? What's a coil?" Elisabeth hoped it wasn't expensive, whatever it was.

Shawn sat down at the table, helping himself to his tea. "That kind of tank has a coil in it—that's what heats the water. They get dirty over time—minerals and such. Anyway, it's such an old tank, you'd be better off just getting a whole new tank, I suspect."

"A new water tank?" Elisabeth snapped to attention. "Oh, no."

"It's possible that you just need to clean out the thing, but it's a tremendous headache. It's pretty ancient, and it's probably never been cleaned."

"You've got that right," Elisabeth said, thinking of her father lounging about in the front room in his robe and slippers, nose in a book, while her mother complained about his inability to maintain the house.

A new water tank, she mused. Yeah, come to think of it, she could do that. *Angela's divorce*, she thought. *Enough for a whole new tank. Wow, hot water 24/7.*

For a moment, she fantasized about hot water

gushing out of the taps, hot showers first thing in the morning. What a concept.

Shawn rose, sauntering over to the stove where he picked up the kettle, weighing it in his grasp before pouring more water into his mug. He returned to the table, having located a teaspoon near the sink, and sugared the weakened tea in his cup. Stirring, he went to the refrigerator, bending over to retrieve the milk.

It was so odd, seeing Shawn at home in her kitchen all over again. She almost liked it. Almost.

He put the spoon in the sink, and seeing her looking at him, gestured with the mug. "The house still looks the same. Like it used to."

The warmth in his tone brought her back to her present reality with a jolt. A voice in her head cried out a warning. The present was bad enough; what if he wanted to talk about the past? She was so afraid of the past. What if he wanted to talk about them? About why she hadn't shown up? Why she'd jilted him? She felt panic growing in her chest, like an expanding bubble, getting larger and larger. It was becoming difficult to breathe.

She should never have invited him in.

Shawn was leaning against the kitchen sink, staring at her expectantly.

"What?" she choked.

"I said, we haven't done this in such a long time."

The tentative, friendly expression on his face faded, to be replaced by something bordering on concern. "Is something wrong?"

"No, I—" She stood up quickly, knocking her injured knee against the table leg. She doubled over in pain, much worse than before now that she was bare-legged.

"Owwww—" She grimaced. Shawn started toward her, mug clattering onto the countertop, but she held up a hand hastily. "I'm fine," she whispered, clutching her knee.

"Did you want to show me that new case?" She tried to speak normally, but her voice was rasping. Shawn's mouth tightened. She saw the veil drop down over his face almost as surely as if she had physically put it there herself. Her heart ached, but she knew he got the message.

"Actually, I put the files in the front room. I take it that's your office?" His voice took on the cool, professional tone she had come to associate with him in the office. Somehow it did not ease the quickening of her pulse. She felt physically ill.

"Yes, that's right. Thank you. Is there anything I should know about it?" She tried to put a note of finality into her voice, the kind that she used when she was trying to end a telephone conversation.

The expression on Shawn's face grew more frozen. He got it, knew that she wanted him to leave.

He shook his head. "No, it's self-explanatory." He put his empty mug into the sink. "Thanks for the tea." He began to head out of the kitchen and down the hall toward the door.

A lump formed in Elisabeth's throat. She hobbled slowly behind him, watching as he picked up his briefcase from where he had deposited it at the foot of the staircase. Elisabeth could see her reflection in the hall mirror. She looked miserable.

"Take care of that leg. Looks like it hurts. And think about a new water tank."

Elisabeth nodded. Shawn put his hand on the doorknob, then stopped. There was a pause. Then he turned to her. He seemed to have made a decision.

"If you have the time, I'm sure Ricky Junior would like it if you just took that case off his hands. As the lead attorney, I mean."

"Really?" Elisabeth stared at him in amazement.

"Don't look so shocked. I was being a jerk when I gave you paralegal work to do. Ricky Junior told me that all the strategy behind his last case was yours. I was just being an idiot. I'm sorry."

"Oh—" she faltered, not knowing what to say.

"I'm sorry if I made you uncomfortable by coming here, Bethie."

Had she misheard him, or had he called her by that fond old nickname?

"I've upset you by coming to the house," Shawn was saying. "But I needed to see you. I needed to talk to you. I didn't want to leave things between us —" He stopped, struggling for words.

Elisabeth opened her mouth, but he stopped her. "No, let me say it. I just—I just—I should have talked to you sooner, Beth. I was stubborn and stupid. Eight years is a long time to be stubborn and stupid. Especially because we were—we were—"

"No, it was my fault," Elisabeth interrupted. "It was completely my fault. I was the one who didn't show up. And I should have explained."

But what could she have explained, she thought. That she'd lived with a noose around her neck? That Shawn could not have set her free? That Greenleigh held her prisoner? Would he have listened? And wouldn't the result have been the same? Wouldn't they still be apart? Wouldn't they still be having this awkward conversation, rehashing the past in order to figure out a way to move forward?

"But I should have dealt with it the right way, instead of getting angry and just cutting you off." Shawn hesitated, and then said, "I want us to be friends again. I want us to start over."

At this, Elisabeth blanched. "What does that mean? Start over?"

"It means start over. Put these years behind us. Maybe—maybe—we can work it out."

Elisabeth felt her hands trembling. She pressed them together, hoping he wouldn't notice. "What do you mean, work it out?"

Shawn threw up his hands in exasperation. "All right, then, you want me to say it? I'll say it. I loved you, Bethie. I thought we would always be together. I don't want to pretend we never happened. Especially with us both living in Greenleigh now. It's wrong. We have to settle this thing that's between us."

"Shawn—" Elisabeth tried to speak, but he rushed on.

"I can't stop thinking about us. Because we never actually broke up. We never ended things. I just want us to be able to—" Here he stopped. He looked at Elisabeth, and she sensed that he was about to step toward her.

No, she thought frantically. *No, if you kiss me, that'll be the end. I won't be able to think. I won't be myself anymore. I'll just be the Beth who belongs to Shawn. Everything will be all messed up.*

In spite of herself, she said it out loud. "Shawn, no."

He stopped. His arms were raised, as if he were going to reach out to her, but he lowered them.

"Why?" he demanded. "We work together. I just want to clear the air. And—I still—I still—you still make me feel—"

If you only knew how much I want you to kiss me, she thought. *I've been so lonely.* But she knew she couldn't say it.

"Shawn, no," she said instead.

"Why? Why won't you talk to me?" he said, angrily. "I got up the courage to come and see you tonight because I wanted us to start over, to not be haunted by mistakes from the past. Why won't you just let us do that? I still love you, Beth. My feelings haven't changed. God, I didn't mean to say all of this." He ran a hand through his hair, then passed his hand over his face wearily.

Elisabeth took a deep breath. Of all the things she'd expected and feared, this had not been one of them. She'd expected his anger and his contempt, and she'd worried that he might want explanations from her, before she knew what to think and how to feel—but love! He loved her still! That, she hadn't expected.

"I'm not in a good place right now," she protested. "It's complicated. So much has changed. You've been gone for such a long time."

"I know things are hard, but—" Shawn stopped, then gestured at the front room. "I saw those bills on your desk."

"You what?" Elisabeth gasped.

"I put the files on your desk, on top of a big pile of bills. I didn't snoop, they were right there."

Oh, my God. Elisabeth put her hand on the coat tree to steady herself. The bills! She had left them scattered all over the desk because she'd been trying to find a way to pay something thirty days late so that she could make the due date for the water bill.

"I didn't know it was that bad," Shawn said. His voice was calmer now. "I didn't mean to look, but I was trying to clear a space for the files and I couldn't help it."

"Well, you knew I needed the work," Elisabeth said. She was trying mightily to keep the emotion out of her voice, and wasn't at all sure if it was convincing. Shawn knew her so well, damn it. "I told you that when you hired me. I only have one client right now. This one client is going to have to pay for the new water tank, incidentally. Thank God I have any clients at all."

Something shifted in Shawn's eyes. He looked disconcerted, as if something had just occurred to him.

"That first day, when I saw you," he said slowly. "You said something about a client."

"Yes. When I made the appointment to see Mr. Murray, I had no clients at all. And I didn't have any prospects. I really had nowhere else to turn, unless I gave up practicing law. That morning, when I was late—I'd just had a potential client show up. And she's all I have right now. Look, Shawn." She took a deep breath. "This is hard for me. It's awful. You know—you're here, trying to help, and it's like I've bared my soul to you. You've seen everything—everything about how hard it is for me to exist in Greenleigh, in this house. I appreciate your help. And I know I did a really, really horrible thing to you all those years ago. But right now—right now, could you save my last shred of dignity and just leave?"

"Beth, I—"

"Please," Elisabeth said. "Right now I don't want to talk about the past. Or about the things that have happened since you left. Or about how I'm going to manage going forward. I just want—some quiet. I need to think. Let me figure my life out."

Shawn stood still, his gaze unwavering. "All right," he said finally. "But I'm not giving up. I still love you, and we still need to talk." He waited, but Elisabeth did not respond. Finally, he picked up his briefcase and left.

9

Shawn sat in his car, not moving, watching Elisabeth's shadow slanted across the curtains of her office. He was parked just down the street, and he had a view of the brightly-lit front room from where he sat. He shivered. It was a clear night, perfect for a hard frost.

"I must be out of my mind." He made the comment aloud, his gaze not moving from the slight figure behind the bulky shape of her desk. Was she working? She was very still.

He'd had every chance to tell her what he had come to say, and yet he had let it slip by. Instead, he had idiotically told her he'd loved her.

At the moment he'd said it, he'd known it was true. In fact, he'd probably known it when she first answered the door and he saw her as the same Bethie he'd tried to marry.

She was so thin. He had seen the inside of her refrigerator when he had gone to get the milk for his tea. It looked like it had a crisper full of vegetables, but not much else. Old Mrs. McPherson next door probably gave her a lot of garden produce, he suspected. There had been a block of cheese and some bread.

He felt weary and frustrated. *She needed me to believe in her, when all I wanted to do was to run away because of my own pain. The only solution I could offer was the coward's way out. The going got tough, so I left.*

The light in the front room switched off. Elisabeth must have gone to bed. He saw a flicker of lamplight in an upstairs window, but his view was obscured by a large oak tree. The house loomed dark against the sky. It might as well have been a haunted house, but for the tiniest glow in that one upstairs window. Shawn glared at it. He hated that house. As far as he was concerned, it was haunted with spirits who wanted nothing but ill for Beth.

Beth, left to face her mother's death alone. Left to muddle her way through law school, alone. Left to concentrate on achieving her dreams for herself, alone.

He felt like a jerk. All these years, he'd been

angry and hurt, not bothering to consider that Beth was the one left behind. Like Bob Stuart.

Shawn started up the engine. It was getting much too cold, and he'd had enough for one night. Tomorrow, he'd corner her and explain to her about the Stuarts. He'd planned to tell her that she couldn't represent Angela Stuart if Lawson & Lawson already had Bob Stuart's construction company as a client. But that was before he'd found out that Angela Stuart was her only client. When he'd realized that Angela was her only client, he hadn't been able to bring himself to tell her that she'd have to give up the case.

That conversation needed to happen, and when it did, it was going to suck.

HE COULDN'T FIND HER AT THE FIRM THE NEXT morning, and when he at last mentioned her absence to Ricky Junior, he was told that she was in court that day. "One of her old clients suddenly called her to help him out in small claims," Ricky Junior said. Ricky munched on a handful of potato chips from a large bag propped on his desk against a jumbo-sized soda container. Shawn viewed the chips with distaste, thinking of the grease stains they were liable to leave. He resolved to keep his personal things out of Ricky Junior's office.

"Incidentally, Ricky, I hired Beth as a law clerk, not a lawyer, but given how busy you are I gave her one of your cases. That ought to take the load off of you."

"Hey, thanks, that's great. That'll help a lot." Ricky dug into the bag for the little crumbs at the bottom. He licked his fingers, then took a swig of his soda directly out of the bottle. He tossed the empty bag into the trash. Shawn watched, revolted.

"Is that your lunch?"

"What? Hell, no. Just a snack. If you want to see her you'll have to call her at home. Or go down to the courthouse."

The courthouse. That was it. He could snag her on her way out. He checked his phone for the time. The judge would probably recess for lunch at noon, so if he wanted to catch her, he knew he had to hurry.

ELISABETH WAS IN THE LOBBY. SHE CAUGHT SHAWN'S eye as he advanced toward her.

"Hello," she said. Her eyes were tired, but she looked calm, matter-of-fact, despite their parting the night before. "What are you doing here? Work? Don't tell me you have a client in small claims?"

"No, actually. I need to discuss something with you." Seeing her expression, he added hastily, "Work-related. Can I take you to lunch?" But Elisabeth shook her head, patting her briefcase.

"I have a date. With peanut butter and jelly."

They stopped in the entrance hall of the building, amidst the sounds of clicking heels belonging to the secretaries criss-crossing the halls at a run as they tried to squeeze their errands and their lunch into the space of an hour, the residents of the county wandering about, trying to settle their real estate taxes or retrieve their drivers' licenses after they'd had one too many and been caught by a trooper on the highway. The din was pleasant, a hum of jobs well done, salaries well-earned.

Elisabeth looked up at him inquiringly. "Did you need something from me?" she asked.

Shawn found his voice caught in his throat. He looked down at her, all serious brown eyes and girlish dress, and he wanted to both shake her and kiss her at the same time. *We need to talk*, he wanted to shout. *Stop pretending that what was between us is gone.*

Everything about their lives had entwined them about each other, as if they together had formed a single tense strand. He bent toward her lips, wanting so much to touch her, wanting to feel that unity again.

But he didn't dare. And especially not in the middle of the Greenleigh courthouse, subject to the curious stares of half the legal community. Instead, he stammered, "Beth, I—I have to confess something—something you won't like." God, he sounded like he was twelve years old.

Elisabeth raised her eyebrows. She glanced at her watch. "I hope you don't mind if I start on that sandwich right here. I don't want to hear anything I don't like on an empty stomach." Her tone was light, but he could see the tension in her neck as she bent her head over the briefcase. She brought out a sandwich and began to unwrap it. She nodded at him to go on.

Shawn watched as she took a bite. He knew he had to just say it, as quickly as possible. He took a deep breath. "Beth, I know you're representing Angela Stuart."

Surprise crossed her face. "You seem to know a lot about my cases. Greenleigh is such a small town." Elisabeth took the last two bites of her sandwich, crumpled up the plastic, and stashed it in the pocket of her dress.

"Actually, I should have told you about the Stuart case last night." Shawn hesitated. "I didn't get around to it. But that was part of the reason I stopped by. I'm sorry I got distracted." There was an uncomfortable pause.

Elisabeth broke the silence. "What do you mean?"

"Bob Stuart—he's a friend of my father's. And a client of the firm. He owns Stuart Construction. He came to me asking for personal legal advice, and I offered to help him out and handle his divorce case. I didn't know his wife was your client." There, he'd said it.

Elisabeth's eyes widened. "I suppose you withdrew after you found out who his wife's counsel was?"

"No. I mean, I thought about it, but it won't help the matter. Stuart Construction uses our firm for all their legal work, and Ricky Junior in particular works on their corporate stuff a lot. You really can't be representing Angela Stuart. I'm sorry."

"And you know she's my only client right now," Elisabeth said.

Shawn nodded. "I'm sorry," he said again. "It turns out I have a personal connection to Bob Stuart, too. He plays chess with my dad at the senior center. This is such a small town, it's hard to tease apart all the different connections. But you can't represent Angela Stuart and work for Lawson & Lawson at the same time."

"So the only way I can help Angela is to quit working for Lawson & Lawson?" Elisabeth said.

Shawn frowned. "Well, I suppose. But—"

"But what? But I'm too broke to quit?"

"Well, no, but—" Shawn began, but Elisabeth cut him off.

"So now that you've seen all of my bills, now that you've seen the whole ugly truth about my life, I guess you can just make all the decisions about everything. Like who my clients should be. Like what I can afford to do. Like whether I need a new water tank." The words came tumbling out faster and faster.

"Hey, I don't—"

"No," Elisabeth snapped. "*You* don't anything. *I'll* make these decisions on my own, thanks very much. Just because you know everything doesn't mean you own everything." She turned on her heel but Shawn grabbed her arm.

"Hold on," he said tersely. "You're not being fair."

She wrenched her arm away and glared at him. "Stop it. You're making a scene. And you're my boss, remember? Just think of what all the gossips will say."

She stalked down the hall, heading for the ladies' room.

Shawn sat down on one of the benches in the courthouse entryway. He was bewildered, but he was also angry. What choice did he have but to ask her to give up Angela as her client? There was no other answer, and it had nothing to do with anything he knew about her finances or her life. Bob's company was too deeply enmeshed in Lawson & Lawson for it to make a difference if Shawn represented him or not. And what was this about "helping" Angela Stuart? Wasn't this a divorce?

The more he thought, the more irritated he became. He waited until she emerged from the ladies room, patting her forehead and neck with a damp paper towel. When she saw him waiting for her, her lips thinned and she lifted her chin.

Shawn almost laughed. He recognized the posture immediately, somewhere deep in his gut. He couldn't even remember when he had ever seen her do that before, but he knew it to be a sign that she was not to be crossed. He rose as she tried to walk by him, and hurried after her.

"Beth. Beth, stop. Just listen to me."

"I'm busy," she retorted. "Leave me alone."

"I'm really sorry about Angela Stuart. But I can't think of any other answer." She kept walking, so he raised his voice and called out, "It's just a divorce!"

At this, Elisabeth stopped. She turned around. Her face was flushed. "How can you even say that?" she said. "That's someone's *life* you're talking about." She seemed to want to say more, but she shut her lips tightly, turned around, and stalked off. This time he didn't follow her. It was probably time for her to get back into court.

What the hell just happened? Shawn thought. *Where did I screw up?*

He walked angrily out the doors of the courthouse, standing at the top of the grand staircase in front, pulling up the collar of his coat against the chill wind. They could expect snow within the next few weeks, he thought, even before Thanksgiving. Bad sign for winter. He thought of Elisabeth's water heater, and wondered whether the boiler was holding up. He wished he had thought to snoop around more when he had been in the cellar. He'd be willing to bet that the boiler needed to be replaced, too. For a house of that size, that would easily run her close to ten thousand dollars. He'd seen the bills on her desk—second and third notices for utilities and property taxes, lots of other smaller but equally urgent bills. There was no way she had a spare ten grand lying around.

Shawn peered into the wind in the direction of Church Street. He could see the gentle rise of the row of grand old downtown houses beyond the Congregational church. His heart still ached for the love he had left behind so long ago. It seemed almost quaint now. He wanted to heal that wound. He needed to either try again, or to close the book and move on.

He sometimes got the feeling that the old Beth was still there somewhere, but at other times, like today, it seemed the very fact that he'd known and loved her for so long was what put her off. As if his love for her was some kind of straitjacket that she was desperately trying to ditch.

He wished he understood better what had caused her to bail on him. At the time, he'd assumed it was her mother. And sometimes, when he was in a bad mood, he'd decided that she basically loved Greenleigh more than she loved him. Weirdly, he understood that. His mother had loved Greenleigh. And that was why he'd felt the need to flee. He got it—love and hate sometimes came from the same strange place.

Looking at that pile of bills on her desk, he'd known it was more complicated than just feelings. There were solid, three-dimensional reasons for her decisions. But he was back in Greenleigh now, back for good. Why wasn't she overjoyed? Why didn't she want to clear the air between them? Wasn't it the best thing possible that he was home to stay?

Had she changed that much?

What he was afraid of was that it was his fault. That he'd changed her, by not reaching out to her over the years to tell her that it was all right, that he'd understood that she wasn't ready to leave Greenleigh. Except that he hadn't understood, and it wasn't all right, so there was nothing he could have done about that.

That was his greatest fear, that perhaps he had destroyed any shot of happiness that they'd had, and that there was nothing he could have done about it. This was why he had felt compelled to tell her that he still loved her. He didn't want to waste any more time.

10

The following morning, Shawn walked into the library where Elisabeth and Ricky Junior were working. He paused in the doorway, silent, and at first Elisabeth didn't notice that he was there. Ricky Junior had one hand on the back of her chair as he bent over where she sat, and she was thinking abstractedly that while she really enjoyed his light-hearted company, she didn't want the relationship to head in the direction he so clearly wanted it to—should she tell him? How should she tell him?—when her skin prickled, alerting her to someone else in the room. She glanced up, words dying on her lips. From the expression on Shawn's face, he was not happy with what he was seeing. Or perhaps he just wasn't happy, she couldn't tell which.

I don't like his haircut, she thought—*it's too short* —then remembered that the length of his hair wasn't any of her business.

Even though he said he loved her. She'd repeated those words to herself over and over again, into the wee hours of the morning as she lay in bed, listening to the wheezing of the radiators. He said he still loved her.

There was a time when she would have leapt at those words, clutched at them for dear life. But now, she didn't know what she felt. It was as if her core were numb and she'd forgotten how to feel pleasure.

And what if she failed him again? What if she allowed this thing to move forward, but he wanted to go in a direction she wasn't ready for? What if she rejected him again? And with them both in Greenleigh, both of them lawyers, both of them at the same firm—it would be awful. It might make it impossible for her to work as an attorney in Greenleigh.

If that happened, where would she go?

"I need to talk to you," he said abruptly, without preamble. "In my office." He nodded at Ricky Junior, who didn't seem in the least bit perturbed by his boss's sudden appearance.

"I'm going out for a five-dollar coffee, Beth,"

Ricky said, his tone a mock threat. "I'm getting you a mocha latte."

"No, don't," Elisabeth scolded. They had a private joke about Ricky Junior's taste for overpriced gourmet coffees. Elisabeth was scandalized by the money that Ricky Junior spent on fancy drinks when perfectly good coffee was available in the office.

"I'm going to wear you down," Ricky Junior continued. "Nothing like a mid-morning latte. I'll win you over to the dark side yet. How about you, Shawn? Latte?"

Shawn was watching them, his eyes traveling from one to the other as Ricky Junior shrugged innocently in response to Elisabeth's frown. "No, thank you," he said, then turned on his heel and left.

"Wonder what's up," Ricky Junior said to Elisabeth. "Let me know if it's something I did. I don't want you to take the fall for me."

"Don't worry," Elisabeth replied, balancing her briefcase on top of her pile of papers. "I'm sure it's me, not you. I've probably messed up on something. No lattes! Okay?"

"No promises," Ricky Junior replied. Elisabeth grimaced. She knew he would be back with overpriced coffees, pastries, and an attempt to take her out to dinner.

She made her way down the hall until she reached Shawn's office. The door was ajar, and she pushed at it slightly with her shoulder, peeking in to see if he was there. He was. His back was to her as he leaned against the credenza behind his desk, gazing off in the distance at something through the window.

She would have knocked, but her arms were full, so she entered quietly, placed her pile on one of the two chairs in front of his desk, and began to sit down, but he half turned around and pointed at the door behind her. Obediently, she went to shut it, and when she returned, he was facing the window again, staring outside.

There was a long silence.

Elisabeth's eyes traveled around the office. There were framed photographs on a side table at the back of the room, and she tried not to stare but she was desperately curious about who was in them. She couldn't tell, but it looked like law school class-mates—smiling men and women in festive attire, clutching champagne flutes. His law school diploma hung on one wall, a bland corporate painting on the other—she was quite sure that was an office fixture, as it was definitely not his taste—and a plant that looked like it had seen better days perched on a coffee table in front of a small couch.

She went to inspect the plant. It was badly in

need of water, and looked as if it had some kind of blight or fungus on the underside of its leaves.

Shawn said, without turning around, "Congratulations on winning your case yesterday."

"Thank you," Elisabeth replied. At the sound of her voice, he looked over his shoulder, noting that she was no longer in front of his desk. She added helpfully, "Your plant. It's dying."

"Yeah. I know. I tend to kill plants."

He turned then, and walked over to the sofa and sat down. Alarmed, she began to retreat to a chair in front of his desk. There were piles of paper and folders on the nearby armchairs, so there was nowhere else to sit—except on the sofa next to him.

He stopped her, gesturing at the couch next to him. "I don't bite," he said dryly. "And I want to talk to you. Come sit down. I don't want to project my voice across the room."

"All right," Elisabeth said. She wondered why he hadn't just sat at his desk so that he could face her across it, but she was determined not to look like it bothered her to sit next to him. She sat primly on the edge of the sofa, facing him. He had tucked himself into his corner, his long legs crossed, one arm across the back of the sofa.

"Who was your client yesterday?"

"Oh. The natural foods store on Main Street. He isn't my client right now, but I've done work for him in the past. It was a slip-and-fall case, and it was just small claims so he didn't originally call me. He just got scared at the last minute. I'm glad I could help."

"Did he pay you?" Shawn asked bluntly.

Elisabeth bristled. "He will."

"In cash, I mean."

"As it happens," Elisabeth said coldly, "I am currently being paid in groceries. And that's fine. They're struggling in that new location on Main Street."

"So you're not actually getting paid for the case you won yesterday."

"For goodness' sake, Shawn." Elisabeth was getting angry. "I thought I made that clear yesterday. Just because you know everything about me doesn't give you the right to judge my business."

"This is about the Stuart divorce." Shawn ignored her comment.

Of course, thought Elisabeth. Of course it was. She studied his face, not trusting herself to reply.

"I've thought about it—carefully. And I keep coming to the same conclusion. We can't be on opposing sides of this case."

Elisabeth remained silent. She looked down at her hands, knotted in her lap. She noticed a small tear on the edge of one pocket, where she had caught it on a chair. Probably time to stop wearing flower-print dresses around law firms with heavy wooden chairs.

"There are all kinds of problems with this scenario, but I'm sure I don't have to go into those. At bottom, you're a contract attorney with the firm, and I'm the supervising attorney on all of your cases. We can't be on opposing sides in a courtroom."

Elisabeth allowed the sound of his voice to fade out of her hearing. She listened to the tiny creaks and sighs of the sofa as Shawn leaned back slightly, waiting for her to react.

The situation was frankly absurd. How had the two of them ended up on the opposing sides of a courtroom? In a divorce case, of all things?

The gods are laughing at me, is what she wanted to say. *Someone up there thinks it's really funny to poke at me and watch me squirm. I'm obviously a source of entertainment for some idle viewer.*

In spite of herself, she looked up at him, and thought about what she would say if she had the courage. His gray eyes were fixed on her, growing increasingly uncertain as she let the seconds tick by.

This is happening because I'm just an organism in this universe, Shawn. Because I don't matter. Because I'm expendable. My mom could have told you that.

But the Stuarts—they matter. They matter to each other, and they matter to me.

She waited a little longer, to make sure he wasn't going to jump in and say more.

"Is that it?" she said, finally.

"That's it," he said.

"I see. And—if I don't give up Angela Stuart as a client?"

"That's fine, but you can't work for me anymore."

"Right, that's what you said yesterday," Elisabeth said, although for a moment she wondered if she had said it out loud or only in her head. "Right," she repeated, just to make sure.

She had calculated her possible future earnings and her bill payments down to the penny, and she knew that Lawson & Lawson wasn't enough to raise her out of the hole. Without Angela Stuart, she didn't know how she would get through the winter.

She let her gaze slip away, to the little display of festive law students on the side table at the back of the room. She could make out their faces more clearly now. They looked so happy. Shawn looked so happy.

She looked back at him. His gaze had not moved, but she was struck by the unhappiness in it. He didn't resemble the Shawn in the photograph at all.

Law school graduation, she thought. *Back then he would have been making plans to take me to New York with him. So that was probably the happiest he'd been since before his mother died.*

And now look at him. I'm really good at making him unhappy. Special talent of mine.

She rose. There was nothing more to be said. Startled, Shawn heaved himself up from the sofa also.

"I understand. I'll talk to Angela, let her know that she needs to find counsel elsewhere."

"Beth," Shawn said quickly. "I'm sorry. I wish—"

"It's okay," Elisabeth said, moving toward her pile of papers.

"It isn't okay," Shawn said, following her to the chair. He stopped, towering over her as she bent over to retrieve her papers. "I could back out of representing Bob Stuart myself, but we already represent his contracting company. It would still be a problem."

"Don't apologize," Elisabeth said, straightening up again. "I understand. I can't afford to give up my work here at Lawson & Lawson. And I'm sorry I lost my temper yesterday. I felt—weird—that you already knew the answer before you'd even spoken to me. It wasn't a conversation. It was more like you were making an announcement. I was kind of put off by that." She took a deep breath. "But obviously, there really is only one answer to this situation. So I understand."

She saw Shawn beginning to speak again and held up her hand. "No, it's fine. Please, it's fine." She turned away from him, saying over her shoulder, "I've got some errands to run so I'll see you later."

Elisabeth could smell the aroma of the mocha latte before she even got to the library, so she walked past without stopping and continued into the reception area. She collected her books and papers into a messy pile and squashed as much of it as she could manage into her briefcase, then realized with irritation that she had left her coat in the library with Ricky Junior. As she walked back to the library door, she could hear Ricky Junior talking with Shawn in his office, so she slipped into the library quickly to grab her coat off a chair. She looked longingly at the mocha latte and chocolate croissant that Ricky Junior had left for her but knew she couldn't stay. She'd have to figure out that business some other time.

"But why? What did you say to her?" She could hear Ricky Junior pestering Shawn in the distance. She shuddered.

She hurried home as quickly as she could muster with the wind seemingly trying to knock her down at every possible opportunity. Throwing her coat over a chair in the hallway, she went straight to the kitchen. She was ravenous. She opened the refrigerator, to be faced with nothing but a small block of cheese and some vegetables. She hurried to cut herself a piece of cheese, setting up the cutting board next to the sink, and in her haste nearly sliced off a fingertip. She jumped, staring numbly at the blood beginning to trickle down the side of her finger and onto the cutting board.

Suddenly, she burst into tears. She looked down at the block of cheese on the cutting board, little droplets of blood scattered from the wound on her finger, and hurled the knife into the sink as hard as she could. It clattered, but with far less sinister effect than desired, and slid slowly down toward the drain, where it rested. Even her rage and frustration seemed to manifest themselves in pathetic ways. She felt a great welling of panic and tension in her chest, and she leaned forward on her elbows on the kitchen counter and sobbed. She sobbed so hard that her shoulders heaved and shook, and she felt her legs wobble and give way beneath her as she slid to her knees, her hands clinging to the polished oak of the cabinets. She tried to wipe at her face with her hands, but they shook so badly that all she could muster was to bury her face in them, pressing the palms against the warm, wet flesh of her cheekbones, rubbing at her eyes, willing the tears to stop.

She remained where she had sunk to her knees, leaning against the cabinets, hiccuping, spent. She couldn't work enough hours at Lawson & Lawson to completely support herself. And now, she couldn't even take the clients who came to her. The whole town had some kind of relationship with Lawson & Lawson—at least everyone in town who could afford to pay her. She wasn't a fool. She knew that this was a trap from which she could never extract herself. She could help the Angela Stuarts of the world and starve, or take the leftovers from Lawson & Lawson and barely scrape by. In either case, the house would tumble down around her and bury her.

Elisabeth glared at the corner of the kitchen where her mother's little bed had been. *All right, Mom,* she said silently. *I know I was boring and not pretty. I wasn't going to make anything of myself. I was going to stay here in quiet little Greenleigh and waste away. And no one was going to love me the way you did, so you made sure that I would always stay by your side. You weren't going to let me take my chances on some man, the way that you did, and lose. So you made sure I would never have the confidence to make the mistake that you made.*

Elisabeth laughed, but it came out like a snort. "I'm still here, Mom!" she said out loud. "Everything happened just the way you said. I'm a failure and I don't have a man. But where are you?" She began to sob anew. "You screwed up!" she screamed. "You screwed up! You weren't supposed to leave me behind! That wasn't the plan!" Her voice cracked, echoing against the shiny hard surfaces of the kitchen.

Shawn's mother had left him, too. And he'd never recovered from that. He couldn't bear to be in Greenleigh without her. Only something extreme like his father's heart attack could have brought him back to Greenleigh. He couldn't possibly be happy to be back. No wonder he wanted to start over with her—he was clutching at any shred of happiness he could possibly find. He was hoping to find something, anything good in coming home to Greenleigh.

When had she been happy? Elisabeth thought back over the years. Hours spent with Shawn. Hours spent with his mother before she got sick. Those were the years when her mother had been alive and nagging at her, but Shawn had been there for her, and all was well. It only got messy after his mother had died, when he tried to tell her that they would never find happiness together in Greenleigh.

He still loved her. And damn it, she loved him, too.

"Shawn, I've missed you," she said to the empty room. "I've missed us," she amended. The words made her stomach flutter. It felt strange, like thinking about a crush or a first boyfriend. It was odd, to think that if she wanted, she didn't have to spend the night alone. Ever again.

The sound of her voice faded away. She listened. She could hear nothing more than the occasional purr of an automobile coasting down Church Street.

The window above the sink rattled with a sudden gust of wind, and she raised her face. There was a crack in that window, and Elisabeth had been putting off the inevitable duct tape repair for months. It was already time to shut the storm windows, and she had been thinking that perhaps it would be enough to leave the cracked window be if the storm window was going to go over it anyway. She slowly heaved herself to her feet, tiptoed to peer at the cracked corner. The crack had gotten worse, and the pane was starting to collapse. She turned away. She felt the draft at her neck, but she couldn't bear to think about it any longer.

She left the mess on the cutting board and went out into the hall. Her finger was still bleeding, so she grabbed a tissue. She went into the front room, directly over to the maple secretary, and scrabbled about until she found what she was looking for.

She was going to take care of Angela Stuart, no matter what Shawn said. She'd have to do it through a back door, but she'd do it.

11

The prediction Friday was for heavy snow, an early storm. Shawn was eyeing the gray skies skeptically as he maneuvered his car into a parking space on Church Street, wondering whether it would be nearly as bad as forecasted. His father had gone to Boston that week on business and was spending the weekend with some Waterstone cousins before he was due back on Sunday.

Bob Stuart had called him first thing in the morning, confirming their appointment at Elisabeth's home on Church Street.

"Elisabeth Burnham called me to ask if we could push the meeting back to noon."

"Wh-what?" he'd stammered, taken aback. He thought that after his conversation with Beth there would be no need for there to be a meeting at all. Didn't she say that she would withdraw as Angela Stuart's attorney?

"It was scheduled for ten, but she said she had an urgent situation come up. I said it was okay—I hope it was okay?" Bob sounded too cheerful, too eager, too energetic. He was nervous.

"It's fine, but—"

"Oh, good. This is better for me. I've still got some snow prep to do at a couple of my work sites."

What the hell? And why hadn't Beth called him to make the change? Why had she called Bob directly?

He glanced at the clock on the dashboard. It was a quarter of twelve. He wondered if Bob Stewart had arrived yet.

Only one way to find out, he decided. He swung out of the car, noting with disgust that he didn't have jumper cables or a windshield scraper. He'd somehow gotten out of the habit of carrying them around, since in New York he had rarely relied on his own car for transportation about the city. Stupid, he thought. He needed to swing by a hardware store before the day was out.

He saw that someone had raked the leaves around the Burnham property, a change from his visit several days ago, when the lawn had had a thick covering. The storm windows had also been put up. *How on earth does she keep all of that straight,* he wondered. Between himself and his dad, the two of them barely kept on top of the seasonal needs of the house, not to mention repairs and maintenance, and they didn't have the added pressure of having to worry about where the funds to pay for it all would come from.

He walked up the stone pathway and onto the veranda, taking care to make enough noise so that his arrival would not be a surprise to Elisabeth. He rang the doorbell, and the door swung open immediately.

"Good morning." Elisabeth greeted him with an excess of cheerful enthusiasm. *Great. First Bob, now Beth. Two sad people pretending to be happy.*

"Good morning. Is Bob here yet?" He tried to maintain a note of formality in his voice. There was a bandage around one of the fingers of the hand which was grasping the door. She had left her hair down this morning, a distractingly cheerful tumble of brown curls, kept out of her face with a plain black hairband. There were dark smudges under her eyes, and her rouge was a touch too bright. He cast his eyes away, fixing his gaze on the knees of her gray wool slacks.

"Not yet. But come on in." She opened the door wider. Shawn considered waiting outside for a moment, but it really was too cold, even to spare them another embarrassing moment. He followed her in, and allowed her to take his coat.

"I've got some coffee on. I'll get you some." She went into the kitchen, not bothering to ask if he was interested. He turned to go into the front room. It had been tidied since his visit earlier in the week, and the pile of bills and papers on the maple secretary was nowhere in sight. Elisabeth had built up a fire in the wood stove, and he went gratefully over to it, extending his hands. She followed a moment later bearing a tray with two steaming cups. He started to reach for one, but Elisabeth shook her head.

"Yours has less sugar," she said, indicating the other cup with her chin. Shawn caught her eye and smiled as he picked it up. She looked away.

"You have a good memory," he said. Elisabeth did not reply. She put the tray down. She stood for a moment next to him, sipping at her own cup. Shawn wanted to put his hand out to her, but he did not dare. She moved away, almost as if she had read his thoughts, and sat down. He decided to ditch the formalities.

"Beth, what is going on? I would have thought we'd cancel this meeting. After we spoke yesterday, I thought we'd agreed—"

"I just wanted to tie up loose ends," she interrupted. "I don't want to leave Angela high and dry. This is my fault, after all."

"It's not your fault," he protested. "I didn't know you were representing his wife—and if the firm weren't representing Bob's company already I would have withdrawn myself—this is no one's fault, it's just—"

"—awkward," Elisabeth finished. "I know. But I wanted to make sure Angela's side of the story gets its due."

"Beth, I want you to know—you're a fine lawyer. Lawson & Lawson—we—we're happy to have you work for us. It's just—the Stuart case—we can't possibly face each other in a courtroom. It would be a mess. And it would be all over the papers, even if it weren't a basically bad idea."

Elisabeth laughed, her voice strained. "Well. Thanks. I guess you're looking out for me. Thanks so much."

Was that sarcasm? That was new. Shawn couldn't remember ever hearing that note in Beth's voice before. She was certainly entitled to feel bitterness, as much as anyone. But he'd always felt that he was the aggrieved party. He'd always thought that he was the one who had to do the forgiving. Not her.

Well, he'd been wrong. The doorbell sounded, and she excused herself.

Shawn didn't have a chance to reflect, because in a moment, she returned, followed by Bob Stuart and someone else. It was a woman. She was tall, golden-haired, wore pale pink lipstick, and a genuine and very expensive-looking camel hair coat with a cashmere scarf tucked neatly about her throat.

The golden-haired vision peeped around Bob, smiling directly at Shawn.

Shawn gaped. He knew that face. Where on earth did he know that face from?

"How are you doing?" Bob was saying. Shawn rose to shake his hand. His heart went out to the man, who had donned a suit for the occasion, awkwardly pumping his hand and looking terribly ill at ease.

"Good. How about yourself?"

"Oh, not bad, not bad." Bob's voice was artificially cheerful. "We're going to have some weather, so I had to do some hammering around the house. I checked up on my job sites. Getting ready for the winter, all those little things. Haven't seen your dad over the past week. He all right?"

"He's fine. He's in Boston on business, actually. He'll be back on Sunday."

"Oh, right. I guess he mentioned that." Bob laughed a little ruefully, and pulled at his ear. "My mind's wandering nowadays."

"Shawn, this is Christine Roberts," Elisabeth was saying.

"We've met," Christine said. She held out her hand, still smiling at him, looking as if she had just been handed a winning lottery ticket. "In fact, we were in law school together."

"That's right!" Shawn exclaimed. "You were in my—" he squinted, trying to remember.

"Contracts class," Christine interjected helpfully. "And then we were in the same study group."

He remembered now. Although her hair hadn't quite been that shade of gold, and hadn't she used to wear heavy glasses? Was he thinking of the right person? He had thought Christine from contracts wore sweats pretty much 24/7, although he also re-membered that she'd trained for the Boston marathon all three years of law school—maybe that was why. He frowned, but Christine was still looking at him, her eyes laughing, so he tried to soften his expression.

"Christine is a marital mediator," Elisabeth said. "I've asked her here so that I could introduce her to both of you. Seeing as I won't be repre-senting Angela," she said, addressing herself to Bob.

Bob looked surprised. "You won't?"

"No, unfortunately not. I do contract work for Shawn, you see. It's a little too—close—to have both of us working on the same divorce, but on opposite sides."

Bob appeared to have shrunk inside of his suit. "Yes, yes. I see what you're saying."

"Christine just signed on with a big firm in Boston—Anderson Associates. They're opening a satellite branch up here and she's in charge of their family law section." Elisabeth's voice was carefully neutral. "I've never worked on a divorce before, to be honest. So this is what will be best for Angela, in my opinion. I've discussed it with Angela and she's open to considering mediation." Christine was slipping out of her coat, revealing a pink plaid suit in a light wool that would have looked appalling on anyone else, but Shawn couldn't help but admire how nice it looked on her. She had a lean athlete's build, and the bold, dark plaid on the pale pink background suited her beautifully. It looked both expensive and edgy, a little too fashionable for the legal field. He surreptitiously checked for a wedding band or engagement ring. None. He immediately hated himself for looking, but couldn't help noticing that she wore a hefty rope of pricey-looking pearls, nestled deep in her cleavage. He turned away, flushing.

"Coffee?" Elisabeth was saying, directing the question toward both Bob and Christine.

"Sure," Christine replied, and Bob nodded.

"It's surprising we've never met, Elisabeth. You've lived here all your life?" Bob said, following her as she moved toward the kitchen. "I thought I knew everyone who lived in these big old houses downtown."

Shawn heard Beth reply pleasantly in return. "We've been here forever, since the early 1800s. But I think we're the only old family left, besides the McPhersons next door. Everyone else has sold and moved on. Maybe that's why you know all the others, but not us."

Christine had hung her coat on a coat rack, and was gazing around the entryway with an admiring expression. "What a lovely old home," she commented. She walked over to a couch and took a seat. She beamed at Shawn. "Fancy meeting you here. Are you from Greenleigh? Is this where you've been hiding all these years?"

Shawn flinched slightly. "No—I mean—yes, I'm from here, at least originally. But I've been in New York until now. I just started at Lawson & Lawson." He hoped he didn't sound too defensive.

"New York!" Christine said appreciatively. Something about the pleasant tone made Shawn think that she was laughing at him. Maybe he was a little too transparent. Did she think he was overly sensitive about being stuck in a small town? "Is that where you went after graduation? Country living sounds good to me."

"It's country living all right," Shawn said, feeling increasingly irritated. "You won't find much going on here."

"Oh, that's all right. I used to do divorces, but I'm really enjoying the marital mediation lately." She leaned in a little conspiratorially. "I think people in the country are saner, though. Maybe the divorces will be less stressful."

"Are you a friend of Beth's?" Shawn asked abruptly.

"No—but I know Ricky Murray quite well. His dad and my dad are buddies from a long, long time ago. Ricky called me to ask if I would take over a case from Beth. And of course I couldn't say no. I could never say no to Ricky. What a sweetie." She beamed again.

Huh. So Beth must have told Ricky that she was being forced to give up her client, and he called in a favor from a childhood friend to help her out. The thought should have made him feel less guilty about forcing her into a corner over the Stuarts, but instead he felt annoyed that she had gone running to Ricky for help.

"If you're a mediator, then Bob's wife still needs an attorney."

"Not necessarily. She can represent herself. Obviously, if you continue to represent Bob, or if you want to attend the mediation itself—then she will probably want someone with her." Christine was still smiling—God, did this woman ever stop smiling?—but her tone was professional and her words succinct. "But people do their own divorces all the time. My job is to keep the cost and the level of animosity down. I do a very good job, if I say so myself."

Shawn walked over to the big bay window and stared outside. He suddenly understood. Beth had performed a superb slight of hand. She'd recused herself from the case, but she'd essentially kicked Shawn off the case, too. If Angela was willing to mediate without an attorney, there was no way Bob was going to bring an attorney in. And if Shawn insisted on staying involved, Beth was going to advise Angela informally, on the sly, without actually representing her.

Checkmate, he thought. Beth had just won this battle. And he had to hand it to her—it was a smart move, calculated to upset no one and to give her client—her ex-client now—an advantage.

So who had thought of this plan? Beth? Ricky Junior? Or the deceptively lovely Miss Christine Roberts?

Christine was speaking to him, so he turned back to face her. "I still don't know many people here. Ricky took me to lunch yesterday and drove me around a bit. It's a cute town. Would you like to grab a cup of coffee some time? I'd love to catch up. It's been such a long time."

"Sure," he replied automatically. He didn't think he cared much for this woman, but he didn't want her to think that he was a law firm reject rusticating in a hick town—he'd show her a good time. "I'd like that. We can do dinner tonight if you'd like. Why don't I come by for you—where are you living?" His mind was still turning over his latest discovery.

"I'm right down the street," Christine said.

Shawn paused, not certain at first that he had heard right. He frowned. "Where?"

"Next to the church. Christine laughed, a light, tinkling sound. "Isn't it funny? Church Street—so there's a church! On Church Street! How quaint." She laughed again.

Shawn wasn't laughing. "You mean the old Webster place? Right next to the church?"

"That's the one! I'm really excited—it'll be so much fun to renovate it. Don't you think? It's a beautiful house."

"But—are you renting it?" The Webster manse was a mess. If Beth's home was run down, the Webster property was a disaster. Old Mr. Webster had died a few years back, but the relations who had inherited the place were not interested in throwing their money down a black hole, and had been looking for a buyer for years.

"Oh, no—I've bought it. I was looking for a property to renovate. Something that needs a bit of TLC. I've always wanted to live in an old house. I'm tired of apartments and condos. So boring. So modern."

"Most of the residents of the downtown are young families now," he heard Beth saying. "There were lots of old families in these houses when I was growing up. But gradually the houses have been getting sold. These places are much too big for elderly people, and the upkeep is difficult unless you have a lot of energy." She emerged from the kitchen with a tray. "I spent all of yesterday doing storm windows, one by one, all over creation. Of course I discovered quite a few places where I never got around to removing them from last year! That was a relief."

"You're just in time for the first big storm," Bob Stuart said, following close behind. "It really is hard to keep up a large house. This is something I've always thought about with regard to our home—the kids are more or less gone for good and we really don't need the space. And I just don't feel like it anymore." He sighed.

"Storm windows!" Christine exclaimed. She accepted the cup that Elisabeth offered. "What are those, and should I get some? Are they for storms?"

Elisabeth gaped.

"Christine just bought the Webster manse," Shawn said. "She's renovating it."

Despite not knowing what storm windows are, he almost added.

"Aren't old houses wonderful?: Christine said, smiling.

Beth turned away, and Shawn did not dare catch her eye.

12

Elisabeth wondered how much longer she could stand breathing the same air as Christine Roberts.

Yes, she was friendly. Oh-so-friendly. The type of golden-haired princess who put her hand on your arm as she reacted with intense interest to whatever you were saying. Touchy-feely.

Yankees aren't touchy-feely, Elisabeth reflected. Christine must be from somewhere outside of New England. Someplace where people don't mind touching each other.

Don't touch my arm. I'll oh-so-accidentally spill coffee on your beautiful skirt if you do.

She smiled at Christine, thinking irritatedly that Ricky Junior could at least have found her a marital mediator who was old and ugly. He'd said she was new in town but an old friend of the family. Ricky Junior had been eager to help Elisabeth out after she'd fled and abandoned the mocha latte at the firm the other day.

Maybe she should let Ricky Junior take her out just once. No...no, that wasn't a good idea. She couldn't lead such a good guy on.

And this thing about being Shawn's classmate. Was she one of the happy champagne drinkers in that photo in his office? Shawn hadn't recognized her right away, so maybe not. But she was certainly eager to be cozy with him. Elisabeth almost sniffed, but she caught herself just in time. Bob was saying something to her about the difficulty of keeping up his house, and Christine was smiling and nodding as if Bob were telling a funny story.

"Have you thought about selling and moving to something smaller?" Elisabeth asked. She gestured toward a comfortable armchair for Bob, leaving Shawn to join Christine on the couch.

Bob shook his head. "No, I've never gone that far in my thinking. You see, I've always viewed that house as Angela's. I was hardly home all those years, and she was the one who held down the fort. I suppose I just assumed that she'd want to stay there."

"You know, Mr. Stuart," Elisabeth said gently, "You should try talking to her about the house. Both of you built it together. It's a symbol of your marriage. You should take care of it. Like taking care of a family, or a child."

"What a lovely thing to say," Christine interjected. Her hand was on Shawn's shoulder as she leaned into the conversation, and Elisabeth tried not to glance at Shawn to see what he was thinking. "I know that this is a very difficult conversation for us to have—especially since Angela isn't here, unfortunately, and doesn't have an attorney to represent her—but Beth is correct. Marriages need fuel. If you don't feed them, they die."

"I know I'm responsible for neglecting the house —and for neglecting Angela. And I've thought and thought about this. But how could it have been different? I had my job, and I was real lucky—we were okay even when the building trades everywhere were doing so badly. I worked my tail off. Although Angela did, too, of course," Bob added. He spread his hands apart. "I don't know what else we could have done. We barely had ten minutes of conversation, total, in a day. Mostly we had less, and it was generally about the children."

"I'm really sorry that Angela isn't here with me today," Elisabeth said. "It took her quite a bit of courage to even come to me. I'm afraid it was asking for more than she could bear to see you under these circumstances. I'm also really sorry that I can't represent her. I think we might have had some good conversations." She nodded at Christine. "But a mediator can help take a divorce out of court and dial down some of the stress."

The wind had picked up outside, and there was a very strong draft in the room. Elisabeth suspected that there was a storm window she had forgotten to install somewhere—*yes, Christine, storm windows are for storms.* She moved forward and opened up the woodstove door to jab at the fire with a poker. Her practiced moves coaxed the flames into leaping with renewed vigor around the main log in the center of the grate.

"I think I need to buy one of those," Christine said brightly.

"They're useful," Elisabeth said, trying to keep her tone light. Why was Christine so intent on playing the idiot? Did she think anyone was going to buy this dumb-blonde charade? Whom was she trying to fool? Shawn? That made no sense—Shawn knew she wasn't stupid. Bob? What for? So the only person left was Elisabeth. And why would Christine want Elisabeth to think she was shallow and stupid?

I don't care, she thought. *I just care about Angela. I'm not abandoning her. And now that I'm not her attorney, I don't have to.*

Elisabeth dusted the ash off her hands and replace the poker on its hook next to the stove. She looked at Bob Stuart, who was gazing absently into the fire.

"Mr. Stuart—"

"Bob. Call me Bob." He was sitting absolutely still, his carefully controlled countenance revealing only the slightest hint of agitated feeling in the light sheen of sweat at his hairline. Elisabeth knew that Bob desperately wanted to be told that there was still hope.

"I'm sure you're thinking that Angela resents you terribly for all that she's suffered." Bob's shoulders sagged, but he nodded without a change in expression. Elisabeth continued, "But actually she's afraid that she'll lose her resolve. This is not something that she's eager to do. It's a desperate act. And yet it was necessary for her, for her sense of dignity and in honor of your marriage. She needed to leave. It was time. It's because her marriage was that important to her. She wouldn't have left if she hadn't cared. Does that make sense?"

Christine, to her credit, had stopped smiling. She was watching Elisabeth with fascinated interest.

"But she left me," Bob said. He seemed caught on this, wanting to repeat it over and over. "She left me, Beth. She's the one. I never would have left her —God help me, I never could have abandoned her. And yet, she left me. Just like that, as if we had never existed."

Elisabeth allowed the silence to take shape around his words, the fire roaring softly in the stove. She was gazing at her shoes, stretching her legs out before her. She held her hands out on her lap, examining the long fingers, pulling down the sleeves of her sweater. She looked up and saw Shawn looking at her, brow wrinkled. She pointed at him. "Now see, Mr.—Bob, I mean. Attorneys are for divorces. Not for fixing things. They take marriages apart. They don't put them together. That's why everything your attorney tells you will be a cautionary tale."

"Shame, Mr. Waterstone," said Christine sternly. Her hand went back on Shawn's arm, and Elisabeth nearly laughed. She was so predictable!

"I didn't say anything," Shawn said in protest. He turned to Bob. "It's not my place to meddle. I'm only here if you need legal advice. And if you feel it's beyond all hope, I'm here to help you figure things out." Bob's expression was bewildered. He turned questioning eyes to Elisabeth, who was watching him. She nodded.

"That's the question, of course. Only you can answer that. Is it beyond all hope?" She addressed Bob.

"God, I don't want it to be," Bob said with feeling. He looked at Elisabeth now with a sudden glimmer of comprehension. "You're right. If the marriage means anything to me, I'll do what I have to do."

Elisabeth was settling in her chair, looking innocent. "Why, Bob, that sounds very romantic. Maybe you can sweep Angela off her feet, drag her off somewhere on horseback."

Bob laughed. "She'd have me committed if I did that! No, I understand now. I spent a long time blaming myself and hating her for leaving. But I see now that everyone loses that way. And I understand the part about her leaving now. I just hope I can tell her that myself." He rubbed sweaty palms on his pants. "God, I'm feeling a bit shaky." He stood up quickly, took a turn about the room, returning to the little knot of chairs in front of the stove, automatically holding his hands out for warmth, even though the red flush on his neck belied the fact that he was not at all cold. He cast a look at Elisabeth.

"So how do I make her agree to see me? I can't try to fix things if I can't talk to her."

Elisabeth shrugged slightly. "You've known Angela for thirty years, Bob. I'm sure you have all the answers somewhere up there." She smiled at him and tapped her head. He smiled back, a new determination creasing his brow.

"You're right, of course," he said, rubbing at his crewcut. "You're absolutely right. I know her better than anyone. I'm the one who needs to fix this. No one else." He swung over to one of the bay windows, gazing intently out at the first fat snowflakes beginning to fall. They hovered and danced and took their time before fluttering down to the ground, where they promptly melted. A light sprinkling was beginning to settle on the leaves of a giant rhododendron bush.

"I need to leave!" Bob said suddenly. He turned around quickly. "Beth, you have saved me."

"Certainly not," Elisabeth said. "I'm just here to help. Any life-saving was done by yourself."

"Thank you." His voice choked, and he turned toward the door.

"Let me get your coat."

Bob turned to Shawn. "I hope I never need your services, Shawn. But thank you."

Shawn raised an arm. "Good luck, Bob. I get the feeling that Dad won't be seeing you much at the Senior Center now."

"I hope not—but I've got a great chess board at home. He'll have to come over and help me to break it in." He waved farewell before heading out into the gathering snow.

Elisabeth watched through the window from her position next to the door as Bob Stuart hustled down the walk, turning up his collar against the blowing snowflakes. There was something hopeful, a little spring in his stride, despite the dismal setting.

"I hope that wasn't unethical," she said, directing the comment to Christine.

Christine shrugged. "I don't know why it would be. You're not anyone's attorney. You're just a friend. I'm here to offer mediation as an option, to answer questions if there are any. But Bob didn't have any questions."

"That's because he doesn't want a divorce," Elisabeth said wryly. "No matter what Shawn thinks."

"Hey, I'm not an ogre," Shawn protested, sounding annoyed. "I'm just representing my client."

Both women looked at him in silence until he coughed and picked up his cup. It was empty, so he put it down again.

"The wind is picking up," Elisabeth said, finally. "You'd better go."

Christine turned to Shawn. "Did you say dinner?"

Shawn looked slightly uncomfortable. "Yes. Beth, would you like to join us?"

"Who, me?" Elisabeth averted her eyes, busying herself with cups on the tray. "No, thanks. I have to connect with Angela, make sure she knows that Christine is available to mediate, and that she can hire another lawyer. If she wants. So I have some clean-up to do this afternoon for this case. You two have fun."

"We will!" Christine exclaimed. She rose and held out her hand. "It was lovely to meet you. I think what you did for Bob was wonderful. Even if Shawn doesn't."

"Stop," Shawn complained. "I'm outnumbered."

Christine laughed her tinkling laugh. She had donned her coat, and she gave Shawn's arm a squeeze with her gloved hand. They walked toward the door, her hand firmly tucked into his arm.

Elisabeth retreated to the kitchen. She could hear Christine laughing again as she and Shawn exited.

Yeah. You two go have fun. I've done my work, and I'm satisfied.

13

When she had spoken to Angela about the scheduled meeting with Bob and Christine, she had met with violent resistance.

"Absolutely not," Angela had gasped. "No. No. I'm not ready."

"I know it's hard," Elisabeth had begun, but Angela cut her off.

"I feel ridiculous," she exclaimed. "I know I came to you—well, Sarah made me—she said that I should—and I was—I was—but no!" she finished, choking on her sentence.

Elisabeth tried again, but Angela cut her off once more. "I don't understand!" she wailed. "Why do I need a different lawyer? Why can't you just talk to him for me?"

Elisabeth explained, but Angela was still upset. "Bob can hire someone else," she sniffled. "I don't understand why he had to go talk to Lawson & Lawson. He doesn't even *like* lawyers."

"Or you can both ask Christine Roberts to mediate," Elisabeth said. "You won't have to accept anything you don't like. It's a way to cut down on the friction between both sides, and to keep it out of the courtroom."

"A kinder, gentler divorce?" Angela's voice was bitter.

"Yes," Elisabeth replied firmly. She'd called Ricky Junior and he'd connected her to Christine. That part of it would work fine. She was almost tempted to give herself a pat on the back for clever thinking. She wasn't a particularly good chess player, but she wasn't too bad at thinking on her feet. She thought that maybe she could continue to help Angela without actually giving her legal advice, and that way she might be able to help prevent this marriage from unraveling.

But this wasn't workable indefinitely. In the future, there would be more Angela Stuarts, more Bob Stuarts. She couldn't keep bailing on clients. And God forbid, if people figured out what was going on, that would be an easy way to disrupt things—if Elisabeth Burnham is representing the other side, then just hire Shawn Waterstone! She'll get kicked off the case! End of story!

She simply couldn't maintain a private practice and keep working for Lawson & Lawson. Even if her personal clients had no connection to Lawson & Lawson, the large insurance companies and other corporations that gave her clients such a hard time were often Lawson & Lawson clients. It was going to be a mess going forward, and she knew it.

She'd arranged to see Angela after the meeting with Bob, Christine, and Shawn. She was able to coax her out for coffee at Pierre's, but she knew it was going to be a difficult meeting.

Fine snowflakes were falling on and off; the forecast said the storm might shift a bit and head toward the sea, in which case they wouldn't get nearly the dump of snow that they had thought. Elisabeth splurged recklessly on a coffee and a croissant, and sat at a table next to a window, watching the flakes dance and flutter before they skittered away across the sidewalk outside. Ms. Tattoo had her head buried in another Russian novel, as was her habit, and merely grunted when Elisabeth deposited her change into the tip jar.

Angela arrived, her cheeks pink with cold, snowflakes in her hair. *She has no idea how pretty she is*, Elisabeth thought, not for the first time. *Why is it that all the lucky ones have no idea how lucky they are?*

Angela ordered tea, and Ms. Tattoo heaved herself up grumpily from her perch, leaving Dostoevsky next to the register. As she stalked over to the cans of tea leaves, Angela came to sit with Beth.

"I'm sorry about the way I acted," she said, before Elisabeth could open her mouth. "On the phone, I mean. I'm so embarrassed. I feel like a teenager. One moment I think I'm in control, and the next, I'm screaming. I'm so sorry." She smiled wanly. "I swore I wouldn't cry anymore, but sometimes—sometimes I just can't keep it under control," she ended in a whisper. She looked around anxiously for eavesdroppers but the shop was deserted.

Elisabeth did not reply, but held out a hand. Angela took it and squeezed it gratefully.

"I just want this all to end," she said. "I just want to start over. I'm so tired, and I want something new for myself."

"What does that mean?" Elisabeth asked, her heart sinking. Perhaps she had been wrong to presume, wrong to give Bob the impression that he had any ability to fix what had gotten so messed up over the years. Maybe Shawn was right. Maybe this was "just" a divorce. Maybe lawyers were supposed to perform surgery, not miracles.

Angela shook her head. "I don't know. I can't explain. I feel suffocated, like I'm about to burst. At the same time, I feel so sad. I don't want this, but I want this. I want something to happen, but I dread anything happening. I want change, but I dread change."

"I know exactly what you mean," Elisabeth said, to her own surprise. She did. She couldn't explain it either, but she felt the same way, as if she'd seen the lightning and was now waiting for a thunderclap.

Ms. Tattoo had returned to her perch, so Angela went to fetch the tea. When she returned, Elisabeth could not bring herself to continue the thread of the conversation. Instead, she stared blankly out the window at the flakes that continued to twirl through the air.

"I wonder if we're going to get slammed," she said aloud. "Or if this storm is going to head out to sea. With all the technology we have, you'd think we'd have a handle on winter storms by now. But there's always the possibility of the storm suddenly veering off somewhere. You can't predict things like that."

"It feels like snow," Angela said. "You can smell it. In the air. You know what I mean."

Elisabeth nodded. She did know. Snow had an unmistakable smell.

"I don't think it's going away," Angela added.

"I just want to know if this is going to be two feet of snow or twenty feet of snow."

Angela nodded. "I wonder that also. I—I wonder if Bob will be okay, taking care of the snow removal for the company, plus keeping an eye on things at the house." She gazed out the window at the falling snow and murmured, "I won't be there to shovel the steps and the walkway."

"I hear you. It's a lot of work," Elisabeth agreed somberly. She hesitated, then said, "Why don't you call him, Angela? Ask about the snow. You'll feel better. You don't have to talk about anything complicated. I think disappearing on him is part of why you feel so aimless."

"But it's so painful," Angela said, searching for her handkerchief. She settled on the napkin under her cup, and pressed it against her eyes. "This just hurts so much. I want it to stop."

"Believe me, I understand," Elisabeth said quietly. "But silence is a mistake. Misunderstanding and pain live in that silence."

Angela peered at her, the napkin crushed in her hand. "I know you're right," she said finally. "But Beth. I feel like—like—" She paused, frowning. "Like having that conversation is another kind of mistake. Like the more I try to explain, the more chance it has of becoming its own thing. Like a nightmare. It's part of sleep unless it's too big, too long—then it's a monster. I don't want a monster. I don't want this to be knotty and complicated. As long as I don't say anything it's just part of my everyday life."

Elisabeth nodded. "Yes. It feels like as soon as you point out the problem—you've just made a problem. But problems can be addressed. If you are just feeling general pain, there's nothing Bob can do about that. He's a problem-solver. Maybe pointing out the problem will be a good thing for him."

The door blew open with a blast of frigid wind, snow whipping around the door jamb and hitting Ms. Tattoo in her black tank top. She cursed, shouting, "Close that door, God damn it! Jesus!" She got up from her perch and hurried over, helping a lean youth in a black leather jacket to push the door shut against the wind. Elisabeth watched curiously as he gave her a hug. Ms. Tattoo almost looked cheerful as she slapped the boy on the back vigorously. They were clearly acquainted with each other.

"Just a black coffee," she heard the boy say. As Ms. Tattoo went in back of the counter and started banging mugs around, the boy turned and caught sight of Elisabeth and Angela.

"Just saying, it's bad out there. Getting hard to walk. Wind was blowing me all over the place." He nodded at the door.

Angela stood up hastily. "I'm worried about Sarah," she said to Elisabeth. "Are you okay? Will you get home all right?"

"Are you kidding—I'm born and raised here—you think a little nor'easter is going to scare me?" Elisabeth tried to joke. She smiled at Angela. "Promise me you won't do anything rash."

"I promise," Angela said.

"No trips to the Bahamas, no plastic surgery, no new boyfriends."

Angela gasped, then laughed. "I promise!"

"And please—think about talking to Bob. Give him a call. Ask about the snow. Nothing stressful. Just a conversation."

Angela nodded wordlessly and gave Elisabeth's hand a squeeze.

The boy in the leather jacket went over to pull the door open for Angela as she left. Elisabeth watched her stagger her way down the walk, pulling her hat firmly down onto her head.

"Hey."

For a moment, Elisabeth thought he was talking to Ms. Tattoo.

"You sure you don't want to get going? It's bad out there."

Elisabeth felt inexplicable irritation. She pulled herself upright in her chair. "I know," she said. "I like snowstorms." *What? Where did that come from?*

She did not like snowstorms. In fact, she was already wondering if any snow was getting into the house.

Leather Jacket was smiling at her, a crooked smile that could have been a smirk. Elisabeth averted her eyes.

"I'll be fine," she said.

Ms. Tattoo was hurrying out from behind the counter. She was wearing a heavy jacket and a gray knit cap.

"I'm closing up," she said toward Elisabeth. "But you stay as long as you want." She gestured with her chin. "He's staying here."

Elisabeth started to rise. "Oh—oh, no, I'll leave."

"It's fine," Leather Jacket said. He sounded slightly bored. "I do this a lot. Gina has to move her car. There's a snow emergency, she's gonna get towed. She might as well leave."

"What about your car?" Elisabeth asked. She had to leave, she thought. This was weird—she didn't want to sit in Pierre's with a leather jacket dude.

"I don't have a car," he said, smiling. The door slammed. Ms. Tattoo had gone.

"Can I refill your coffee?"

For a moment, Elisabeth wanted to run away. Everything about this setup felt wrong. But she looked at the Leather Jacket dude. He had slick black hair, an earring, and from what she could make out at his wrists, a length of tattoos on both arms. He wasn't very tall, taller than she was, but mostly just lean and compact, in jeans and a plain white tee shirt that set off a slight tan nicely.

She felt dowdy and old in her scuffed boots and homemade scarf. And this leather jacket dude—he wasn't Shawn. He was the wrong guy.

"Here you go," he was saying, putting a fresh cup on the counter.

How could the wrong guy be the one who was here, right now, serving her coffee?

Maybe the guy who was here, was the guy who was here.

"Thanks," she heard herself say.

"What's your name?"

14

Greenleigh had exactly one fancy restaurant. It was a nouveau American-style place with prime rib, cavernous ceilings, and candlelight, and it was the one restaurant that Shawn absolutely did not want to be caught at with Christine. He knew that gossip would fly fast and furious around Greenleigh, and the last thing he wanted was to be paired up with the beautiful lady lawyer from Boston before he had even been home for a couple of months. On a Friday night, the Mill House Tavern on Water Street was going to be packed full of expensive suits and pearls and heels.

He thought he remembered something about Italian—hadn't Ricky Junior and Beth gone to some Italian place for lunch once? But when he shot Ricky Junior a text, he was nettled to discover that the Italian place was actually much fancier than he'd thought. Why the hell had Ricky Junior and Beth gone to such a fancy place for lunch?

He was annoyed when Ricky Junior cheerfully texted back, "Great place for a date, Beth loved the scampi." Date. This was not a date. And Ricky Junior and Beth were not dating. Definitely. Not. Dating.

Then a moment later, "Expensive but maybe it was the wine. Fun to treat Beth to a good wine tho."

Jesus. Shawn shoved the phone back into his pocket, fuming. Okay, then.

He knew that it wouldn't be wise to drive out of town on a snowy night where the nor'easter could take a turn for the worse at any moment, so that meant they were stuck with the Greenleigh options.

The Mill it was.

He had dropped Christine off at her office across town and spent a fitful afternoon wrestling with the pile of work on his desk, uncomfortably aware of both Beth's and Ricky Junior's absence. He knew that Ricky Junior was responsible for Christine's sudden involvement in the Stuart case, and he wondered if Beth had gone off to meet with him. *I'm paranoid*, he told himself. She'd said she needed to speak to Angela, which sounded likely. Angela had not shown up herself, so there would be loose ends to tie up there. One thing about Beth, she did not leave any loose ends.

Except...for them. *They* were loose ends, weren't they.

Shawn shook his head to clear the cobwebs, but the thought persisted. It was strange. He knew her now as an attorney, as a fully-fledged adult with adult responsibilities. When he'd left Greenleigh, she'd still been connected to the nexus of her family, that awful mother of hers and that ramshackle old house. He'd been all too ready to ditch his family, the family business, the town, the entire lifetime of connections—none of which were awful. What could have been so hard for her? As far as he could tell, nothing she had in Greenleigh was good for her. It didn't help her to grow. It just tied her down.

How had Beth grown in a person who left no loose ends untied—at least when it came to her clients—when she'd been able to abandon him in a parking lot and never speak to him again?

The snow appeared to have slackened some-what, but it was bitterly cold and getting colder by the time he stopped by Christine Roberts' office to pick her up for dinner. As much as he hadn't wanted this to appear to be a date, when he poked his head in her office door, he knew that there was nothing he could do about the gossip. He shook hands with the other two young attorneys who had been tasked, along with Christine, with setting up the new satellite office for their big city firm, and once his back was turned he could had sworn he could feel their smirks. The fifty-something-year-old receptionist was the wife of his dentist, and she seemed particularly interested in Shawn's lame attempts to downplay his connection to Christine—oh, did he know her? from school? from work? how nice that he was taking her out to dinner! The delivery guy stacking boxes in a corner of the posh new suite was the same guy who delivered to Lawson & Lawson, and he gave Shawn a knowing look as Christine emerged, donning her coat.

To be fair, anyone looking at Christine would have had a hard time looking away. She was wearing the same pink plaid suit but had changed her hairstyle. It was now in an upswept chignon, with shiny blonde strands falling about her face. It looked carefully casual, exactly the way she sounded. She was also wearing giant round glasses.

"I just had to take my contact lenses out," she apologized. "The air is so dry when it snows." Shawn was reminded that Beth also occasionally wore round glasses, except that hers always looked as if they were a little warped. They never sat quite right on her nose. Christine's glasses looked like a fashion accessory from the pages of *Vogue*.

"What a pity Beth couldn't join us!" she said

brightly as they walked out the door. "Although I suppose she really did need to connect with Angela today after that meeting. Maybe she can calm her down. I hope Angela gives me a call. I think I can help the Stuarts work things out. If I don't hear from her in a little bit, I'll call Beth and see what she's thinking. Do you have her cell?"

Shawn shook his head. Did Beth even have a cell phone? He had no idea. He never seen her with one. "She's kind of analog," he said, then regretted it when Christine threw her head back and laughed. Hard.

"Really? What a curious person! But—that's kind of awesome!"

"She does her own thing," Shawn said tersely. He started up the car. "She works from home. You can always find her. She's at home, in the library, or at court."

"That's lovely. I wish my life were that simple." Her words ended on a sigh, and for a brief microsecond, Shawn thought she sounded almost genuine. He decided not to pursue the opening. It was too small. And he didn't care. He was in pain, and he didn't really want to hear about whatever minor woes someone like Christine Roberts could possibly be facing.

"It's been a long time," he said. "What have you been up to? Were you in Boston all along?"

"For a little while. Then I went to California." Christine was peering out the passenger-side window. "What a lovely town Greenleigh is."

Was she trying to change the subject, or was she just a ditz? Shawn felt more irritation bubbling up, then tamped it down firmly. That wasn't fair, he knew. He hated it when people wandered off topic during a conversation, which Beth never did. Okay, never had, he amended. And maybe that was because of him. Maybe he was just an egomaniac and wanted a captive audience at all times. If that were true, he was a real jerk. In fact, he kind of did think he was a real jerk.

He answered patiently, "It's not California, that's for sure."

Christine put her window down, and the snow that had been gathered against the glass fluttered into her lap. She put her cashmere-encased hand out into the frigid air, then pulled her hand back in to inspect her palm. Shawn glanced at her. Her lap had a considerable dusting of snow in it now. It was going to melt and make a mess on her coat. Clearly, she was much too fascinated with snow to be a real New Englander.

"You look like you've never seen snow before, but you were at law school in Massachusetts."

"I never had a car, though," Christine countered. "It's neat how the snow is lying flat against the window in a sheet, and if you put the window down, it's still standing there. Like a sheet of paper made out of snow."

"Until it falls in your lap."

Christine giggled. "Yes. I'm going to be all wet. It'll be okay. I'll survive."

Shawn didn't comment. He could have told her that once she got her gloves wet, it was all over—she'd be cold for the rest of the evening—but he refrained.

There was valet parking at The Mill, so he left the engine on and the keys in the car in front of the restaurant. As he escorted Christine through the door, he realized that she was wearing heels that matched her suit, not boots, and that her feet were soaked.

California, he thought scornfully. *What was she thinking, wearing heels during a nor'easter?*

"This is lovely!" The Mill had dim interior lighting, multiple fireplaces, and heavy wooden tables and chairs. The maitre'd wore a tux. The tablecloths were dense and white, and each table had a candle and fresh flowers. It was a touch above your parents' steakhouse, more like a scene from a movie featuring D.C. lobbyists bribing corrupt politicians. The level of dress was sophisticated, but most of the guests wore practical boots for the weather.

"It's nice," Shawn agreed. He looked around

anxiously. It was a bit thin for a Friday night—thanks to the snow—but it was still busy. He recognized a dozen people right away, and weighed the risk of asking for a quiet table and making this seem more like a date against the risk of being seated in the thick of things and being openly ogled. He chose the former, and the host escorted them to a far corner of the back room, next to a small window with a view of the falling snow. There was a crackling fire in a huge fireplace right behind them, and the host clucked as he observed that Christine's coat was soaked down the front, promising to hang it carefully in hopes of drying it off.

"You might want to leave your gloves out," Shawn said, then wished he hadn't, because Christine turned to him with that fascinated expression that he was starting to understand was her way of laughing at him.

"They're in my purse, is that bad?"

"No," he muttered. "Just—when they're wet, they're useless. Gloves like yours, anyway."

"Oh." Christine observed his gloves with interest, lying on the table beside his water glass. They were lined deerskin, worn but still nice to look at. She reached for her purse and removed her gloves. She held them up. "Should I spread them out to dry? You're right, they're soaked. It's nice that we have the fireplace right there."

She carefully spread them out next to her, adding, "You people up here in Greenleigh are so practical!"

"We are that," Shawn agreed. "Hard to do otherwise when the weather rules everything. What made you come here to practice law? California sounds good to me. None of this." He gestured at the window.

"I was done with California and nice weather," Christine said. She still had a pleasant smile on her face, but her voice had changed into the businesslike tone that she had used back at Beth's. "I was ready to come back. My family's in New Jersey. My dad is a lawyer—he does business stuff—and he convinced me to come back east. California was interesting, but I'd had enough of it."

The wine menu arrived. He guessed—correctly—that Christine would know how to choose a wine, and let her handle it. He wasn't a big wine drinker himself and thought the whole process was mostly pretentious.

"What did you do in California? Family law?"

"I actually clerked for a year."

"Really?" Shawn sat back in his seat. He knew that Christine was hiding her brains behind a ditzy-blonde act, but judicial clerkships were extremely competitive, and reserved for the top students in class. He hadn't been interested in a clerkship at all

—he'd wanted to climb the law firm ladder ASAP and make huge amounts of money ASAP—but he was impressed by anyone who had done one.

Christine laughed. "Oh, don't pretend you aren't shocked. Yes, I originally wanted to do complex litigation. If it was hard, I wanted to do it. That's why I ran so many marathons. If it involved pain, I was there."

"That's right. I remember you were a runner. You ran the Boston Marathon every year. I'm not a runner," Shawn said apologetically. "I don't know what that's like. Just not a thing I ever did."

"Well, let me tell you, running is kind of masochistic. It's hard on the body. Hard on the mind. It's good for you, helps you to push yourself. But as a mindset, it's something you have to watch out for. It can go to all kinds of dark places." She beamed.

"I can't believe someone as cheerful as you ever goes to dark places," Shawn said honestly.

"Oh, I'm a pro at dark places," Christine replied, still beaming. "So when I started practicing in California, I did celebrity divorces."

"Seriously?"

"Seriously. The most famous, wealthy movers and shakers you can think of, with the most deeply tangled, bizarre, disturbed relationships that you *can't* think of. I mean, talk about stuff you would never have imagined. Stuff that would fill the tabloids many times over. I made partner and then left. I was done." Christine nodded out the window. "This is nothing. I can handle a little snow." She took a sip of wine.

Shawn also reached for his wine glass, feeling simultaneously impressed and humiliated. He'd been mentally dissing her all along, annoyed that he had to have any kind of interaction with this annoying society chick, but clearly she had one-upped him. That dumb-girl air was mostly preservation instinct, he suspected. A veneer that she used so that she could get the work done.

"So you bought that house on Church Street. That's going to be a project. You like challenges, it seems. That one is going to be a hell of a challenge."

"Do you know anything about old homes, then?"

"Yeah, I guess I do. My dad's house isn't as old as yours is, but it's old. And Beth's is old. Really old. She can tell you something about keeping up an old house."

Christine closed her menu and set it aside. She leaned forward. "Do you think Beth would be okay with me asking her about house stuff? She's very sweet, but she's kind of reserved. I don't want to be pushy. But I don't know anyone here. I'd love it if we could be friends. All of us." Shawn looked up from his menu, expecting to see her beaming again, but to his astonishment, she was not smiling at all. She was serious.

Oh, my God, you don't know the half of it, Shawn thought. What to say? He couldn't figure out if he was envious of Christine, if he loathed her, if he admired her—and mostly, he ached for Beth and wished that Christine would go away and stop complicating everything.

On the one hand, he hated it that everyone in Greenleigh had known him his whole life and knew all of his business. On the other, it was so helpful that no one ever asked him about Beth, because that was a subject that people had politely relegated to his past. If it was one thing you could count on in a small New England town, it was that people didn't say things to your face. This new person coming into town, who knew nothing of Greenleigh, New England, or even snow—this made it all so much worse.

But Beth was alone, he thought. She didn't have family, and she hardly seemed to have friends, except for the many people she helped and took care of every day. Maybe there was a remote chance that Christine could be her friend. It was worth a try.

"Sure," he said finally. "You should just knock on her door this weekend, go out for coffee. Beth is a great person. She'll be glad to help."

A little rashly, he downed his glass of wine all at

once, and instantly regretted it. His head swam. Christine was reaching out for his hand, and he was too fuzzy to think about whether that was a good idea or a bad idea.

"You're a great guy yourself, Shawn Waterstone. I think we're going to be very good friends."

15

"What's your name?"

He had to repeat himself, because at first Elisabeth didn't answer. She sat in her seat next to the window, frozen with indecision.

"Elisabeth. Elisabeth Burnham."

"Nice to meet you, Elisabeth Burnham."

She wasn't used to being addressed by cute guys in leather jackets, but there was no one else in the shop, there was a nor'easter starting up outside, and he had just poured her a second steaming cup of something hot and black. It smelled fantastic. Ms. Tattoo must have done up a fresh pot just a little while ago.

She could just leave, she supposed. And avoid the temptation to get friendly with this kid.

She got up slowly.

"Actually, let me bring it to you. Don't leave. Really, it's okay. I watch the place for Gina all the time. In fact, let's eat all the cookies." He nodded toward the cookie jar on the counter and reached for a plate.

"Uh—I've been here for a while, I should get going anyway," Elisabeth said, trying to disguise her alarm.

"Don't make me eat all the cookies by myself," Leather Jacket continued. "I'm hungry, I'm gonna go for it. Mmm. Looks like snickerdoodles. Sorry, I'm going to stick my hand in here—oh, wait. There are wax paper things." He fished out a stack of cookies and set them on the plate, then brought the plate and coffee over to Elisabeth's table. To her dismay, he pulled out a chair, flipped it around, and sat down, leaning his arms against the chair back. He helped himself to a cookie.

"Thanks," she said, but merely watched as he munched. He had a flop of dark hair over one eye and had clearly not seen a shave in a couple of days. The leather jacket that had looked threatening from a distance looked comfortable and worn up close, and she saw that one of the pocket zippers was broken and had been mended with a safety pin. His eyes were dark, his lashes long, and his facial features were strong, but he seemed younger than her

—or at any rate, younger than she felt. He vaguely resembled a movie star whose name she couldn't remember, some Italian guy. He'd be gorgeous if he didn't remind her of a mischievous younger brother.

"Do you live around here?" he asked, reaching for another cookie.

"Church Street," she answered.

"Oh. Not far, then. You'll be okay getting home. Walking?"

"Yes."

"It's bad out."

"It's always worse when it starts. It'll get better when there's enough to plow."

"Yeah."

Elisabeth looked out the window, for lack of anything to say. She was uncomfortably aware that it was her turn to say something, but she wasn't the one who had plopped down at someone's table and initiated a conversation over a plate of snickerdoodles. *This isn't fair*, she thought irritably. *I didn't start this.*

"Elisabeth."

Startled, she turned back. Leather Jacket was now gazing at her, hands folded on the table in front of him.

"I just wanted to say your name."

Flustered, she stammered, "Oh—okay—why?"

"It's pretty. Old-fashioned."

"Do you mean pretty and old-fashioned? Or pretty old-fashioned?" She spoke rather more harshly than she had intended, and immediately wished she hadn't.

"Pretty. And. Old. Fashioned." He spoke slowly. There was an amused grin spreading over his face.

Elisabeth stiffened. She didn't appreciate being laughed at. She reached for her coffee.

"Thank you," she said primly.

"You're funny," he said. He was still grinning. "All tough girl. Are you a teacher? Teachers scare me."

"No," Elisabeth said. "Why do teachers scare you?"

"They all have a power trip. I never made it through high school. Had my ass kicked too many times. After a while, I stayed away." He shrugged, but he was still smiling. He pointed at the plate. "Cookie?"

Something about his smile made Elisabeth reach for a cookie.

He was sweet, this kid. And she had to be four, five years older than him at least. Maybe more.

"Did you go to school in Greenleigh?"

"Yeah. But I've been living in Worcester. I'm a city guy now."

"So what are you doing back here? Working?"

Leather Jacket shrugged lightly. "Yeah. More or

less. When I can." He nodded toward the register. "Gina's a friend. I did her tats."

"Excuse me?"

"Tats. You know." He pointed up and down his leather-jacketed arm.

Elisabeth looked at him blankly.

He sighed. "Tattoos. I did her tattoos. I'm a tattoo artist."

"Oh. Oh, all right," Elisabeth said. She blushed and knew she was betraying her naïveté, so she bent her head over her coffee cup again.

"Have you ever had a tattoo?"

"What? Uh, no."

"Would you like one?"

"Um—" Elisabeth shook her head. "No. No, thanks."

"I'm really good. Promise. You look like you could use a—" He tilted his head critically, peering at the small areas of exposed flesh at her neck and wrists.

"No, thanks," she interrupted hastily. "I can't. I'm a lawyer. I think I'd get into trouble."

"Ha! You think? Like I haven't worked on lawyers?" Leather Jacket was laughing.

"It's not that," Elisabeth protested.

"Then what? No one has to know. If you don't want anyone to know." He was smirking, and the mischievous, crooked grin had her. She laughed.

"You make a good lawyer yourself. Okay, I admit it. I don't have a reason. I'm a coward? How about that?"

"You're not a coward," he said. "You're a tough girl. Why do you say you're a coward?"

"Because tattoos hurt."

Leather Jacket shrugged. "Life hurts."

Elisabeth paused. He had a point there. Damn it.

"Well, it's extra pain. Extra pain on top of life's pain. How's that? I don't want any more pain than necessary."

"But at least tattoos are beautiful. Here."

He shrugged out of his jacket. He was wearing a plain white tee under it, and Elisabeth could see colorful swirling designs starting at his wrists and disappearing under the sleeves of his shirt. More color and flowing cursive script peeped out from under the collar.

"That's impressive," Elisabeth said, as he held out both his arms for her inspection. "Did you do your own arms?"

"No, I had a friend back in Worcester do them, but I designed them. I drew the artwork and he did the ink. He's pretty good. I'm better, though." He extended his arms as she leaned forward to get a closer look. One arm featured peacocks, dragons, a knight in shining armor, a princess in a gown of rainbows and stars. The other had a sparkling phoenix exploding into a ball of flame.

"You have a lot of talent. You can do a lot of different things with talent like that," Beth said, marveling at the fine details and gentle gradations of color.

"You sound like my teachers," he said indifferently. "It's all BS. The world doesn't appreciate talent. It's all who you know, how much money you have, blah blah blah. There's no-talent crap all over the TV, and I can't get a decent job if I try." He reached for his jacket again. "I might as well do tattoos for people who appreciate them. I'll never get rich, but hey. Whatever." He shrugged.

Elisabeth gazed at him, fascinated. "Do people in Greenleigh get tattoos like those?"

"Yeah. They do. Not sleeves like mine, most of the time. They kinda can't afford me. They walk in and have twenty bucks to spend, and I have to do something small. It's hard to get creative for twenty bucks. But at least I won't screw up their design."

"Have you thought of going to a bigger city? Why did you leave Worcester? And come back here? This is such a small town."

There was a pause, and Elisabeth detected a slight, uncomfortable break in his careless, bad-boy facade. He didn't meet her eyes, but was turning the last cookie over and over in his hands.

"I came home," he said finally, "because I wanted to say goodbye to everyone." He raised his eyes. "I'm headed to the West Coast. Seattle."

"What's in Seattle?"

"I think I'll fit in better there." He broke the cookie in half and offered her a piece. "What about you?"

"What about me?" Elisabeth took the cookie from him.

"Why are you here? As you put it, it's such a small town."

"I've always been here," she said.

"I'm sorry, but that's a dumb reason."

"Well, it's the only reason," she said, trying not to sound offended.

"You got that right," he agreed. "There is no other reason to be here, except that you've always been here. And that's not a reason to stay."

"I don't have anywhere else to go," she protested. "My family has always been here. Why would I leave?"

"Why wouldn't you leave? Are you happy?"

"Happy? What do you mean, happy?" Elisabeth put the cookie down.

"Don't get all offended," he said. "I'm just asking."

"You never told me your name," Elisabeth said, changing the subject.

"It's Gunnar."

"Gunnar. That's an unusual name."

"My grandma was Norwegian."

"Wow, that's really unusual."

"Yeah." He smiled at her, a frank smile that lit up his eyes. "My grandma died when I was ten. She was cool. She told me that my name meant 'warrior.'" He held out one of his arms. "That's why I have a dragon on this side."

"Oh, right. The dragon and the fair maiden. Who's the maiden?"

"I don't know. Haven't met her yet." He paused, looking intently at her. "Maybe she's you. She's got dark hair and eyes." He leaned back a little, cocked his head. "She could be you, actually. If your hair were down."

Elisabeth laughed. "Not likely. I think I'd re-member if I'd seen a dragon. But thanks. So I guess you're the knight?"

"Yeah," Gunnar said, laughing. "I guess I am. Pretty lame, huh?"

"What? No, no, not lame at all. Don't say that. But why Seattle? What's out there?"

"Everything's new out west. I'm sick of all this old stuff." Gunnar waved an arm vaguely in back of him. "It's all crap. And I'm sick of small towns, small imaginations. I just want a lot more. Don't you want more than this?" He waved his arm again.

"I guess—well—well, no, not really. I don't know what I'd do in a place like Seattle."

"You'd be a lawyer. Like you are here. But you could change directions, expand your thinking— people out there are doing cool things all the time. You could do a lot of different stuff." He laughed. "Maybe you already do a lot of stuff here, but I doubt it. This town is as boring as sh—" He stopped and looked self-conscious.

"I'm not a prude," Elisabeth said. "You can swear. Although I'd rather if you didn't."

"I like you, Elisabeth," Gunnar said. "You're classy."

"I like you, too," Elisabeth said, laughing. "You're —cool."

"So I'm not classy?"

"I think classy equals boring in your universe."

"Classy equals classy. Do you have a boyfriend? Or—oh, God. A husband?"

"No," Elisabeth said. She smiled at him. "No boyfriend, no husband."

"Oh, good. Why don't you have a boyfriend?"

"Do you have a girlfriend?"

"Not really."

"Okay, wait. What's 'not really?'"

"I have some girls I hang out with but I don't have a girlfriend."

"Gina?" Elisabeth prodded gently.

"No way. She'd eat me for dinner. She's like a really mean big sister. But she takes care of me."

"You're funny."

"No, *you're* funny."

They both laughed. Gunnar reached out to grasp her hand. "I want to take you home," he said. "It's dark out. And I'm going to lock up. You said Church Street, right?"

Elisabeth tried to pull her hand away, but Gunnar caught it back. He was smiling at her, and she felt a little light-headed. She wasn't ready for this, she thought. This was too weird, too powerful, too scary. And he was a kid. She didn't want to hurt a kid, especially one who was hightailing out of Greenleigh forever—but her heart was not available, and he needed to know that. There was no point in even getting started. They'd never see each other again anyway.

"How old are you, Gunnar?" she asked.

"Why? How old are you?"

"I think I must be a lot older than you."

"Why? Am I acting like a punk?"

"No, but I went to high school in Greenleigh and I don't remember you. So I must have graduated before you. Which means you're at least four years younger than I am."

"You're wrong, actually. Because I dropped out. Remember?"

"Oh! Right!" Elisabeth shook her head. "I guess I wouldn't have known you from school."

"Nope," Gunnar said. "But I don't think I'm as young as you think. I'm twenty-four."

"Ha! You're quite a bit younger than me, actually."

"What, like—ten years? fifteen?"

"Thanks a lot," Elisabeth said, offended. "No, not that much. But I'm closer to thirty than you are, how's that?" She decided that being thirty qualified as "close to thirty."

"Jesus. I thought you meant really old." Gunnar laughed. "I'm going to lock up. And then I'll take you home. I've got my bike."

"Bike? In the snow?"

"Motorcycle. Jesus, I have to keep translating for you. It's like you don't speak English. You don't understand anything I say."

Elisabeth knew he was joking, because he was whistling as he took the dishes back to the sink and started loading up the dishwasher. She was too busy fretting over the motorcycle to reply.

Motorcycle? She was going to ride on the back of a motorcycle up to the house on Church Street? What if Angela saw her? What if Sarah saw her?

Thank God Shawn wasn't going to see her!

16

It was a crazy spin through town on a motorcycle in a snowstorm. The roads were empty, the shops shut, and not a pedestrian was in sight. Elisabeth alternated between abject terror and an adrenaline rush that made her feel as if she were flying. She would have screamed, except that she knew she'd be screaming right into Gunnar's ear, so she merely clung tight to him and wondered what had happened to her ordinary life. She knew Gunnar would not let anything happen to her, but she also knew that he was making fun of her. He clearly felt that there was something lacking in her universe, something fundamental, something basic, and instead of wasting the time and the words to try to persuade her to live on the edge, he'd decided to show her.

She suspected he was right, that something was missing in the world she knew, but a high-speed motorcycle journey through Greenleigh, at night, in the middle of freezing temperatures and snow, would not have been the way that she would have chosen to test out that thesis. She'd known him for all of an hour, but she'd already entrusted him with her life. That wasn't the Elisabeth Burnham that she thought she knew so well.

"That was fun. But now you're all wet," Elisabeth said. She was walking across the front room, holding two steaming mugs, as Gunnar turned away from inspecting the framed photographs propped up on the mantelpiece.

"So are you," he said, taking the mugs from her. He put them down on the coffee table as she walked away to switch on another lamp. There was no overhead light, in typical old-house style, and the lamp bulbs were very dim.

"Yes, but at least I took off my coat. My clothes aren't too bad, it's just my hair that's wet. Let me take your jacket."

Gunnar shed his jacket obligingly, and she went up to take it from him. She paused, admiring the tattoos running up and down the length of both arms.

"Can I be blunt? Those are beautiful. Do you have any others? No—don't take off your clothes!"

she laughed as he started to lift up his shirt. "Just tell me." She walked away to hang up his jacket.

"Better if I showed you," he teased. He eased his shirt back down his torso. "Nah. Just kidding. I think you'd faint if I showed you."

"Why?" Elisabeth countered. She returned, folding her arms and eyeing him speculatively. "I'm not such a wimp. Are they naked ladies? Or the grim reaper? Some kind of monster?"

"I only do joyful art. So no monsters."

"But wait, you have an exploding phoenix on that arm. Can I?" Elisabeth came up to look closely at his arm; he held it up for her. She put her hand on his arm gently, then led him over to a lamp to get a better look. "Okay, that's not exactly joyful. It's terrifying, actually."

"It's not terrifying. He's just doing what he does. He's a phoenix, so his job is to make a statement. He wouldn't be a very successful phoenix if he just stood there."

"But you said you only do joyful art. And he's not joyful," Elisabeth said.

"How do you know? Maybe that's how phoenixes act joyful. It's art, right? I'm the artist. I get to decide what joy looks like."

"Right. I suppose so," Elisabeth said. She took a couple of steps back and leaned her head to one side. "You have a rather—violent interpretation of joyful. So you don't do unicorns and rainbows then."

"Ugh. No way. That's not joyful, that's saccharin."

"And an exploding phoenix is more joyful than a unicorn?"

"Yeah. He's doing what he's supposed to do. So even though he's self-destructing, he's fulfilling his destiny. It's all good."

Elisabeth took a sip from her mug. "So why would I faint if you showed me your other tattoos?"

"Because you're a good girl, and they're in places that good girls wouldn't normally see."

"Oh. Ha ha." Elisabeth blushed and turned away to put down her mug. When she turned back, Gunnar was grinning.

"See. You're a good girl. I make you nervous."

"I thought maybe they were on your back. Or your legs."

"That too."

"You're just making fun of me. You think I'm fun to tease."

"You are definitely fun to tease." Gunnar drained his mug and set it down. He looked around the room. "Can I get a tour? I've never been in one of these places. I've seen these mansions on Church Street my whole life, but I've never been inside one."

Elisabeth made a face. "Sure. There's nothing special to look at, though. What do you think you'll see? It's just an old house. It's a mess, just falling down around me."

"Yeah. I know how that goes. My folks have an old house."

"Where are your folks?" Elisabeth asked curiously.

"They're in East Greenleigh. On the way out of town. You know, where all the cows are."

"You're funny. So you guys have cows?"

"Nah. Our house is beyond that bit with all the cows."

"So your family has been in Greenleigh for a long time?"

"Yeah. I guess. My grandma used to live with us. And my grandpa grew up in Greenleigh, too. My dad is Greek, though. He's not from Greenleigh. My mom's family is from Greenleigh."

Elisabeth decided to stop asking questions. Gunnar seemed disinterested in discussing family history, and was examining the hardware on the door that led out of the front room.

"That's original," she said. "That's why none of my doors shut. Because my dad had a thing about keeping the original hardware on all the doors. And the house has shifted, so nothing clicks into place."

"I can fix that," Gunnar said, nodding at it as he passed through the doorway. "It's not hard. In fact, you could fix it." He gave her a meaningful look.

"So what's that supposed to mean?" Elisabeth responded irritably. "That I could be doing more? Yes, I could be doing more. But I can't do it all fast enough to keep it from dominating my life. And I do have to work."

"Where do you work?" Gunnar followed her into the kitchen, but was clearly uninterested in her response. "Wow. That's a hell of a wood stove. Do you heat the house with that thing?" They paused to look around the kitchen, with its giant cast-iron wood stove, the small wooden drop-leaf table in one corner, the rickety old baking cabinet with its metal countertop, and the huge, old-fashioned sink.

"Ha. I try. It's complicated. Wood is expensive, too. I use it when I can. It's not on now, obviously. I wasn't home to light it, and it takes a long time to heat up. There's no point to lighting it now. I'd be up all night dealing with it."

"Yeah."

"There are two ways to get upstairs. We can go up behind the kitchen, behind the bathroom, but it's really ugly. So let's go this way. Oops. Sorry."

Elisabeth pushed her way around him, back toward the front room, and led him up the front staircase.

"What is it you're so curious to see?" she asked over her shoulder. "There's nothing much that's interesting. Bedrooms and old furniture and boxes of stuff."

"I like old houses." His voice was right in her ear, and she jumped. "Sorry, did I scare you?" He sounded amused, and this annoyed her.

"No," she lied. She stopped at the top of the stairs and pointed to the door directly in front of her. "That's the attic. Nothing up there but junk."

"How many bedrooms does this place have?"

"Um. It's hard to say. There are a couple of rooms that are a little weird. Like, they're rooms in between other rooms, so the only way you can use them is by entering from the room on either side. If you count those, then eight bedrooms."

"Are you freaking kidding me? Eight? That's crazy." Gunnar was trying one of the door knobs. "Is this a bedroom? Or a closet? The doorknob needs to be screwed in right."

"Original hardware," Elisabeth said, sighing. "There's a trick to that door. Let me show you." She walked over and put her hand on the knob, showing him how to rotate the knob once completely to the left before feeling it catch and turn. She pushed open the door, but it was dark inside.

"No light?"

"No ceiling light, if that's what you mean."

Gunnar peered into the room. "It's huge. Master bedroom?"

"Not really. They didn't have master bedrooms in the old days. It's just a big room." It had been her parents' room, but Elisabeth didn't mention that detail.

Gunnar turned around suddenly, and Elisabeth found herself leaning against him in the doorway. She backed away into the hall again.

"It's really cold up here," he said.

"There's no heat in the hall, that's why. And I haven't been home, so the downstairs heat was turned down. The upstairs hall only gets the left-over heat from downstairs. And it's cold tonight." As she said the words, it occurred to her that she had taken a whirlwind ride through Greenleigh on the back of a motorcycle, and hadn't been the least bit cold. Mind over matter, it seemed. She had too much fun on that motorcycle. So much fun that her mind had forgotten to remind her body that she was cold.

"Where's your bedroom?"

Elisabeth pointed. "The door's open." It was the next room down, in the middle.

"Has that always been your room?"

Elisabeth nodded. "Yes."

"So you've been living here since—when? You grew up here, I assume."

"Yes, I've lived here my whole life."

"You're worse than me. At least I left and went to Worcester for a while."

"Why am I worse than you?" Elisabeth demanded. "This is where I'm from. Why wouldn't I have stayed here?"

Gunnar paused in front of her bedroom, his hand on the door frame. He said without turning around, "Elisabeth. You know you need to get out of here. This place is a tomb."

Elisabeth opened mouth to retort sharply, but stopped herself. Gunnar had left her bedroom and was trying the doorknob of the next room. He managed to unstick the door, but as he pushed it open, it knocked heavily against an obstruction on the other side. Gunnar stopped pushing.

"Closet?" he asked.

"No, something must be blocking it," Elisabeth said. She went over to slip her hand around the door and push aside whatever piece of furniture was preventing the door from opening. She managed to get the door to open a little wider and gestured inside.

"More furniture and junk."

"There's probably a treasure trove of antiques in this place. You could make a lot of money, I'll bet. You should call in one of those guys, you know, those guys who deal in antiques."

"I know I should." Elisabeth started to back away from the door, but Gunnar caught her arm. She looked up at him.

"I mean it. This is no place for someone like you to hide. It's just wrong." He looked and sounded serious; she didn't know if she'd seen him look serious yet this evening. She was reminded that she hardly knew him, and that no one knew that they were together in her house that night.

Maybe he's an axe-murderer, she thought. Or a thief. Scouting out Church Street for a raid. Well, now he knew there was nothing to steal in the Burnham manse. And the axes were in the shed outside, so he would have a hard time laying hands on one at the moment.

"Don't take this wrong—I don't want you to be upset with me or anything—but this is messed up. I mean, you in this big old house. All by yourself. As if you're waiting to die."

Elisabeth tried to move away, but his hand was still on her arm.

"You also said you didn't have a boyfriend. But you're lying."

"I am not," Elisabeth gasped. "What makes you think that—"

"I don't know, but something's not computing." Gunnar nodded toward her bedroom. "And there's a picture of a guy in there. A young guy. Not your dad, not a friend."

Elisabeth gaped at him. It was true. There was a single picture of herself and Shawn, taken in high school, on her dresser. But her room was dark save for the dim hall light seeping in, and she couldn't imagine how Gunnar had gotten a good enough look to decipher the photo by standing in the doorway.

"He's not my boyfriend. He's a guy I dated in high school," she said finally. "It was a long time ago. Were you looking for pictures of guys in my room? How did you even see that?"

Gunnar shrugged. He still hadn't let go of her arm. He leaned in close, so close that Elisabeth could feel the damp on his hair. He was not nearly as tall as Shawn, and she could feel his breath on her face as he spoke.

"I have excellent eyesight. I draw for a living, and I don't make mistakes. I also know what I'm seeing when I see it. Listen, Elisabeth. I'm going to kiss you. Hold still."

Before she could react, he had leaned down to kiss her. Very gently. It had been so long since she had been kissed, she was too shocked to move, even with his admonition ringing in her ears.

The kiss seemed to last an eternity before he lifted his head and looked at her intently. "You really needed to be kissed. And I'm really happy to kiss you. You deserve so much more than to be stuck in this place."

The distant sound of the wind rattling the glass in the windows was getting louder, and Gunnar was bending down to kiss her again when Elisabeth realized that the rattling was actually the sound of someone pounding on the door downstairs. She broke away from Gunnar, wondering what was wrong that she felt such regret over interrupting a kiss she had neither expected nor wanted.

"Someone's at the door," she gasped, before hurrying down the stairs.

17

They were slowing down in front of the big old mansions on Church Street. A couple of the Victorian-style street lamps were flickering, in need of repair, but the one in front of the Burnham manse was bright, casting a circle of light onto the wet snow surrounding it.

"Hey, does Beth have a motorcycle?" Christine craned her neck, peering around Shawn as she spoke. "There's a motorcycle—right there in front. There's almost no snow on it. Someone's just parked it there, within the past hour."

"Beth? On a motorcycle? Are you kidding?" Shawn started to say, but his voice faded as he looked up at the windows of Beth's front room. The curtains were only partly drawn, and he could see shadowy shapes coming together, separating, and coming together again.

Who was that? And what the hell were they doing?

He dropped Christine off at her home, further down the block. Because of the snow emergency, there were no other vehicles parked on the street, other than the motorcycle in front of the Burnham house. Shawn turned the car around and parked in front of the house, then got out, surveying the motorcycle critically. Who on earth could be visiting Beth on a night like this? It was a big bike, probably belonging to a man. There was a dusting of snow on it, but Christine was right—it was still warm, so the snow wasn't accumulating.

He had no right to expect anything from Beth and he knew it. And it was weird to be upset that some guy was visiting her during a snowstorm. He didn't own Beth. She had no obligation to him. It was her right to have a guy over at her house if she wanted. She was thirty years old and single. They hadn't dated in years. And knocking on her door to find out what was going on—well, it was borderline like stalking. It was controlling and not at all okay. He should just leave.

But he couldn't stand it. Something felt so wrong. And what if this was a break-in? Everyone in town knew Beth lived alone. A big snowstorm would be the perfect time to break into one of these houses, when the town's emergency services would be busy.

That settled it.

He went up the steps and knocked. There was no answer.

He knew she was there. He'd seen the shadows. She wasn't alone.

He began to pound, his heart racing. He looked around, wondering if he could break in, or possibly get in through the kitchen entrance in the back of the house. Maybe she'd left that door open. Or there might be a window he could break.

Suddenly, the door opened, and he nearly fell into the house and on top of Beth.

And as soon as he saw her, Shawn knew. Her guilt and her confusion were written all over her face. She'd been with someone. He could see it. Regardless of what exactly had been going on, she felt guilty. And he was the last person in the world she wanted to see right now.

"Hi," Elisabeth said breathlessly.

"Beth," Shawn said. "I saw the light. There was a motorcycle outside, and I got worried—"

"I'm fine," Elisabeth interrupted. She wasn't meeting his eyes, and she wasn't inviting him in. And the confirmation was when he looked up and saw him.

He found himself momentarily unable to breathe, his next words dying in his throat without sound, the wind completely knocked out of him. The guy descending the stairs behind her was the kind of cocky thug he would have avoided on the subway in Boston for fear of getting a knife between his ribs. He was dark-haired, with a flop of hair covering his eyes as if he had something to hide, tattooed heavily on both arms, and wearing a thin white tee shirt and jeans. He ambled casually down the creaky staircase, one hand sliding with intimate familiarity over the glossy wood of the rail. He was caressing it, running the palm of his hand back and forth as he glanced once at Elisabeth, carelessly, then fastened his gaze on Shawn and nodded.

There was the faintest touch of a smile on his lips.

What was that? A smirk? A challenge? A "welcome to my lair" nod?

Shawn transferred his shocked gaze back to Elisabeth, who didn't seem to know where to look.

Seriously? Beth was into this kind of guy? They had been upstairs together. That pretty much spoke for itself.

His mind was trying to imagine them together, this punk with his well-muscled arms and the hair in his eyes, actually kissing Beth. Why he was torturing himself, he didn't know—just he felt as if he needed to actually see it in order to believe that this was really happening—

He felt as if he were going mad. What had he missed? There must have been something, a signal, a detail, a gesture. Beth must have tried to tell him, somehow, and he hadn't been paying attention. She wouldn't have abandoned him and his hopes without a word.

It was Christine, he thought. She was distracting, and it must have been her fault he had missed a signal somewhere. Jesus, was it that same day that he had been in this very house, meeting with Beth, Christine, and Bob Stuart? It felt like a century ago.

He tried to remember the last time he'd been upstairs in this house, and couldn't. Even when they were young and crazy in love, their kissing games had been restricted to the front room, the parlor, or on rare occasions, the kitchen. Her mother was often shut away in an upstairs room, doing God knows what. Upstairs was not an option for a couple of kids in love. Not in this house. In those days, they were forever sneaking around and laughing about it. He couldn't figure out what was funny, now that he was looking back on it. Sneaking around was not funny, not at all.

Maybe that had been the problem with their love, maybe the sneaking around had been the thing that killed it. Maybe if they had been more open, if they had challenged her mother and told her what they were planning—maybe then Beth wouldn't have abandoned him like that. Maybe he could have given her the courage to stand up to everyone around her.

He dismissed those memories out of his mind. They hurt too much.

When had this happened? This guy—where had he come from? How was Beth, his Beth, his innocent Beth—how was she mixed up with this tattooed creep?

She still wouldn't look at him. She looked miserable.

"I'll get my jacket," the man was saying.

"Oh, I'm sorry," Elisabeth exclaimed. She turned away from Shawn and went to the coat rack. She handed the man a black leather jacket and watched as he slipped his arms into it and pulled up the zipper.

"Think about what I said," he said to her softly. He touched her elbow lightly and leaned forward, and for a moment, Shawn thought he would kiss her, but instead, he smiled and winked.

Elisabeth didn't reply, just looked up at him with an expression that seemed to border on the edge of terror. Shawn felt an empty drop in the pit of his stomach, as if he were on a roller coaster.

"See ya," the man said. He nodded at Shawn

again as he brushed by, walking out into the damp, cold evening without so much as a hat or pair of gloves. For a moment, Shawn hated this nameless figure, casually strolling out into the winter world with minimal belongings, minimal baggage, and hopping astride his motorcycle in preparation to roar away into the night.

It looked so easy. How dare anyone live such an easy life when complicated crap was right around the corner?

"I'm fine," Elisabeth said loudly, and he turned back to her, startled. He'd forgotten that he was standing in front of the open door, letting the cold in. He heard the motorcycle start up easily, the engine revving gently in the quiet of the winter night. He turned again to see the motorcycle glide away down the street, pause, signaling right, before disappearing into the darkness.

"Thank you for checking up on me," she said, a little louder, and he turned back to her again.

"Who was that?" He hadn't known if he should ask, but the words came out before he could pause to think about it.

"Just a friend. He brought me home—we got all wet in the snow, he just stayed to dry off." Elisabeth shuddered and wrapped her arms around herself. "Are you coming in? Are you leaving? Please pick one, it's really cold."

Shawn hesitated. He hadn't been planning to stay—he'd just wanted to make sure she was all right, and after catching sight of the guy, he'd been too stunned to think—but this felt too much like an interrupted conversation, and it would be better to finish it now than to have it hanging over their heads at the office.

He stepped into the entranceway, pulling the door shut behind him.

"Is your heat on?" he asked. "The boiler—is it firing up?"

"Yes, I think so. I heard it go on a little earlier. It takes a while, and I haven't been home long."

She hadn't been home long. So maybe—maybe he'd gotten the wrong impression—maybe it was innocent—

He thought again of Elisabeth's panicked expression when she answered the door, and the man's hand caressing the wooden railing. They'd been upstairs.

No. No, something was up.

"What are you doing here? Were you just driving by?" she asked.

Shawn remembered with a start why he was even on Church Street at all.

"Actually, I brought Christine home."

"Oh. Right." Elisabeth's smile was pained. "Storm windows."

"Yeah. She's going to need a crash course in storm windows." Shawn followed Elisabeth into the kitchen, where she automatically turned the kettle on. "Her place has been restored somewhat but it's still going to be a headache this winter."

Elisabeth did not reply. She was searching through a cupboard, pulling out several boxes of teabags.

"I won't stay," Shawn said quickly. "I didn't mean to cause you any trouble. I just saw the motorcycle and I got worried. I didn't know if someone had broken into the house, or who knows what."

"I'm fine," Elisabeth said once again. "I appreciate you checking on me. But I'm okay. I can take care of myself. I've lived in this house my whole life, remember."

"Still, you never know," Shawn said, trying to keep his tone even. "Who's the guy?"

"Just a friend, I told you." Elisabeth sounded weary. "No one you know."

"Come on, Beth." Shawn felt his temper rising. He was feeling both impatient and full of dread. He felt he needed to know, but he didn't want to know, and felt both of these things at the same time. He could hear the little pinging noises in the kettle as the water heated, and thought that it sounded much like his chest felt at the moment—hollow and hot.

"Stop questioning me!" Elisabeth snapped irritably, her voice rising. "Stop! He's just a friend. And he was being nice by bringing me home."

"On that motorcycle? In the snow?"

Elisabeth did not reply, but she pressed her lips together mulishly. She brought down two mugs from the cupboard but made no move toward the boxes of teabags.

"Look, you can't blame me for worrying. Christine and I saw you in the window, and we saw the motorcycle outside. How was I to know who that was? For all I knew he could have been a burglar or something."

"You can thank Christine for me—such a neighborly gesture," Elisabeth replied tightly.

Shawn cursed himself inwardly for mentioning Christine.

"You know I worry about you," he said softly.

"You do not need to worry about me," Elisabeth responded. "I am fine. I've lived in this house my whole life, and I've been alone for a few years now —if I need your help, I'll let you know. But for now, I'm good, thanks."

"I wish you'd listen to me," Shawn exclaimed. "I'm just trying to tell you—I'm trying to tell you that—"

"Oh, stop!" Elisabeth cried. She clapped her hands over her ears. "I don't want to hear it! Don't! You'll just make it worse!"

"Worse? What are you talking about? I'm just trying to tell you that I care about you—is that something bad? Should I stop?"

"I don't want you to care about me!" Elisabeth said, her hands still covering her ears. She hunched herself over, her elbows tight to her sides. "This is all bad enough without you adding to the problem."

"I don't understand why I'm adding to the problem," Shawn persisted. He approached her, but stopped as he saw her shrink away. "Beth, this is terrible. Don't do this. I can't stand it when you act like you're afraid of me. I want to help."

"You are not helping!" Elisabeth cried. "You're like a—like a big black shadow hovering over my life! You're a reminder of everything awful, everything bad that has happened to me—right down to, I can't even make a living without your permission!" She gasped for breath. "I just want—I just want to live, Shawn. Let me start there. I want to do my work and live my life. Please. That's all. Please just let me be."

"I don't want to let you be," Shawn said, his frustration rising. "I can't stand to watch you live like this. This house—it's—it's falling down around you. And you're barely making ends meet. You're a great lawyer, you could be doing so much more, but you're staggering along. You don't have to live like this. People who are much less capable than you are

—they're earning more money and living in houses that aren't decrepit. They're moving forward. You're not moving forward. You're trapped in some kind of —some kind of time warp, and I want you to get out of it."

"I'm trying to move ahead, Shawn! It doesn't help that you're here to drag me backwards!" Elisabeth pressed her hands against her eyes. "I'm trying my best."

Shawn turned away. He couldn't bear to see her in so much pain, pain that he knew he had a large role in creating.

But what about MY pain, he wanted to shout at her. *What about ME? What about the man you left behind that night? That man never recovered from what you did to him.*

I know you were the one who was left behind. But that man is STILL a mess. And meanwhile you've moved on without him.

Don't you care, Beth? Don't you care that you hurt me so badly? I know I hurt you. I'm ready to make it up to you.

You hold the answer to all of this pain.

All you have to do is to just love me again. I promise I can fix everything, take it back in time to where we were before, fix all the mistakes I made.

Just love me.

In two steps he had crossed the space between

them and grabbed her roughly. He wanted to shake her—for some reason he felt furious, furious at her, furious at himself for all those wasted years—but instead he kissed her. He wasn't nice, and he wasn't gentle, and he didn't care.

He felt her resist, stiffen in his arms, but he knew she was fighting against a losing battle, because her mouth was not resisting. However, at the same time, she was crying, and he couldn't bear to kiss a woman in tears.

He let her go. The pinging noises in the kettle had given away to the steady rhythm of bubbles at the bottom, but the water was not yet boiling. She pulled away, tears streaming, leaned against the wall next to the stove and sobbed.

"I don't want this," she sobbed. "I don't want this. It hurts. I want this to just stop."

"What can I do?" he begged. "I'll make it stop hurting, I promise. I love you, Beth. I can take care of you. None of this has to continue—I can make it stop."

"I don't want that!" she shouted. "I don't want you to take care of me!"

"But I want to help," Shawn protested. "I love you, Beth." He paused. But she didn't respond, and a choking sensation threatened to take over his chest as he considered the scene he had interrupted earlier.

"Is it him? That guy? Are you in love with him?" Just saying the words made him gasp.

Elisabeth shook her head, wiping her eyes with the edge of her skirt. "No," she whispered. "We just met."

"Please tell me you still love me." Shawn said the words softly. "Please just say it. Say it and I'll go away and leave you alone. Just give me something to go on."

Elisabeth reached out to turn off the burner under the kettle, which was starting to whistle softly. She shook her head wordlessly.

"Please."

Elisabeth shook her head again. "No," she whispered. "This hurts."

"I'll make it stop hurting," Shawn promised. "I'll fix everything. I know I can."

"You can't," Elisabeth said, her eyes brimming. "I need to find my own way first. This is something I have to do myself."

"I don't believe it."

"Then you don't believe in me," she whispered.

"I believe in us."

"Shawn," Elisabeth said. "There is no us."

"You don't believe that. I don't believe that. You just never gave us a chance."

"But I'm not that person anymore. You can't keep thinking about the past." Elisabeth sank down onto the floor and put her head in her arms. "Just go," she said, her voice muffled.

Shawn felt his emotions threatening to choke him, making him dizzy with pent-up frustration. This whole conversation was stupid, and he wanted her to just listen to him. He knew what would make all of this go away, and that was for Beth to just shut up and listen to him. What was her problem? Why was she being so difficult? He knew he'd been stubborn, he knew he'd been wrong. She just needed to give him the space to apologize.

There was a pause. She wasn't sobbing any longer. She gave a deep sigh.

Shawn knelt down to put his arms around her. "Please. Let me just take care of this. Trust me to fix it. You used to trust me. Remember?"

Elisabeth raised her head. Shawn leaned in to kiss her, but this time he was careful not to be too rough. He wished that he could stay with her, but it would be unconscionable to take advantage of her when she was so lonely and unhappy. He would have to leave her tonight, but he knew, absolutely, that this was a beginning, a crack in her armor. He could feel her responding to his kiss. He was too cautious a man to be happy quite yet, but he knew the tide had turned. She loved him. She did.

"We are going to be okay," he whispered into her ear. "I love you. And you love me." He felt her yield to his embrace, and she momentarily rested her head against his chest, turning her face inward to press her lips against him.

His heart was overflowing.

"Thank you," he whispered.

18

The snow piled up overnight. While it had been a sloppy mess during the evening, when the temperature settled into the upper teens, it turned fluffy and thick, and fell fast. In typical nor'easter style, when it came in, it came in with attitude. It waited until after midnight, and then briskly took over.

After the snow, the temperature did a classic New England downturn into the single digits, causing schools to close and gas stations with tow trucks to enjoy a spectacular rise in business thanks to the cars stalled out on every road. As accustomed as they all were to fickle winter weather, a pre-Thanksgiving snowstorm of such magnitude was still worth plenty of space in the papers and lots of talk time on the television.

Mr. Kelly at the town hall had sent his second son Robbie and a high school buddy of his to dig Elisabeth out. There had to be at least a couple of feet of snow piled up about the house in drifts, and the low temperatures following the storm had created the usual hazard of crusty ice, frozen solid beneath a layer of brittle snow, and the source of many a broken hip at the emergency room. Mrs. McPherson next door, in fact, had not salted or sanded her walkway sufficiently and was the unfortunate victim of a nasty fall. No broken bones, fortunately, Elisabeth learned when she went to call, but lots of bruises, including on one very tender ego.

Angela Stuart telephoned, apologizing that the weather made it difficult for her to come in person. She mentioned that she'd taken Elisabeth's advice and called Bob because she was concerned about the storm. He'd responded pleasantly and had not been awkward or pushy. Angela was relieved, but also disappointed. Elisabeth bit her nails and worried. Was Bob going to get his act together and start taking charge of his marriage? Or was he going to completely muck this up by maintaining a facade of pleasant indifference? He needed to convince Angela that he still loved her, that she was as important to him as she'd ever been. He wouldn't succeed at getting her back by being polite and gentlemanly.

Angela claimed to still want a divorce, but was

now willing consider having Christine mediate. Elisabeth wrote out a frighteningly large check to Angela and put it in the mail. She took a deep breath and put the new water tank out of her mind. The tank was on the blink but it wasn't completely gone yet. And mediation was the best thing for Angela.

Elisabeth avoided Lawson & Lawson for a few days. In her mind she felt somewhat justified given the bad weather, but she was eventually overcome with guilt. After all, Ricky Junior was still counting on her. She also needed the money.

On her first day back in Lawson & Lawson's offices, she stole in guiltily very early in the morning, and hid in the library. When she emerged at about eleven o'clock to deliver a sheaf of paperwork to Ricky Junior, she heard Shawn's voice down the hall, and ducked into the ladies' room. She ended up scrawling Ricky Junior's name on an envelope and depositing her research on the receptionist's desk, receiving a very hostile look in response. Elisabeth fled.

She drummed up the courage to go in to see Ricky Junior several days later. Shawn, she discovered, was not in that day. Taking care of something at the factory, Ricky Junior said. He seemed almost a little relieved. Shawn was watching his every move, he complained mildly to Elisabeth, as if he were a junior attorney rather than a competent attorney of nearly ten years' experience. "Something's up with him," he said to Elisabeth.

They hadn't spoken or seen each other since that night, but she felt as if she were waiting for a bomb to drop.

This had to stop. Shawn could not continue to think that they were going to get back together like nothing had happened, like those intervening years could be disappeared with a kiss and a snap of the fingers. She wasn't the same person, and doubtless neither was he. She'd once decided not to invest in him, and that had wounded him so deeply, he had not spoken to her in years, not even during his vacations home. They'd severed their connection neatly, surgically. What made him think that it could be put back together? Why did he think he loved her still?

She blamed Gunnar. Shawn had seen him and gotten the wrong idea. Men. They were stupid and competitive, even when it didn't serve their interests.

She wasn't good for Shawn, she said to herself. She wasn't smart, fun, sophisticated, the kind of person he could laugh with. She was too anxious, too negative. And she wasn't sure what she thought of him anymore. He made her nervous. His suits were too nice. His car was too nice. He belonged with Christine—someone like Christine, she amended—not with a lame excuse of a lawyer from Greenleigh.

Did she love him? Yes, of course she loved him! How could she not love him? Every inch of her ached to return back to those comfortable old times, when she was sure of him. But now was now, and then was then. She could not trust him to still love her the way she was now. She'd changed. She felt shriveled, small, weak. She didn't want him to know her the way she was now.

She walked home slowly, exhausted by the mental pressure of dealing with both the reality of her current life and the unknown prospects of the life she faced in the months and years to come. The chill of the house in the wake of the first storm of the season and the feeble groaning of the old boiler as it tried valiantly to heat up the drafty old mansion all but convinced her of the futility of trying to carry on the fight any longer. Young Robbie Kelly and his buddy spent some of each afternoon chipping away at the ice on the sidewalks and clearing the gutters so that any melted snow would drain properly, but these gestures of kind neighborliness from her clients only served as embarrassing reminders to her of her professional failure as a lawyer. Such a failure, she thought, that her clients felt obliged to feed her and shovel the snow around her gloomy, drafty home. As grateful as she was to them all, it only sank her spirits deeper to imagine how they must all be pitying her. Poor little Elisabeth Burnham, orphaned young, left with responsibilities greater than anything she could bear.

Coming up the curve of Church Street, Elisabeth paused to check the mail, bracing herself for the uneasy moment when the newest sheaf of bills would be gathered up into her gloved hand and carried into the house for further inspection. She struggled a moment with the hasp of the mailbox, its post leaning precariously in the snow, before pulling the little door open. With a practiced eye she leafed rapidly through the small stack, willing herself not to dwell too closely on any one of them, lest she become nervous before she could even enter the house and take off her coat. She began to walk slowly up the front path toward the house and up the porch steps, kicking snow off her boots as she did so. As she dug in her coat pocket for her key, her eye fell upon an envelope with an unfamiliar scrawl across the front.

It wasn't a bill at all. It was an envelope with only her name written on it. She flipped it over. No return address.

She struggled to get the key to turn in the lock, but finally got the bolt unstuck. Once in the house, Elisabeth went straight into the front room without bothering to remove her wet boots or her coat. She threw the mail onto the maple secretary, peeled off her gloves, then picked up the envelope on top. She ripped it open and pulled out a single sheet of white paper, folded neatly in half and then in thirds.

When she opened it up, her jaw dropped.

It was a beautifully detailed color portrait of—

—her.

Except it wasn't her.

She stared at it in amazement and confusion. The profile was hers, definitely, but it had been— cleaned up? The markers of cares, worries—gone. Her skin was silky smooth, her lips rosy. She was wearing makeup, her lashes were longer than they really were in real life. Her hair had been lightened by several shades and she wore a crown of flowers, gold, and jewels.

But what caused her to gape in astonishment was that she wasn't the only person in this portrait.

Gunnar was gently grasping her chin and gazing into her eyes. Except that it wasn't Gunnar. It was Gunnar as a Greek god, his dark hair long and windswept, his strong nose definite but his eyes outlined with eyeliner and eye shadow. He was dressed in black with a crown of black flowers and—ram's horns?

The image was painted in vibrant watercolor, and she could see the marks of colored pencil under the layers of paint. At the bottom of the sheet, there was a caption in blocky print:

HADES AND PERSEPHONE

Elisabeth let out a surprised laugh. What? Was this a weird fancy of Gunnar's? Was he bored? Was he taunting her? Was this a prank?

It was a spectacular piece of artwork, but it made her feel funny all over, as if it were exuding some kind of malicious force. She shuddered. Maybe it was because Hades—Gunnar—whoever—looked so fierce, and Persephone—Beth—looked as if she were more than ready to be kissed.

Elisabeth shuddered briefly at the memory. She didn't want to remember that Gunnar had kissed her. That was awkward. She should have stopped him.

She went to hang up her coat, but as she did so, she saw a shadow through the window, making its way up her front steps. She knew exactly who it was, and went to open the door.

"Did you like it?" There was no preamble as Gunnar opened the storm door and went past Elisabeth into the house. He started to take off his jacket, but paused and looked around.

"It's fricken cold in here. Sorry, don't look at me like that—I talk like a grownup, not like a baby. I should have used the real word, too, not a pretend swear word. And—is that dude here? Cuz I don't want to be here if he's going to kill me. That was just bad, the other night. He didn't upset you, did he?"

"No, not really," Elisabeth lied.

"Why the hell is it so cold?"

"Because it's an old house and they're always cold," Elisabeth said shortly.

"That's not true. My parents' house is old and the heat works. You've got a wood stove, is it on?"

"No. I just got home."

"I'll start it." Before she could stop him, he was in the kitchen. "Where's your wood pile?"

"Out the back. But it's a mess."

"Yeah. I'll bet," he said over his shoulder. In a moment, he was back, hauling an armload of split wood easily. "Kindling? Come on, don't just stand there—I don't know where anything is."

Elisabeth had been staring at him blankly. She roused herself. "Oh. Sorry. Kindling is in that metal tray right there. Sorry. It's a mess."

Gunnar looked over at her from where he was crouched on the floor in front of the stove. "Your two favorite phrases. 'Sorry' and 'it's a mess,'" he teased. "Matches?"

"Oh, sorry! Uh—right—they're over your head, on the shelf. Here—" She went to get them and handed them to him.

"See? Done. Fire's going. How can you stand it? I hate being cold. Man, I can't wait to get out of

Greenleigh. This weather just sucks. It'll be cold until May, too." Gunnar rose, dusting his hands off.

"Not May," Elisabeth chided. She went to get the kettle, feeling oddly cheerful.

"Please tell me you're making coffee," Gunnar said, plopping down at the kitchen table. Elisabeth stopped.

"No, actually. I was making tea. Did you want coffee?"

"Kind of. But tea's okay."

"I don't know why I was making tea, I do have coffee—" Elisabeth slowed, realizing what she was saying. She was making tea because she always made Shawn tea, almost reflexively. They'd spent years having tea right in this spot.

She felt a little lightheaded. She put the kettle down.

"Hey." Gunnar waved a hand at her. "Are you okay? You look like you've seen a ghost."

"No—no, I just decided on coffee after all," Elisabeth said. She went to grab the coffee from the cupboard, and set about pulling filters out of a drawer. "I haven't seen a ghost, just Hades," she said, trying to joke.

"What did you think? Did you like it?" Gunnar sounded bored. He had picked up a legal journal from the table and was leafing through it. "This looks like crap. I can't believe you like this stuff."

Elisabeth glanced over. "Huh? Oh, I don't. It's boring. But I have to keep up with the news. Greenleigh isn't exactly the center of the universe. I have to make sure I know what's going on everywhere else."

"Why are you here anyway? This place just sucks the life out of you."

"Yeah. Well, don't hold back. You told me last time what you thought, too." Elisabeth handed him a mug. She went to get the drawing from the other room, and when she returned, he had shed his jacket. He was wearing a bright white tee shirt again.

"It's getting warm in here," he said, seeing her raised eyebrow.

"I thought you hated the cold," she said. "It isn't that warm."

"You're just a wimp. I thought you were from Greenleigh. Feels better now. It was awful before I lit the stove."

"You know what? You're a pain," Elisabeth said. "You walk into my house without an invitation and then you moan about how cold it is. You could've just stayed home." She sat down at the table across from him and put the drawing down between them. She smoothed out the folds and looked up at him. "But this is beautiful. Thank you. Did you do this for fun? Or were you trying to convince me to get a tattoo?"

"Sure." Gunnar picked up the drawing and gazed at it critically. "This would work. I'd need a lot of room for this one. But it's you."

"And you." Elisabeth watched as he frowned over the drawing.

"Yeah. More or less. Kind of a better looking version of me, huh?" He held the drawing next to his face and struck a pose. She laughed.

"It's definitely a better looking version of me."

"Well, it's fantasy."

"How did Hades end up being a fantasy? And for that matter, why are you Hades? Are you that bad?"

"Nah." He shook his head. "Hades isn't about me, it's about you."

Elisabeth was taken aback. "Me? What do you mean? Why is Hades about me? I'm not Hades, I'm Persephone." She pointed at the drawing.

"Yeah, but—" Gunnar put the drawing down. The aroma of coffee was filling the room, and his distracted gaze wandered around the kitchen until he found the coffee maker. "You're the earth princess. That makes me Hades. So it's your fault I'm Hades."

Elisabeth got up to fill the cups, laughing. "What? You're crazy."

"Hades persuaded Persephone to leave Earth. And I told you, you need to leave this place."

"Yeah, you said that last time," Elisabeth said, concentrating on the coffee pot. She brought the cups over and sat down again. "I remember, you like it black."

Gunnar was reaching for his cup but he paused. He smiled at her. "Yeah. Good memory."

"I'm an attorney, it helps," Elisabeth said, picking up her own mug.

For a moment, they sat in silence. Then Gunnar spoke, gesturing at the drawing with his chin.

"That really is you and me."

"I know, Gunnar, but why?" Elisabeth put her cup down. "You worked really hard on this. It's beautiful—all the watercolor, the shading—it's just amazing. This must have taken a long time."

"It did."

"So why?"

"I did it for you. It's a gift. So you'd come with me."

Elisabeth knit her brow. "What do you mean? To Seattle?"

"You need to leave this place. I'll take you away."

"Gunnar, that's absurd—I'm not leaving this place."

"Just listen to me. I'll change your mind."

Gunnar reached out for her hand and grasped it before Elisabeth could pull away.

"Gunnar, stop," she said severely.

"It's not like that, Elisabeth. I'm not coming on to you."

"You're not? That's what it feels like." Elisabeth tried to pull her hand away but he tightened his grip.

"Hold on a moment. Just listen. You're so deep in your own head, you don't listen."

"Gunnar, stop. Let go."

"I'm not letting go. If I'm not touching you, you're not listening."

Oh, my God, Elisabeth thought, *how did I get myself into this?* Gunnar was gazing at her steadily; the intensity of his expression matched his depiction of Hades. Momentarily, she chuckled, and he loosened his grip. She took a moment to admire the bright colors of the tattoos covering his arm, all the way down to where his hand lay over hers.

"You really do look like Hades."

"It's the Greek in me. I'm going to kiss you again," Gunnar said, reaching out for her. Elisabeth started to rise in a panic, and he laughed. "Kidding. But I'm taking you with me. I'm getting you out of this place."

19

In spite of herself, Elisabeth put her other hand over his. She took a deep breath. She needed to just nip this in the bud. She liked him. She knew he liked her. And God, she was lonely. She didn't want this—this—whatever it was—to get out of hand.

"Listen. Gunnar."

"No, you listen," Gunnar shot back, but she could tell he was teasing. "Is there any food around here?"

Momentarily distracted, Elisabeth paused, looking around the kitchen. "Uh—sure—"

"Shall I make something?"

"Gunnar!" she exclaimed in exasperation. She pulled her hand away but he kept hold of her other hand.

"What?" He pretended to be equally annoyed, but he was grinning.

"You are all over the place! You can't stay on a topic for more than ten seconds."

"Yeah, all the teachers said that. Screw'em." He released her hand and stood up.

"I'm hungry. I'll make something. Omelet?"

"You're nuts," Elisabeth sighed. "We need to talk, Gunnar. We need to talk. I'm not going to Seattle with you. We hardly know each other. And I have a life here. I don't know what you plan to do in Seattle but—"

"You have eggs, right?" Gunnar was peering into her refrigerator. "Okay, you do have eggs. But Elisabeth—" He straightened, turned to her. "There's hardly anything in here. You can't live on this."

Elisabeth looked away.

"I'm gonna say it, because maybe no one ever says it to you. But you can't live like this. I can see what's going on."

"Maybe," Elisabeth said, trying to keep her voice steady. She looked up at him, which took effort. "But things are better. No—they really are," she said hastily, as Gunnar frowned at her. "They were much worse, and now I've got—" She paused, not knowing what to say. How to explain this situation to someone who clearly had never bothered with any kind of structure or rules—how to explain the fact that being independent was sometimes worse than just knuckling under and taking whatever lumps you had to take, even if it meant humbling yourself to an old boyfriend—she couldn't think of a way to explain that would make any sense to Gunnar. He was so young.

"You know what?" Gunnar was pulling the eggs out of the refrigerator, along with a block of cheese. "You're having trouble explaining things to me because you don't believe any of it. It's crap."

He spoke matter-of-factly, as if he were discussing the weather. He wandered around the kitchen, looking at the various pans and utensils hanging up on the walls.

"Elisabeth Burnham. This is a disgrace. These pans are so dusty, I'll have to wash'em before I can use'em."

"No one said you had to cook anything," Elisabeth said defensively.

"I'm hungry. I came as soon as I finished my last client. I didn't even stop to pick up food. I should have, though. Elisabeth, I'm gonna make omelets, but there isn't much of anything for tomorrow. How the hell does that boyfriend of yours let you live like this?"

"He's not my boyfriend," Elisabeth muttered.

"Well, whatever. I dunno, ex-boyfriend? I don't care what he is. What the hell is this anyway?"

Gunnar gestured vaguely with a stick of butter, and plopped a pan into the sink. He opened the tap and turned to face Elisabeth as the water filled the pan. "Do you wanna fill me in?"

"Why should I?" Elisabeth burst out. "Why should I tell you anything? I don't know anything about you, either. I just met you a few days ago!"

"Yeah, but I get you. I know what's up inside here." He tapped his head with the stick of butter. "And in here." He tapped his chest.

Elisabeth tried not to laugh, but it was too ridiculous. She chuckled and rose from the table. "I'll help you."

"Don't," Gunnar said, placing the newly rinsed pan on the stove. "I'm a little scared of what you'll do to my omelets. I take it you don't cook."

"Not much," Elisabeth agreed.

"You don't like to cook?"

"I guess I don't care about food. My mom wasn't a good cook, either."

"Where's your mom? Is she still around?"

"No. She died a few years ago."

"Mine is still in that old dump. I hate that place. Check this out." Gunnar was cracking eggs expertly with one hand.

Elisabeth laughed. "Okay. You're a genius in the kitchen, too. What can't you do?"

"Uh, sit in a classroom? Read law crap? Lie?"

"What is that supposed to mean?" Elisabeth said, affronted.

"Elisabeth, you're a liar. If you were honest you'd have left this dump ages ago. How long have you been here alone?"

"A few years, I guess."

"And doesn't Lover Boy help you out?"

"Stop calling him that," Elisabeth said irritably. "He's not my boyfriend."

"Anymore?"

"Stop. I won't talk about him."

Gunnar did not reply, but squinted at her as he tilted the pan over the flame. The silence was unusual, so it felt uncomfortable to Elisabeth, who had grown accustomed to Gunnar's absurd chatter. She added hastily, "He's someone I knew a long time ago. He just moved back to town."

Again, Gunnar said nothing, but Elisabeth realized that his silence, too, was a statement.

"All right," she said, giving up. "I'm lying. What do you want me to say? That he's my boyfriend? He's not. He'd like to be. He's trying to be."

After the words were out of her mouth, she felt queasy. She hadn't admitted this to herself, never mind to a stranger.

Shawn wanted her back in his life. He wanted her. Oh, God. He wanted her. He still wanted her.

"And you? Do you want him to be your boyfriend?"

"I don't know. Oh—I just don't know. I can't go back there—it was a long time ago. Years and years. Like, another lifetime. Things are so different. And we're in such different places. I just don't feel right about any of it. It just feels weird."

It was the longest and most complete confession of her confusion that she had ever made out loud to anyone, even to herself, and she heard herself out with amazement.

"You don't trust him."

"I don't trust myself."

It was as if she were listening to herself speaking in another room. Eavesdropping, that was it. It was like she was eavesdropping on her own thoughts.

Amazed, she looked at Gunnar, who was sliding his creations onto plates.

"You've got some salad stuff, I'll make a salad. It's a little weird to just have eggs. But you should eat this before it gets cold. I'll be quick."

"I don't know why I said that."

"Said what?" he asked innocently.

"Oh, Gunnar. You are so full of—" Elisabeth shook her head.

"Yeah, I know. I told you, you're a liar. But you're doing better. I heard what you said." He brought over salad plates filled with lettuce and cucumbers. "See, I told you I'm quick."

"Did you even wash that?" Elisabeth pointed at the plates, and bent to examine them.

"Don't ask."

They sat down to eat. For a few minutes, they were both quiet. The omelets were superb, topped with a cheerful sprinkle of paprika that Gunnar must have found in the cupboard. The salads were the perfect foil for the rich, creamy eggs and cheese. All they needed was some chilled white wine.

So many hours at this very table with Shawn.

The thought floated into Elisabeth's head unbidden.

She looked at Gunnar, who had no idea of any of the history of this house, of her history, of her history with Shawn. No wonder he was calling everything right. He had no way of understanding the baggage that held her back, and why should he?

This was no way to live.

She was in so much pain. And there was Shawn, ready to make it go away. Why wouldn't she let him? Why was she trying to make him the bad guy? He was trying. He was doing just as Gunnar said, trying to fix things. Trying to apologize for leaving her, even though she was the one who'd refused to go with him. What was wrong with her?

Elisabeth put her fork down and burst into tears.

"Jesus!" Gunnar exclaimed. "What'd I do?"

Elisabeth shook her head. "I feel like—like—" she tried to say, but the words seemed to stick in her throat.

"Don't," Gunnar interrupted. He pushed the plates aside, leaned over to put his arms around her.

For a long while, he stroked her hair as she sobbed. He had a completely different feel from Shawn. Shawn was tall and lean, but Gunnar was sturdy and muscular. Shawn smelled of soap and laundry, but Gunnar smelled like something musky, like aftershave or cologne. He was a kid, she thought, but he somehow understood her. What was wrong with her, rather. And he made her feel safe.

Safer than Shawn did? She didn't know. All she knew was that Shawn's love made her feel stupid and miserable, and Gunnar's silly, scattered commentary made her feel like she was a capable grownup. She sobbed into his shirt until he protested and complained that he was soaked. This made her laugh, and she pulled away.

"So now you get to see me ugly cry all over you," she said, her voice muffled as she wiped her face.

"Eh. People do that all the time when they get tattoos," Gunnar replied. "Shit hurts. So people cry."

"That sounds about right," Elisabeth said. She

gave her face another swipe with her sleeve. "And I'm just so done. With everything."

"Elisabeth Burnham. Darling. You need to leave. You are buried alive. I feel like I've said it ten times. I feel like a broken record. Would that be a skipping CD? Defective download? What's the modern metaphor? Anyway. Get out of Greenleigh."

"How will leaving Greenleigh help? I've got this house. It's such a headache, but it's all I've got."

"Sell it."

"I can't."

"What do you mean, you can't? As in, what? Like, it's mortgaged and you're upside down and you owe more than you'd get from a sale?"

"No, no. Just—this is my family home."

Gunnar picked up his fork. He shrugged. "So it's not that you can't. You won't. Look, Elisabeth, if you sold this house, you'd have plenty of money to start over in a new city. You're a lawyer and you've got lots of courage and nerve. Lawyers aren't timid. I know you can do anything you set your mind to. Whatever you think is holding you back—it's just not real. Just because it hurts, doesn't mean it's real. It might just be in your head." He began to eat again.

"Right," Elisabeth said tentatively. This was new, this commitment to not lie. It felt both crazy and re-assuring, so long as Gunnar was there to catch her when she slipped back into lying, she thought.

"I could actually leave," she said, half to herself.

"It's a wide, wide world out there," Gunnar said. "I've got some friends in Seattle, and I can stay with them for a while. You can come with me, look around, see what you think. You can always come back. But you won't." He looked around at the kitchen. "You won't be back."

"You sound so sure."

"Elisabeth, if Lover Boy isn't a thing, if he isn't doing something for you about this," he nodded toward the front room, "—then there's nothing for you here. Life is not about real estate. Life is about people."

"Gunnar." Elisabeth pushed her seat back from the table. "Why are you here? Why do you want me to go with you? I mean—we don't really know each other."

"Aw, come on, Elisabeth. Do you believe that? Do you think we don't know each other?" Gunnar leaned his chair back on two legs. He folded his hands over his midriff and grinned. "I feel like we're old friends."

"I guess, what I want to know is—" Elisabeth hesitated, then reminded herself that she liked Gunnar. She didn't want him hurt. "I don't want you to get the wrong idea. About us."

"You still love that guy, don't you?"

Confused, Elisabeth shook her head. "That's not

what I wanted to say," she began, but Gunnar was laughing. He pointed at her.

"Did you tell him? That you don't love him anymore? That he makes you miserable? That you want him to stop coming by?"

"No, I—"

"See what I mean?" Gunnar interrupted. "You could sell this house and leave. You could tell Lover Boy to leave you alone. You could do a lot of things. And you haven't done any of it."

"It isn't so easy!" Elisabeth protested.

"Yeah, and you think it's supposed to be easy? Please. What garbage." Gunnar got up from the table, the chair legs crashing to the floor with a loud thump. He wandered out into the hall, then eyed the stairs. "Let's go upstairs."

"Gunnar, stop."

"Do you want to know how I feel about you? Is that what you're asking? Let's go upstairs and I'll show you. Or maybe, you're not asking a question—you're trying to tell me to get lost? Because you're saving yourself for Lover Boy?"

"You've got some kind of attention deficit disorder, I think," Elisabeth sighed. "You can't stay on topic."

"Yeah, well, neither can you. What the hell do you mean, you don't want me to get the wrong idea about us? Like, do I work on drawings for all the girls I meet? Do I make dinner for all the girls I meet? What do you think?"

For a moment, he actually sounded annoyed. Elisabeth rose from the table.

"I'm sorry," she said. "I'm just trying to make sure I'm not messing with your mind. I don't want you to be hurt. But I'm in a rough place right now." She walked over to him, put her hand on his arm.

"I'm listening," she said meekly. "I'm listening. I'm thinking about Seattle, and selling the house. Really I am."

"You still love that guy." He wasn't looking at her.

"Yes—maybe. He thinks I love him. I wish I loved him the way he should be loved. And I don't want you to get some cheap substitute for what you need. It's not fair. You're a great guy. If I weren't in this situation—maybe."

He looked at her, and just for a moment, he had ditched the wise-ass demeanor. He just looked young and lonely, a hungry expression in his eyes. He reached out and pulled her to him.

She couldn't help it. He reminded her of what it was like to be twenty-something and to have the world before you, before too many really bad things could have happened to you. As he kissed her, she remembered other kisses in this kitchen, other conversations filled with plans and promises.

Elisabeth put her arms around Gunnar's neck. It

wasn't right, it totally wasn't fair to him, but she'd warned him, she thought. And this felt so good. She hadn't been in a man's arms in so long. She should have felt nervous, but perhaps the evidence that she wasn't in love with Gunnar was that she wasn't worried in the least. His arms felt kind, hopeful, in a way that Shawn's did not. In Shawn's arms she felt worried, guilty, confused, afraid that she couldn't live up to the level of passion and spark that she felt there. In Gunnar's she felt companionship, camaraderie, and an unexpected innocence.

Looks are so deceiving, she thought. Who would have looked at Gunnar and used the word "innocent" to describe him?

Right on cue, however, she felt his kiss change and deepen, and knew this was her signal to pull back. "Gunnar," she murmured against his lips.

"I know. Stop," Gunnar said, releasing her. He walked away, put his hands on his hips, stared down at the floor for a moment. He took a deep breath, then lifted his head and stared out the window next to the door, before returning to where she stood. He ran his hands through his hair, sweeping it off his forehead and out of his eyes, then smiled at her.

"I wish that other guy were out of the picture," he said. "I feel like I should have met you earlier, before he came back to town."

"He's not out of the picture, though, Gunnar. I'm

sorry. Maybe you'd rather not talk me into going to Seattle with you," Elisabeth said timidly. "I can't be the person you want."

"Not right now," Gunnar said.

"Gunnar—"

"I can hope, right? It's not against the law to hope."

"You need to understand, Shawn and I—"

"Don't," Gunnar said. He put two fingers over her lips. "I'm okay as long as I don't hear about the two of you. I can be your friend, but not that friend. Not the friend who hears about you and Lover Boy, gives you advice on your problems. Not that friend." He took his hand away.

"All right," Elisabeth whispered. She tried to smile.

I could really fall in love with you, she thought. *But I like you too much to let this happen.*

This was the moment where she realized that she really could make any decision she wanted. For herself. For her life. For her past and for her future.

"Gunnar," she said suddenly.

He looked at her, his head cocked, waiting expectantly.

"I can do this. I can sell this house. I can leave Greenleigh."

He nodded, saying nothing, but his lips twitched, as if he were holding back a smile.

She added, a little breathlessly, "I can find work in Seattle, or anywhere else. I can live a better life. Than this." She gestured.

"You can rule the world," Gunnar said. He caught her in his arms. "We can rule the world. Maybe the underworld. Hades and Persephone."

Elisabeth laughed. Something melted deep in her chest, and warmth spread throughout her body. She allowed Gunnar to kiss her cheek, then her forehead, then her nose.

"Sweetheart, it'll be hard," he said. "It's going to hurt. You're going to need me to help you. So let me help you."

"Okay," Elisabeth said. She tried to pull away, but Gunnar held her tight. For a moment, she thought she should remind him of her earlier warning, that she couldn't promise him anything, that her heart was taken. There was a tense note in his grip. Then he released her.

"I'm getting out of here," he said. "I'll text you tomorrow. Oh, I don't have your number." He was shrugging into his jacket, reaching into a pocket for his phone.

"My phone sucks at text," Elisabeth said. "Can you just call me?" She gave him the number and he punched it into his phone.

"What do you mean, your phone sucks at text? That's not a thing. Let me see your phone."

Elisabeth pointed at the flip phone lying on a small table in the front hall, plugged into an outlet.

Gunnar viewed it with disbelief. "Are you kidding me? That's your phone? What is it, circa 2000? Jesus. Does it even hold a charge?"

"Not too well," Elisabeth confessed.

"That, my dear, has to change. But never mind for now. We'll take care of it." He turned to her and gave her a kiss on her cheek. "I'll change your mind about us yet, Elisabeth Burnham."

As the door clicked shut behind him, Elisabeth felt a twinge of worry. Was she playing with fire? She'd been honest, as honest as she could be. Beyond that, she didn't know what she could do. He was a grownup. He needed to quit taking dumb risks on women who were unavailable.

But more importantly—she was leaving Greenleigh.

As she went to the sink to start washing the dishes, she looked around the kitchen. She would miss the house. It was her entire life, the life of her parents, and the life of generations of Burnhams before her. She wasn't sure she would actually have the courage to sell it. But it was the right thing, she thought. This was how she would become a grownup. This was how she would shake herself free of all the baggage of her life.

And as for Shawn—she knew he couldn't be the

reason why she didn't make this decision. She couldn't let him become an obstacle. It wasn't fair to him, because he wasn't an obstacle. The obstacle to growing up and moving forward had always been herself, her own heart. It was time for her to grow up.

20

"I don't know, Shawn." Bob Stuart was shaking his head. "I'm trying. She still doesn't want to see me." He wouldn't meet Shawn's eyes, choosing to hunch forward and fiddle with his substantial key ring instead.

"I asked Christine to call her. She might be able to get her to come around." Shawn tapped his pencil against his desk, eraser side down. He waited for Bob to look up, but Bob concentrated on switching his key ring from hand to hand, methodically going through the keys one by one, as if mentally cataloguing them. He did not look up.

"I don't think she's going to change her mind. She's so evasive."

"At the very least, the two of you need to meet

and talk," Shawn argued. "You can't just throw in the towel."

Bob finally looked up at him. In the slanted morning light of November, his face looked lined and worn. The blue in his eyes seemed pale and diffuse, and they were rimmed with the red of sleepless nights, making him look like a much older man.

Was it really November?

Shawn glanced outside. The trees were bare. The early snow had long since collapsed into hard, dirty piles, but the ground remained wet and slushy, and a thin coating of frost covered the evergreen corporate shrubbery surrounding Lawson & Lawson. Yes, it was November, and it felt like it had been November for months.

"I'm not throwing in the towel. But I think it may be too late for me to convince her. I'm at a loss. I'm afraid she just wants the divorce."

"Are you ready for that?"

"No." Bob was blunt. "No, I think Angela is wrong. I don't think our marriage is over. But I don't know what to do. I feel like—"

There was a long pause.

Shawn raised an eyebrow.

"I feel like I should talk to Beth," Bob finished. "She would know what to say to get Angela to talk to me."

Shawn stopped tapping.

Bob continued, "I know that Angela talks to Beth. And—and Beth doesn't represent Angela anymore. So there's nothing wrong with talking to Beth —is there?"

Shawn did not reply. He picked up the pencil, examined the eraser carefully, then put it down.

"I should talk to Christine, see if she managed to get Angela on the phone," he said, not answering the question directly.

"I'll do whatever she wants," Bob said. "I'll go for counseling. I'll do mediation. Whatever she wants." He leaned forward. "Make sure Christine knows that." He started to rise.

"Are you going to talk to Beth, then?"

Shawn's question stopped him. He sat back down, looking at first awkward, then determined.

"Shawn. I don't mean to pry."

Shawn took a deep breath. He tried to let it out without sounding as if he were annoyed. He nodded.

"I know you and Beth must have some history."

Shawn nodded, keeping his face impassive.

"I know there's something going on—you don't have to tell me, of course. It's none of my business."

"I know this isn't ideal," Shawn admitted. "Beth works here—she's not on staff, but she does contract work—and we've known each other a long time. It's awkward."

"That's not what I meant," Bob interjected. "I didn't mean this." He gestured behind him, to the rest of the offices beyond Shawn's closed door. "I know you said Beth needed to stop representing Angela, because she works here. But I mean—you and Beth. Your dad mentioned it."

At this Shawn looked at him sharply. "My dad? What did my dad say?"

"I saw him last week at the senior center, and he wanted to know if—" Bob smiled, a little ruefully. "Well, he wanted to know if you were doing a good job. I had to say that we weren't exactly having a rousing success at trying to get this thing cleared away. He wanted to know who was causing trouble, and I said, no one. That Angela didn't have an attorney, that Beth Burnham had been helping her, but was just a friend. That's when he said he thought you and Beth had a relationship going way back."

Shawn sat back in his seat. Well, heck. His dad knew? He hadn't thought his dad noticed a damned thing in those days. Ever since his mom had died, his dad had been a workaholic. He never came home from the factory at any decent hour. He'd practically skipped Shawn's teen years. It had only been recently that he had persuaded his dad to indulge his chess obsession at the senior center from time to time. That was all the time he took for himself.

Maybe he'd gotten the gossip from the guys at the senior center, he thought. He could have sworn his dad had no idea what was happening in the world outside those factory walls.

He was going to get Beth back, he thought. He hadn't spoken to her since that night when he had found her with that kid, that tough with the motorcycle. He had needed the cooling off time, the space to be alone and figure out what the hell he was going to do. All he'd needed was Beth to agree to let him fight for her. If he could fight for her, he knew he'd win. And she'd given him that—anyway, he thought she had. He wasn't sure. He hadn't pried anything out of her beyond a nod, but he knew her. He was sure she still loved him.

He hadn't seen her around the office much, and he'd been busy. He'd met Christine for coffee a couple of times and then driven her home, but he hadn't seen that stupid motorcycle around, so he hadn't stopped by to check on Beth. After all, what could he say? Until he could tell her how things were going to be, he didn't think there was much point. And he just wasn't sure how he would untangle everything. All he knew was that it was inevitable. He would fix things.

"I didn't know if it was okay to bring this up," Bob was saying. "But—Beth called me last week."

Shawn tried to bring his focus back to the conversation at hand; he was still preoccupied with thoughts of the motorcycle dude. "She did?"

"Yes." Bob hesitated, as if trying to figure out what to say.

"About Angela?"

"No—well, yes, I asked about Angela. And she didn't really want to say anything, other than she thought I shouldn't give up. She was calling to ask if I would do an inspection."

"An inspection?" Shawn frowned. "Inspection of what?"

"An inspection of her house." Bob waited, but Shawn was still frowning. He shook his head.

"Why? Is she trying to get things fixed? A good idea, if you ask me," he added, "before winter really hits. She has a crap boiler. You should look at that. And that damned water tank."

Bob shook his head. "No, actually. I thought that, too. I thought she wanted to make sure all her systems were in good order. But that's not it. She wants a formal house inspection."

Shawn was still frowning. "I don't understand. Why would she—" His brow cleared. "Wait. A house inspection? A house inspection, as in—"

"She's selling the house." Bob waited for Shawn's response.

She's selling the house. The words died on his lips while they echoed in his brain. He gaped at Bob in amazement. His breath seemed shallow in his chest.

Selling the house?

Bob spoke into the void. "She doesn't plan to fix it up. But she wanted to have the inspection on hand for the realtor. It's on the market."

On the market?

Shawn sat back in his chair. He ran his hand through his hair, trying to think.

Beth couldn't sell that house. It was impossible. This had to be a mistake.

Had he said it out loud? He wasn't sure.

He tried again. "This has to be a mistake, Bob. That house—it's been in Beth's family for generations. She'd never sell it."

Bob was gazing at him with sympathy. He nodded. "It's a beautiful house. It's got some problems, it's had years of neglect. But it's a fine old home."

"She'd never sell it," Shawn repeated. "Never." His mind was reeling, clicking along furiously. That house! That house and that awful mother of hers. The things that had held her back from leaving this stupid town with him. Eight years. Eight years of doing without her, trying to move forward, not calling her, speaking to her, or trying to understand.

He hadn't bothered, he'd borne the awful pain of knowing that she hadn't chosen him. She'd chosen Greenleigh, her family, that house. She'd opted to stay behind, when he had crafted those beautiful plans, not just for the two of them, but for her. For her.

Her mother was gone, so that was one noose less. The house—the house was the last thing. And now she was selling it.

Why?

"It's listed and it's being shown," Bob said. "The realtor called on Monday because she wanted to pass along some questions from a few potential buyers."

Shawn shook his head. "This can't be true," he objected.

Bob lifted his shoulders. "I guess she didn't tell you?" He ended the statement on a questioning note. He might as well have asked whether Beth had said anything to him.

She doesn't tell me anything, Shawn wanted to shout. *She doesn't tell me a damned thing.*

Does she tell that thug of a boyfriend things, he wondered? No, he wasn't her boyfriend. She'd denied it. He wasn't her boyfriend. And he, Shawn, was going to put an end to this rot. All of it.

He'd made some mistakes. Bad ones. He'd been angry and stubborn all those years ago. He'd waited, thinking she'd change her mind, call him, apologize, beg to start over. She hadn't. He hadn't called from his own end. That was a mistake, too. Again, because he was stubborn and vengeful. Ugly emotions, both of them. And clumsy, for a lawyer who was in the business of making careful moves. Just stupid.

He'd been mean to her when she showed up to ask for work. He'd disrespected her, treating her like a temporary clerk, when she was a perfectly good lawyer. She'd done that all by herself, without him! Without anyone to help her.

And he'd almost been too late. He'd swooped in just in time to grab her out of the arms of some creepy kid who was going to do who knew what to her.

All of this ended now.

He stood up abruptly. Bob jumped up also, looking both relieved and anxious.

"Thank you," he said, holding out his hand. "Thank you for telling me."

"I didn't know whether I should," Bob confessed, as they shook hands.

"Beth and I—we were engaged. Once." There, he'd said it, and it wasn't as hard as he'd feared. He needed to practice putting things out into the open. Secrets were just a bad thing.

Bob's brow cleared. "So that's it," he said slowly. "I thought something was—"

"I've got to go to her," Shawn interrupted. "She didn't tell me about the house. I need to stop her."

"You do that," Bob said. "I'll leave you to it. But you don't mind if I talk to her about—"

"No, you go ahead and talk to her. I'll call Christine. We'll get this sorted out with Angela. You might have to lie in wait for her outside of old Mrs. Miller's house. Just swoop in and grab her, make her pay attention to you." He turned to grab his suit jacket from the back of his chair and shrugged into it. "That could get nasty. She's an old bird." Shawn shuddered at the thought of an altercation with Mrs. Miller.

Bob laughed. He turned to leave, saying over his shoulder, "I won't give up if you don't."

"I won't," Shawn said to Bob's retreating form. "The hell. I'm not giving up. I've hardly gotten started."

He gave his desk a quick glance to make sure he hadn't left anything sensitive on it, and strode out the door. As he made his way down the hallway, he glanced quickly into the library. He stopped.

Elisabeth's slender form was hunched over a computer terminal, a stack of books beside her.

"Hey," he said softly. He walked into the room.

She looked up.

"Hey," she said. She looked better than usual, as if she'd been getting enough to eat for a change. Her cheeks were rosy, possibly chapped from the cold. Her hair was down, and it had been cut recently. Instead of a schoolmarm-ish voluminous dress, she was wearing a light sweater, a short skirt, and dark tights and boots. She looked almost fashionable.

Shawn found himself wondering—was this all because of That Guy? Was that why she looked as well as she did?

"Where's Ricky Junior?"

"I don't know," she replied. "I haven't seen him. Maybe he's in court."

"I thought you two were as thick as thieves," he teased.

Elisabeth smiled. "We are. But then I wouldn't give him up to the authorities, would I? You should know better than to ask me things I won't answer."

"Touché," he said, smiling. "I suppose he must be out grabbing a latte." He sat down at the big conference table, not too close but close enough to show that he wanted to have a conversation.

"I wanted to ask you something."

Elisabeth raised an eyebrow. She put down her pen.

"Yes?"

"Are you selling the house?" He'd decided to be blunt. He was all in, now. No reason to pretend he wasn't in the game. This was one battle he planned to win, and he didn't see the point to trying to deceive her.

"Yes." She was calm, meeting his gaze frankly.

"When did you decide this?"

"Recently."

"Does this have anything to do with—" Shawn tried, but couldn't bring himself to say it. The Guy? The Creep? The Dude? Did he even have a name? He couldn't remember if Beth had said what his name was.

"It's a lot of things," Elisabeth was saying. "You know it is. Trying to stay afloat, make a living, taking care of the house. It's just a lot."

Did he ask about the guy? It sucked that everything she said made so much sense, seemed so rational. All he cared about was the guy, all he cared about was winning against that guy.

"Isn't it hard to sell that house? It's been in your family forever."

"Yes. It's hard. I didn't want to do it, but I can't justify keeping it. It's kind of silly, actually. A single woman doesn't need such a massive house. A family would do it justice."

We could be a family, Shawn thought. But he didn't say anything. He watched the expression on her face, wondering what she thought of his interest, wondering why she suddenly looked healthy and normal, not the badly dressed waif who had wandered into Lawson & Lawson just a couple of months ago.

"So I listed it, and we've had some interested people walk through. I asked Bob Stuart to do an inspection. I can't fix anything up, so I won't get as much money as I probably should. But it's a good house. It's solid."

Shawn nodded. "It's that," he agreed. "And then you must be looking at some neighborhoods to buy in." He wondered if she were buying an apartment for one, or a family home. He suddenly felt ill at ease. What were her plans? What was she counting on for her future? Was he included?

He suddenly realized that he had made a mistake. A very grave mistake indeed. He should have taken over her plans much earlier, he realized. She was at the point of planning for her future, and he hadn't jumped in to make sure she included him. In fact, she probably didn't even realize that he assumed that he was in the picture.

"Beth—" he began, but she stopped him.

"Shawn. I'm leaving Greenleigh."

"You're—you're what?"

"I'm leaving Greenleigh." Elisabeth looked away, as if the expression on his face was causing her pain, and she couldn't bear to look at it.

He wondered what he looked like—it must be

horrible, he thought, if she couldn't stand to look at him.

"You're not leaving Greenleigh," he said, but his voice sounded odd and tinny.

"I'm leaving," she said gently. "I'm going away. I'm taking the money from the house and starting over. Somewhere else."

21

"You can't be serious."

There was a pause as Elisabeth seemed to consider his words. She was looking at her hands on the computer keyboard, stretching her fingers out and gently spreading them over the keys. She ran them over the smooth surface, keeping her index fingers on the "f" and the "j" keys, but letting her other fingers travel.

She looked up at him.

"I'm serious," she said.

"Where did this come from?" Shawn tried to keep his voice down, but his throat hurt from the effort. He wanted to shout at her. *What the hell was this*, he wanted to shout. *What the hell?*

He didn't want to ask about that guy. He was afraid of what she might say.

"I've been thinking about it."

Shawn looked at her sharply. And what he saw dismayed him.

She was lying.

Why was she lying? Why?

This was almost an out-of-body experience. He could swear that he was leaning back in his office chair, watching Shawn Waterstone and Beth Burnham sweat it out, as if it were a movie.

Take a breath, he thought.

He took his breath.

She had gone back to evaluating her hands on the keyboard. He leaned over, reached out, picked up her left hand. He ran his thumb over her ring finger, rubbing it gently. His mind traveled to that long-distant day, when he had carried his mother's wedding band safely in his pocket as he waited in a darkened parking lot.

"This has all gone wrong," he said softly.

Startled, she looked up at him.

"I'm sorry. I feel like I've done this to you." He hadn't been able to afford an engagement ring in those days, but he could more than afford one now. How he would love to buy her a diamond, he thought.

"You haven't," she protested, a little too quickly. "It's just the right thing to do."

"I don't agree with you," he said, trying to keep his voice steady.

Breathe, he thought.

He waited until he'd taken another calming breath. Then he put her hand down and leaned back. "Can we talk about this?"

"I've—I've already listed the house," she said, looking away. "I've made up my mind. It was hard. But I think it's best."

Relief flooded through him. She didn't want to sell the house. He could see it in her body language. It was making her sick to do it.

He knew her. He still knew his Bethie. Regardless of whatever was going on with that other guy—he knew Beth. He wasn't going to lose her.

Shawn rose. He knew that it was the better part of wisdom to leave a negotiation while he was still ahead.

"We'll work through this, Beth. Don't rush into anything. You're a lawyer, you know better than that, right?" He tried to grin, although his face felt oddly stiff.

Elisabeth didn't smile. She nodded. "I know. I haven't had any offers yet. I can't fix the house up properly so I know people are going to make all kinds of crazy underpriced bids. I didn't even bother cleaning it—"

"Most people know exactly where the house is

and what it looks like, cleaning it would be besides the point," Shawn said wryly. "There aren't many people around here who wouldn't recognize your house in a real estate listing. You won't need to pretend that it's a showcase—that's not why people would want to buy it."

"Shawn—" Elisabeth looked up at him. "About —about last time—at the house—"

"Let's talk about this somewhere else," Shawn interrupted. "I've got an engagement tonight, but I'll cancel it." He'd been stupid to let the whole thing lie for as long as he had, but he'd just catch up—he'd bring her flowers, yellow roses like the ones in his mother's rose garden, the ones that she'd treasured, the ones Beth used to help her prune. And he'd take her to dinner, he'd convince her that things were going to be okay. And the key part of this was not to panic, not to get upset, not to scare her off. If he acted like a crazy person, she would use that as a reason to avoid him.

"I can't," Elisabeth said. She hesitated, then said rapidly, "I've got an auctioneer coming in to sign a contract."

"What?" Shawn exclaimed. He had been ready to believe his own self-talk, that all he had to do was calmly remind Beth that he was there for her, that they belonged together, that he was going to fix everything—he was mentally buying her a diamond, in fact. He'd get her the biggest goddamn stinking diamond that Greenleigh had ever seen—

"It'll be hard to sell after Christmas," Elisabeth said. "That's what the realtor said. This is the last chance I've got until spring. I really want to get through all of this now, so I don't have to wait 'til next summer."

"Beth—" Shawn groaned. He ran a hand through his hair. "You're just moving too fast—you've got to slow down. This is a big deal."

"I know it is. But it—it feels right. I think I need to do this."

"Why?" Shawn tried to control his voice, which threatened to rise again. "Why do you need to do this? And now? Why now? I thought—I thought—"

"That's why I wanted to say something about last time—" Elisabeth interrupted. "I feel bad about that—it wasn't—it wasn't right." She rose and faced him. "I think I led you to think that we—we—"

"You didn't lead me to think anything," Shawn snapped. "I know exactly what I think." He had given up trying to control his temper—he was ready to pound his fists on the table in frustration.

"But I did," Elisabeth continued. "I know you think we can just go on like we were before. And I didn't argue with you—but things are different. We just can't pretend they aren't."

"Are you telling me that you don't love me,

then?" Shawn demanded. "I don't care if they hear me," he added, seeing Elisabeth's eyes dart to the open door behind him. "Let 'em all find out. Let 'em talk about how the managing partner is in love with one of his attorneys. I don't give a shit. Tell me you don't love me and I'll just go away. I'll go away and leave you alone. I'm daring you."

Elisabeth remained silent.

"You can't say it, can you? That's because we belong together. See, even you can't disguise the truth. This is the most frustrating, the most pointless argument—just stupid—" He paused for breath.

"It's so much bigger than that, Shawn," Elisabeth said. Her voice was quiet, her expression sad. "You suck the air out of the room. I can't say anything to you. You're always right, no matter how I feel, no matter what I try to say. You just don't see it."

"Listen. Listen to me, Beth." Shawn approached her, his jaw set. "I'm happy to shut up and let you have your say. Any time. But you have to accept one point. Which is that—listen to me carefully—we belong together. Got that? We. Belong. Together. We have to solve this. Together. Together. I'll say it again if you don't get it—"

"I hear you," Elisabeth said. The color in her cheeks was gone, and she was back to looking like the fragile Beth that he knew. He was struck with the thought that however right he was—and he knew he was right—he was making her unhappy.

He suddenly felt terrible. And exhausted.

"Bethie. Let's not talk about this here. You're upset, and I'm upset. And whatever is going on, I'm sure we can fix it—together. Let's sit down and just go through everything and work it out. We can do this."

Did she really say that he sucked the air out of the room? He was suddenly conscious of how stifled he felt in the law firm library. Did she feel stifled? Rather, did he stifle her?

"Will you talk to me? Will you just sit down with me and talk to me? I promise not to suck the air out of the room. I'll hold my breath."

He was hoping to get a chuckle out of her, but she merely shook her head.

"I have nothing to say, Shawn. My mind is made up. I need to move forward, and this is the best way. It's the only way."

"It's not the only way. And you're accusing me of not listening, but you're not listening, either."

At this, Elisabeth looked away.

It was true, and her silence showed that she knew it.

She didn't want to listen.

I know you, Beth, Shawn thought. *If you listen,*

you might change your mind. Because I love you and you love me.

But if this was true—and he was absolutely positive that it was—then why? Why leave? *Is it that guy?* Shawn wanted to ask. *Is he the reason why?*

He was finding comfort in her refusal to say that she didn't love him, but he couldn't fit that new guy into this picture. He was convinced that Leather Jacket was at least partly responsible for this sudden plan. Beth was hurting for money, and her legal career was in limbo. Despite her skill and her popularity with locals, she was barely holding things together. It wasn't unreasonable for her to think about making a career move elsewhere.

Well, it wasn't unreasonable for most people. For Beth Burnham, though, it made no sense. She belonged in Greenleigh.

With me, Shawn thought.

"I'm cancelling my engagement tonight. Can you call the auctioneer and reschedule? Let's do this tonight."

"I don't want to," Elisabeth said. "It's after hours, and I felt bad having him come tonight as it is."

"Then I'm going to just come over in the middle of things and make trouble," Shawn said, turning to leave. "I'll be there tonight. Let's go to dinner after I chase that guy away."

He meant to take a light tone, but when he

turned back to look at her, she had a stricken expression on her face.

"Hey," he said gently. "I'm kidding. I won't be rude."

"It's not that," Elisabeth choked. "It's Gunnar. I don't want the two of you to argue."

Shawn let the words hang in the air. Gunnar. So that was his name.

"He's a kid," she was saying in a rush. "He's just a kid, and he's a pain in the butt, but I don't want you to scare him. He acts like such a wise ass, but I'm sure you must intimidate him. I don't want you to come over when he's there."

"Will he be there?" Shawn asked slowly. *Why? Why?* his mind screamed. *What is it with this kid? Why will he be there?*

"He's emptying the carriage house for me," Elisabeth said. "It's full of junk. Most of it can probably go on a bonfire. He's been working on hauling that stuff away—he knows someone with a truck—"

"I see," Shawn said.

"Just—just don't. Don't come over. We can talk another time. I know you're right, Shawn. I know I'm just running away, and I'm not being fair to you. But—I don't want more messes to deal with. It's enough for me as it is."

Shawn mulled this over. It was a fair request. And he wanted to know more about this Gunnar kid. If he manhandled Elisabeth, she would just shut down. And she was serious about her plans. If he couldn't get her to open up to him, she'd sell the house and leave.

"All right then," he said. "Not tonight. Tomorrow?"

"I can't."

"Thursday?"

Elisabeth nodded. "Thursday is fine," she said softly.

"So tell Gunnar that you're spoken for on Thursday night."

She nodded again.

Shawn walked out of the library, trying to keep his stride confident. But inside, he was smarting.

His rival was a tattooed kid named Gunnar, probably from the wrong side of town. What hold did he have over Beth?

22

The pickup truck was pulling away when Beth walked up to the house. She had fled from the office early, not able to concentrate on her research. Maybe doing some manual labor would clear her head.

She hurried up the steps and found the front door open, but no one appeared to be in the house.

"Gunnar!" she called softly, but there was no reply. She dumped her coat and briefcase on a chair in the front room and went into the kitchen. There was an espresso pot on the stove and the strong smell of coffee; a small jar sat beside the stove. Elisabeth picked it up, unscrewed the lid, and lifted it to her nose to sniff.

Milk? she wondered. The jar was warm. She shook it slightly before she set it down again, then

opened the lid of the espresso pot and peered inside. It was empty.

She didn't own an espresso pot, so Gunnar must
have brought it over. Unless he'd found it in the
shed? He'd promised to clean out all the outbuild-
ings of ancient Burnham junk, and she'd told him to
keep or dispose of whatever he found. There was
nothing valuable out there, she knew. But an
espresso pot? She couldn't imagine her father or
anyone else in her family brewing espresso.

Where was Gunnar?

She went out the back door of the kitchen, down
the steps into the back yard. She heard voices in the
carriage house.

"So how much would you want for that?"

Elisabeth paused. It was a female voice, brimming with amusement.

"Probably about two hundred. Give or take. But
I'd give you a discount."

"That would be sweet," the female voice continued. "Can I just walk in?"

"No, you should call first. What's your number?
I'll call your phone and then you'll have mine." A
second later, Elisabeth heard a tinkly melody sound.

Elisabeth walked into the carriage house and
stopped short. It was mostly empty, and she had to
take a moment to collect herself. When she'd
brought Gunnar in, it had been so crammed with

junk they'd had a hard time forcing the door open. They'd had to squeeze into the cobwebby interior, pushing their way around boxes of old *National Geographic* magazines and broken lamp shades, sneezing along the way—but now it was a wide-open space, with beautiful wood floors that had been swept clear of dust and debris.

Gunnar was standing in the middle, leaning on a broom, talking to—Christine.

"Oh, hey," Gunnar said.

"Hi," Elisabeth replied. She looked at Christine, who was dressed in cropped jeans and a tight white sweater. She'd done something to her hair—it was shorter, and almost platinum blonde. She looked like Marilyn Monroe, complete with bright red lipstick. "Aren't you cold?" she asked, eyeing her cropped jeans and sneakers.

"Hi!" Christine said brightly. "I just ran over to ask a question. I took the day off—I have to get a plumber in—and I saw Gunnar out here. Can I borrow him? He's awesome."

Gunnar was watching Elisabeth, a lazy smile playing about his lips. He was so annoying! She knew he was laughing at her because Christine was so not her type.

"Sure," she said, trying to keep her voice friendly. "I don't keep his schedule."

"He said he's here every day," Christine said. "So

if you can spare him—" She looked at Gunnar, then leaned toward Elisabeth conspiratorially. "He's going to do a tattoo for me," she said in a stage whisper.

"Oh, really?" Elisabeth replied. She looked at Gunnar again, who had started sweeping the floor and had his back turned.

"I have a small one," Christine confided. "I got it after I ran the New York City marathon, but I had just turned eighteen, so I had to hide it from my parents. They would have freaked. I was able to keep it under my bikini bottoms, though. It's tiny and not very good."

She patted her hip bone. Elisabeth turned to look at Gunnar again, but he was studiously avoiding her gaze, sweeping further and further away from them.

"I was thinking I'd like something really awesome, like a tiger. If he could incorporate that old tattoo and do something new around it, that would be great."

"I can do that," Gunnar said from a far corner, continuing to sweep.

"I think it'll be great," Christine said. "I'm so excited!" She beamed.

"It'll probably show around your, uh, bikini bottoms," Elisabeth said. "I guess you're not planning on hiding it anymore?"

"Oh, pfft." Christine waved a hand. "Too bad if people don't like it. No one at work will know it's there, and who cares if people at the beach see it. And anyone else—well, it'll be a case-by-case basis. If guys don't like it, then they can go away." She winked.

"I'm going in," Gunnar announced. "Elisabeth, this place is done. And the garage and the shed are both done. All empty. We can hit the attic next. Maybe after the auction house people take a look tonight."

"I can't believe it," Elisabeth gasped. "That's nuts! All those boxes?"

"Gone. Gone, baby, gone." He paused next to the door. "You're fine with not seeing them before they go? I just sent Eddie with the last truckload, but if you wanted to see anything—"

"No," Elisabeth interrupted. "No, just get rid of it. Get rid of it all."

"This is a huge change, Beth," Christine said. "Are you sure you're okay just throwing everything away? You can put things in storage. I've got a storage locker with my California stuff in it. It's easy." Gunnar walked out, slamming the door behind him, and Christine watched through a dirty window as he strode toward the kitchen door.

"No, it had to go. All of it," Elisabeth replied curtly.

"When did you decide to sell? I was so surprised when I got here and Gunnar was loading up the truck! I thought there was a robbery going on. But he's cute. Gunnar, I mean." Christine was smiling, but Elisabeth was not fooled. She wasn't going to be tricked into saying more than she intended. She shrugged and began to walk toward the door, but Christine blocked her way.

"I know you don't like me," she said. "But I needed to talk to you, so I waited around. It's about Angela Stuart."

Elisabeth flushed. "It's not that I don't like you. I'm sorry, I just don't know you very well."

"I could say the same for you and Gunnar—he told me you met a couple of weeks ago, but you seem to be pals. So I know it's not that you don't know me very well." Christine was no longer smiling. "Let's cut the crap. I know I've stumbled into something, and I'm sorry—I don't mean any harm —but I've got a client who only talks to you, and the guy she's trying to divorce also only talks to you. So what gives? I'm a mediator, but I can't mediate between two silent people. And Shawn can't violate Bob's confidences, so he can't tell me anything. Do you want to help me out or no? Because if not, I've got to tell Angela that this is a lost cause, and then there's going to be a messy divorce. When people refuse to deal with each other, that's the worst kind of divorce there is. It's expensive and complicated."

She stepped back a little, folding her arms. She shivered slightly as a draft puffed under the door. "You're the one who called me, remember?"

"I know I did," Elisabeth said. "And I feel like I've tried to talk sense into Angela. But she isn't listening to me, either. I suppose I should talk to Bob. He needs to just go to Angela and force her to have a conversation." She hesitated, then added stiffly, "I'm sorry if I've not been—welcoming."

"It's okay," Christine replied. "I'm a divorce lawyer, this is old stuff. I've had much worse. But I didn't expect to have such a hard time with people who just won't confront each other. Usually confrontation is all I've got. Frankly, unless she has a boyfriend I don't know about, I don't understand Angela at all. I think Bob's ready to give her anything she wants, and she doesn't even want to talk to him."

"That's probably the worst kind of problem to try to fix," Elisabeth said. "Angela is actually being pretty radical—after all, she up and left. Maybe this is the person she used to be, way back before she got married. Maybe she's turned into a person she doesn't like, after all these years of being married to Bob, and she's just trying to get back to the old Angela. If that's the case, this ought to look familiar to Bob."

"Well, whatever it is, I need a remedy. Otherwise Angela and Bob are doomed, and we need to call the lawyers back in." Christine shivered and rubbed her arms. "Damn. It's cold. But I'm not done. I wanted to ask you about the house sale. Why so sudden? I could swear this wasn't in the works when we met."

"It wasn't." Elisabeth tried to sound casual. "It's the right thing to do, though. I don't have much of a private practice, and I'm kind of tired of taking care of this place. It's much too big for me anyway."

"I don't agree," Christine objected. "I just bought my big old project, remember? I think it's an awesome thing, to restore an old house to its former glory. Ha. Listen to me. As if I know what I'm doing."

"It's a lot harder than you think," Elisabeth said. "Of course, if you're willing to spend the money, it's easier. But even there—it's a black hole. You can spend and spend and still have a dump. It's so depressing." She was suddenly astonished at her frankness—she hadn't planned on saying any of this out loud. But this was why she was leaving Greenleigh—right? It wasn't about Shawn—or her failure of a law practice—right?

Christine heaved a sigh. "I know. And lots of people told me I was crazy. The realtor who sold me the house told me I was crazy. And right now, I've got no heat. Which is what brought me here to begin with—and then I got distracted by Gunnar and his biceps. Very nice biceps, actually."

"What?" Elisabeth started. "How long have you had no heat? Because your pipes are going to burst overnight if you don't figure something out. You've got to get someone over right now. Have you got a plumber?"

"No, that's why I came over. And it's almost the end of the day, so I was thinking it would be hard to find someone who would come right away, unless you had a name you could give me."

"Yes, I'll call someone for you. We'd better get into the house. You're freezing anyway. For future reference, you don't just dash down the street without a coat at this time of year."

Christine was laughing. "Yeah, it's hard to take the California out of me. I spent too many years there. I'm really from New Jersey, so I ought to know better."

"New England is nothing like New Jersey," Elisabeth said severely, as they left the carriage house.

"Yeah, I know." They were outside the kitchen door, and the strong smell of espresso hung about the steps. Christine put a hand out to stop Elisabeth from opening the door.

"Just a second. Before we go in. Listen, I'm sorry

about Shawn. I can tell you guys have a history. I feel like I stepped into something and I don't know what it is. Is he part of this? Selling the house?"

"No," Elisabeth responded quickly. "No, he's not."

Christine squinted at her. "Really?"

Elisabeth shook her head, not trusting her voice.

"Do you mind if I date him? He's pretty cute."

Elisabeth hesitated, and Christine laughed. "Okay. I know the answer, then. I'll stay away. And I'll stop prying. I just wanted to know if I could help."

"Wait, you didn't give me time to answer," Elisabeth objected, but Christine had pushed in front of her and had her hand on the doorknob.

"How about Gunnar?" she said over her shoulder.

"Gunnar's a kid," Elisabeth returned. She decided not to think about him kissing her—twice.

"You must know that he has a crush on you."

"That's just stupid. I don't believe it. I'm so much older, and not his type." Elisabeth hoped she was telling the truth. She wanted it to be the truth. She thought she had nipped things in the bud the night of the second kiss.

"Just be careful, he's crazy about you," Christine said. The tone of her voice changed abruptly as she charged into the kitchen stairwell. "Gunnar!" she squealed. "Oh, my gawd. You made me a cappuccino! I'm so freaking cold, it's not funny!"

Elisabeth pulled the door shut behind them. The odor of wood smoke was pungent, and the kitchen was almost too warm. Gunnar stood at the stove in his shirt sleeves, shaking the jar of milk until it foamed up. Christine held her arms out to Gunnar in a mock hug as he handed her a cup.

"I'll get the plumber over there," Elisabeth said, brushing past Gunnar in the kitchen. He grabbed at her arm before she could slip away.

"Hey, I have a cup for you," he said.

She shook off his hand. "I need to call the plumber, Christine's going to have a problem if she doesn't fix her heat by tonight. Christine, do you have wood stoves? If I can't get someone in, you'll have to light your stoves. I hope you know how that works. You'll need wood." She went into the front room, rubbing her arm where Gunnar had grabbed her. Christine was right, she needed to be careful. He was a kid, but that second kiss was a bad mistake —it hadn't felt like she was kissing a kid, and she was lying—again!—if she pretended that he was just a kid. The first time, he'd taken her by surprise, but the second time was on her. He'd done it, but she'd let him do it. She had to make sure it didn't happen again.

What kind of a crazy guy falls for a screw-up like

me? He must be hard up, she thought. She shook her head as she punched a number into the phone and waited. No, he wasn't hard up. He could have a lot of girls. He was good-looking, charming, and knew how to do things. He was artistic, but he actually had a trade he could earn an income from. He was reliable—he'd shown up to help when he said he would—and he clearly had lots of friends.

Why the heck was he so into her? He made more money than she did and had a better wardrobe! She chuckled, then jumped as she felt an arm around her waist. Gunnar was sliding a steaming cup onto the desk in front of her with his right hand, but had reached around her waist with his left arm, as if to steady her.

"Wanted to make sure you didn't jump and spill this," he whispered.

Elisabeth nodded, but she caught his eye and saw his knowing smirk.

She had to be careful. He acted like such a know-it-all punk, it would be easy to believe that version of him.

The first place wasn't answering, so she hung up and tried another number. This time the guy answered—he was the father of a high school friend, and he was on his cell phone on the road, but was willing to stop in and take a look at Christine's boiler.

Elisabeth returned to the kitchen, where Christine and Gunnar were having a lively argument, their voices climbing louder and louder as they each tried to talk over the other.

"You don't know the first thing about the West Coast!" Christine complained. "I don't know why you think it's better out there—it's not, it's a lunatic asylum."

"At least it's not boring," Gunnar countered. He glanced mischievously at Elisabeth, who was adding sugar to her cappuccino. "Did Elisabeth tell you that we're headed out there?"

Elisabeth froze in the middle of stirring her cup. She was afraid to look up and meet Christine's eyes, so she took a sip of her coffee for lack of anything else to do. "No! Why on earth are you going out there?" For once, Christine sounded genuinely shocked.

"Seattle, actually," Gunnar said. "I have friends out there. Elisabeth is coming with me. We'll have a lot of fun."

Elisabeth cringed.

"Beth, is he just pulling my leg?" Christine still sounded shocked. "I can't tell when this guy is making stuff up."

"Hey—um—I've got someone coming over. He can take a look—Roger Milton of Milton Heating and Plumbing. I know his daughter, he's a good guy.

He's kind of expensive but—" Elisabeth felt herself blushing. "I'm sorry, just—he's on the road and headed to your place."

Christine rose from the table. "Oh, my gosh, thank you! Thank you so much, Beth—that's so awesome—I'd better get home—but listen, are you guys really leaving? Together? Beth?"

This time Elisabeth made herself look at Christine. "Yes. That's why I'm selling the house."

"Holy crap," Christine breathed. "Does Shawn know?"

"Kind of," Elisabeth said. "Some of it."

"Listen, Beth. If you need something, come find me. You know where I am—close enough that I didn't wear a coat. Okay?" Christine walked up to Elisabeth and put her hands on her shoulders. "Okay? I feel like I've only got a fraction of this story —and I've only just gotten to know you—but if you need something, come find me. I owe you now, too."

"Okay," Elisabeth nodded, trying to smile. She didn't hate Christine—she didn't think she liked her, but she hadn't done anything actively despicable, anyway.

"Nice meeting you, Gunnar. Thanks for the coffee—" There was a sudden banging at the front door. Christine hurried over to open it, and in a moment, she turned around, a long florist's box in her arms.

Elisabeth stared, perplexed. Only Shawn had ever given her flowers. But those had been garden flowers, not florist flowers. Who on earth could be sending flowers now? She racked her brain. She couldn't think of any clients who would have a reason to do so.

"Open it!" Christine urged, handing her the box. Elisabeth put it down on the hall credenza, and opened the box. Nestled among the tissue paper were a dozen yellow roses. There was no note, but she knew who they were from. "Yellow roses," she said aloud. Shawn used to bring her roses because he took great care of his mother's rose garden, wanting to make it as vibrant and as beautiful as she had kept it when she was alive. And for whatever reason, the yellow ones had always smelled sweetest. He would bring her armfuls of them all summer long. But these were different—long-stemmed, thornless, the yellow a smooth golden cream rather than the slightly battered lemon-yellow that she remembered from days long past. Maybe this was what happened when you had lots of money—and it was November. You sent florist roses.

She lifted one tenderly out of the tissue, bringing the blossom up to her nose, breathing deeply. She could barely catch a whiff, the very faintest whiff of perhaps what this flower's ancestors might have smelled like on a brilliant summer's day. The smooth petal brushed against the top of her lip. It was enough to evoke a surge of remembrance, a welling of emotion from somewhere inside her, a place where she kept her passions and beliefs sacred and hidden from day-to-day life.

She could feel it so intensely, that shimmering, glowing feeling from long-ago summers. How strange that the touch of a rose petal, the faint scent of perfume could do what no amount of rational conversation with herself could prevent. They took her back, back to a time when her understanding of the world was far more innocent, back to a time when she had been tempted to follow her heart. Her heart had been so sure.

Shawn remembered. And she knew exactly what he was saying. He wanted to go back to a time when she had trusted him. He wanted to give her the opportunity again to make the fateful decision to believe in him. She shook her head. She felt dizzy from the intensity of the remembrance, as if she had stayed out in the sun too long. A wry laugh escaped her. Sun was a funny thought when one was standing in a drafty hallway.

She bent her head to the flower again, closing her eyes. In her mind's eye she could see him outside, laughing, overloading her with his flowers as she squealed and tried not to get pricked by the thorns. He had been so boyishly handsome in those days, not the cool, distinguished man in the Italian suit that he was now. Age had improved him, like a mellowed sherry. Eight years ago, he still had that eager edge to his personality, all afire to see the world, try new things. Now he was more sedate, less inclined to jump in with a comment or a joke, even though Elisabeth could always tell by the quick movement of his eyes and the restless motion of his hands that while he seemed more pensive, it was merely the exercise of a choice. His mind remained as active and as incisive as ever.

Elisabeth opened her eyes. It was not an option, she told herself. It was simply not an option. He said that he loved her. And once she had believed him with all her heart. Why should he love her now? He was just reaching back for the past.

The past was gone. His mother was gone. And they themselves—were gone. They weren't the same people anymore.

"Well?" Christine said impatiently.

Elisabeth had forgotten momentarily about her two visitors.

"I can't believe you even need to ask," Gunnar said dryly. "It's Lover Boy. He's the only one who can make Elisabeth look that unhappy. You were wondering why she's leaving town? So now you know." He went over to Elisabeth and gently took the limp rose out of her hand. He replaced it and closed the lid of the box.

She looked up at him. There were tears in her eyes.

"Am I making a mistake?" she whispered.

"It'll be okay," Gunnar said. He put his arm around her and nodded at Christine. "You've got two witnesses now. Someone needs to make you happy, and it's not Lover Boy."

23

"This is a mess."

Christine leaned forward on her arms. Her expression was grim. He hadn't even known her face could look like that, frowning and tense.

In her heels, she towered over his desk, and he normally really disliked it when visitors stood up and loomed over him in his office. It felt like a power play, and he wasn't caving to any stupid power plays, not from anyone, and certainly not from Christine. But he didn't feel inclined to stand. He was tired. Really, really tired.

"I didn't make the mess," he argued. "If it's a mess, it's that guy, what's his name—"

"Gunnar."

"Yeah, right, whatever." The hell kind of name was that? He'd never heard of it before.

"I didn't make any of this mess," he repeated.

"What a stupid answer," Christine responded. "Excuse me, but you're not a stupid man. Please don't give me dumb-ass responses like, 'it's not my fault.'" She said the words in a baby voice. "And anyway, who cares whose fault this is? You need to fix this. Now. You don't have any time. I'm serious."

Shawn remained seated, although it was costing him considerable effort. Christine had barged into his office right as he was thinking about going out for coffee, slamming the door behind her and effectively preventing him from taking the coffee break that he felt he'd earned after a hard morning trying to wrap his head around a piece of complex litigation that was going south on him. He had a headache from insufficient sleep and insufficient caffeine, and he was thinking that he was going to do the unthinkable and pass this big case off to an associate who was chomping at the bit for a meaty assignment. He could just come in at the last minute to oversee it and look for holes in strategy, he thought, then was disgusted that the thought had even passed through his mind.

What had happened to the aggressive, hungry legal perfectionism that had helped him to climb that impossible New York law firm partnership ladder? Why was he so distracted and irritable over a case that would have taken about five minutes for one of his New York colleagues to dissect and dispense with?

Why the hell had he even come home? This town was a dump. He was bored. He was lonely. He was angry. And yes, he hated waking up alone. He was sick of it. It sucked.

Was that the reason why he was so bent on getting Beth back? Was he just bored and lonely?

Or did he hate losing? And did he especially hate losing to a tattooed punk with a weird name like "Gunnar?"

That kid looked young, certainly younger than himself, and younger than Beth. What the hell was up with that? Did Beth really like that guy? She never would have talked to a guy like that back in high school. She'd have run screaming in the opposite direction if a dude with tattoos and a leather jacket had even looked at her.

All of these thoughts crowded his mind as he sat, playing with the fancy pen that his father had given him for law school graduation years ago. He twirled it around in his fingers, noting vaguely that it was looking a little scratched up. Just like his ego, he thought. He smirked at nothing in particular.

"Stop," Christine commanded. She reached forward to grab the pen from him and slammed it on the desk. He winced.

"You've got to go to Beth and stop her, or she'll make a huge mistake."

"I'm already seeing her tomorrow," Shawn complained. "I'll talk to her. But her thought process isn't flawed. She's having so much trouble with that house, no wonder she's thinking of selling. You just don't have a clue. Yeah, yeah, I know you bought a big old house—you have no idea what you're in for this winter. Just you wait."

To his surprise, Christine leaned back from his desk, flushing. "Yes, I'm finding that out," she said, her voice curt.

"Uh-oh. Has something happened? Is everything okay?" Shawn sat up in his seat.

"Barely. I am the proud owner of a new heating system today. Nearly had a dramatic freeze-up in the middle of the night, too. Fun stuff, holding blowdryers on pipes. Just so much fun."

"Oh, shit. That's awful. I'm sorry."

"Yeah. Well. I wanted a hobby, and I got one." Christine laughed, but she didn't sound amused. She sat down in one of the chairs in front of his desk. "So I get it, but I think you're the one who doesn't get it. It's not the house. It's not about the house at all."

Shawn didn't want her to say it. He needed to

take a minute, just a minute, to let the screaming in his head calm down. He held up a hand, but Christine raised her voice.

"No. No, you have to let me say it. It's Gunnar. You have to stop Beth, or she'll make a big mistake. With Gunnar."

Shawn felt the blood rush to his face, and his collar suddenly felt tight. He pulled at his tie with two fingers, trying to loosen it. He realized that he already knew what Christine was going to say, and marveled that he hadn't figured this out earlier. Maybe that's what those shapeless anxiety dreams were trying to tell him? Why had he been so stupid?

He'd just listened to the surface of what Beth was saying, without paying attention to what was underneath. All she'd said was that she was leaving Greenleigh, and he'd accepted it, he'd let it percolate in his mind, confident that he would find a way out...but he suddenly knew—she wasn't leaving alone.

"She doesn't realize what's happening," Christine was saying. "She thinks this is just about getting rid of the house and everything that ties her to this place. It really isn't. She'll break Gunnar's heart. It'll kill her when she's in Seattle and she figures out that she's got to hurt him badly. And then she'll never love anyone again."

"Hold on, hold on," Shawn said, rising. "You're

—you're exaggerating. Don't get all dramatic, Christine. You don't really know—"

"I'm *not* being dramatic!" Christine gasped. She rose again, her whitened knuckles gripping the edge of his desk. "Don't tell me I don't know! I do know! You're the one who doesn't know anything! Jesus Christ! How is it that I know Beth for a month and everything going on with her is as plain as day— and you've known her your whole life and you can't figure this out? You're a *moron* if you don't see it, Shawn!" She paused for breath, bent over the desk, her blond hair, loosened from its usual ponytail, falling forward over her face as she attempted to compose herself.

For a long moment there was only the sound of her breathing. Shawn was facing away from her, staring out the window.

"What's your stake in this?" he said finally, not turning around. "Why do you care so much?"

"Oh, my freaking *lord*," Christine breathed. "I can't even believe you said that."

"Is this how you act during your client meetings? Do you name call? Throw insults? I thought you did divorces, Christine. Celebrity divorces—I would have thought those required more finesse? If you hammer clients the way you're hammering me, I don't know why they put up with you," Shawn snapped.

"You're just so stupid," Christine retorted. "I can't stand it. You're the one being insulting. Do you think I've got some kind of ulterior motive? Like maybe I've got a crush on that kid? Listen, you jerk. He's the best thing that's happened to Beth in a long time. He's taking care of her—which you're not, I might add. You're too busy thinking of yourself."

Shawn did not reply. He was smarting. Take care of her? She didn't want him to take care of her. He'd tried repeatedly to engage her, and all he got was the sense that she was terrified of him and wanted him to go away. Oh, and right, he sucked the air out of the room. Had to remember that one.

Apparently she was fine with that punk taking care of her, but didn't want anything to do with him, Shawn, the guy who actually knew what she needed. Only, she wouldn't listen to him. She wanted very little to do with him, unless it had to do with work. Even work—she would get out of her Lawson & Lawson job in a hot minute if she could. It was convenient for her when times were hard, that was all.

Oh, Bethie. What the hell. Where were all of those wonderful memories? Why had everything gone so wrong?

It was his fault, he knew.

Christine was right, damn her. This was his fault

and he was the only one who could make it turn out right.

"The auctioneer came last night and she's signed the contract," Christine was saying. "Everything is going, Shawn. Except for a few antiques that she's leaving in the house for buyers to see, it's all going. Every bit of it."

Shawn turned around. He'd known about the auctioneer, but he still couldn't believe it. He tried to stay calm. "How's that?"

Christine shook her head. "It was those flowers."

"The flowers? What do you mean?"

"The flowers, Shawn. The flowers came and Beth broke down. She held it together until the flowers came." Christine was speaking softly now. She eyed Shawn with compassion. "I'm sorry. I know you wanted to make her happy. And maybe if you had sent her flowers—earlier. Like a long time ago. It might have worked. But last night, it just sent her over the edge. She loved you so much. But it's too late for flowers. They just made her remember —something she couldn't bear to remember."

"Oh," Shawn said slowly. "Oh." He realized the magnitude of his mistake. His mother's yellow roses were precious to him, the last happy memory of those pre-cancer days. Her garden meant everything to him, and Beth knew that. Those roses were the deepest, most meaningful gift he could give her, an invitation to pick up where they'd left off. They were a symbol of the ties that bound them, ties that would never be forgotten. But now they were a noose, a source of pain.

He'd moved too decisively, much too late. He needed to have sent her yellow roses eight years ago.

He needed to have forgiven her. And he needed to have asked for her forgiveness, for his impatience and his lack of understanding.

It was long past the point where it made any sense to send her flowers. Christine was right. He was a moron. An utter idiot.

"So the auctioneer," he said finally.

"Yes," Christine replied. She sank back down in her seat. She seemed too weary to stand any longer. "He came over and Beth told him to just take it all away. He was a little surprised. He said she'd make a good amount of money if he held an auction right there, in the house. But she told him to take it. He'll hold it in consignment." She shrugged. "I guess the good thing is that most of it will probably just sit in a warehouse for a while. So she won't have to rush into anything. She'll get a chunk of whatever he eventually sells. Maybe it's too painful for her to actually witness an auction in her own home, of stuff that's been in her family forever."

She looked up at him. "Shawn, I thought about whether I should even be telling you this. I didn't know if it was the right thing. I just happened to be at Beth's because of my heat failing—I just wanted her to help me find a plumber who would make a house call after five o'clock. I figured that if anyone could persuade someone to stop by after hours, Beth could."

"And you were right," Shawn said dryly.

"I was," Christine agreed. "I feel like I'm going behind her back by saying any of this to you. But Beth—she's part of what makes this town work. I've been here for only a couple of months, and I see the signs of her everywhere. I can't stand it that she's about to run away. And it's even worse that she's gotten Gunnar all tangled up in this. You have to fix this. I don't know how—I wish I did—you'd think after doing all those divorces I'd know something about relationships." She chuckled, but a note of bitterness had crept into her voice. "Mediator or not, I seem to only know about how to take them apart."

"I'm supposed to see her tomorrow night," Shawn said.

"Be careful," Christine warned. "Right now she's trying to muscle her way through the pain. She's probably not going to listen to half of what you say. Talking at her won't get through to her right now."

"I know. Oh, hell. Maybe I'll cancel."

"Cancel? But...why? Don't do that. You need to work this out. Don't lose any time—it gets worse every day." Christine stopped speaking abruptly, as if she had said more than she'd intended.

"Worse—you mean Gunnar. He's in love with her."

Christine shrugged again, but Shawn could see the truth on her face. He sighed, then said, "And Beth? If she wants to be with him, I should stay out of this."

"I think Beth only loves you," Christine said. "But she doesn't know what she thinks or how she feels. She needs to be able to figure it out, and for that, you need to take her back in time and fix everything that went wrong."

"You have no idea how hard that's going to be," Shawn groaned. He shook his head. "It's been a long time. I think it may be too late."

Christine suddenly rose from her seat, looking at her watch. "Shoot. I have a mediation in half an hour, and I'm going to be late, speaking of late. Shawn, you need to try. Some things are too important. You can't not try. Even if you fail, you can't not try."

For a little while after Christine left, Shawn stood, staring vacantly into space.

Beth...going to Seattle with another man, to start a new life.

It was surreal.

What if she actually did it? What if she actually

left? She would get a nice sum of money for that house, and still another good chunk for all the antiques that she had told the auctioneer to take away. She lived frugally. She could take her time, start over, look for work that made her happy. Gunnar had friends—they'd be safe, and there would be time for Beth to think about what she wanted to do with herself. She'd never been able to do that. She'd just been trying to pick up the pieces after her mother's death and the albatross of that old house.

It was flat-out bizarre, because if he were giving advice to a friend, he would tell her to do exactly what Beth was doing. It was not a stupid plan.

Except for the Gunnar part, which he just had no idea what to do with. That depended on Beth and how she felt about Shawn, how she felt about their past, and whether the past meant as much to her as it did to him.

Should he let her go?

And if she left, could he possibly drop everything he had in Greenleigh and run after her? Because that was an option, too. He could just drop everything and follow her. It was exactly what he had asked her to do for him all those years ago. Just leave his job, his elderly father, and everything he was angry at in good old Greenleigh. It was what he had demanded of her, so why not him?

He was in exactly the same spot she had been in

eight years ago. She had tried to leave Greenleigh to follow him, but had been pulled back by her mother and her own ties to her home. And now that she was the one ready to leave, he didn't think that he could follow her, either.

This is it, he thought. It comes down to leaving, and following, and coming back home. All of us, executing pieces of this infernal, never-ending puzzle. Damn this blasted town. Greenleigh just won't let go.

Who would be able to leave, and who would drop everything and follow? Who would come back? What would be enough proof of a devoted heart? He needed to decide. This was a new turning point, one that would take over responsibility for the future from that tired old moment all those years ago. Would they join together? Or once more, would someone be left behind?

24

There were no lights on in the house. Shawn walked up the sloping path, his pace slowing as he craned his neck, searching for any sign of life. A single lamp was lit in one of the bay windows in the front room, but he knew that Elisabeth would have left the lamp on if she had gone out, so that wasn't proof of anything. The other windows were dark, and the porch light was on.

He stomped up the porch steps. There was a new film of light snow coating the walkway, and more snow was predicted for the evening. Not much, apparently, only an inch or two, but this was considerable for pre-Thanksgiving weather. And it was cold, bitter cold. The mercury would be dipping down to zero that evening.

He was a day early because he couldn't stand to wait. Beth had agreed to see him tomorrow, but after Christine's visit this morning, he couldn't keep away. He needed to see her.

Shawn went up to the door and jabbed at the doorbell. He waited. He tried again. Usually he could hear the echoes of the bell reverberate in the front hall, but it was silent. Broken, he thought. Damned old house. Falling apart like crazy. He lifted the knocker on the door and banged.

No answer.

Shivering, he stood, shoulders hunched, hands thrust deep into his pockets. He knew he'd messed up on those flowers but he'd been operating on instinct. It had been a silly, sentimental thing to do, perhaps, but he had been daydreaming in his office about one occasion when he had surprised her in the carriage house with an armload of yellow roses from his mother's garden. She had been so touchingly pleased. And he remembered a particularly nice kiss that had followed.

He should have known better.

He shuffled back down the walk, noting the fine little flurries beginning to float down from the sky. It was just too cold be out and about. Where on earth had Beth gone? Was it possible that she had a business appointment? Shawn doubted it. But he wondered where she could possibly be on such a bitterly cold evening. With Gunnar?

He realized that his curiosity stopped right there, with Gunnar. He didn't want to know.

Shawn scrounged around for his car keys, fumbling with gloved fingers at the button. Once he got the door open, he didn't waste a second. He yanked the door closed behind him, started up the car, and set the heater to full blast. An icy stream of cold hit him full in the face until he aimed the vent away, coughing. It would take at least couple of minutes before the engine would warm up enough to send any heat into the body of the car. Shawn contemplated his direction. He couldn't think of what to do with himself. Go back to work? He nixed that idea immediately. He couldn't work. He didn't think he had the mental stamina to force himself back to the office for an evening of management headaches.

Perhaps he should just go home. But he knew his dad was at the senior center, and Shawn didn't want to be alone tonight in that big old house. The idea of wandering about downstairs, television blaring, trying to force down one of Martha's saltless, fatless meals was just not very palatable.

Shawn gripped the steering wheel. He could feel bone-numbing cold penetrating his gloves. He'd pop by the senior center for a bit and see his dad. Maybe he'd come to the Athena Diner with him. He released the brake and turned the car out into the street.

He gave a last glance in his rearview mirror at the dark shape that was the old Burnham place. He could see the bright little light in the front bay window and the softly glowing shape of that ugly snow-covered rhododendron bush that he hated so much. So much had happened as they'd gone marching along their separate paths, he and Beth. So much time, so many experiences that the other would not share. A waste, Shawn thought, grimacing. A waste which he could have prevented. An acknowledgment that he could not have made a mere month earlier, but it was the truth. He had been stubborn, and she had paid for it. She was what she was, after all—she had been afraid, and no amount of lecturing on his part would have changed that. He should have been more understanding. He should have been more helpful.

He had to tread carefully.

Shawn tried to concentrate on the fact that the road was slick and icing over, and that the giant digital clock at the bank on Main Street was flashing a temperature read-out of nineteen degrees, "and have a nice day." The streets were deserted. He noticed that Corbett's grocery store had a large Thanksgiving Day cornucopia in the window, and wondered where Beth would spend the holiday.

Alone? With Gunnar? Who was that guy, anyway? Where did he live? Where had he come from?

He pulled into the parking lot beside the senior center. Surprisingly, there were a fair number of cars in the lot. Shawn surmised that there must be some special program going on.

Several of his dad's friends greeted him loudly as he entered the room. His dad, he could see, was in his usual spot in a far corner of the room, bent over a chessboard. His opponent was a stout woman with steel-rimmed glasses, wearing a formal-looking gray suit.

Sam Waterstone looked very grumpy. Shawn guessed that he was losing. He plunked himself down on a sofa and was promptly joined by Joe Peterson, blue baseball cap firmly perched atop the shock of white hair. Shawn was tempted as usual to ask about the baseball cap. He refrained, although not without an internal chuckle.

"I guess Dad's losing."

Mr. Peterson rolled his eyes. "How can you tell?" He sounded both amused and disgusted.

"So who's the lady?"

"Rose Pelletier. Kindergarten teacher for forty-five years. No one ever beats her. Not even your father."

Shawn grinned. "That's good to hear. Keep him going. He'll never rest until he figures out her secrets." He glanced over at his father, who was scratching his head, brow furrowed. His contemplation of the chessboard was intense. Rose Pelletier, on the other hand, looked cool and comfortable, her gaze drifting over to a knitting circle chatting away on a set of couches in a corner of the room. She smiled and made an "OK" sign with her fingers, causing them to titter. Sam Waterstone scowled in response.

"How long's he been here?" Shawn returned his attention back to Mr. Peterson, who shrugged.

"Dunno. Maybe an hour."

"He isn't ready to leave, then."

"Oh, no. Not nearly. They'll be at it all evening. I'll take him home, Shawn. You don't have to stick around."

Shawn rubbed at his head wearily, then ran his fingers through his hair. He was tired. "I'm just wondering about dinner. Has he eaten, do you know?" There was an ominous silence. Shawn cast a look at Mr. Peterson, who was studying his shoes.

"Uh-oh. I know what that means. Mr. P, did he eat something he wasn't supposed to?"

"Burger and fries," Mr. Peterson said reluctantly. "I tried to stop him, but—er, Martha's dinner tonight made him really mad. He threw it at the cat." He looked up, a guilty grin on his face. "And the cat wouldn't eat it, either."

Shawn knew he ought to be absolutely furious. The doctors had put his father on a very strict low-salt, low-fat diet. A burger, probably with gobs of grease and topped with a huge piece of cheese, plus fries cooked in who knew what kind of fat—it was a nightmare meal for his heart. But Dad loved to eat so much. The switch in diet had been quite possibly the worst consequence of his heart attack, and he was constantly wheedling at Martha about her "heatlhy" meals. Shawn repressed a smile at the thought of the cat's revolted countenance as it surveyed the remains of what should have been dinner for two. No way the cat would eat anything his dad had rejected.

"Was it green? Dinner, I mean?"

Mr. Peterson's eyes widened slightly in surprise. "Actually, it was. Extremely green."

Shawn nodded. "Martha's special spinach soufflé. No eggs, cheese, or milk. It's awful." He cast a sidewise look at Mr. Peterson and sighed. "Okay. I guess once won't hurt. I can't blame anyone for wanting to hurl that soufflé at the cat. Can't blame the cat for running, either."

"I try to keep an eye on him, Shawn. He's got a mind of his own." Mr. Peterson shook his head.

Shawn stood up. "Well, I guess I'll go on home, then. Make sure the cat's still alive—he might not be if he ate any of that soufflé. You'll bring Dad home?"

"Sure. You go on. Is it slick out?"

"Yeah, getting bad. Couple more inches overnight, they say."

The door opened and several people clattered into the multipurpose room, engaged in a loud and animated discussion. Shawn recognized Bob Stuart among them.

"Looks like our worthy town selectmen are through for the night," Mr. Peterson said, holding his hand up in greeting.

"I was wondering what all the cars in the parking lot were here for," Shawn said. "Some kind of town business?"

"Dunno. Don't think it's anything too major or they wouldn't be meeting here—they'd be at town hall. Hey there, fellas." The little knot of selectmen advanced toward them. Bob Stuart glanced in their direction, and his eyes fell upon Shawn. He beamed.

"Shawn! How are you doing?" He reached out and pumped Shawn's hand, pulling away slightly from the other members of the group, who were gabbing in a leisurely fashion with the others in that corner of the room.

"Not too bad, Bob. And yourself?" Shawn regarded him thoughtfully. He didn't look like someone who was going through a painful divorce. He was wearing a sweatshirt that said "Berkeley" on it, and the sweatshirt seemed to encourage his relaxed stance. Bob smiled at him.

"Wonderful, Shawn, just wonderful."

Shawn tried to wipe the dubious expression off his face. When he'd seen Bob earlier this week, he hadn't been in the best of spirits.

Bob laughed. He took Shawn's arm and steered him a little further away from the group. He said in a low voice, smiling, "You must think I'm in denial."

"Of course not!" Shawn said, embarrassed. "I'm glad everything's going well."

"Everything is going wonderfully. Planning a trip out to California. Ever been there?"

"California? Sure. Just for work, but I really enjoyed it."

"Our daughter Grace is in school there. And you know, Angela loves to travel, but we haven't been anywhere in years. Work and all that. Winter weather. I was always worried about weather emergencies and delays." He paused, then went on, reddening slightly. "You know, I'd clean forgotten how much Angela loves to travel. When we were first married we used to go on little jaunts all over creation. Somehow after the children came, all that went away. My fault, thinking that we were both too busy. So this time I decided to just buy the tickets and take her. It's a surprise, but she won't be able to say no. I know she wants to see Grace. And we'll have some time together that way." He grinned. "I decided to just do it. I'm going to drag her out there for Thanksgiving. If she still wants a divorce after that—well, then I'll figure that out then. But I'm going to sweep her off her feet. I'm sure this is the right thing to do."

"Bob, that's a great idea!" Shawn blinked in surprise. It really was a great idea. Angela couldn't possibly avoid talking to him that way. He knew Bob would do his best to please her. And their youngest daughter would be there to remind Angela of all that she and Bob had worked for over the years.

"I never would have thought of this myself. Never would have thought it was worth trying if it weren't for Elisabeth Burnham. This was her idea."

"Really?" Shawn frowned. It didn't sound like Beth at all. Spring a surprise trip on Angela? Beth was such a cautious person.

Bob Stuart nodded. "She's smart. And kind."

Joe Peterson poked his head into the conversation.

"Whatcha guys all hush-hush about here?"

Bob turned to him. "Just talking about Elisabeth Burnham. Lawyer in town. Do you know her?"

Mr. Peterson was nodding his head. "Yep, I know her. Not personally of course, not being someone who likes to hang around lawyers much—" he winked at Shawn "—but she helped out Tony Pirelli when his landlord tried to raise the rent on his shop. Bought him a lot of time. Tony ended up moving his shop anyway after that whole affair, but the landlord was beggin' him to stay by that time. And I think Walter over there knows her, too."

"Who?" Walter, a slight, skinny man in a neat flannel shirt and corduroys, wandered over to join the group. Shawn recognized him as one of the selectmen.

"Elisabeth Burnham. The lawyer."

Walter was nodding his head. "Sure. All of us downtown know her. The Burnhams have lived in that house forever. My wife knows her really well. Beth helped her when her contract at the hospital ran out and Annie didn't know what to do about getting a new one. Beth negotiated the whole thing for her. Barely charged us for her time. I don't know how she keeps going." He shrugged.

Bob looked at Shawn. "Seems like the whole town knows Beth. I'm surprised I didn't know her before now." Shawn felt his own gaze falter under the older man's scrutiny.

In the hallway, Shawn found his feet numbly walking in the direction of the building exit. He pushed through the door, finding himself in frigid cold, snowflakes gently fluttering to the ground, a half-inch coating on the walkway. He slipped a bit heading for the car, digging in his pocket for his gloves, and huddled himself against a gentle but bitter cold breeze. Climbing into the driver's seat of the car, he turned on the engine and listened to it sputter once before starting to whir. Once again a cold blast of air hit him in the face from the vent, and he muttered a curse as he pointed it away. He shivered in his seat, waiting for the car to warm up, and wished he'd sprung for the model with heated seats.

One part of his brain felt hopelessly scared and muddled. The other felt absolutely calm and sure. It was his intellect warring with his heart again.

He knew what he ought to do, and he just wasn't sure he could do it. If he failed, it was going to mess him up, maybe for a long time. Maybe forever. *Rejection scars like nothing else does*, he thought. He was afraid of more rejection.

He turned the car out of the lot and onto the street, noticing with disinterest that the anti-lock brakes were engaging as the car slipped ever so slightly with the turn of the wheels. Bad weather to be out and about.

Shawn drove slowly, grateful for the absence of traffic. The traffic lights were all set to blink, urging drivers to use caution and their own judgment of how safely they could brake at the intersections. On Main Street, he slowed before one such intersection, the yellow lights casting their cheery glow on the snow. He crawled into the intersection, checking for oncoming traffic in the other directions. The streets were empty. Near the new Italian restaurant, his eye caught a small figure huddled against the icy wind, trudging along the cross-street and occasionally slipping in the thin layer of snow. He let the car trundle along at its own momentum for a moment, squinting out the passenger-side window. It was really too cold to be out walking, he thought. He let the car roll to a gentle stop on the right side of the road, and waited. He glanced at his rearview mirror and froze. It was Beth.

What he hadn't seen until now was the motorcycle pulled over to the side of the street, and the figure that was sitting astride it. He was waving at Beth as she slipped and slid along the sidewalk and hurried toward him.

Shawn couldn't bring himself to watch. He put the car into gear and drove away.

Mentally, he made his decision. No more small stuff. He was going to cast his chips just to see where they landed.

25

"We've got several interested buyers," Betty McClintock was saying to Elisabeth as she shuffled through the papers on her desk. She peered at her over her reading glasses. "In fact, a couple of them sound as if they're willing to offer more than your asking price."

"Really?" Elisabeth shook her head, confused. "That is so strange. I can't imagine why."

"You've got yourself a wonderful old home," the realtor said. "It's beautiful, and it's a historic fixture on Church Street. As soon as it was listed I had a long line of people waiting to see it. And I'm really glad I convinced you to raise your price. You're going to do really well with this sale."

"It's in terrible shape," Elisabeth said honestly. "I don't know how to maintain it, and all of the systems need an upgrade. I didn't clean it or hold an open house. I didn't even put vases of flowers out the way you suggested—I ran out of time—" Her voice faltered as she recalled the one vase of yellow roses in the front room.

Mrs. McClintock waved away her concerns. Her snow-white hair was tinged with blue, set off perfectly by her pearls and black brocade pants suit. "That's of no consequence. No one cares about decorations in a fine old home like yours. People are interested in original period details and you've got all of those because you've never done one of those terrible rehabs where they knock down all the walls and make it 'modern.' Your house is basically strong and well-designed. It's withstood the test of time. It's not going to fall down, and as for upgrading systems—" She shrugged. "People finance upgrades. That's no problem. It'll just get folded into the mortgage."

Elisabeth nodded. "Well, that makes sense. And that's why I can't go replacing them all. I wouldn't be able to afford it, but someone else can."

"You know, Beth," Mrs. McClintock began. She hesitated, then continued. "You could always mortgage the house and upgrade your systems yourself. Have you thought of that?"

"Oh, I could never," Elisabeth said. She chuckled. "I wonder if that house has ever had a mortgage on it. Like, it was probably built with cash. Back in the 1700s. Mortgaging it would be really—"

"But why not? That's what people do. All the time."

Elisabeth struggled to find the words. She shook her head. She didn't know why, but the thought of borrowing money, making changes to the house, moving into the future with a plan for a modern rehab—it felt impossible.

"I've known you for a long time, Beth," Mrs. McClintock said. She took off her glasses and steepled her hands. "You've pulled through for my business any number of times, and you were there when Bert passed away. I don't even remember that phase of my life, my God—it's a blur. You were so helpful, I had no idea so many things had to be resolved when someone dies. I've tried to keep my opinions to myself, but I'm wondering why you need to take care of all of this so quickly. Thanksgiving is next week. It's a quiet time for real estate, but you've gotten so much interest in the house, it's surely going to sell. You don't need to be in such a rush. And there is nothing disgraceful about a mortgage! That house was left to you in a state of disrepair and neglect. No one would fault you for financing a new heating system and some carpentry work properly, through a bank. You can even sell it after you've done some repairs."

Elisabeth nodded. Mrs. McClintock was an old friend of the family. There wasn't much she did not know about the Burnhams. When she had called her to put up the house for sale, Mrs. McClintock had been suitably surprised, but in classic Yankee fashion, had not pried, and had been brisk and professional about arranging the necessaries.

She decided to tell her the truth.

"I'm leaving, Mrs. McClintock. That's why I'm selling. I'm leaving next week."

"Next week?" Mrs. McClintock sat back in her chair. She looked genuinely shocked. "You know that a house sale requires a lot of paperwork. And waiting. Your purchaser needs to get financing in order, and things do fall through. We almost certainly won't be finished with all of this next week."

"I'll have Ricky over at Lawson & Lawson take care of everything." *Oops*, Elisabeth thought. Ricky Junior was going to be stunned when he heard that he was going to handle the sale of her house—and completely gobsmacked when he heard that Elisabeth was leaving Greenleigh. Uh, with a tattoo artist she'd just met. That wasn't going to go over well.

She shook herself slightly and tried to pay attention.

"Is there something I can do to help, Beth? It just seems that all of this is so sudden," Mrs. McClintock was saying as the string of bells on the door jangled. Someone was entering the tiny storefront office.

"Good morning!" a friendly voice called.

"Oh, that's Angela Stuart," Mrs. McClintock said, rising from her desk. "I promised to help her find a house sitter. Beth, please think about what I've said. You don't have to rush. And as for leaving next week—when will you be back?"

At this point, Angela had stuck her head into the office and was smiling at Elisabeth. She looked more cheerful than she had looked in a long time.

"Hello!" she said.

Elisabeth decided to drop the bomb and get it over with. It couldn't be worse than getting called on in contracts class after an all-nighter, she decided.

"I'm not coming back," she said, looking from one friendly face to the other. "I'm leaving for good."

"What?" both women said in unison. The smile fell from Angela's face.

"Please don't try to talk me out of it," Elisabeth said in a rush. "I've already decided. I want to start something new, do something for myself. This is why I'm selling the house."

"Selling the house?" Angela gasped. "But Beth— when did this happen? I just talked to you—last week? When did you decide this?"

"Round about last week," Elisabeth said, trying

to smile. "Sorry. I should have told you. But things have been crazy."

"Can we talk about this?" Angela was clearly flustered. "I feel I must be missing something."

"I have to go—I'm meeting someone. I'm sorry, I should have said something, Angela. But why are you getting a house sitter? Are you going away for Thanksgiving?"

Angela nodded. "Bob sprang tickets to California on me. He just went ahead and bought them —you know I have a daughter in California at school—he said he was taking me for Thanksgiving week. Just like that." She snapped her fingers. "I was really thrown for a loop. I didn't know what to say. And then I thought, what the heck. That's my daughter, I haven't seen her in a while, and I love travel. Maybe Bob thinks we'll work things out during the trip. I don't care. If he wants to talk, we'll talk. I decided thinking too hard was a bad idea. And that getting out of Greenleigh for a week would help get my head straight."

"You're so right," Mrs. McClintock said. "Overthinking leads to all kinds of confusion."

"Absolutely, and that's what I've decided, too," Elisabeth said. "I'm avoiding the overthinking. And getting out of Greenleigh will help. There's too much—too much stuff here. I decided to just sell the house and start over. It seemed like the right answer to all my problems."

"But leaving Greenleigh permanently! Selling the house! That's so final, Beth!"

Elisabeth opened her mouth to reply when the door jangled again. All three women turned to peer into the storefront.

Gunnar.

"Hey," he said. He nodded at Mrs. McClintock, who looked at him sharply before looking back at Elisabeth.

"Oh, hi. I'm sorry, I know I'm late."

"No problem," Gunnar said. He was wearing his usual black leather jacket and white tee shirt, hands thrust into the pockets of black jeans. His tattoos peeked out of the edge of his shirt neck, which was spotless, practically starched and ironed, bright white against his olive skin. A row of diamond piercings glittered along the edge of one ear, accentuated with a bright silver hoop. He'd clearly just cut his hair, which was shorn almost to the scalp on one side and slicked with styling product on the other.

He beamed, looking almost like an eager puppy waiting to be praised.

Elisabeth sensed the sudden current of disapproval in the room. She raised her chin, indignation swelling in her breast. "This is my friend Gunnar. Gunnar, Betty McClintock, Angela Stuart."

The two ladies smiled and nodded, but Elisabeth was not fooled.

She knew what they were thinking and it made her furious. It was the same disapproval she had sensed from Shawn, something beyond basic jealousy. It was good old-fashioned Yankee snobbery.

They were blaming him for messing around with a Burnham of Greenleigh, when he clearly wasn't good enough for her. They were blaming him for taking her off on a crazy jag, maybe even suspected him of trying to grab her house or the money from selling it. They were looking at his tattoos and piercings and judging him for not being a dude in a suit with a fancy degree. They were scrutinizing his year-round tan and wondering what country his people came from and how many generations back they went.

Even nice people, good people, were biased and unfair when they were afraid that someone they loved was about to get hurt.

Screw that, she thought. *This is wrong. **You're** wrong.*

"Gunnar and I are off to Seattle next week," she said, keeping the anger out of her voice. "He's helped me to get the house details all nailed down, and I think I'll be all set when I leave. The furniture is going out to the auction house, and I've got most of the junk thrown out—Gunnar's done most of the work."

Gunnar looked a little surprised, but said nothing. He nodded, turning a curious gaze onto the two ladies. He seemed fascinated by them.

"I'll call you, Beth," Angela said in a stage whisper. She looked distressed, her mouth turning down at the corners.

Elisabeth turned on her. "You don't have to whisper. Gunnar and I have everything under control. Nothing is happening that he doesn't know about. Oh, and have a great trip, Angela! I might not be around much, so if I don't return your calls...." She let the words trail. "And Mrs. McClintock, if you need me, you can always get me through Ricky Junior at the law firm." Nodding, she excused herself from the office.

"Jesus!" Gunnar was saying once they had emerged from the storefront. "You are one scary lady. Remind me not to piss you off. What pissed you off, by the way?"

"Nothing," Elisabeth said, irritated. "Just the way they looked at you, I guess.

"Ha! I hadn't even noticed. That's my everyday life. Don't let it bother you. It won't be like that in Seattle. Yankees are so damned conservative. Speaking of which, I got our plane tickets." They were walking down Main Street in the bright sunlight, headed toward Lawson & Lawson. The sun was turning the snow to slush in gray piles along the sidewalk.

"Oh, shoot. I'll write you a check," Elisabeth said.

"Sweetheart, you're adorable. No one writes checks anymore."

"That's not true—I write checks all the time."

"Elisabeth, you are living in the twentieth century, and it's the twenty-first century now. I don't even have a bank in town."

"What? How do you handle your money?"

Gunnar shrugged. "I have a bank in Boston and people send money to me electronically in whatever way they want—but I haven't darkened the door of an actual bank in years."

"I'm going to have to write you a check, because I don't have any other way to give you money, unless you'd rather have the cash," Elisabeth said.

"You need a smartphone, my dear."

Elisabeth sighed. They slowed their pace as they reached the corner. "Stop, we've been through this. I don't need a smartphone."

"You're going to need one to apply for jobs in Seattle. Seattle is actually in the twenty-first century, unlike Greenleigh."

"Well, I'll cross that bridge when I get there."

"Actually, we're crossing that bridge now." They

stopped walking. Gunnar's motorcycle was parked in a space at the corner.

"What? You're always saying weird things," Elisabeth started to complain, but Gunnar was pulling something out of his pocket. It was a phone. He handed it to her.

"What am I supposed to do with this? Why are you giving me your phone?"

"It's yours."

Elisabeth looked down at the phone. It was white and slippery, and still had a film of plastic over it. It appeared to be brand-new.

"What the heck? Why? Gunnar, I don't want it." She tried to hand it back, but he stepped back from her.

"I'm tired of trying to track you down," he said lightly. "And I'm worried that you won't understand how things work when we get to Seattle. You need to join the twenty-first century, Elisabeth. You need to leave all this crap behind." He gestured around him. "My number's in there. It's the only one you need. But you can at least give your number to other people." He nodded toward the facade of Lawson & Lawson in back of her.

Did he mean Shawn? She couldn't remember telling Gunnar that Ricky Junior would be handling her house sale. Although it wouldn't be unreasonable for him to assume that Lawson & Lawson would take care of it.

She looked at him uncertainly.

"Don't look so terrified," Gunnar laughed. "You just gave a virtual middle finger to a couple of old crones back there. You're not a shrinking violet. You can handle a phone, trust me. And anyway, plane tickets show up—guess where—on *phones*. They're e-tickets. Ever heard of them?" He shook his head at her in mock dismay.

"So I'm going to go talk to Gina about selling my bike. I know you've got stuff to do at the law firm. I just wanted to tell you that we're all set to leave on Thanksgiving. Next Thursday."

"Thanksgiving? Why Thanksgiving?" Elisabeth said in surprise. She'd been wondering where Gunnar would be having Thanksgiving, in fact, but this was unexpected.

"Because it's almost impossible to travel comfortably any time this week or next, until Thanksgiving itself. The entire country is traveling right now, and it's a bear to get a good routing. Thanksgiving Day early was good, so I grabbed the tickets." He leaned over and kissed the top of her head. "Don't worry. Everything is going to be fine. I know what I'm doing. You just clean up your stuff and stay happy. Don't let those stuffed shirts at the law firm get you down."

He started to walk away, then seemed to re-member something and turned around. "Hey! I wanted to tell you that I hate your clothes! Throw them all away!" he called, walking backwards down the street.

"What?" Elisabeth said, laughing. She was still trying to get a handle on the thought of traveling on Thanksgiving—skipping Thanksgiving in Green-leigh, which seemed inconceivable to her for some reason—and now Gunnar was talking about her wardrobe?

"Yeah! Get rid of all of it—it's awful."

Elisabeth looked down at her coat and her long corduroy dress and tights. "Gee, thanks, Gunnar," she called back.

"NP," he replied, turning around again. He jogged lightly down the street and jaywalked across the middle, ignoring the crosswalk.

Elisabeth turned away, shaking her head. She was still smiling when she walked into the velvety silence of Lawson & Lawson and said hello to the receptionist.

"Oh, Beth, there's a note here for you," the re-ceptionist said. "It's from Mr. Waterstone."

Shawn? Elisabeth tried to breathe deeply. She had to get used to thinking about him without feeling so nervous. She was seeing him tonight, and she needed to be emotionally prepared to deal with whatever he was going to say to her about Gunnar and leaving Greenleigh.

The note was on law firm stationery, scribbled hastily with a pen. Shawn normally had beautiful handwriting, somewhat unusual for a man—this had always stood out to her—and this scrawled note was almost indecipherable. She paused to frown over it.

"Beth, I've got a lot of stuff going on, so I'll have to cancel tonight. Sorry. I'll try to call you later if I can. Shawn."

Canceled?

She didn't know what to think of this. Was he busy with work? Was he sick of dealing with her? Was his dad all right?

Slowly, she pulled the glossy white phone out of her pocket. She gazed at its shiny face for a moment, then walked over to the receptionist.

"Hey, would you help me out? I've got this new phone. Where do I find my number? I'd like to leave it for Mr. Waterstone."

26

This is it, Elisabeth thought.

She looked about her at the front room.

Normally, it was cluttered and messy, dust balls catching at the corners of the furniture, piles of paper sliding off the old oak-top desk. But right now, it was as neat as a pin.

In other words, it had been emptied of every bit of its identity. No more Burnham clutter.

The papers were gone. The dust had been swept away. She could even see that the tops of the ancient, heavy drapes had been feather dusted for cobwebs.

That would have been Gunnar's handiwork— she couldn't remember the last time she'd wielded a feather duster. Perhaps never. And to be fair, she didn't know if Gunnar himself had done any dusting. He seemed to have friends in every conceivable profession and owning every conceivable vehicle—what he wasn't willing to do, he always found someone willing to donate.

The furniture was all there. The auctioneer had priced some of the more valuable items, saying that he would conduct private showings of the house after Thanksgiving. The realtor thought the house would show better with the old furniture in it, so she'd shrugged and given the auction house man a key.

Thank goodness she would be gone. She didn't want to see any of the activity. Somehow, her conscious mind could handle what she was about to do, but she didn't know if she could actually stand to see it happen.

Elisabeth wandered aimlessly from room to room, trying to remember all the instructions. Gunnar had told her repeatedly that she needed to make lists, take pictures with that new phone, record what was there and what wasn't, keep an inventory—all of it blurred into an impossible jumble of chaos in her mind. She paused in each doorway, staring blankly at the room before her, trying to grasp at why she was there, what she was looking at, and what on earth all of it meant.

Instead, she remembered odd bits and pieces of things—middle school science projects spread out on the dining room table, the Burnham family Bible with its pages of births and deaths, her mother and father guffawing loudly during the occasional late-night talk show. She remembered that there was once a green shag rug in front of that television set —where had that gone? There was also a hideous gray vinyl arm chair that had sat in the same room. She couldn't remember what had happened to it, but she felt as if she had spent her entire childhood in that chair in front of reruns of bad sitcoms.

There was no longer a television at all in that room, and the gray armchair had been replaced by an antique bentwood rocker that the delighted auctioneer had found in the attic. He had placed it lovingly next to the wood stove, which when he had discovered that it not only worked but could easily heat up half the ground floor, had sent him into raptures.

Elisabeth walked slowly up the stairs, reluctant to open the doors of the abandoned bedrooms. Her parents' room was nearly empty. She'd boxed up what remained of her mother's knickknacks and tucked them into the attic. Nothing valuable or sentimental there. She paused in the doorway of her own room, which looked odd and starkly empty in the dim half-light of the afternoon.

She'd listened to Gunnar and thrown out most of her wardrobe, replacing it with a set of short wool skirts and turtleneck sweaters, which served to make her look more bohemian chic than she felt. She hoped that she'd be taken seriously in Seattle. Gunnar told her she absolutely would be, if she would stop assuming the worst and remember that she was a competent professional.

Elisabeth knew that she could stand up for the little guy—she wasn't afraid of any courtroom, any judge, if it meant protecting someone weaker than herself. But she wondered if there was a place for someone like her in a big city in the west. And if there wasn't—what new part of society would she inhabit?

She couldn't even fathom what that would be like, and she didn't know how she felt about the strangeness of all of it.

Someone was banging on the front steps. She recognized Gunnar's heavy tread—he always wore army surplus combat boots and would ritually kick the snow off of them before entering the house. He didn't bother to knock on the door anymore, but would shout her name into the hallway when he entered.

"E-lis-a-beth!" he bellowed. His voice echoed off the newly bare floors and walls.

"I'm up here," she replied.

He bounded up the stairs two at a time.

"Yo," he said, coming up behind her. He bent to

kiss her neck and she shrugged him off auto-matically.

"Stop."

"Why?"

"You know why."

"You're such a prude."

"Maybe I am."

"Huh." But he didn't sound upset. "Are you done?"

"I think so. I don't even know what I'm looking for."

"Do you have pictures?"

"I think so."

"We can catalogue things later. I'll help you. It's the easiest way to take an inventory."

Elisabeth sighed. She went into her room and headed for the bedside lamp. She clicked on the light. "I did what you said, but Gunnar, no one is going to steal anything."

"I never said anyone was going to steal any-thing," Gunnar objected. "An inventory is just so you know what you own. Are you really a lawyer? I have to tell you everything, like. Someone should give me a law degree."

Elisabeth was opening drawers and shutting them. They were all empty.

"Someone should," she said. "Why don't you go

back to school? You'd make a great lawyer. You'd kick my butt."

"No school," Gunnar shuddered. "No way."

"Can you just leave the tattoo shop? Just like that?"

"Yeah. They can always find someone else."

Elisabeth held up a piece of paper. "I don't think so. Not many people can do this." It was Gunnar's drawing of Persephone and Hades.

"Oh. Ha ha. Yeah, well." Gunnar shrugged. "Nice that you saved it."

"Of course I saved it. It's beautiful. Listen, Gunnar—"

"Uh oh." Gunnar had followed her into the room, but now he retreated backwards several steps. "I don't like the sound of this."

"We have to talk."

"Not now. I'm closing a deal on my bike. I just stopped in to see if you were okay."

"We have to talk," Elisabeth repeated. "We're leaving tomorrow and we haven't discussed—us —yet—"

"Let's talk about it on the plane," Gunnar said. "They always serve free wine on the plane. We can get buzzed and then talk. You know, I've never even seen you drink."

"That's because I'm too broke to drink," Elisabeth said curtly. "Listen, I don't want to wait until tomorrow. I want to get this straight before we leave."

"Elisabeth, there's nothing to get straight. Okay? Let's just leave it as it is."

"But why?" Elisabeth persisted. "What are you avoiding? I just want to—"

"We have lots of time," Gunnar interrupted. "Lots and lots of time. We've got a long flight and then a long trip into the unknown. It's awesome. No one and nothing from the past to get in our way. We've got plenty of time, Elisabeth. Don't rush. Rushing is bad."

"You've said that to me so many times," Elisabeth said, running her hands along the insides of her wardrobe. She pulled out a single sock and tossed it onto the bed.

"You've said that to Angela Stuart a lot of times. It's good advice. You're a good lawyer. A great lawyer, in fact."

"But I'm rushing through all of this now. Selling the house, leaving town—in a rush."

"Ha. You know better than to say that this is a rush. You've been wanting to leave for years. You just haven't done it."

Elisabeth did not reply. He was right. She could have left with Shawn. And she could have left after Shawn. She'd been trying to leave Greenleigh for years, but had never had the courage.

"I really have to go sign the papers for my bike," Gunnar said. "But I'll see you tomorrow. The taxi will be here first thing. And then we'll lock up and get the hell out of Greenleigh."

Elisabeth shuddered slightly.

"What, scared?" Gunnar came over to her and put his arm around her. "It'll be fine. Trust me."

"I do trust you," Elisabeth said. "God knows, it makes no sense— I don't know why I trust you, but I do. For all I know you're totally screwing me over somehow—convincing me to sell my house, quit my job, go to some city I've never been to without a place to stay or a plan—"

Suddenly, Gunnar was kissing her, and before she could pull away and scold him, she responded. Both arms went around him, and when he leaned her back onto the bed, she didn't protest. In that moment, all she could think was that she was in her room, on her bed, and this was Shawn and not Gunnar. Somehow, Shawn's words were in her mind— he loved her, he loved her, he loved her still. And she wanted those old days back, those long-ago days among the roses, when even the most difficult things in life seemed surmountable.

She wanted this man, the one who was here with her, to be Shawn. She wanted to believe that she could go back in time, fix the things that had gone wrong. Maybe all it took was one kiss. Maybe all it took was for her to stop struggling, to believe. She knew that Gunnar would say that.

But even though it was her familiar world, this was an unfamiliar guy with a completely different feel and build. Wiry and compact, not tall and lean. The scent of a well-worn leather jacket and hair gel. As she slid her hands over his shoulders, down his arms, she knew that this wasn't Shawn.

She wanted to believe, but it was Shawn whom she wanted to believe.

What was she doing?

She longed to be close, to be close to someone who loved her.

But this was Gunnar. *Oh, God.* Confusion filled her mind.

By the time she realized that this wasn't what she wanted at all, he had wrenched off his jacket and was lifting up her sweater.

No. It was the wrong guy.

"Stop!" she gasped. She tore her mouth away, but he merely transferred his kisses to her jawline, behind her ear, down her neck.

"I don't want to stop," he murmured. "I don't think you do, either."

"This is a terrible idea!" But before she pushed him away, she saw the look on his face and knew that something on her own face had given him permission. He relented easily and let her straighten her sweater and get up from the bed, but she knew that he didn't believe for a minute that she really thought it was such a terrible idea.

This was why he had been so patient, so persistent. He knew that she wasn't as indifferent as she claimed, and even if she told him no tonight, he would just try again. He knew that she was still in love with Shawn, and he was going to be there for her when she finally shut the door on that old affair. He wanted to keep reminding her that he would be there when she was ready. One of these days, her need for love and warmth and human feeling would override her common sense, and he knew it.

No, she thought. Maybe if Shawn hadn't come back. Maybe if she hadn't pulled the trigger on the sale of the house. But too many things were going on, too many big, scary things. And she suspected there was chaos in Gunnar's life as well, chaos that he was not admitting to her.

Where would we all be if we just followed our hearts, she thought. *Or even worse, our bodies? We'd be a complete mess!*

Or would we?

"I'm meeting the buyers at Gina's," Gunnar was saying. He was shrugging into his jacket as if nothing had happened. She had to give him that—it was hard to feel self-conscious around him.

She smoothed her hair and cleared her throat.

She was going to try again. "Gunnar, we need to talk. You know that."

"I think you know what I know," he said. He leaned over to kiss the top of her head and leaned his cheek against her hair for a moment. The gesture was sweet and comforting, unbelievably innocent, almost brotherly. "It's okay, I should have restrained myself. You just make it hard." He winked. "I'm Hades, right? He's a bad, bad guy."

After he'd left, she sat staring into space for a while, wondering what kind of craziness lay ahead for her.

Maybe this was all a terrible mistake, she thought. *No, no. It couldn't be. It all sounded so reasonable in broad daylight.*

She was not in love with Gunnar. But he had a heart of gold, and she didn't want to break it. She'd be careful. And eventually, she would need to settle things with Shawn. She would tell him that there was still hope, that she just needed to sort herself out.

Elisabeth could hear her phone buzzing downstairs. She'd turned off the ringer but text messages still caused the phone to vibrate. What did Gunnar want now, she thought. Maybe he needed a witness for the bill of sale on that bike.

She walked down the stairs to the kitchen,

where her phone was lying on the table. She picked it up, but didn't recognize the number of the text.

"Dinner tonight?"

Who could that be from, she was wondering, when another message came.

"Sorry, this is Shawn."

27

———

"Take a deep breath," Christine advised. She was pacing restlessly in his office, her bright red stilettos occasionally catching on the carpet and nearly yanking themselves off her feet. She flicked them free automatically and continued to pace without missing a beat.

"I'm fine," Shawn said. He was shrugging into his jacket, pulling down the shades, nearly knocking over the potted plants behind his desk as he did so. It was dark outside, but the lights in his office were off. He'd been sitting at his desk for the past two hours, in the dark of the gloomy November afternoon, staring into space, with his phone resting silently on the credenza behind him, ringer switched off.

Christine had found him there, after the receptionist had told her that she thought Mr. Waterstone hadn't come back after lunch. Apparently, he had never gone out to lunch at all—but with the lights off in his office, everyone thought he was gone. In truth, he was sitting quietly in the dark, thinking. And waiting.

Two minutes ago, his phone had finally lit up with a response.

Game on.

"You need to take a deep breath," Christine insisted. "I do this for a living. Trust me. Get your heart rate down."

Shawn gave her a sour look. "My heart rate *is* down. I'm a litigator. I like adrenaline. It's fun."

"Adrenaline means your blood pressure is up. Man, I don't know what she sees in you. You won't listen to anyone but yourself. You're such a pain."

"Yeah," Shawn agreed. He looked around the office, then patted his jacket pockets for his phone and wallet. Check. They were there.

Christine stopped pacing.

"God. I'm sorry. I'm such a witch. Listen to me. You've just made me so nervous. I'm much better than this. I don't even know why I'm so nervous. I've negotiated divorces between really awful people with lots of money and property at stake, and I don't get this nervous. I'm sorry. I just want this to work. It's killing me."

"Yeah," Shawn said again. He smiled wryly. 'Yeah, I do, too. I don't know what I'll do if it doesn't."

"It was her idea," Christine said for the thousandth time. "She thought it was a good idea."

"Yeah. I know. It has her written all over it. It's just like her. But I don't know how she'll feel about having her own tricks played on her."

"You won't know unless you try," Christine said, again for the thousandth time." And you can't not do anything."

"Yup." *I can't not do anything*, he repeated to himself, but he was inwardly terrified. *This might push her over the edge, and then it's all over, for good. And what the hell will I do if it's all over? How can I stay in Greenleigh without her?*

"Are you going to be all right?" Christine reached down to pick up two shopping bags, which she handed to Shawn.

"I hope so. And thanks, Christine. You've helped a lot. And the shopping. I couldn't have managed that part." He looked into the bags. They were filled with tissue paper so that he couldn't see what was inside, but he wasn't concerned. He knew Christine would have handled those errands for him beautifully.

"You're such a liar," Christine said. "You knew exactly what you wanted me to buy. You were just pretending. But it's okay. I know it's awkward. It's all good." She reached out to give him a hug. "Good luck, big guy. You can do this."

"I hope so," Shawn said.

"Please let me know how it goes. I'll be dying until I hear from you."

"I will."

They went out into the hallway together. The staff was gone, but some of the attorneys were still in their offices. Shawn could hear Ricky Junior's booming laugh behind one of the doors. It was the day before Thanksgiving, and many of them had left earlier that week for the holiday weekend, so activity at the firm had been at a crawl. It hadn't been difficult to keep a low profile.

He'd been shocked when Beth had left a cell phone number for him at the reception desk last Friday. He'd been very deliberate about cancelling their date; he knew that he couldn't see her until he was ready, for once and for all, to make his move. So he decided to quietly make his plans and wait for the right moment. He'd made sure his dad was taken care of, the factory was taken care of, and the law firm was taken care of.

Thanksgiving Eve, and Thanksgiving weekend, was the right moment. It was a time for gratitude, and a time for family. She thought she didn't have family anymore but that was a construct in her mind. He knew it was, but he wasn't sure she would buy it. In fact, he knew she was conflicted about whether she was happy or upset not to have family —but he could settle that for her.

Christine was right, he would just have to wait and see. This plan would work or it wouldn't work —and he couldn't know until he'd tried.

His original plan had been to wear her out with his logic, but when he'd seen her with Gunnar on the street that night, it was clear that compared to Gunnar he was all talk and no action. Words weren't going to change fate—only action would do that, and Gunnar knew how to play by those rules. So he'd cancelled the plan to meet and talk. He'd decided to take a step back and think. But he hadn't expected her to suddenly leave her cell phone number for him. And he could see when he texted her new number that it was a smartphone, not her old flip phone. When had she gotten a fancy new phone?

When he mentioned it to Christine, he saw the look of comprehension in her eyes, and it made him feel queasy. It was obviously for Gunnar. She had gotten a new phone because Gunnar wanted her to have one. He was changing her. Elisabeth Burnham of old would never have a smartphone. She didn't need one because her clients always knew how to reach her. But now she was embarking on a big city adventure with a slick operator—sure, she needed a smartphone. Obviously.

He just hoped that she had left her number for him because she was sorry that he had cancelled their meeting. She hadn't said, but he hoped that was the case. It would really help if she at least wanted to see him one last time.

He walked out to his car, and put the shopping bags in the back seat. He consulted his phone to check the time, then got into the car. He was as ready as he'd ever be, he thought. Full tank of gas, the insides vacuumed, new pine-tree-shaped-de-odorizer-thing dangling from the rearview mirror. For the first time in his life, he wished it were a BMW or some such fancy car. He'd never been a car guy, largely viewing vehicles of that sort as a ridicu-lous waste of money—but today he wanted perfec-tion, and he wouldn't have minded leather seats and a better stereo.

He pulled out into the street and glanced into the rearview mirror to check his hair. His face was taut and unsmiling, little stress lines at the corners of his eyes, so he brought his brows together and scowled deliberately, just to make it worse.

Bring it on, he thought, then laughed at himself

for being dramatic. He was a courtroom lawyer even at the height of pain.

When he pulled up outside the Burnham manse, he saw her figure at the window, waiting. He was momentarily taken aback by the bright light in the front room—previously it had only had lamps with 40-watt bulbs, and now it appeared that someone had changed out all the weak lighting for something stronger. Possibly the realtor had insisted. He could see Elisabeth clearly, and he could see the room in back of her. It looked strange. Some of the chairs were gone, and the china cupboard in the neighboring dining room was empty.

He found himself feeling grateful that he had skipped this part of the past two weeks. He didn't think he could bear to see the Burnham home being dismantled.

Elisabeth emerged from the house. He was struck by how different she appeared. She wasn't looking frumpy or hesitant—in fact, she was wearing a new winter coat. It was a conservative charcoal gray and practical, but it was stylish. She was still wearing snow boots, but frankly, Christine's stilettos always seemed ridiculous to him. No amount of stiletto-wearing was going to chase a New England winter away one minute earlier, and in the meantime she was stuck with wet feet. Elisabeth also wasn't wearing her usual voluminous corduroy frock, but what looked like gray wool shorts and tights.

Shorts? Winter shorts? Was that really a thing? In New England?

Shawn forced himself to acknowledge that if this was Gunnar's influence, it was a good thing. He'd never felt the urge to criticize Elisabeth's clothes choices, but he'd also felt that she used frumpy clothes as an excuse to hibernate. All those years ago, when they'd made their plans to flee Greenleigh, he'd dreamed about the new personae they would inhabit when they reached the big city. He imagined them in a Fred Astaire-Ginger Rogers sort of sequence, he with a top hat and she with a feather boa. Obviously that wasn't reality, but if Gunnar was of the same mindset, he couldn't blame the guy.

"I'm so glad you got back to me," Elisabeth was saying. "I know I left you that weird phone number. Thanks for reaching out—"

"Yeah, I didn't recognize it," Shawn said, pulling the car into the street. His pulse was racing. This was harder than he'd thought. So strange. Christine was right, he needed to take some deep breaths.

"—but I really wanted to see you," she concluded.

I really wanted to see you, too, he almost said, but bit his tongue. He didn't want to say anything too loaded. He was determined not to manhandle Beth. Not tonight. He would show her the life he wanted to give her, and then he would let her decide.

He let the silence settle around them like a blanket. He was nervous, but the silence itself felt good. It felt—peaceful.

It was Beth, he thought. She was calm. Over the fall, he'd felt her anxiety every time he spoke to her, but right now she wasn't anxious, and that made such a difference.

This, too, he knew he could attribute to Gunnar. Son of a bitch. He'd rather not have anything to thank him for, but if this was what he did for Beth, then—

—then what?

I can't let myself lose the battle before I've had a chance to fight, he thought.

He headed toward the highway.

"Where are we going? Someplace new?" Elisabeth asked. She had settled back in the seat comfortably, and was loosening her scarf.

"I don't know how you manage without a car," he replied, evading the question.

"It's a bit challenging," Elisabeth admitted. "I sometimes have to get a cab. But you know Charlie—"

"—from Greenleigh Taxi," Shawn finished. He felt his face relax into a smile.

Elisabeth laughed. "How did you know?" she teased. "Yes, of course. He comes by and checks in with me."

"I thought he'd be retired by now."

Elisabeth shook her head. "No. It's really hard to retire. People don't have enough money. They basically work until they can't work anymore. Charlie's got a disabled kid, too."

"I remember," Shawn said. "But he's not a kid, I would think."

"No, he's well into his forties, but he isn't self-sufficient. We talk about the alternatives for when Charlie is gone. There aren't many options. It's hard."

"So Charlie takes care of you, then."

Elisabeth nodded. She looked out the window at the countryside passing by. "He does. So what's the point of me getting a car I can't afford, right?"

And what will Charlie do when you're off in Seattle with Gunnar, Shawn wanted to ask, but he didn't. He stared straight ahead, thinking about the effort it took him not to judge, not to lecture, not to scold. He really needed to learn to keep his mouth shut, he thought. It was just that much better when he didn't talk so much. It had been a long time since he and Beth had an encounter that was this peaceful.

"You're not taking me anywhere too fancy, I hope," Elisabeth said. She leaned over to check her lipstick in the rearview mirror, and he could feel her warmth invade his space. Her elbow pressed against his arm as she flicked a hair out of her eyes. "Oh, sorry."

"It's okay." *When should I tell her*, Shawn thought. *Now?* "I don't mind," he added, trying to buy time so that he could decide.

"I'm not all that hungry. I had a late lunch." Elisabeth sat back in her seat. When Shawn didn't reply, she looked at him. He could feel her staring at him, so he glanced at her.

"Sorry. What did you say?"

"You're distracted."

"I wanted to turn on the jazz station and I couldn't remember what number it was," he lied. *Jeez*, he thought. *That's really lame.*

"Oh?" She reached over to switch on the stereo. The sound of violins filled the car. "That's loud!" she exclaimed. "Do you always listen to music this loudly in the car?"

"Well, it's only me in the car," he said. "I don't have many passengers."

This time the silence was awkward, backed up by the refrains of Mozart.

Elisabeth broke it. "I can look for jazz if you want."

"Sure."

For a minute or two, Elisabeth went through the channels, and finally hit upon the jazz channel.

"I think I've got it."

"That's it."

"Remember that jazz concert you were in? The one where you had to switch instruments because someone didn't show? Like, in the middle of a song?"

Shawn laughed. "How could I forget? That was a disaster."

"No, it wasn't. It was great. You were amazing. And you got an award."

"Ha. I'd forgotten about the award. That was funny." It had been a bottle of scotch from the rest of the guys, proclaiming him the Greenleigh Jazz Notes MVP. It was a joke, because Shawn enjoyed his scotch and was a snob about it.

"Have you learned to drink scotch yet?" Shawn asked, remembering that she'd declined to have any from that particular bottle.

"Not really," Elisabeth said.

"You can't just drink sweet things, you know."

"Why not?" Elisabeth said. "I like sweet things."

That's because you're sweet, Shawn thought. *Corny, but true.*

It was time to tell her. He didn't know how he would do it—he didn't have the words, and he hated to ruin this mood. Would she hate him for this stunt? He didn't know. But the stress was killing him, Christine be damned—he hated it when Christine was right, she was too smug about it—and he needed to just get this over with.

"Beth," he began. He glanced at the speedometer. He was going a comfortable 75 mph, and he knew an alternate route where he would avoid holiday traffic. They'd make it in under three hours. Their reservation was for eight and they'd be right on time.

"I'm taking you to my favorite restaurant."

"Oh! Where's that?" Elisabeth looked out the window but there was dark countryside and nothing else in sight.

"New York. New York City."

28

There was a long moment, with nothing but the sound of wind whistling past the side mirrors, the rumble of highway pavement under the tires. They hurtled through the dark, mysterious shadows of pine trees high overhead on both sides of the highway, headlights beaming at them from the oncoming cars in the distance.

Shawn was driving fast enough that no one was passing them, although possibly it was just that the road was empty, which should have been a little strange for the night before Thanksgiving. But Elisabeth didn't own a car and hadn't been out of Greenleigh in a while, so she didn't know if the dark stretch of highway on a late autumn evening was normal or not.

And what was he talking about? It wasn't making any sense.

New York City. That was a place, a place far away from Greenleigh. She'd never been there. How could Shawn be taking her to New York City? How was that supposed to work? For dinner?

"I don't understand," she said, finally. "What do you mean by New York City?"

"My favorite restaurant," he said slowly, one word at a time, almost as if he were reciting. "It's in New York. And I want to take you there." He glanced at the display on the dashboard. "Our reservation is at eight."

Eight? Elisabeth glanced at the clock. That would mean a three-hour drive, more or less. And then a three hour drive back? All in the same night? Technically possible, she supposed. But why? Why was he so eager to take her to New York, so much so that he wanted to drive six hours? They wouldn't get back until well past midnight, maybe even one or two in the morning.

"Are you sure?" she said tentatively. "It's a long drive."

"I'm sure," he said. "Are you hungry?"

"No—I had that late lunch," she said. She was still perplexed.

"Good. Because I want you to be hungry for dinner, but I was worried you'd be starving all the way there." His voice was careful, controlled, his tone light, as if the issue were food.

Elisabeth wasn't fooled. There was nothing casual about this conversation and it had nothing to do with food. But she still couldn't figure this out. Had she misunderstood? She was tempted to check the phone to see if she had somehow missed something in their brief back-and-forth about dinner tonight. She didn't think she had, but she was new to texting, and maybe she'd missed one of his texts. Maybe that would clear it up.

She slipped her hand into her purse.

It wasn't there.

Damn it! She suddenly remembered that she had plugged it in to charge—the phone was in the kitchen, exactly where she had left it.

All right. Until now, she'd lived without taking her phone with her everywhere. She didn't need a phone just to go out to dinner. She would look at those texts later.

"Shawn, why are we going all the way to New York for dinner?" she asked. "We could have gone somewhere closer." The wail of a saxophone interrupted her and she leaned over to turn down the volume on the radio.

"Because," Shawn began, then stopped. He seemed to bite back the words that were at his lips.

Elisabeth waited. When he didn't continue, she

said, "It's a lot of driving, New York and back in a single night."

Shawn didn't reply, so she turned to scrutinize his profile. She could see the rise and fall of his chest, the grip of his hands on the steering wheel. He was nervous, she realized.

"What is it?" she asked gently. "Is there something wrong?"

As soon as she said the words, she regretted it, because she saw him frown. And it clicked for her. The last time he'd looked so upset was when he'd raised the question of Gunnar. *Oh, no.* She realized exactly what was wrong—but she didn't want to talk about it. Not now. She didn't want him to start on about Gunnar again.

Gunnar.

She hadn't thought about Gunnar once since getting into the car. She'd been paying attention to Shawn, feeling butterflies in her stomach every time he glanced over at her, wondering if she would be able to have an honest conversation with him. About the past, the present. And maybe the future.

That near miss with Gunnar had brought her to her senses. She wanted Shawn to know the truth, that she loved him still.

But she was leaving Greenleigh tomorrow with Gunnar. Butterflies or not, this wasn't just a date. It was goodbye.

Maybe—maybe it would be as if that terrible thing had never happened. And he would forgive her.

And she could forgive herself. And they could move forward. In what way, she didn't know. But she felt stronger, stronger than she'd ever felt— knowing that he loved her, and knowing that she couldn't go forward in that relationship until she had fixed everything else in her life that was a mess.

The chance of wiping away that long-ago terrible night—it seemed too good to be true.

As she considered the situation, however, she knew it really *was* too good to be true. And what's more, Shawn didn't want to wipe it away.

That, she realized, was what this was all about. He didn't want to erase that night at all. Her stomach tightened. *Oh, my God. This isn't goodbye. Not for him.*

Damn it, this is why texting is dumb, she thought. *We were talking but we weren't talking. Those messages didn't convey anything of the truth. It was all smoke and mirrors and confusion.*

He had no intention of bringing her back to Greenleigh at all tonight, of getting rid of the past and parting as friends. It was actually the reverse. He'd spirited her away to New York in order to re-write history. His way. What she had thought would be the end of that awful story was his attempt to start the story all over again.

Only now, someone else was going to get hurt.

"Shawn," she said, her voice choked. "Shawn, stop."

Shawn finally glanced at her, and what he saw on her face made him slam on the brakes. He swerved into the breakdown lane.

They rolled to a stop.

"Are you all right? You're as white as a sheet—you look like a ghost," he exclaimed.

As a giant tractor trailer rig roared by in the lane next to them, the car rocked. Shawn turned to look behind them.

"I need to move the car. This is a bad place."

"Shawn, no. We can't do this. I'm leaving Green-leigh tomorrow." Elisabeth was either going to faint or throw up. The image of Gunnar knocking at the door and finding her gone—it was making her nauseous.

She couldn't do this to him. She'd done this once already—stood up a man who loved her—and she couldn't do this again. Another life, another person, betrayed.

It was like some kind of evil cloud descended every time someone reached out to her.

"Beth. I'm sorry. I had to try." Shawn sounded desperate. The words came tumbling out over themselves. "When I was talking to Bob Stuart last week, and he said he was taking Angela to California—he said you told him to do it—and it was so obvious, it was so smart. He was saying how it made sense, that he had to do something—I realized I had to do something, too—I haven't actually done anything, just talked a lot, tried to control you—"

"How is this not controlling me?" Elisabeth interrupted. She wasn't angry—she felt sick. Her head swam. She couldn't meet his eyes—she couldn't bear to see his expression while she still held the image of Gunnar and her empty house in her mind.

Shawn shook his head, held up his hands. "I know. I know. I thought about this—for hours, just —staring into space, just hours—I couldn't decide if this was okay, if it made sense. But I decided—I finally decided, after I cancelled our date and I sat around all weekend and thought about it, that if you would even see me again, I was going to take us back to the beginning and fix it."

Another *whoosh*—a trailer with a giant bulldozer whizzed by and the car seemed to jump.

"This is dangerous, I have to move," Shawn muttered. He checked behind him before pulling into the slow lane. He gunned the engine, trying to get up to speed with the traffic around him.

Elisabeth said nothing. She leaned her head back, closed her eyes, tried to breathe deeply. The nausea was still there, lurking in the pit of her stomach. She reached out to lower her window a crack. Cold air shot into the car, fanning her face. There was moisture in the air. Snowflakes? No, it felt like rain. Somewhere in the back of her consciousness she heard a light spatter on the windshield.

"I can turn around," Shawn said finally. "I can turn around and we can just go out to dinner closer to home. But I want more than that. I want the chance to make things right. And we can't do that unless we just—start over."

"We can't start over in Greenleigh, not now," Elisabeth whispered.

"Yes!" Shawn exclaimed. "Exactly!" She felt him turn to her, even though her eyes were still closed. "You were right about the house. I don't like the idea of you selling it—I could have helped you figure something out—but we can't even have a conversation in Greenleigh without all the baggage—"

"It's raining," Elisabeth murmured. She could hear the raindrops hitting the windshield steadily now, followed by the sound of Shawn turning on the wipers. "So weird. It must be warm."

"Or about to ice over," Shawn said. "The temperature will drop overnight."

There was silence.

It took several minutes for the sick feeling to fade away. She kept thinking of the car pulling up to the house, Gunnar trying to peer into the window, calling the phone that was lying in the kitchen. She thought of Shawn, so many years ago, sitting in the parking lot and watching the clock. Wondering where she was. Until he realized that she wasn't showing up. Until he drove away, washing his hands of her. Of them. Of Greenleigh.

Elisabeth opened her eyes. The rain had stopped, and there seemed to be a lot more traffic than earlier. Were they hitting the holiday rush? This part of the highway was more brightly lit than the area directly around Greenleigh. Shawn was driving more aggressively, passing slower cars and ducking into the left lane to get around anyone traveling more slowly.

She put her window up and stared outside.

"Gunnar and I are leaving tomorrow," she said, finally. She turned to look at Shawn. She wanted to say the words out loud, and to make sure he knew that she had made that decision herself. This trajectory was her life.

"I know," Shawn answered. He glanced at her, his face stark. Perhaps it was the highway lights, but he looked haggard. She hadn't noticed that he looked so much older tonight.

What was she doing to the people she loved?

Love was a two-way street. As much as her mother had tormented her, she herself as a daughter must have been a source of torment, too. Kids always worried their parents. And her mother could not have wanted to leave her daughter behind in such a parlous state. In fact, all those years, she had kept saying that Elisabeth should stay away from men who claimed to love her. That was not an effort to make her daughter unhappy. That was for her protection. It was all her mother had to offer her after a lifetime of disappointment. Only those words, nothing more.

And that house.

"I can't—I can't do to him—what I did to you. It would destroy me," she whispered. "It just—it just ruined my life. For years afterward. What I did to you. It was so wrong of me, but it was the only thing I could think to do at the time. And Gunnar—he's a kid. I just can't do this to him. I don't want to be the reason that he never trusts anyone again."

Shawn inclined his head.

After a moment, he said quietly, "Shall I turn around?"

Elisabeth did not reply. What did she want? If she went with Shawn to New York, could they fix things? What did it even mean, to "fix" things? She loved him. She wanted him to know that. But going back in time—was that possible?

"What does it mean to start over? And how do we—how do we make things right?"

"I don't know," Shawn said. "I feel like—I feel like I've talked enough. And I've just made you unhappy. I feel like I've tried to own this thing. Whatever this thing is. And it's not working. And I can't just manhandle this thing and fix it. I've treated it like a legal problem, and it's not a legal problem. Like there's justice and a right and wrong answer. But if we can just stop talking and just—be with each other. The way I'd planned. Like we used to be. I don't know. Maybe this is stupid." He sounded exasperated. "It sounded like the only answer when I thought about it. Bob said he just wanted to be with Angela, and then whatever she decided would be okay. But maybe it's just dumb for me to think it would work for us."

"I can't hurt him, Shawn," Elisabeth said. "That would be like what I did to you. All over again. Not showing up, not keeping my promise. Not being there because somebody stopped me and I couldn't decide for myself what to do. It's just wrong."

"I know. And I guess—I just didn't think about Gunnar. I just didn't care what his part of your plan was." His voice caught.

Elisabeth paused. She forced herself to think about Gunnar for a moment, picture his cheerful grin and his various earrings and tattoos. *Ouch.* It hurt just to imagine his face. No. She was going to force herself to think about him, even if it hurt.

She remembered that day when he'd come over to talk to her at the coffee shop and that first motorcycle ride. The time he'd kissed her upstairs at the house, because she "needed to be kissed." That beautiful watercolor of Hades and Persephone. All those hours he had put into cleaning, fixing, and getting the house ready. How he'd bought the plane tickets and then given her a phone, so that she could finally join the twenty-first century.

She took a deep breath and forced herself to remember him kissing her on her bed, and how close she had been to letting go. He'd reminded her that while she'd been stuck in her regret and continuing to apologize for a crime she'd committed years ago, she was still a warm-blooded human being. Human beings needed love, and he'd offered it to her.

It was his generous nature. He didn't want her to be stuck in her grief. And she wasn't going to let him down. If anything, her courage would be her tribute to him.

He hadn't believed her for a minute when she'd said Shawn wasn't her boyfriend. He'd been right.

"Lover Boy," he called Shawn. Momentarily distracted, she almost laughed, but checked herself.

"I need to get back to Greenleigh tomorrow," she said. "Can you do that?"

There was a heavy pause.

"What time tomorrow?" Shawn's voice was hoarse.

"Gunnar hired a car to take us to the airport at ten."

"I can get you back in plenty of time," he said.

Gunnar's not a coward, she thought. *And I'm a different person now, thanks to him. I'm not going to be a coward, either.*

29

At first, he was dizzy with relief, as if he had stood up too fast. Then the adrenaline of victory hit him. *I am going to show her the best damn time ever*, he thought, jubilant. *I want her to know what I wanted to give her. Everything that I can give her, that no one else can. I'm winning this one.*

Then five seconds later, a panicked: *Oh, my God. What the hell am I doing?*

For all of his cynical, confident New York patina, he was just a Greenleigh boy underneath it all. He had no idea what he was doing.

He'd lived in New York City for eight years. Eight long, tortured years. He'd worked himself into the ground, sometimes sleeping at his desk and using the gym on the fourteenth floor to shower and change into the extra shirt he kept bundled in a drawer. It was always somewhat wrinkled but could be made to work under a suit jacket.

He'd made partner in record time. He'd dated a dozen of the young female attorneys before they all figured out that he was a waste of their time, because he was still stuck on someone back home.

"Someone in his law school class," they said.

"Someone really smart. She edited the law review."

"Someone really successful. She was an appellate court clerk."

"She left him and went to L.A."

"She went to London."

"She went to Buenos Aires."

"I saw her picture," one woman said. "It's on the lamp stand in his office."

For a while, there was an inexplicable traffic jam in the hallway outside his office as people knocked on his door and wandered in and out, bearing coffee and bagels, trying to get a look at the framed law school photo on his lamp stand.

Shawn wasn't sentimental. He was not a dreamer. He had some high school photos of himself and Elisabeth, some snapshots that various people had grabbed of the two of them during his college years, when he'd come home during every vacation in order to see her. Some shots of the two of them during a hike they'd done the summer before that. But he hadn't brought any with him when he moved to New York, because he'd thought *she* would be with him. Photos were for memories. He'd left them all at home, and when she'd abandoned him, he hadn't bothered to look at them ever again. They were in a pile somewhere, and for all he knew maybe the housekeeper had thrown them out.

Ironically, the photo on his lamp stand in the office had been a gift from one of the classmates in the picture. She'd sent it to him care of the law firm, so he put it on the lamp stand and forgot about it.

Life was all about work. When he wasn't working he was wining and dining clients, going to the opera with clients, and learning to golf with clients.

Shawn hated golf. It was boring and barely qual-ified as a sport, as far as he was concerned. But for some reason, old guys always liked him and wanted to "teach" him things, so he went along when he was invited and obligingly listened to them wax on about the "old days." He found it easy to get along with them. He could tune out and respond automat-ically, just as he did when he was with his dad. He was an indifferent golfer, which made his clients happy, because they were always better than he was.

He wasn't tempted to reach out to Elisabeth. He was busy, and never alone. He knew why she hadn't shown up, and he felt like an idiot that he'd even thought she would choose him over that disaster of a house and shrew of a mother. It was all good. He would move on. And he had moved on. Life had treated him well. And when his dad's heart condition had forced him to reconsider his fast-track New York existence, he hadn't been too worried about digging back into all that old stuff. He should have been worried—he knew that now.

Of course Beth hadn't left Greenleigh. That part wasn't a surprise. That she had grown, changed, and was running her own life—that was a surprise. She'd retained her sweet nature even in the face of obstacles that would have made most people cynical and hard. But she was a different person now. She was still quiet, but she knew who she was. And she was finally trying to express herself.

Shawn wanted her back, but he knew now that he wanted the new Beth, not the old Beth. Once upon a time, he'd angrily accepted leaving her behind because he was leaving his old self behind, too. She wasn't ready for the bright lights of the big city, while he, on the other hand, had absolutely needed to get out of Greenleigh. But now that she'd realized that it was time for her to leave, he didn't want to give her up. Not yet. Not until he'd had a chance with the new Beth.

Tonight would be his only chance. If he was

going to convince her to change her mind, he had exactly one shot.

Beth had gone silent after she'd agreed to go with him to New York. He glanced at her now, wondering if she was thinking about Gunnar, and wondering what kind of an idiot he was to agree to take her back home to Gunnar at the end of the night.

She was gazing straight ahead at the road, the highway lights playing over her face. There was a slight frown on her brow, but she didn't look upset. In fact, the lines on her face had softened since he'd pulled back onto the highway and continued driving south. She seemed to have relaxed into her seat, and her hands, which had been tightly gripping her gloves, were now limp in her lap.

If I were braver, I'd just keep her with me, he thought. *I'd say, hell, no, I'm not taking you home just so that you can go make a mistake with your life. There's no way that she'll be happy with that guy. And all that talk about him being a kid—he's not a kid. He knows what he wants. She's just naive. Why doesn't she see that?*

"I didn't bring much money with me," she said suddenly. Her tone was light, conversational.

"I'm not surprised," Shawn replied. He tried to match the evenness in her voice, but he had to clear his throat. To make up for the awkward moment, he reached over to turn up the radio. He missed the volume button and ended up turning up the blower. Dry, hot air blasted out of the vent.

"Damn it," he muttered.

"Let me. You need to watch the road." Elisabeth leaned forward to turn down the heat again, then started to flip through the radio channels. She ended back up at the jazz station and turned it up slightly.

In for a penny, in for a pound, Shawn thought. *Might as well go for it.*

"I guess I should tell you. I have a hotel room booked."

To his surprise, Elisabeth laughed. In spite of himself, he turned to look at her, concerned that she was mocking him. She gestured frantically.

"Watch the road!" she exclaimed.

"I thought you might be mad, but I didn't expect you to laugh at me," he objected.

"I'm sorry." She didn't say anything more for several moments, and he was too uncertain to continue.

Finally, she said, "I'm not mad. But I don't have any clothes or anything with me."

"Yeah, I know." He felt her turn to look at him, and forced himself to keep his eyes on the road. "Why'd you laugh? And why aren't you mad? I thought you'd be furious. It's like I've cornered you."

"Wasn't that the plan?"

"Huh. Yeah—yeah, I guess it was."

"Then you've done a good job."

He was puzzled. She sounded amused.

Maybe that's how it is. Maybe we're just friends. Maybe things with Gunnar are so far gone, she's not even worried about spending a night in New York with me.

He didn't want to consider what she and Gunnar might have done together, or whether they had made any plans beyond travel to Seattle. He wanted to pretend it all away, whatever "it" might be. On the other hand, she wasn't acting like a scared rabbit for a change. Was that because of Gunnar? Was he giving her the confidence to just be herself?

This is all screwed up, he thought. *I don't know what's good and what's bad, for me, for Beth, for us—*

"I just need to get back to Greenleigh tomorrow in time for the car. As long as that happens—it's fine."

"I'll get us back to Greenleigh in time," he said.

"I know," she said. "But other than that—I like being here with you."

Shawn wished he could look at her, but there were big rigs in the lanes on either side of him, and he didn't dare. He gunned the engine, hoping to lose them.

"Really?" he said after a moment.

"Really."

"Even though—I tricked you?"

"I didn't like that part," Elisabeth admitted. "But I think I wouldn't have come if I'd known. And—I think I should have come."

"You do?" He was losing the battle to get in front of the big rigs, so he eased off the gas. If Beth was willing to spend the night with him in New York, he didn't want to waste the opportunity by killing them both in an accident on the highway.

"I just would have been too scared to say yes. So it's fine." She paused, then added, "I wish you'd picked a better day, but I think it's my fault that you had to do it this way. I didn't give you a chance. And every time we met—I don't know, it felt all wrong."

"That's because we were at home. Beth, I wanted to get us out of there."

"Do you mean now? Or back then?"

"Both!" he exclaimed. "Greenleigh—it's like slow death."

"But—you came home again."

"I had to, Beth." How to explain? His dad needed him, true. But it was also the emptiness of his life, his all-too-successful life, with all the money, wine, and women he could stand. It was empty. It was use-less. He'd had enough.

He decided not to explain. She understood, he knew she did. There was Greenleigh, ready to take care of you when all you wanted was to fall into a deep, uncomplicated, dreamless slumber after going through hell. And there was Greenleigh, your nemesis, the albatross around your neck, preventing you from getting out of bed every day.

Someone you loved, who loved you—could be the very thing suffocating you.

I'm not going to be that person, he thought. *This decision is not in my hands. It's in her hands.*

He glanced at her hands in her lap, and thought about putting his hand over hers, gripping it tightly and never letting go. It would be so easy, and he needed to feel her warmth. They were flesh-and-blood human, not mere ideas of humans, but real people.

But he thought about the gesture, and he knew that it wasn't right. She didn't need him to put any of his weight on her. What she needed was lightness of spirit, of heart, so that she could do what she needed to do. No wonder she liked Gunnar so much. He didn't weigh her down.

He felt a little sick as he considered all the things he could do to improve his odds with her. But he wasn't going to do them. He would let her decide.

At any rate, he was going to try his best to let her decide.

Shawn took a deep breath and hoped she didn't notice. He stared straight ahead at the road.

"Shawn," he heard her say quietly.

He nodded without replying, thinking that he was glad their hotel was downtown and that they would be out of the city in the morning before the Thanksgiving parade traffic snarled everything up. They would have to be up early, but he knew how to zip through the back streets of Jersey City so that they could get themselves onto the turnpike headed north without crossing any major arteries.

He felt her hand on his arm, and then covering his hand on the steering wheel. He sighed. Then he put his hand gently over hers and linked fingers, turning her hand so that his was palm up on the seat beside them, hers resting on his. No pressure, not from him. She could reach out for him and he would respond. But she could leave and he would let her go. He would be the vulnerable one tonight, instead of the one always setting the agenda, always pushing her around.

It was enough. He would just let himself feel the hurt, if it hurt, and the joy, if it didn't.

30

They made good time into New York City. As they approached the city from across the river, Elisabeth wondered what had gotten into her, that she had agreed to what was essentially a harebrained scheme on Shawn's part. He was going back in time, to see what would have happened if she had shown up as she'd promised.

The kiss from Gunnar had shocked her into realizing that she only wanted Shawn to kiss her like that. Sure, Gunnar tempted her. He would tempt any red-blooded human. He was sweet and sassy, sugar and spice at the same time. She could see it for what it was. And if she'd tumbled forward into her own harebrained schemes, she might have gone there with him, because she was lonely and scared.

That would be a mistake, she knew. And she

would need to corner him into an honest conversation that he wasn't going to enjoy.

But she also needed to respect Gunnar and show up when she said she would. Shawn said they would make it on time, and she chose to believe him. There was a small, niggling voice in a far corner of her mind that observed that it would be to Shawn's benefit if they didn't make it in time for her rendezvous with Gunnar, but she ignored it. That wasn't true, because she wasn't going to abandon Gunnar regardless of what Shawn did. He surely knew that. He wouldn't win her by trying to keep her with him by force.

Something was different about Shawn tonight, and she wondered why. He'd never accepted that she wasn't the same Beth that he'd left behind in Greenleigh. He had treated her as if she needed constant babysitting, and she'd felt awkward, because she did need help, and he'd helped.

Were things different because they weren't in Greenleigh anymore? That's what Shawn was trying to say. He blamed Greenleigh.

Maybe he was right. Maybe things would be different without Greenleigh weighing them down.

"So," Shawn was saying as they ducked into a tunnel to make the river crossing into Manhattan. "I brought you something."

"Oh? A present?" Elisabeth teased. "For me?"

"Kind of. Don't take this the wrong way."

"Uh-oh."

"I knew you wouldn't have brought anything with you. Clothes, shoes—a toothbrush—"

"Most of the time, when you kidnap people, they don't bring a change of clothes," Elisabeth said.

"Well, I took care of that."

"What? What do you mean?"

"I brought things for you to wear. Because we're going to a—er, kind of a fancy place. I thought you'd like to wear something nice."

"Okay, is this a commentary on my sense of fashion?" Elisabeth demanded.

"See, that's what I meant, I don't want you to take this the wrong way," Shawn complained. "But I wanted this to be—perfect." He glanced at her, and his face softened. "I just wanted everything to be perfect."

Elisabeth didn't know what to say. She felt both annoyed and touched. He was sweet, but he was pushy and aggressive, too. Had he always been this way? She thought back over the years. Eight years was a long gap of time not to be with someone, she reflected. So much had happened, so much that he hadn't been there for—finishing college a few courses at a time, the fight to go to law school, the fight to afford law school, the realization that she had to stay in Greenleigh to take care of her mother

and couldn't apply for any decent jobs anywhere—
Shawn couldn't possibly know what all of that had
done to her.

And Shawn had turned into a big-city attorney
with sophistication and polish. She wondered what
kinds of experiences he'd had. Had the city made
him aggressive? Or had he always been aggressive?
She mulled that one over, concluding that he'd always been kind of pushy. After all, he'd been the one
to order her to come with him to New York so that
they could start their lives somewhere other than
Greenleigh.

Eloping. What an old-fashioned idea.

She laughed, then was startled when she realized she'd laughed out loud.

"You keep laughing," Shawn complained. "This
is about the third time in the past hour."

"Not at you," Elisabeth countered. She paused,
because she realized she was lying. Gunnar would
have rolled his eyes at her.

Not gonna lie, she thought.

"Okay, kind of at you," she amended. "Sorry. But
you're so pushy. I was wondering if this was new, or
if you were always that way."

"And?"

"You were always that way."

"Humph." Shawn shook his head, but he was
smiling. "I guess."

"So what's this place we're going to? I thought I was dressed okay."

Shawn glanced at her. "You look beautiful."

"I wasn't fishing for compliments. I—" Elisabeth realized that she'd thrown away most of her clothes and bought new things because Gunnar had told her to. She decided not to elaborate on her new wardrobe. "I was wondering what you got me."

Shawn nodded in the direction of the back seat. "I hope the shoes fit."

"Shoes? You got me shoes? What is wrong with my boots?"

"Boots would be awkward with the dress I got you."

"You got me a dress?" Elisabeth gasped. She reached behind her and felt the crackle of paper under her fingers, so she turned around. There were two large shopping bags on the floor behind her seat.

"Shawn! What kind of place is this? Why can't I wear what I'm wearing?"

"It's the most romantic restaurant in New York. And I wanted this night to be special. I didn't want you to say we couldn't go there because you weren't dressed for it. Which is something you would say."

"But—but how? Do you even know my size?"

She pulled one of the bags into her lap and began to root around in it.

"Shawn, this is amazing. You got me a dress. I can't believe it. And shoes. And—is this lingerie? Seriously? Okay. You didn't actually go into a shop and buy these things. Please tell me you didn't. Especially if you did this in Greenleigh. Oh, my God. I just realized—if you bought these in Greenleigh, you are the subject of gossip right this very minute. All those old biddies." Elisabeth looked up from the bag, suddenly distracted at the thought of Shawn buying women's clothing on Main Street in Greenleigh.

"All right, all right. I had help."

"Who? Someone from the office?"

"I'll come clean. It was Christine."

After a startled moment, Elisabeth found her voice. "Christine? Really? She knows? About—about us going to New York?"

Shawn nodded. "I'm sorry if that makes you feel uncomfortable. But as you pointed out, I couldn't exactly do the shopping myself. And I really wanted everything to be just right. I was afraid you wouldn't come with me to this restaurant." He shrugged, but Elisabeth could see the tension in his shoulders. He was nervous, wondering if she would be angry, she thought.

This is ridiculous, she decided—again. *I'm a hell of a friend if Shawn can't tell what will make me happy and what will make me sad. It's like I'm a time bomb that could go off without warning. Does he really not understand me? Am I really so random?*

This is where I make my decision, she thought. *I'm not going to be that person, that Beth. I don't like her.*

After a pause, Shawn glanced at her. The look on his face caused her to catch her breath and look away—she didn't like seeing him look so obviously vulnerable. She knew he wasn't only trying to make her happy—he also wanted to win her back. She didn't want to give him false hope, but she also knew he couldn't help but hope.

And this feeling inside her—she couldn't give it a name. Hope? Excitement? Expectation?

She wasn't going to ditch Gunnar and cancel Seattle, no matter what Shawn said or did. But this was where her heart was. With Shawn. She hoped that he could understand how she could love him and leave him, both at the same time.

She gathered up her courage and said, "Everything looks perfect." She wasn't at all sure that it was, but she figured she could put up with whatever strange fashion choices Christine might have made for her.

"I'm going straight to the hotel, and then we're walking a few blocks to the restaurant. We can change in the room."

"Oh, you mean you have to get dressed, too? What's wrong with what you're wearing?" Elisabeth turned to look at him, trying to figure out if he was wearing a tie.

Shawn laughed. "I didn't want to drive to New York in a suit. That's all."

They pulled up in front of the hotel, a beautiful brick façade in Greenwich Village. It had a distinct 1920s vibe, complete with copper-trimmed bay windows and a pair of grand glass doors. There was stone trim, antique glass, and gas lanterns flanking the doors, and a uniformed valet was opening the door before Elisabeth had time to stop staring and gather her things.

"I'll just check us in," Shawn said over his shoulder. He pulled a garment bag out of the trunk before tossing his keys to the valet, and strode ahead. By the time Elisabeth had wandered through the double doors and into the vestibule, he was holding the door open for her as she descended into a sunken sitting room decorated in red velvet, with art deco hangings adorning the walls. A fireplace crackled invitingly, and she paused for a moment, admiring the scene. It was busy, with guests gathered to sip wine and chat, and there were strains of jazz emanating from a small lounge off to the side.

"We've got time before dinner, but not that much," Shawn said in her ear, and she jumped. She hadn't felt him come up behind her, and when she turned, he was watching her face anxiously. In spite of herself, she reached up to put her arms around him, letting the shopping bags drop to the floor as she did so.

We're a spectacle, she thought, sensing that the lobby crowd was beginning to notice them, and she realized that it was important that she not care. She needed to prove that Shawn was more important than her embarrassment, so she pulled his head down to kiss him on the cheek. For a moment, as she began to withdraw, she felt him resist, felt his arms tighten around her before he seemed to catch himself and let her pull away.

"Thank you," she whispered. "It's beautiful."

"We're not even there yet," Shawn said, sounding embarrassed. "Let's go upstairs and get dressed."

The room was much larger than Elisabeth would have expected for a hotel room in downtown New York City, decorated in porcelain blue and white and dark wood furnishings. Shawn walked across to the floor to ceiling windows and pulled open the curtains, revealing a glittering display of Manhattan skyline after dark. He stood for a moment, staring out at the city view.

"I'd forgotten how beautiful New York is at night," he said, half to himself.

"Do you miss it?"

"Yeah. I guess sometimes. Well. No, not really."

"Which one is it?" Elisabeth said. "Yes-some-times or no-not-really?"

"I think it's both." Shawn did not turn around. He continued to stare at the view, one hand on the curtain pull.

After a moment, Elisabeth said, "Did you not date anyone, Shawn? In all those years?"

Shawn was silent for a moment, continuing to gaze out at the view. Without turning, he said, "I went out with lots of women. But I was a real jerk. I wasn't serious about anyone, and they all eventually figured that out. I was messing around. I just couldn't get past—us."

Elisabeth walked over to where he stood and looked out at the sparkling towers around them and in the distance. "I'm sorry," she said. "I hate that I did that to you. I have to admit—I assumed you had just erased any thought of me from your mind and moved on. You didn't call. You didn't try to see me. It was as if we'd never known each other."

"Just the thought of seeing you—it hurt so badly, I couldn't deal with it. You must think guys don't have any feelings," he said bitterly. "That I could have wanted to marry you one day and then the next day just changed gears and found someone new. You must have really thought very little of me."

"I didn't say that!" Elisabeth exclaimed, hurt. "But I stayed behind. You went off to start a new life.

A completely different life. There were so many new experiences waiting out there for you. It was what you wanted. It was different for me."

Shawn kept his eyes on the view and shook his head. "I think you're wrong. I don't think it was different."

"It is different," Elisabeth insisted. "When you're living in Greenleigh—being left behind is not the same as being alone anywhere else. Being left behind is its own special hell."

At this Shawn turned to her. She realized what she had said only a moment after saying it, and felt her next words die in her throat. Tears sprang to her eyes. This time he was the one being left behind. This time he was the one who would be alone in Greenleigh, inhabiting that special hell. The hell that belonged to those who were left behind.

"I'm sorry," she whispered. "It was my own fault —I was the one who didn't come to New York with you. I could have come. You tried to make me understand. And I wasn't brave enough. I couldn't do it. I wasn't ready."

"Listen, Beth." Shawn said. "I get it now. It wasn't right for you." He looked miserable, Elisabeth thought, but his voice was calm, resolute. "When I saw you that first day, when you came in to ask for work, I was so angry. I couldn't believe that you had to open up that raw wound all over again. After I'd avoided it for so long. So I wanted to believe that you were still stuck in the past, that you were still the same person who couldn't leave Greenleigh, not even for me. But you'd changed. You weren't the same person anymore, and I didn't know who you were. You were this lawyer—someone that everyone in town seemed to know—someone who had her own independent role to play." He laughed a little. "I was stupid to think you would have stayed the same."

"Have you stayed the same?" Elisabeth asked.

Shawn did not reply for a moment, then shook his head. He turned back to the view. "I don't know," he said quietly. "I think maybe I lost myself. I'm not proud of the person I was during those years. I was aggressive, working around the clock. I kind of had no life. I was a great lawyer, but not a great human. I couldn't keep a relationship going. I didn't make many friends. I hope I'm not that person anymore. I hope I can recover something of myself. Now that I'm back home."

Damn Gunnar, Elisabeth thought. Her friendship with Gunnar had given her the inner courage to come to New York with Shawn, to tell him how much she loved him, how much he meant to her— and to say good-bye. It was going to hurt. All of this was Gunnar's fault, for making her realize that she needed to be honest with herself and with the world.

She didn't want any of this. She momentarily regretted reuniting with Shawn, meeting Gunnar, selling the house—all of it.

But Shawn must regret this, too, she thought. *He must regret ever meeting me again.* And that thought suddenly trumped everything else.

I don't want him to regret taking this step. I don't want him to feel that his last ditch effort was nothing but humiliation. Because I love him. And no matter what happens, he needs to know that.

She slipped her hand into his and leaned her head against his shoulder. He squeezed her hand hard.

"Let's get dressed for dinner," she whispered.

She was going to make sure that this last night together wasn't going to be about who abandoned whom. Both of them needed to face the future with as much courage and honesty as they could muster. They could both do this.

31

Christine had impeccable taste. Of course he'd always known that—she was a sharp dresser, much too fashionable for Greenleigh—but when Elisabeth emerged from the bathroom, his hands were suddenly fumbling with his tie as he stared.

The dress was perfect. The shoes were perfect too, giving her legs a long, slim line beneath the edge of the royal blue silk of the dress. Christine had nailed the color exactly right—a jewel tone that brought out the subtle auburn highlights in Elisabeth's brown hair and tamed her skin's tendency to look sallow by balancing the rose in her cheeks—although perhaps the heightened color was just embarrassment. She had probably never worn anything that short before, he thought.

"I wish I could help you with that tie, but I don't know anything about tying a tie," Elisabeth said, as he looked nervously back at the mirror and tried to fix the mess he'd made.

"Sorry," he muttered.

"So, can I keep this?" She was trying to joke, making light of an uncomfortable moment as she sat down on the bed, watching him re-do his tie. "I kind of like it. Although I would never have worn anything like this on my own."

"Of course." Shawn tried not to think about the possible occasions in Seattle when Elisabeth might have cause to wear a sparkly blue beaded dress that was cut very high above her knees. Maybe to a charity function, he consoled himself. A fundraiser. A wedding—someone else's wedding, he amended.

"I wish I didn't have such bad eyesight," Elisabeth lamented. She looked around the room, squinting. "I look better without glasses so I try not to wear them, but I have a hard time seeing well after dark."

"Contacts?"

"No, I'm too scared to put things in my eyes." She laughed.

"Fear is relative," Shawn said, shrugging into his jacket and adjusting the cuffs of his shirt. "You're not scared of being grilled by a judge. You're not scared of putting your name on those briefs."

"I'm scared of lots of things, though," she replied.

Shawn decided that he didn't want to pursue that line of conversation. He took one last look in the mirror, and observed that his eyes looked tense, his jaw tight. He rubbed his face with both hands, but when he looked up again there was no improvement.

The closer he got to the big moment, the more nervous he got.

He hadn't discussed it with Christine, knowing too well that she would veto the plan. *Beth is fragile*, she would argue, automatically donning her marriage counselor hat. *Don't do anything that'll upset her.*

But she didn't seem fragile, he argued in his mind. In fact, she seemed more relaxed and happy than he'd seen her in—well, years. He wouldn't do it if it would cause her distress.

And—he could feel it. She loved him. He knew she did. In her heart. Somewhere. There was a bond between them, built on waiting. He'd waited for her, even though he'd pretended he'd moved on. And she'd waited for him, even though she thought he'd left her for good. They'd both tried to stay in the same emotional space, but they'd been unable to, because time just doesn't work that way.

It was no wonder that when they'd finally met, it

had been a disaster. He'd been taken aback by how powerfully he still loved her. She'd been devastated at the thought of the person she'd tried so hard to outgrow—that she was still in Greenleigh, in the old Burnham manse, alive and well. She didn't like that person, she didn't want to be that person, and yet when she'd seen Shawn after all those years, she gone right back to being scared and shy.

The question was whether she would back out of her deal with Gunnar.

She was different tonight—unexpectedly different. He was afraid to allow himself to hope, but hope he would. He was nothing if not hopeful.

Elisabeth was laughing at the appearance of her practical coat over her skimpy beaded dress.

"Shawn," she scolded. "The next time you kidnap someone, make sure she's wearing the right coat for the dress. I look like a catalogue mistake. L.L. Bean meets Dior. I'm about to provide Manhattan with its evening entertainment. I'm a walking comedy. And how do I walk in these shoes, by the way?" She extended a foot, frowning. Christine's choice of shoe was a sandal so frail and glittery, it was barely footwear. Its only concession to shoes was a thin, high, silvery heel.

Shawn stared, then started to laugh. "Christine didn't know about the walk to the restaurant. Maybe we should take a cab."

"No!" Elisabeth exclaimed. "That's absurd. I'm not taking a cab for a few blocks. But I'm not sure I'll make it down to the lobby in these."

"I'll hold your arm."

"I just hope I don't bring you down with me," Elisabeth said.

It really was only a few blocks, but by the time they got to the restaurant, Elisabeth's feet were wet and she was out of breath from stumbling and catching hold of Shawn as they slowly made their way through the heart of Greenwich Village. Fortunately, it felt relatively warm compared to Greenleigh, and any previous snowfall had apparently melted away, because the sidewalks were wet, but there was no snow or ice.

Shawn slowed down his pace, enjoying the feel of Elisabeth clinging to him as she winced and tried not to fall, tottering and wavering on her heels. At one point, he turned to look at her, and she glanced up at the same moment, catching his eye. He smiled at her, and she tightened her grip on his arm. He loved the fact that she wore sturdy New England outerwear and ethereal silvery sandals; the incongruence was one hundred per cent Beth.

You can take Beth out of Greenleigh, but can you take Greenleigh out of Beth, he wondered, amused. *Would she always wear practical coats and boots? Would she be willing to morph into a chic Manhattan professional? No*, he decided. *Not Beth.*

Wasn't that a problem? How would they ever escape this box that they were in? Was it even possible to become a new person at this point in life? God knew, she was trying. She was trying hard. She didn't want to be the old Beth. He understood that. The old Beth had hidden herself from the world. She was ready to move forward. She was an adult now.

He couldn't agree that Gunnar was the man to guide her through this new chapter in life. He couldn't accept that, and he knew that he would nurse that resentment in his heart forever. But he was going to offer himself to her, and if she said no, he was going to pull back and let her go. This was the big decision that he had made without telling Christine. He knew that he had made serious mistakes. He knew that Gunnar had jumped into the breach, doing what needed to be done to really help Beth. But he needed to let her know that he was ready to apologize and start over. Whenever she was ready.

It really was the most romantic restaurant in New York. The exterior was unassuming, red brick and what looked—hilariously, to Elisabeth—like weathered barnboard doors, but the interior was all candlelight and white tablecloths, a beautiful curved wooden staircase leading to an upper level, fireplaces and wide pine floors. Sets of French doors led out to a garden, but although there was mood lighting and carefully trimmed plantings, it was not in use during the winter months. The spray of pink roses on their table was gloriously out of season, but Elisabeth didn't care. It was beautiful, and she bent her head to sniff the flowers again and again.

"Those yellow roses you sent me," she said, not lifting her eyes from the menu.

"I'm sorry," Shawn said. "I know I shouldn't have. Christine told me it was upsetting. She chewed me out."

"Oh. Right, she was there, wasn't she." Elisabeth looked up, then paused. "I guess I was upset. But that wasn't what I was going to say." She reached out to touch one of the pink flowers, rubbing a petal lightly between her fingertips. "I remember your mother's roses. I remember that whole awful summer. I'll never forget it. When she was so sick. And you worked so hard in her rose garden." She reached her hand across the table, and Shawn took it. His throat hurt.

"Yeah," he said huskily. "We were kids, weren't we."

"We were," she said, lost in the memory, her voice fading. "We were kids."

There was a quiet moment, with just the barest

hum of dining room conversation in the background, the fire crackling in the fireplace next to them. He tightened his grip around her hand.

"I'm sorry," he said. "I'm sorry I wasn't around for you when your mother died."

She laughed a little, tried to shrug. "Yeah," she said. "It was okay. She was sick for a while, but it didn't last that long. I had a lot of help from all the old church ladies."

"I still feel bad. I didn't know." *And I should have known*, he thought. *What was I doing when Beth was dealing with all of that alone? Probably squiring some partner's daughter to the Met Gala and getting very drunk on pink champagne.*

Shawn bent over the menu again. He felt unaccountably nervous. *Mom would not approve of any of this*, he thought. *She always did think I needed to slow down and think before I acted. Mom, if you're watching—I'm sorry. But I've got to jump in and do this.*

Had he ever told any of his lady friends about the summer that his mother died? He was sure he hadn't. Why hadn't he? Probably because it hurt too badly to talk about it. But also, because those memories were for him and for Beth, for the two kids who'd struggled through it together. He didn't think he would ever tell anyone about it. It was like looking into a snow globe, a shop window, a museum display—there they were, two teenagers helplessly lost in a sea of terrifying emotion, trying to play the grown-up, trying to act like they knew what they were doing and that everything was going to be okay. It really wasn't okay. It couldn't possibly be okay. If he'd told anyone, there would have been reassurances and encouraging speeches. He didn't want to be encouraged. He had borne witness, and so had Beth, and that was enough.

They talked about nothing in particular, laughed about the legal gossip in Greenleigh, discussed Shawn's dad. His health was indifferent, and Shawn admitted that it might be time to let the factory go.

"It's not easy to produce textiles in New England," he said. "We've got a niche market in high-end athletic wear, but even that's hard to maintain. There's a lot of nice stuff coming in from all over the world. Our things are already insanely expensive. There's really nowhere to go, price-wise."

"Aren't you attached to the family business?"

"Of course," Shawn said. "But I don't want to run a factory. And Dad has never pressured me about it."

"Do you still want to practice law?"

"Not the way I was doing it here, in New York," Shawn found himself saying. He paused, a little surprised at himself, then continued, "It's been nice, in Greenleigh. I didn't expect it."

"You're not actually doing as much actual litigating, though, are you?"

"No, I'm not," Shawn admitted. "I'm doing a lot more management. I guess maybe it's less stressful. But also—it seems to be where I'm useful."

"Ricky Junior loves being in the courtroom," Elisabeth chuckled. "You can let him do the stressful stuff."

"You're way too friendly with Ricky Junior," Shawn complained. "I should have separated the two of you."

"Right," Elisabeth laughed. "Yeah, the pair of us, getting up to no good. Don't worry. He's much too invested in the courtroom. He'd never do anything to mess up his work. He hates to lose."

"So do you," Shawn countered.

Elisabeth looked surprised. "Do you think?"

"So when is the last time anyone made you do something you didn't want to do?"

Elisabeth pondered this. Then she laughed. "Tonight? When you kidnapped me?"

"Touché," Shawn said. He decided not to say the obvious—that he'd done his best to make it difficult, if not impossible, for her to get out of this weekend with him. Sure, he would have taken her back to Greenleigh if she'd really objected strenuously. And that was exactly what he'd needed to know.

She was here with him. She hadn't insisted on going back. Was there any hope?

If this goes well, we'll switch to champagne, he thought.

He procrastinated until the desserts came out, and he knew he couldn't procrastinate any longer. They were tipsy on their wine, and it was already time to order coffee. There wasn't much time left.

I've got to do this.

"Beth," he began unsteadily.

She didn't try to respond, just cocked her head and waited. Her cheeks were flushed with wine, and she'd pulled her hair back with an elastic to keep it out of her chocolate mousse.

"I'm going to ask you something," he began.

Her reaction time had definitely suffered due to the alcohol. He watched as she frowned in concentration for a long moment before he saw the worry enter her eyes.

"Shawn," she began. "I don't—"

"You know I love you," he said, interrupting, then regretted the alcohol and his lack of finesse. *Damn*. Their waiter was approaching, but seeing that they were lingering over their coffee, paused, then turned away to retreat to the kitchen. The restaurant was still busy on a Friday night, with new diners continuing to walk in and take their seats, despite the fact that it was well after 10 p.m.

"I will always love you," he continued. He reached into his jacket pocket and brought out an envelope. "This is for you." He slid it across the table.

He watched as she gazed at the envelope, a troubled shadow on her brow. She raised her eyes to his, uncertain.

"I'm not trying to trap you," he said. "I just need you to know that I understand that you have things you need to do. And I'll wait for you."

"Shawn, I'm not planning to come home. When the house is sold—I won't have anywhere to come home to anyway. I'm leaving for good." As she said the words, her lower lip trembled. It was as if she had never said the words out loud before, as if she had practiced them in her mind, but had never really tasted them. She gave a little gasp, clutched at her napkin.

He didn't reply, just watched as she fought down her emotions. When he'd judged that she'd regained her self-control, he reached out for the envelope and picked it up. It was a small manila envelope, of the sort that the jeweler back in Greenleigh would put repair items into. Carefully, he opened it and shook a ring into the palm of his hand. He held it out to her, and she bent to look at it. Recognition crossed her face.

"Let me put it on you," he said.

She began to shake her head, her eyes stricken, but he reached out to gently remove her hand from her mouth, pushed the napkin aside on the table. Out of the corner of his eye, he could see the waiter's discreet form hovering near the kitchen doors, probably wondering if he needed to congratulate a newly engaged couple or quietly pretend he hadn't seen a thing.

"Here. I'll put it into your hand, and you can look at it."

It was his mother's ring, an oversized opal surrounded by tiny diamonds, bluish purple in normal light, but when held up to the candlelight, full of fiery orange sparks. He'd had it cleaned and the diamonds checked, and the ring sparkled with life. He picked up her limp hand and put the ring in it, and she held it up to her wondering gaze in spite of herself. She held it before the candle on the table, and he could see her expression change as the orange veins leapt into view.

"Oh!" she whispered. She turned the ring carefully, this way and that, to try to recapture the spark of orange. "I can't even tell what color this is—there are so many—" She looked up at him. "This is your mother's ring. The one that used to be your grandmother's. She showed it to me, one time when we were sitting outside in the garden. She was wearing it but she was so thin, it was falling off—" She choked, a tear trickling down her cheek.

"She wanted someone to love this ring," Shawn said. "She wore it night and day, she loved it so much. She used to say it was full of fire. But you had to hold it a certain way, or it was like looking at rain clouds."

"Yes," Elisabeth said, continuing to hold it up to the candlelight. "And I remember she said it was fragile. That she couldn't wear it while she was gardening. She was afraid she'd chip it."

"I will wait for you, Beth," Shawn said. "As long as it takes. I took a long time to come home to Greenleigh. You should take the time that you need. I can wait."

Elisabeth stammered, "Shawn, I—I don't want you to wait for nothing. I don't know what lies ahead for me. I don't know when I'll be back. Or if I'll be back."

"Are you marrying Gunnar?"

At this, Elisabeth gave a startled laugh. "Marry Gunnar? No! No, it's not like that between us." But even as she said it, he saw the hesitation in her eyes.

So I'm right, Shawn thought. *There's some kind of unfinished business between Beth and Gunnar.* He didn't want to know what it was—he could almost say he didn't care—because he knew that he and Beth were tied together with bonds that Gunnar could never break.

But he needed to say it out loud. "Beth, Gunnar is in love with you. I know you don't want to hear it —it makes things complicated. But I know when a guy is in love."

"Oh, God." Elisabeth started to shake her head.

"You know it's true," Shawn said gently. "And it's okay—I can't blame a guy who falls in love with you, after all. Will you take the ring? You were the only person with me the summer that my mother died. And I don't think I'll ever be able to tell anyone about that summer. That ring should be yours. It was meant to be yours. I'm patient, and I can wait for you to figure things out. When you return to Greenleigh, after Seattle—I'll be there."

"But Shawn," Elisabeth said. "Shawn, you said that it was Greenleigh that did this—that ruined everything. You said that we couldn't talk, we couldn't figure things out—because of Greenleigh. I don't understand. How can I go back? How can we be together? I just don't know what to think any-more." Shawn felt his chest tighten, and he held his breath. If he screwed this up now, he would never forgive himself. This was it.

"Bethie," he said, "Do you want us to be together?"

"Oh, Shawn," she whispered. "I do. I just don't know how. And I'm scared. Greenleigh is such a big part of all of this and it's bigger than both of us. How do we escape whatever hold it has on us? How can we make this work—in Greenleigh?"

32

After a moment, during which the murmur of the other diners faded into the background, blending in with the occasional clangs and raised voices from the kitchen, Shawn said, "You need to trust me."

Elisabeth waited for him to elaborate, but he stopped.

She reflected on this.

Trust. He said the answer was trust. And not just trust, but trust *him*.

It was hard to breathe. Elisabeth took a breath, and another, and another, but her chest wouldn't hold the air. The dining room felt warm and close, despite the fact that they were seated a distance away from the other diners.

She remembered that she had accused him of

sucking all the air out of the room. She regretted saying it; it had hurt him. But she had blurted it out, and at the time, it was the truth. And now, again, she wasn't able to breathe—was it him? Was it that troublesome word, "trust?"

Could she trust him?

Elisabeth turned the ring this way and that in front of the candle. The little diamonds sparkled, and a deep orange glow leapt from within. It was a big stone, assertive, even with its mild, cloudy exterior. It presented itself with all of its possibilities, and if you took a moment to really see it, it would gift you with that special orange glow. If you didn't take that long, slow moment—it was just a pretty, milky stone.

I can be assertive, too, she thought.

If you take a long, slow moment with me, I have possibilities. Shawn always knew. And Gunnar knew. Good things take time, and careful observation.

And trust.

This lack of air in the room—was it him? Or maybe, it was *them*. Maybe it was something combustible, between the two of them. She never felt this with Gunnar. Gunnar was like a clean, cool breeze, like a window left open on the other side of the house. Unseen, but felt. He never made her feel responsible for his thoughts or his actions. He urged her to be brave, to take bold steps.

To be assertive.

She put the ring down on the table between them.

She hadn't trusted Shawn. She looked at him now, and saw the hope in his eyes.

He knew that he was making a big ask, because it was a lack of trust which had caused their love to derail.

But it had to be about her, not him at all. She had to continue to learn to believe in herself, to trust herself, before she could allow him in. When she was solid—only then could she take a chance and trust him. And he needed to understand that.

She knew what she needed to do. Damn it, it was all so complicated. But the answers were clear, and she needed to tread carefully and get them all right. It was important that she not trample on anyone's tender feelings, and it was also important that she remember who she was and why she was doing any of this at all. *Once upon a time*, she marveled *—once upon a time, I was the one with all the delicate feelings.* It almost seemed unreal now.

"Beth, I can't leave Greenleigh right now. My dad, the factory, this job at Lawson & Lawson—I need to sort everything out. But eventually we can leave together. When you're ready, we can go any-where you want. The West Coast, Texas—or even New York." Shawn leaned forward. "I didn't burn any bridges when I left. I thought I'd never be back, but—well—I can come back. I made partner when I was here. I could go back to the same place. We could start over here. Just like we'd planned."

"Were you happy?" she asked.

Shawn hesitated, looked down at his hands smoothing and re-smoothing the envelope for the ring.

"No," he said finally. "No, I wasn't. But truthfully, I don't know if it's because of the way I was living, rather than the work. Beth, if you were with me—"

Again the hopeful note in his voice. She almost couldn't stand it. She didn't want to be responsible for anyone's happiness. It was just another cage, a different kind of box from the one she was finally going to escape. And she had to be so careful, not to upset this balance of feelings. So many difficult things to do, all at once.

She stood, pushing her chair back, catching her napkin in one hand before it fell from her lap. She placed it on the table and picked up the ring. Once more, she held it up before her, the glow of the table's candle sparking the orange highlights deep within the stone.

"Thank you," she said. She slipped it on the ring finger of her left hand, but finding it too loose, removed it and put it on her right hand, which had always been a little larger. It was still loose, so she shook her hand lightly to make sure it wouldn't come off.

"I loved your mom. I'll always remember her," she said softly. Shawn had risen slowly, his face taut. He waited for her to speak, as if he were afraid of what she might say next.

"It's time to go," she said. "We have an early morning tomorrow. Thank you for such a wonderful evening. I'll never forget it." She tried to keep her tone light, but she could hear the strain in her voice, and she knew that Shawn had heard it also. She cleared her throat, hoping that she didn't look as scared as she felt.

But she needed to get home to Greenleigh. So that she could leave Greenleigh. So that she could leave Shawn. In order to become the person she needed to be.

It was what she had promised, and she wasn't about to renege on a promise—again. She was done with all those years of struggling to forgive herself.

She knew that Shawn wanted her to recognize her decision to leave as a mistake and to put all her trust in him. But that wasn't the person she wanted to be, someone who would casually ditch a friend and break a promise because something more interesting turned up.

She loved him. She had finally come to this point because her decision to leave Greenleigh had made her stronger. He needed to see that—that Gunnar had helped, not hurt, their relationship or their future. But words seemed to be a flawed way of communicating this. It was too complex, too delicate for conversation.

She would just have to show him that she was a better person, someone who was strong enough to put her trust in a man. Someone her own mother had not believed in. But unlike her mother, Elisabeth wasn't going to be a victim. Her mother's form of insurance, of guarantees against heartbreak, involved shutting out all possibility of love. And that was no way to live life.

"It was my pleasure, Beth," Shawn said quietly. The hopeful light had gone out of his eyes, but he was calm. "I've been wanting to bring you here. And my mother would have wanted you to wear her ring. No matter how we ended up."

He thinks I'm rejecting him, Elisabeth thought. She excused herself to go to the ladies' room as he handled the check. Washing her hands, she looked at herself in the mirror. She did not look as if life's problems had been solved. Sometimes the right answers were the hardest answers. She hoped that Shawn would forgive her, but she knew she had to make the best decision she could in a sea of possible bad decisions.

It's just how it is, she reflected. *And I can't waste*

my energy worrying about whether something is a good or bad choice, without actually making any choice at all.

When she returned, he had her coat ready. She tried to smile. "L.L. Bean meets Dior," she quipped. "I have to remember this. It might be the next fashion trend."

Shawn smiled. "It's easy to live in a fantasy in New York City. Can't do that in Greenleigh."

Elisabeth nodded. She took a deep breath as she zipped up her coat and adjusted her gloves. It seemed silly to suit up for a quick walk up the street on pavement. Just think how awful it must be tonight in Greenleigh, she thought. Slush and sleet. Her mind went to Gunnar, probably calling her number and wondering where in heck she was.

It would be okay, she reassured herself. She was never late to anything, and she never missed appointments. He knew that much about her.

As they left the restaurant, Elisabeth reached out for Shawn's hand. They linked fingers.

"Remember how we couldn't hold hands in public?" Shawn grasped her hand more tightly.

"I'm surprised you remember that, when I was the one who was going to get into trouble for having a boyfriend," Elisabeth said. "It isn't a funny memory for me. I was scared witless most of the time."

"You used to always be scared witless of everything that wasn't us," Shawn reflected. He looked over at her as they hurried toward the hotel. "No more."

Elisabeth smiled to herself. He was wrong. She was plenty scared of so many things. It was just easier to act when you knew where true north was on your compass.

Once in the room, Elisabeth disappeared into the bathroom to change. When she emerged, Shawn was still on the bed, exactly where he had flung himself when they had arrived, tie askew and shirt bunched up around his middle, aimlessly flipping through channels on the television.

"Hey. Aren't you going to change out of that?" Elisabeth had put on the clothes she'd arrived in, but she held one of Christine's shopping bags in one hand.

"Yeah. Just tired." Shawn reached out a hand, but seemed to think better of it and let it drop. "What's up with that? Did Christine get you the wrong size of something?"

"Ha. No. But she has definite ideas about nightgowns that I don't share. Like, she must think they don't need to actually cover any skin."

"Please don't tell me that you wear L.L. Bean nightgowns at home. Mother Hubbard dresses. Not flannel, I hope."

"Um. Well. Let's not go there." Elisabeth flopped down on the bed beside him.

"Beth." He reached out again, and she leaned obligingly into the crook of his arm. She rested her head on his shoulder, and a deep sigh escaped her.

For a long moment, they were silent.

"Can I kiss you?" he said finally.

"Please kiss me."

As she tilted her face up to receive his kiss, he reached his arm around her to pull her closer. She could sense him waiting patiently for permission to touch her, and she revisited her earlier mental logic from the restaurant. She could feel the sharp edges of the diamonds on his mother's ring, still some-what loose on her right ring finger. Was it unfair of her to express her profound love for him in this moment right now, knowing that this evening would end without a happy resolution for him?

"Shawn," she breathed.

He pulled back.

"I love you."

"I know."

She laughed a little. "You're vain."

"I know what I know."

"You've always known."

"Yes."

"I never stopped. I was just scared."

"Yes."

"I'm still leaving tomorrow."

"I know. I tried my best. But you're still leaving. And I'll wait."

He inclined his head, but the watchful expression never left his face. He reached out to touch her lips with one finger, then apparently unable to contain himself, leaned in to kiss her again. She allowed it, then murmured, "I just want you to know that I love you. And I haven't forgotten how much you love me. I just need to do this for myself."

It was somehow easier to say the words with his arms around her and his lips on hers. She had thought it would be hard, but strangely, it was much better this way than across a table in a restaurant. This felt real, and his arms made her feel strong. She wasn't alone in this. Not at all.

But he was devastated, she knew. She could feel it in his tightening arms, in his kiss. She told herself that he was strong, she knew he was. And she didn't want to be responsible for his happiness. She wasn't going to let Gunnar down. Shawn was going to have to take things in the moment, just as she was, and to believe that every decision would be the right one. It would be hard for both them to let go of any sense of long-term control, but this was something she was learning from Gunnar, that long-term control was an illusion, a straitjacket, a trap.

Just as Greenleigh's benign, loving stability was an illusion.

"This isn't goodbye," she whispered. "I promise." She reached up to put her arms around his neck, to rub her face against the sandpapery feeling of his cheek.

"It is goodbye, at least for now," he said. His voice was thick. "You're leaving."

"It's just like—like turning a page. Not like closing a book."

Shawn shook his head. "I know. But it feels like closing a book. I have to worry that you'll never come home again. Even though I'll be there waiting." He was beginning to pull away, so Elisabeth pulled him back.

"Please don't. We have one evening, and I want it to count."

"I'm just distracted," he said. "It's hard to stay in the moment when I know you're leaving."

"Every moment we have together counts."

"Sometimes I think you have no feelings." He sounded bitter. He began to pull at his tie, loosening the knot further. Gently, she took over, her fingers deftly tugging and pulling, until she was able to slip it loose and pull it through the collar of his shirt. She folded up the tie and placed it neatly on the end table.

"Shawn. Listen. Did you really bring me here

and think you would change everything in an evening? You didn't, did you?"

There was silence. She watched the emotions cross his brow, changing from sadness to frustration to defensiveness to hope to resignation. She almost laughed. He was such an open book.

Finally, he shook his head. "No. No, I hoped. I wanted to take you away from Greenleigh, give you space to think. But I knew that giving you space might just end in the wrong answer. For me, I mean. Maybe it would be right for you, but not for me. I just wanted one shot, one good shot—but no, I'm not a fool. I knew this might end badly. I was—am —ready for it."

Elisabeth held up her hand, showing him the opal ring, and he caught it in his. They admired it together for a moment. Elisabeth pulled his hand to her chest. She leaned across him to turn out the light on his side before turning out her own. For a moment, there was only the sound of breathing.

Finally, he turned to her and grasped her face in his hands to kiss her. She responded hungrily, wrapping her arms around him and pulling him closer. She could sense a distant reluctance, a fear, and she wanted to dispel it. Yes, the future was scary. Living anywhere but Greenleigh was terrifying. But she wasn't going to let it get to her. For a change, she would be the actor, she would be the one who made decisions, rather than the one who waited for life to be kind to her. She would be kind. She would be generous. She would be strong.

"Beth," he was whispering. "I love you."

"Yes," she whispered back. "I know."

33

I t was the hardest wake-up of his life. He did not sleep well, but when he found himself staring at the ceiling in the dark, the gray edges of the hotel room drapes revealing the warm glow of street lamps outside, he realized he must have fallen asleep after all.

How long would the drive home take? He guessed at most three hours, maybe not nearly that long given that it was Thanksgiving and practically no one would be on the road, at least once he got past the environs of New York City. Thanksgiving! He could not even comprehend that he would be sitting down with his dad and eating turkey that very evening, talking football and arguing with him over whether the holiday was enough excuse for a

438

double dousing of gravy on his entire plate. It was surreal.

He felt the warm pressure of Elisabeth's head in the crook of his left arm, her face pressed against his side. She'd slipped off the pillow, fitting neatly in the hollow between his arm and his chest, her right hand clutching his arm, her left arm thrown over his chest. She was sound asleep.

He hated to wake her. *What if*, he thought. *Just, what if I didn't wake her up and she missed that flight?*

He already knew he wouldn't do it. He couldn't do it. She trusted him and he wouldn't sacrifice that. But oh, it was tempting. Last night, with its crushing disappointment, had been just as she'd said, a turn of the page, not a book slammed shut and put back on the shelf. After their conversation, he'd managed to persuade her into the silk negligee that Christine had picked out for her, and she'd laughed at herself as she'd tried to pull it down to her knees. Shawn observed that she was clearly not seeing the point of that category of garment, that it wasn't meant to cover much at all, but all he got in return was more laughter.

"This is not me," she'd gasped. "Sure it is," he'd countered. "Why shouldn't you wear something pretty and sexy to bed?" He'd felt a twinge of anxiety —he didn't want her wearing it to bed with Gunnar, that was for sure—but reminded himself that he was trying to stay in the moment. All that mattered was right now, when she loved him and he loved her. He needed to concentrate on not grabbing her and kissing her all over as she stood laughing at herself in the mirror. She trusted him not to try to change her mind, to respect her decisions.

But when she came to bed once more, she'd turned to him and kissed him, and all his willpower had fallen apart. He couldn't be with her like this and not want her. He had her in his arms and never wanted to let go. He asked her if it was all right—he didn't want her to refuse him, because that would just destroy him—and she'd looked up at him and said, "Of course."

She knew what he was feeling and that this was going to hurt, and she accepted it—it came with the territory, and he knew that she'd known that back on the highway, when she'd told him he could carry on to New York. She'd known what she was getting into and she'd known that it would make their eventual parting unbearably painful. Perhaps he was going to be unreasonable, perhaps he was going to be angry, but she'd taken a chance anyway. Because she loved him.

Their joining was blissful and it was awful. He'd wondered if he should be delirious with joy or weeping. As he'd kissed her, feeling the touch of her hands on his chest, thinking about the smell of sunshine on her hair and stolen kisses in a garden long ago and far away, he hoped that she wouldn't cry, because if she cried he would cry, too. And she hadn't. She was so much stronger than he was, and he had never known. This fact filled him with so much admiration, he hoped that there wouldn't be a lot of space left for despair. As it happened, he still felt the pain, but it wasn't despair. It was bittersweet sadness for things that had gone by and would never be again, but despair was something else, a pessimism in the world and the belief that things would never be right again. He wasn't in despair. He was just sad.

One sleeve of the lacy gown was falling down, and he gently pulled it up and smoothed it over her shoulder. But while his mind seemed to want to sink into dismal reflection over his failed attempt at recreating that long-ago elopement, his heart was full. He'd shown up for her. She'd shown up for him. They'd been honest. And they loved each other. Today he would trust his heart and see if he could ignore his mind.

He stroked her hair, and felt her stir. "Good morning," he whispered.

"Good morning," she murmured. Then her eyes flew open. "What time is it?"

"Don't worry," he said soothingly. "Everything's

under control. It's still early. I'll get you back in plenty of time."

He felt her relax. *This is so warped*, he thought. *Here I am, making sure that she gets to Gunnar so he can take her away from me. The world is a weird place.*

They were showered and out the door by six. The air outside was damp, the skies were heavy, and the streets empty. It wasn't going to be that cold, which boded well for the Thanksgiving Day parade onlookers, although it looked as if it might rain. Greenleigh, however, would absolutely be cold. It was always cold on Thanksgiving. It seemed fitting that they would journey north, into a frozen landscape.

To Shawn's frustration, his usual route out of the city was blocked due to streets shut down for the parade, so he ended up driving around and around lower Manhattan before going through the Holland Tunnel and over to Jersey City. There weren't many cars about, but the Chinatown traffic lights seemed to take an interminably long time, and for some reason the tunnel felt longer than he'd remembered. When they emerged from the tunnel, they were startled to encounter bright lights and what appeared to be the entire street under excavation.

They slowed to a stop, and Shawn pulled over to check his phone for directions.

"What's going on?" Elisabeth asked.

'I have no idea. I didn't know anyone did road work on Thanksgiving." He put his window down as a policeman in a bright yellow raincoat approached.

"How do I get out of here?" Shawn called. The policeman pointed behind them, and Shawn turned, perplexed.

"What the hell?" he muttered.

"I think he's telling us to turn around?" Elisabeth turned also, but there appeared to be only further construction and a backed up line of cars as far as the eye could see.

"Water main break!" the policeman was shouting. He pointed again at the presumed detour, but that wasn't where the problem was. Elisabeth grasped Shawn's arm and yanked. He turned back around.

"Look," she said, and this time they could see a fountain of water spouting into the air in the medium distance before them.

"Hey! How do I get out of here?" Shawn shouted back, but the policeman was turning again, headed in the opposite direction, toward the cascade of water, which showed no signs of slowing. Clearly he had satisfied himself that the car with the New England plates wasn't in any particular trouble and could figure things out on its own. Meanwhile, they could see several inches of muddy water swirling about in front of them.

"Damn it," Shawn muttered under his breath. The cars behind them had by now figured out that traffic was not going to move forward and had rapidly begun to scoot around and crowd themselves into the pile of cars headed toward the detour behind them. Grumbling, Shawn reversed and tried to turn around, but found his path blocked by a Jersey City Municipal Utilities Authority truck immediately to his left. The driver waved apologetically, then turned his hazards on and climbed out of the truck. He sauntered over toward the retreating figure of the police officer, waving and calling. He was not going anywhere soon.

"Damn it!" Shawn banged his hand on the steering wheel in frustration. They were hemmed in by the truck on one side and piles of construction debris on the other, with honking cars clogging the detour behind them.

"It's okay," Elisabeth said, but he knew she was spooked. "Relax."

"We've got lots of time," he said, trying to sound reassuring, but he wondered if he was going to get the worst of both worlds: he would be late getting Elisabeth to Greenleigh, and it wouldn't even be by design, but because of something as infuriating as Jersey City traffic, and on Thanksgiving morning!

444

He didn't think he could cope with that. It was cowardly to blame metro New York City for failing to get Elisabeth to Greenleigh on time, and he'd rather die than fail her this way.

He pondered the narrow space in front of them. This wouldn't be the first time that he'd been crossed by a stupid external problem while in pursuit of something important.

"Well. I can't go backwards. I'll just go forward," he mused.

"You can't go forward," Elisabeth pointed out. "There's a big truck next to us."

"Watch me," Shawn said grimly.

"But you're not going to fit in that space."

"Watch me," Shawn repeated. He started up again, moving slowly toward the truck, gently edging the car forward into the gap between the truck to the left and a pile of orange cones on their right. Elisabeth gasped as the pile went crashing in front of them and a loud screech of metal upon metal began on the left side of the car. The tires crunched as orange plastic exploded beneath them. Elisabeth jumped, her hands on her ears.

Shawn grimaced. "I'm sorry," he said, raising his voice. "But there's no other way."

"Hey!" The policeman was shouting and waving his arms, but he was too far away to do anything more than stare in hostile annoyance. Shawn continued to grind the car past the truck, and once he was clear, he found open pavement before him. It wasn't exactly the road, which had been closed off, but there was a concrete median strip to his left, so he sped toward it and managed to bump up onto the strip and then across the other side of the boulevard before gunning the engine in order to zip into the relatively quiet side streets of Jersey City on the far side of the Holland Tunnel mess.

"I could only do this because it's Thanksgiving," Shawn muttered. "It's usually a zoo around here."

"Your poor car," Elisabeth said.

"It's just a car. Nothing important. Dents and paint. I'll fix it."

Elisabeth reached out to him. She leaned in to kiss him lightly on the cheek. "Thank you. I know you did that for me."

Shawn did not reply. The truth was, he'd done it for *himself*. For his own sense of right behavior and integrity. If he was going to give her up, he'd do it with class.

Regardless, the hang-up at the tunnel slowed them down. It took Shawn some maneuvering to find the right entrance to the right highway, as the one he would otherwise have taken wasn't an option. Overall, he calculated that he had probably lost forty-five minutes on the tunnel and the subsequent hunt for the right highway, maybe even an hour, but he kept his eyes deliberately away from the dashboard clock in order to keep his spirits calm. It was a trick he'd learned when dealing with the most stressful deadlines in law practice in New York. *Don't watch the clock, lest you go mad.*

Elisabeth needed to be at her home in Greenleigh, ready for the car that would take her to the airport at ten o'clock sharp. All of her things were packed, and she was ready, both physically and mentally. She had disposed of her business with Shawn and said goodbye. There was nothing left for her to do. She tried not to watch the clock, but he knew she did, and he wondered whether it was because she dreaded their leave-taking or whether she was worried about being late. They wouldn't be late, but they weren't going to be early, either. He would have reassured her, but he found himself unable to speak.

They made it into Greenleigh at twenty past nine, and were pulling up before Elisabeth's door at nine-forty.

"I'm sorry. I thought I'd get you here much earlier so that you'd have a moment to catch your breath." Shawn found that he'd been gripping the steering wheel tightly, and when he took his hands off, they were slippery with sweat.

"Thank you for everything. For last night, especially."

Shawn nodded. "Yeah." He did not make eye contact with her, choosing to stare straight ahead into the distance.

"Please don't be that way," Elisabeth said. "I'm just so glad that you kidnapped me. It was the right thing for us. I'm glad we had last night—"

"Stop," Shawn said. "You don't have to say any more." He nodded toward the door. "Do you need help with your bags?"

Elisabeth shook her head. "Gunnar will take care of it," she said. "It's fine."

There was an awkward pause before she leaned over to kiss his cheek. "Thank you," she whispered. "And thank you for this." She picked up his hand, put it to her cheek, then put his hand on hers, on the opal ring. "I'll treasure it."

"Wait," he said, his voice choking. "Don't go, Beth. Don't."

She just looked at him, her face pale and her jaw set.

He knew he was wrong to ask. He shook his head.

"No. I'm sorry," he whispered. "I know you have to go. I just want to kiss you one more time."

She smiled, almost in relief, and reached out for him. He kissed her hungrily, but she broke away before he felt he'd had enough, and he felt his chest constrict.

"Thank you, Shawn," she said.

She opened the door and got out, then paused, wrapping her coat more securely around her. It was cold, as they had known it would be. She walked around the front of the car, clutching the now-crumpled bags from Christine. Would she ever wear those clothes again, Shawn thought? Probably not. And maybe that was just as well.

This is it, Shawn thought. *This is really it. I can't believe it. She's leaving me for Seattle. For Gunnar. For something that I'll never share.*

He couldn't bear to watch the last few moments of her receding figure. As she walked up the stairs, Shawn reached into the back seat automatically for his coat. His phone was in the pocket, and he hadn't looked at it since before they'd left New York this morning. He'd silenced it at some point the previous day, and other than a "hey, just checking up on you" text from Christine, there hadn't been anyone trying to get in touch.

He was startled to see that there were twelve messages from Christine, and seven missed calls from her, all from earlier that morning.

"OMG you're not picking up. Call me!"

"PLEASE CALL ME!"

"WHERE ARE YOU???"

"I can't text you this kind of stuff, please please please call me!"

"I just talked to Gunnar, you've got to warn Beth—"

At this, Shawn looked up at the house. Elisabeth had disappeared. The door was shut. He sat, feeling his stomach churn, knowing that within seconds—

The door flew open and Elisabeth stood in the doorway, her gaze searching for him, her face white. In her hand was her phone.

As their gazes locked, she burst into tears.

34

"He's gone!" she cried. His window was up and her voice did not reach the car, but he could read her lips and see her trembling hands.

Gone? What did she mean by gone?

Shawn stared, uncomprehending, his grip on the phone slackening. Elisabeth was holding out the phone, saying something, but he couldn't hear her.

Then he saw a figure running toward them from down the street, wearing some kind of flapping garment, sliding precariously in the icy slush on the pavement. It was Christine, in a bathrobe and slippers.

"Shawn!" she called, a high, desperate squeak in her voice. She, too, was holding a phone in one hand, waving it frantically.

The world is crazy, he thought. *What the hell? We're all three of us out in the Thanksgiving cold, waving our phones at each other. Crazy!*

He fumbled at the switch on the door for what felt like an impossible length of time before he managed to put the window down. Christine was still jogging toward them, gasping out clouds of white mist, still trying to spit out words that he couldn't quite make out. As she got closer, he could see her lips moving, and the words started to coalesce into sounds he recognized.

"I tried—to call you—" she wheezed.

He didn't feel like yelling back in the Thanksgiving morning silence in Greenleigh, so he said nothing, inwardly cringing as he thought of the neighbors parting their curtains and gazing in horror at Church Street's latest homeowner running around half-dressed in the cold. He turned instead to look at Elisabeth, who was staring in frozen shock at Christine.

Maybe Elisabeth's boiler had finally given up the ghost—perhaps the heat had failed, her pipes had burst, her roof had caved in because the ice dams were finally diverting snow melt and rain into the house. But no, he realized. The house looked fine. And she had unloaded all those problems. She didn't need him to take care of the house. That couldn't be the problem. She was done with all of that, had done the smart thing and gotten out from under all of her Greenleigh woes.

Wasn't that what all of this was about, anyway?

Christine had stopped running and was walking now. She was clutching her side, her breathing ragged. "Shit," he heard her mutter, and he almost laughed, remembering that she had once run marathons. Except this wasn't funny.

"I tried—I tried to get you," she gasped. "You didn't pick up."

"Sorry," Shawn said. "But you knew we were gone. We were coming back this morning. It's hasn't been much over twelve hours—"

"Yes—yes—I know." Christine was at the side of the car now. She wore a thin pink silk nightgown and matching pink silk slippers, which were now ruined with mud and wet. She had pulled on a thick white robe but she was both sweaty and shivering. She reached out to the car door with one hand to steady herself, pulling her robe more tightly around herself with the other hand.

"Isn't the car coming at ten? Beth?" Shawn glanced at the dashboard clock, then up at Elisabeth, who had started down the steps in front of the house. "It'll be here soon."

"He's gone, Shawn. He's gone." Elisabeth choked on the last word. "Gunnar's gone."

"I saw him," Christine said, still breathing hard.

"He came over this morning. Early. Banged on my door like a crazy person."

"He left all these messages." Elisabeth held out the phone. "I didn't bring my phone to New York. I'd forgotten it, it was charging in the kitchen."

"Wait. Wait. I don't get it. What do you mean, gone? Where did he go? And isn't the car coming in —" Shawn looked at the clock "—ten minutes?"

"There's no car, Shawn. This is all my fault," Elisabeth said, her voice breaking. "I was so stupid—"

"Let me, Beth." Christine held up a hand as she struggled to catch her breath. "Be quiet. Let me explain." She turned to Shawn. "Last night, Gunnar must have been trying to get in touch with Beth. He was calling her and texting her, and she wasn't replying. I don't think he thought that was a big deal. Beth probably forgets she even has a phone half the time. But eventually he started to think something was wrong, so he showed up at her house this morning. And she wasn't home. And then he—he just knew. He knew that you two were together. And he went nuts."

"He thought I had skipped town. That I was ditching him, ditching our trip to Seattle." Elisabeth said.

Christine turned to her. "Well, are you?" She looked back at Shawn, then at Elisabeth again.

"No!" Elisabeth cried. "No! I'm here! I'm ready to leave!"

"This—is—all—stupid," Shawn said tightly. "I don't know what Gunnar's deal is, but Beth is here and ready to leave. I got her here on time, and it's all good. If he wasn't acting like an idiot, everything would fine. Jesus Christ."

"Well, he's canceled the car and he's gone," Christine said. "He was shouting at me at six in the morning and I had no idea what he was talking about, except—obviously—I knew where you were last night. I didn't tell him, but I didn't have to. Listen, Beth—" she turned to her again "you've got to stop being in denial about Gunnar. He is so in love with you. You've got to clear this up with him. You can't pretend you're someone not worth loving. It's never been true for him. He's known the real you all along. You just wouldn't accept it. You have to put a stop to this. It's cruel."

"I know that," Elisabeth snapped. "I know. I was going to make sure he understood that we were never going to be a thing. I kept telling him and he wouldn't listen. But I should have made him listen. I told you, this is all my fault. I screwed up. But what do I do now? He's gone, and I'm here. I tried calling him but he's not picking up. I'm getting this weird robot voice, and I've left messages, but I don't know if I'm getting through."

"Why do you have to do anything at all?" Shawn demanded. "He's ditched you. Stood you up. We've driven like crazy from New York in order to make that flight. I don't see why you owe him anything. Screw him."

Elisabeth shook her head wordlessly. There was a long silence. Then she said, "No. I need to see this through. I made a promise. I upended my whole life so that I could make a change. He helped me do it, and I owe him. I can't bail on him now." She looked up at Shawn. "I can't bail on someone again. Even if it scares me. I need to do this."

At this moment, he was close, so close to having Beth stay, spend her life with him in Greenleigh. Gunnar was the bad guy now. Why couldn't she just let him play the villain? Why couldn't she just accept this happy accident? They were meant to be, he and Beth. It was as if the gods were writing their story with exactly the ending they needed.

It sucked that he understood exactly why Beth needed to do this. It was because she knew what it was like to ditch someone, and she knew what happened when someone got ditched. The silence that followed could ruin all chance at happiness forever. She wasn't going to do that to Gunnar. Not to mention, he had misunderstood. She had upheld her end of the deal, and she was angry that he thought so little of her as to assume that she had ditched him.

Aw, hell.

"Grab your bags. I'll drive you. You'll have to have this out with him at the airport. Or God forbid, on the plane," Shawn said, getting out of the car. Christine leapt back just in time to avoid her hand being slammed into the door. He leapt up the stairs, pushing past Elisabeth and into the house. She followed.

"Where are your bags?" he called.

"Front room," she said, her voice hesitant. "But Shawn, are you sure? It's Thanksgiving."

"Yeah, I know what day it is. What airport?"

"Boston."

"Boston! Are you freaking kidding me? Why the hell are you flying out of Boston? He could have picked somewhere closer!"

"I don't know, I don't know. Please, Shawn, don't scold me, I don't know! He bought the tickets, I have no idea why he had us fly out of Boston."

"That's over two hours away," he muttered. He picked up a suitcase in each hand. "Is this it?"

"Yes. I've got a carry-on, but this is all. Are you sure you want to do this?"

"Beth, if you want to be in Seattle with Gunnar, you have no choice." He tried not to sound sarcastic and wasn't sure if he had succeeded, but she backed away from the doorway and let him pass.

Shawn paused, took one last look around. The house was swept clean of knick-knacks and personal items, although there was still furniture in it, awaiting valuation. It looked sanitized, like a hospital room. Its personality was largely gone, without the detritus of the history of the Burnham family lying about, collecting dust. The dust, he realized, was part of the Burnham legacy. A new family would create a new legacy, minus the Burnham dust.

I keep thinking that this is it. But there's another painful step. One more Band-Aid to tear off.

He turned away. "We need to hurry," he said over his shoulder.

"You guys. Please tell me what happens," Christine was saying. She was shivering, hopping from one foot to the other as she stood watching Shawn load the suitcases into the trunk. "I am going to go mad from worrying. I'm having Thanksgiving with my cousin in Vermont, but you have my number. Please don't forget."

"I'm sorry, Christine," Elisabeth said. "Thank you for everything. I know you did all the shopping for me."

Christine's face brightened. "I hope everything fit."

"Yes," Elisabeth said. "Even the ridiculous nightgown."

Christine beamed, then threw her arms around her. "I am thinking about you. Every minute. I'm sorry you're not staying. But I'm happy if you're happy."

"We need to get out of here," Shawn said. He opened the driver's side door, but paused for a moment before leaning over to hug Christine. He did not speak—he wasn't able to say the words, but he knew she understood. He'd tried his best, she'd tried her best. He was going to see this through to the end, no matter how much it hurt.

"Don't crash the car," Christine whispered. There were tears in her eyes, but she sniffled and stepped back from the street.

"I won't," he said.

He fastened his seat belt, adjusted the rearview mirror. Another long drive, only this time to take the woman he loved to a man who loved her. His enemy—no, that sounded too strong, his rival. Would she have the courage to do the right thing, he wondered. Would she be able to break up with Gunnar in an airport? On a plane? On a friend's couch? What if she fell in love with Gunnar after all?

How was one supposed to do this, anyway? Was there a playbook for awkward breakups? If there was, he felt he was probably the author. But he wasn't going to help Elisabeth out with this one. She was on her own.

Elisabeth had gone up the stairs again. He watched as she pulled the door shut, then tried the knob to make sure it had latched. Her back was to him, but he knew that this was the most difficult moment of this entire process. She was leaving Greenleigh, and not even able to borrow Gunnar's strength with which to do it. He knew she hadn't planned on doing this by herself.

She turned and caught his eye. She gave him a little nod, then descended the staircase.

The sound of the car door slamming. The click of the seatbelt. Then a deep breath.

"All right. Let's do this," Shawn said.

35

There was grim silence for the first thirty minutes of the drive. Elisabeth glanced at Shawn's profile once or twice before deciding that she did not want her last memory of his face to be frozen into that furious glare, a muscle working in his cheek, his teeth clenched. She looked at her hands, out the window at the watery gray view, at her shoes, anywhere but at him.

If he was going to be so deeply angry, she thought, he ought not to have insisted on driving her all the way to Boston. She could have managed on her own—

No, she could not have, and she knew it. If not for Shawn, she wouldn't have been able to chase Gunnar down. What an irony.

"I can't believe you did this." That was Gunnar's last message.

He viewed this as a betrayal. He thought she'd left town with Shawn and had no intention of going to Seattle with him. She felt awful, and yet she traced her actions in her mind over and over, and she still couldn't figure out the exact moment when she had hurt him. It didn't matter that he hadn't been there to see her do it—she had definitively turned her back on him, and he had known. Gunnar had always known just how much she loved Shawn. He'd been fighting a losing battle, but with his cocky confidence, he thought that maybe he could break down her resistance. If he could just get her to leave Greenleigh! But he hadn't thought she would stand him up. And Elisabeth didn't want him to think that she was that person. Once, she had let Shawn walk away from her, and years of pain had followed. She would not do that to Gunnar.

Elisabeth imagined Gunnar turning up on her doorstep at six in the morning with two cappuccinos, getting the key from under the mat, letting himself into the house, finding her phone on the kitchen table, seeing her untouched bed. He'd left the cappuccinos on the table, next to her phone. How long had it taken him to figure out where she was, and with whom?

Probably about half a minute. And then he'd

gone to Christine's house, banging on her door and getting her out of bed, demanding to know if he was right—that Elisabeth was with Shawn, had spent the night with him, was not coming back. For once, Christine would have been without makeup and with her hair askew, minus her pearls and heels, startled out of her smooth-talking, wise-cracking veneer. He would have asked, to her face, if he'd been made a fool of, if this had just been some kind of sick game, if the entire town had been conspiring to keep him away from Elisabeth, so that he would just leave her be. That way they could keep hold of their precious charity project, the historic Burnham manse, and their precious charity lawyer—

Elisabeth gasped.

"What is it?" Shawn said curtly.

"Nothing," she said.

But she was thinking of the reaction that Mrs. McClintock and Angela Stuart had to Gunnar, the frosty response to his tattoos and diamond piercings, their startled protests when she'd told them she was leaving Greenleigh.

Of course Gunnar would think that the town was arrayed against him, because it was. They'd decided he didn't belong. Angela Stuart, with her custom cherry cabinets and selectman husband, only had to pretend that they were perfect in order to earn her position in Greenleigh. The truth was that the Stuarts were human and they screwed up and felt pain like anyone, but because the Stuarts made Greenleigh look good, the townpeople would give them a place of honor. But if someone like Gunnar threatened to mess with the tranquility of their town, the claws would come out.

But it wasn't true, Elisabeth thought, confused. It wasn't true. Gunnar wasn't an outsider at all. Why would they think he was? Because he tried to act like such a bad boy? How stupid! And anyway, she didn't care what Angela thought, what the McClintocks of the world thought. Yes, she knew Shawn was on their side—he, too, didn't think a tattoo artist was good enough for her—but Gunnar was from Greenleigh. His dad was Greek, but his mom was old Greenleigh family, he'd said. He was as much a Greenleigh native as she was or Shawn was. He belonged in Greenleigh, even if he'd come and gone over the years.

Gunnar had an uncanny ability to guess at Elisabeth's pain. She'd assumed that it was because he was just like her, someone trapped by the somnolence of Greenleigh. She'd never thought for a moment that Gunnar wasn't good enough for her because he hadn't finished high school and didn't wear a suit to work.

Her head hurt. This was all messed up. Too many things going on at once. She wished it were just about money, or about that broken-down old house. But it was about so much more.

She needed to see him, to talk to him. She needed to explain. She would straighten it all out with him, convince him that she wasn't one of "them." Just because she was a Burnham of Greenleigh didn't mean that she was better than anyone else. She didn't care where Gunnar was from. That whole Greenleigh thing was bullshit, and even Shawn knew it. Wasn't it Shawn who'd said that he needed to get them both away from Greenleigh? Wasn't it Shawn who'd said that the town was the toxic reason for their unhappiness? Maybe it was all about Greenleigh after all.

Elisabeth rubbed her forehead with both hands, feeling the worry lines etching grooves into her skin. She was going to look like she was forty, at this rate.

"Shawn, thank you for doing this."

"Yep."

She stole a look at him then. He still looked furious.

"I'm really sorry."

"So am I."

Timidly, she reached out a hand, but he jerked away.

"Don't," he said tightly. "I can't handle it right now. Just—just let me take you to the airport. I'll do that much for you. But I can't do any more. Don't ask me for more than this."

She nodded and turned away.

He was right. He was going all the way out on an emotional limb in order to do the right thing, but it was only the right thing because he was respecting what she said was the right thing. He didn't agree with her, but he respected her.

It was the right thing, she thought, because she was going to keep her word. She wasn't going to leave another man high and dry, dangling after her because Greenleigh would not release its claws—or more accurately, because the good folk of Greenleigh would not let her grow up.

I am going to see this through, all the way through. To the end. If it's the last thing I do.

It actually took less than two hours to get to Logan Airport, despite a brief holdup as the Massachusetts Turnpike entered Boston, with road construction forcing three lanes to merge into a single slow-moving lane. But it cleared up fairly quickly, before Shawn had time to expound on the absurdity of Thanksgiving Day construction, when all decent citizens should have been at home watching football and vying for a second piece of pie. When they had gone through the tunnel and taken the airport exit, Shawn headed for the central parking lot.

"Shawn. You can drop me off. I'll be all right."

Elisabeth was looking at her phone, trying to make sense of the ticket.

"I'm taking you all the way in," Shawn replied tersely.

"Really, you don't need to. I'll be fine." Elisabeth looked up from the phone as a thought struck her. "I should just text him, shouldn't I. He's either here or on his way here."

"Yeah. Do that," Shawn muttered. He had entered the central parking facility and was slowly accelerating the car up the ramp.

Elisabeth looked down at the string of texts, all from Gunnar between eight and midnight. The cheerful emojis and random conversation starters—they sounded just like him. Then the growing confusion. And the last awful message.

I can't believe you did this.

"I kept calling him. That was a mistake. I should have texted him when I first got home," she said.

"You should have," Shawn agreed. "But we had to just get you here on time. More drama was—unnecessary. You need to let him know you're here. And then we'll meet him in the terminal. I promise I won't punch him," he added, when Elisabeth looked up in alarm.

She typed out, "Hey Gunnar. I'm here at the airport. Where are you?"

She waited. They had parked, and Shawn was opening his door. She typed again.

"I'll wait for you inside by the ticket counter."

She replaced the phone in her purse, and got out of the car.

"Did he answer?"

Elisabeth shook her head.

"Let's get you to the ticket counter then." He turned abruptly, heading toward the elevator bank.

They had a bit of a walk to the ticket counter, which was empty. Shawn went to check the flight board, while Elisabeth glanced again at the phone. Nothing.

"They're not calling your flight yet. You've still got time."

"Shawn, he's not answering."

"Give him a few minutes. Sometimes the signal in the parking garage is wonky." Shawn looked around, then pointed at a row of chairs. "I'm going to sit over there with your bags."

"Should I check in?"

Shawn held his hand out for her phone, and she gave it to him. He examined her ticket, then handed it back.

"I'm not sure you can. It's his itinerary. You're on it together. And they might want to see the credit card he used to book it. You might have to wait and check in together. It really depends." He turned away.

Elisabeth went to check the flight board. Boarding in half an hour. What? Why so soon? The flight wasn't due to leave for almost ninety minutes. She decided to go up to the ticket desk.

"Hi, I'm on the flight to Seattle that departs at one-thirty," she began, but the man behind the desk was already holding out his hand for her identification.

"I'm just asking a question," she continued, "because my—my travel companion isn't here yet, and he's the one who bought the tickets. Do I have to check in already?"

"Do you have bags?"

"Yes, I do, but—"

"That aircraft is due in at the very last minute from Chicago," the man said. "We need to clean it and refuel and turn it around very quickly, so we'd like everyone checked in and ready to go well in advance. We're closing check-in soon. You really should just check your bags right now."

"Can I do that? My friend isn't here."

"Let me look at your booking." He tapped a few keys, then frowned.

"This itinerary has been canceled."

36

"What?"

"Canceled. Didn't your friend tell you?"

Elisabeth stepped back slightly from the counter. "No," she whispered.

"Canceled within the last few minutes, from the looks of it." The man looked at her curiously. "Are you all right?"

Elisabeth looked over her shoulder. Shawn sat staring at his phone, her bags next to him, his shoulders slumped. His body language telegraphed exhaustion. As if on cue, he looked up, and their eyes met. He rose slowly.

She took a deep breath. "Yes. I'm fine. Thank you very much."

She turned away from the counter, stumbling

slightly as she walked over to where Shawn stood with the bags. She scarcely felt her feet. It was as if the blood had drained out of her and she were floating on air.

"Canceled," she said.

Shawn said nothing, his gaze holding hers.

"Did you suspect? That he would cancel? That I would end up at the airport, dumped?" Elisabeth tried to say the words lightly, tried to smile. It was ironic, was what it was. First, she was supposedly the one who'd dumped Gunnar. And now, Gunnar had dumped her.

"No."

For a moment, Shawn struggled to speak. Then he said quietly, "Beth, if it were me, I would never let you get away from me. But I've already done this thing. I made a mistake. And I wouldn't make the same mistake twice. Maybe Gunnar was afraid to be the one who was abandoned. So he abandoned you instead."

Elisabeth nodded. There was a long silence as she thought.

"I don't know where to go," she said finally. "I don't know what to do. I've shut every door, dotted every i and crossed every t. I don't belong anywhere anymore. This feels so weird."

"You could go home."

"You saw the house."

"Yeah. I did. It's empty."

"I guess I can just—just move back in." Elisabeth frowned. Could she just move back in, then? Rewind time, abandon plans to sell? She could, she supposed.

But that didn't seem right. All of this—Seattle, selling the house, getting straight with Shawn—was supposed to be about her. *Her.* Not Gunnar, not Shawn. Her. If she just quietly went back in time, wouldn't she end up as the same timid Beth? What would happen to all the strength in herself that Gunnar had helped her to discover?

She'd be broke, working for Lawson & Lawson, and trying to keep the roof from caving in.

But if she sold the house—what then?

She didn't know the answer to any of this. Previously, she hadn't had to think about it.

She knew she could figure this out, but she didn't think she could figure it out during a two-hour drive back to Greenleigh.

Shawn broke the silence. "Why don't you come home with me, Beth. And you can figure this thing out. Stay with us, and you can sort out the house after the weekend. No one's around anyway because of the holiday."

"A staycation at your house?" Elisabeth said. She shook her head. "I don't know. It seems weird."

"I promise I'll leave you alone. You need to figure

this out on your own. It'll probably do you good not to be in that house for a few days."

She hesitated. Shawn was already walking toward the elevators. As far as he was concerned, the matter had been decided. She remembered her conclusion that he'd always been pushy, and almost smiled.

Elisabeth took a moment, watching him. Was he smug? Happy? Thinking to himself that Gunnar was not to be trusted after all, and here was the proof?

Did he think that he'd won?

After the initial shock, the initial sense of mounting fear and dismay, anger began to well up in her chest. Anger toward Gunnar. She had kept her promise. Why hadn't Gunnar done the same?

After all that I've been through, she thought. *After all that I've had to figure out and overcome. Selling the house. Getting rid of everything I own—everything the Burnhams have owned for centuries. Losing my literal place in my town, my hometown, the only home I've ever known! I did this because of you, Gunnar! You didn't have to change a damned thing in your life, but look at everything I've done and everything I've thrown away! Now, what?*

She walked over toward the elevators, feeling her cheeks burn as she realized how angry she was. Anger wasn't an emotion she was used to, but she had turned her life upside down because of Gunnar, and she didn't feel she'd done anything to deserve being dumped at the airport, a two-hour car journey from home on Thanksgiving Day. Okay, she'd left town with an old boyfriend but it was none of his business. She'd made it back on time. She'd rushed to the airport to make their flight. She'd upheld her part of the deal.

Shawn was stabbing at the elevator button. He wasn't looking her way, but was studying the lack of progress of the floor number indicators as the elevator sat at the street-level baggage claim level for what seemed like an inordinate amount of time before starting its journey up toward their floor.

"I'm really sorry that you drove out all this way."

"Yeah. Sucks."

If there had been any hint of a smile on his face, or a lightness in his tone, she would have instantly decided to have him drop her off at a hotel in Boston, where she could sit alone and figure out what the best course of action was. But there was nothing, not even a carefully blank expression. As best as she could tell, he was pissed for her, pissed for himself, and thinking about how to get the hell out of the airport. Maybe even Shawn could be pushed too far.

Maybe that was a good thing for her to notice. The limits of love. People had their limits. They thought that love melted everything away, but clearly that was not how it worked.

She had never thought of herself as having limits before. She could set limits, and expect people to respect them.

"Are you sure your dad won't mind if I stay with you for a while? I don't know how long it will be until I can sort out the house. It's not under contract yet but there are so many interested buyers, there's no question about it selling."

"My dad loves having company, you know that. He'll talk your ear off, though. You won't get anything done. You'll have to avoid him or he'll pester you into playing chess with him."

Shawn still sounded annoyed. Elisabeth decided to stop questioning him.

The elevator doors opened. Inside the elevator there was a woman in a sari holding the hands of two angry toddlers who were trying to make a dash out the doors. Shawn plunked the bags in front of them just as one of them managed to slip his hand out of his mother's. She cried out in alarm, but the boy was unable to get around the suitcases, and began to howl.

"Thank you," the woman said in relief. Shawn smiled down at her as she began to scold the child. His sister stopped tugging, gazing up in fascination at Shawn, who towered above her mother. Shawn pulled a pack of gum from his pocket and offered it to her, and the little boy stopped crying when he saw his sister eagerly helping herself.

"Here you go," Shawn said, offering a stick to the boy. He did not reply, but snatched at the gum, and his mother apologized before scolding him once more. The boy chomped at his gum, then noticed that his sister had folded the silver gum wrapper into a triangle, and began to fold his own wrapper as well. Elisabeth and Shawn left them as they began to shout over each other's voices and show their harried mother their creations.

"I was that kid once," Shawn said as the doors closed behind them. "I hope they don't try to make a break for it through the parking lot. Too bad they didn't get off on our floor, I have some more tricks up my sleeve."

"I think the gum will last long enough for them to get to their car," Elisabeth said. "That was clever of you."

"Well. It takes one to know one. Aw, hell. I hope I remember how to get out of this place. I don't want to end up out in Revere somewhere." He backed the car out of the space, then realized he couldn't remember where he'd put the garage ticket, so he stopped to rummage through his pockets before putting the car back in gear.

This was the old Shawn, not the angry Shawn that had taken two hours out of his life to get her to an airport so that she could leave town with a man he didn't like. He was just the usual level of angry now, and she could deal with that.

Maybe she could handle her life on her own. She wasn't sure, because she'd never done it with any modicum of success before. Before Gunnar, she was broke, humiliated, desperate—all words that she didn't want to think about. Everyone who tried to help her seemed to be filled with pity for her. She didn't want pity, but frankly, her earlier life was pitiful.

Was this it, then? All the adrenaline that had built up around a move to Seattle—gone, poof, just like that? Was it back to the old life, helping out her neighbors and negotiating small claims court?

Elisabeth reached into her purse for her phone, and taking a deep breath, checked her texts. Nothing. He could have at least told her that he was canceling, she thought irritably. She was momentarily tempted to tap out an angry message. But she didn't know what to say.

I was here, she thought. *I never abandoned you. You were the one who abandoned me.*

They were out of the parking facility and zipping along the empty highway, headed back out to the Mass Pike before she'd made her decision.

"I'd like to stay with you. If it's really okay. And if it's not—you need to tell me. Because—"

"Because it's not going to be like New York." Shawn finished the sentence for her. "Yeah. I know that. And I'm okay with it."

"Really? Just because—"

"Yeah," he interrupted. Was he trying to avoid hearing her say the words? Was he heading off her statements because he wanted to control the direction of the conversation?

She waited, because he sounded as if he had more to say. After a few minutes, she grew impatient.

"Every time I talk you interrupt," she said irritably. "And then I wait for you to keep talking, and you clam up."

"Talk, then."

"Nice to see you're back to normal," she retorted. "I thought you were being a little too nice in New York. This feels more like the Shawn I know."

He glared at her briefly before returning his gaze to the road. He clamped his lips together, and the silence grew.

Finally, he spoke, his voice carefully controlled.

"I don't want you to think I'm playing a game. I'm not. But Beth, I'm tapped out. I can't ride this kind of emotional roller coaster forever. And it's not like I had a plan to wait for Gunnar to flame out. You made your choice, I respected your choice. But this is a whole new situation now. I want to help, but

I'm trying to help without you thinking I have some kind of ulterior motive."

"But I thought you loved me," she protested. "What changed between last night and today?"

Silence. Then Shawn heaved a sigh.

"Look," he said. "I love you. I will always love you. We're always going to be connected—somehow. It doesn't matter where you are and who you're with. But you need to get through this. On your own. I think I understood that last night. Finally. You convinced me. And nothing has changed about that today, never mind what Gunnar said or did. So I'm trying to help. And I'm trying to tell you what I think is best. Which is for you to hang out at my house for a while. Figure out what you want to do. You shouldn't worry that I'm trying to get you to go back on your decision from last night. It's not like that. But if I'm not exactly friendly—you can't blame me. This is going to be hard. But I'm not going to hassle you to be with me. And that's all there is to it."

Right up until the last minute, he had begged her to stay. Right up until the minute he'd dropped her off at her house. She had his heart, she knew, but Gunnar was still in their way, even invisibly. Not only did she need to finally decide on Greenleigh, but she needed to resolve things with Gunnar before she could settle anything with Shawn.

Things were not so bad, she knew. She was smart. She was a lawyer. She had—temporarily—rid herself of the house as an albatross about her neck. She wasn't broke anymore. Shawn loved her. And now she had to deal with Gunnar. He had disappeared, but if she could just find him, even if it meant hunting him down in Seattle, she could clear this whole thing up.

For a change, she wasn't the pathetic one who needed his clarity and purpose. He was the one who needed her to set him straight.

She could do this. And then...maybe Shawn would still be there for her.

She was so tired. Elisabeth turned to look out the window at the gray, cold New England landscape. Massachusetts in November was butt-ugly. No leaves on the trees. Ponds slushy but not frozen. Yellow tufts of grass.

She leaned back in her seat and closed her eyes. It was home. It was what she knew.

37

"You know," Sam said conversationally. "I like her."

Shawn nodded. "Yeah." He knew where this was headed, and preferred not to engage. It was Saturday afternoon, and he was driving Sam out to one of the malls, where he was going to undergo the grueling annual ritual of Thanksgiving weekend holiday shopping. Sam refused to participate in any Black Friday mania, but he did prefer to get his purchasing over with before the holiday season hit in full force. This was a family tradition dating back decades. Shawn's mother had always decorated the interior and exterior of the house throughout the month of December, and getting the shopping out of the way early made it easier for her to indulge in what she regarded as the truly fun part of Christmas.

When his dad had come downstairs and said that he was headed out shopping, Shawn had felt his stomach drop. He usually came home to spend a few days with his father at Christmas, but the pain of the undecorated house was something he could quickly shed if it only lasted a few days. This year, he would have to face an entire season of missing his mother and the festivity of the season, unable to anesthetize himself with work, champagne, and the craziness of December in New York City, not to mention female company at every glitzy, drunken office party, and afterwards.

Without his usual bag of tricks, it was going to hurt. And what was more, that he even recognized that they were ruses was a painful dose of reality.

"Burnham," Sam mused. "Funny, I didn't know them at all. Thought I knew everyone, but I suppose Greenleigh's a little too big for that."

Shawn shrugged, not answering. As he pulled into the mall parking lot, he tried not to shudder with distaste. It was crowded. People's expressions were not cheerful. If anything, they looked harried and stressed as they rushed past. Twice, Shawn had to stop in order to avoid a collision with a shopper who walked slowly while gazing at his phone. It was clear that people weren't here by choice, and that they were also trying to anesthetize themselves from whatever unpleasant reality they faced.

He rolled to a stop before the big box store at one end of the complex. "Listen, Dad. I don't want you to walk through this entire place from end to end. I'm dropping you off at one end, but don't get crazy thoughts about trying to do it all at one go. I'll bring you again if you want. And don't backtrack! If you missed a store, leave it till next time."

"You're such a nag," Sam grumbled. "I'm the parent here. And I don't nag. Maybe I should."

"I don't want you to drop dead," Shawn said. "It would ruin my week."

"Ha," Sam said. He opened his door, saying over his shoulder, "I didn't nag you about Beth. Maybe I should have. Life's too short."

"Wait, what? What do you mean?" Shawn demanded.

"You heard me. Life's too short."

"Yeah, well, tell her that. She's the problem, not me."

"I did."

"What?" Jeez. When had his dad spoken to Beth?

"You heard me. I'll be done in a couple hours."

The door slammed, leaving Shawn with his mouth hanging open as his dad strolled away. He saw him raising one hand as he apparently recognized someone in the distance. Hmm, it was a woman? Who was she? Wait, was this a plan? A date, even?

He watched as his dad walked up to an attractive older woman in jeans. They greeted one another cheerfully and proceeded into the mall, chatting.

Wow. He'd somehow missed this detail. Dad hadn't mentioned having company at the mall. Shawn sighed. You just never knew with him.

He was tired. He was tired and he was over it. Not over Beth, just over all of this mess. If she'd agree to marry him, he'd do it tomorrow. Okay, wait, tomorrow was Sunday. Monday, then. Whenever. Just—he wasn't going to think about this anymore. He was there for her and he would wait for her, but he was worn out trying to fight the Gunnar/not-Gunnar, Seattle/Greenleigh battle. He didn't want to do this anymore. He'd done his best, he'd exorcised the demon of that long-ago elopement, he'd taken them to New York, and he'd even proven himself by delivering her to the airport.

No more. The ball was in her court. He felt as if the past decade had been one long marathon, and he had crossed the finish line, but the officials were arguing whether the race counted because he had taken too long.

He understood far too much now about the callowness of youth, the mistakes that pride and passion could cause, and that silence was like rust, a disease that would eat away at even the strongest foundation. He could see all of his mistakes, as clear as day, and he could see Beth's, too. But there was no real point to seeing the mistakes, because there was no hope of rectifying them. They might have learned things from them, but they couldn't fix them.

The only person who wasn't making mistakes, it seemed, was Gunnar. He'd known what he wanted, and he went for it. He didn't have to live with any regret, even if he'd lost Beth. He hadn't been sly or deceitful. He'd asked for what he wanted, and had shrugged when he didn't get it.

The only thing, Shawn thought, was that he had hurt Beth. That wasn't right. Yes, she'd hurt him also —but he shouldn't have ghosted her like that. It made him look sulky and childish. He should have had a final conversation with her. Beth would have been ready for it.

His phone buzzed, but he paid it no mind because he was driving. He had no particular plans for the day, and he sure as hell wasn't going to go into the office, which is what he would have done back at the firm in New York. Today he could just recover from his ordeal, maybe veg out on the couch in front of the television—no, Beth would be around, damn it. That wouldn't be relaxing at all. Maybe he could take in a movie.

In which case, he shouldn't leave the mall, he thought. The multiplex was next door, and he needed to pick up his dad in a couple of hours, so if he wanted to see a movie, he ought to check the listings before driving in the opposite direction and having to turn around and drive back.

He pulled into a space, and reached into the cup holder next to him for his phone. Before he could look for a movie, however, he noticed that he had a text message from an unknown number. A junk text, probably. He opened up the messaging app in order to delete it but paused when he saw the message.

"Shawn, it's Angela. Sorry to bother you. May I call you?"

Angela Stuart? That was weird. Why would she be trying to reach him? As far as he knew, she was in California with Bob.

Suddenly concerned, he typed, "Sure." He hoped Bob hadn't taken ill or that something hadn't gone wrong during their trip. Given that he was representing Bob during his divorce, he particularly hoped that Angela wasn't calling him behind Bob's back. He would have to tell her that he couldn't talk to her. Awkward.

His phone rang, and he patched the call through

to the car's audio system. He put the phone back in the cupholder.

"Hi Angela."

"Shawn. Thank goodness. I got your number from Bob. I'm sorry to bother you during the holiday weekend."

"Not at all, Angela. Is everything all right? You're still in California? Is Bob there?"

"Bob is here. He gave me your number. And yes, we're still in California."

Phew. Okay, he didn't have to worry that she was going to question him about Bob, then.

"Shawn, I had to call. Bob and I have been talking. Talking a lot, during this trip. I wanted to thank you for helping him—helping us, rather. Your dad is a good friend of his, and I know you must have felt like you had to represent him. Greenleigh is such a small town."

Shawn stretched out his legs and adjusted his seat to lean back a little. This call might take time, but what the heck. Definitely not the kind of client call he used to get in New York! This was far more enjoyable, for sure.

"Yeah, Greenleigh is small," he agreed. "I hope you're working things out."

"Well—I'm glad I came. I think things will be a lot better going forward." She sounded embarrassed, then hastened on. "Actually, I'm not calling to talk about us. We're in a good place, and we'll figure this thing out. But this is actually about Beth."

Uh-oh. Here it comes. Shawn almost groaned. No, he thought. He wanted to stop thinking about all of that. What could he say to make this call less unpleasant, he wondered.

But before he could reply, Angela continued. "You know my daughter is here in California. In school. That's why Bob decided to bring us out here." There was a pause. Shawn could almost hear her thinking about what to say next. He glanced at his reflection in the rearview mirror and realized that he hadn't shaved that morning, nor the day before. The last time he'd shaved had been Thanksgiving morning. In New York. Right before they'd left.

Man. That was some drive.

He rubbed at his chin. *I look like heck. I should have looked in the mirror this morning.*

He knew he would have cared more if Beth had been around, but he hadn't seen her at all today.

Angela cleared her throat, and he was jolted back to the present. Had she said something, and he hadn't heard her? But before he could make a tentative comment, she said in a rush, "I ran into Beth right before Bob and I left for California. She said she was selling the house and leaving Greenleigh. I was so shocked. And I didn't have a chance to talk to her about it."

Shawn waited. He was not eager to jump into this conversation. Better he hold off until he knew what she was trying to tell him. Or perhaps she was just asking for information. In either case, he was reluctant to join in.

He close his eyes, leaned the seat back a little further still. He was tired of this subject.

"I know that—Bob said that you and Beth knew each other from way back. And I'm worried about her. Do you know when she's supposed to leave for Seattle? I think she said it would be next week."

Shawn heaved a sigh. He rubbed at his face with both hands, and wondered how much Angela could hear over the car's phone connection. He was so tired and so done with all of this, he didn't think he could be tactful if he tried.

"Angela, that's been canceled. She was supposed to leave on Thanksgiving Day, but things didn't work out. She's here in Greenleigh."

"Oh, I'm so glad!" Angela burst out. "I know that house has been causing her problems, and—well, we can help. That's what Bob does, and he's good at it. He would love to help her out. But when she said she was leaving, I didn't know what to say! It was so sudden, and I was in the middle of my own...." Her voice trailed off, then sharpened suddenly. "That boy, Gunnar. What about him?"

"I don't know," Shawn said wearily. "I don't know what happened to him. He might have gone out to Seattle anyway, who knows." He stretched further back in his seat, nearly lying down now. God, he was tired. Maybe he should just nap until his dad was done.

"Without Beth?"

"I don't know. Maybe."

"I didn't recognize him when I saw him," Angela said. "Took me by surprise."

Shawn sat up. "Do you know him?"

"Yes. And actually it was my daughter who re-membered him first. Gunnar is a name you don't hear too often. I was talking to Bob and saying that Beth was leaving town with some guy named Gunnar—a guy I wouldn't have expected her to be with—you know, all those tattoos, he looked like such a rough kid—and then my daughter said she knew him."

"How?" Shawn frowned. Gunnar, from Green-leigh? He hadn't thought much about that fact be-fore. In fact, he hadn't thought to ask Beth where in heck the guy had even come from. He just thought of him as a sketchy dude from the wrong part of town. He didn't know anything about him. But if he was from Greenleigh, he should have known who he was. And Beth should have been able to get in touch with him in order to ask him what was going on with Seattle. Shawn had asked Beth if she was going to demand an explanation for being abandoned at the airport, and she had replied wearily that she didn't know where he was.

How had he managed to disappear like that? Who was he?

He thought backwards in time. He was several years older than Beth, and Gunnar was younger even than she was, so it was unlikely that he would have run into Gunnar at any point during his high school years. And Beth had never mentioned anything like that. She wasn't one to bring up Gunnar's name voluntarily, it was true—but if Gunnar had been someone she'd known for years, he surely would have heard about it.

"So this is what Grace said. He got kicked out of school. She remembered that he was a really talented artist, but never did any schoolwork. And he was always giving the teachers trouble. I never knew his name, but I'd seen him around. I didn't recognize him, I suppose, because he wasn't tattooed in middle school." She chuckled.

Shawn relaxed back in his seat. Oh. Was that all? A Greenleigh high school drop out? Big deal. That was boring. Then he was just another guy from the wrong side of town. Not helpful.

"But she's seen him on social media, connected to other people she knew from Greenleigh. And what she told me was that he ended up at a fancy boarding school outside of Worcester."

Shawn sat up again. "What?"

"Yes, I was shocked as well! Grace says his family is extremely wealthy. His father's family is from Greece, and they own various businesses around New England. And their Greenleigh home is more like a country estate. She said she actually heard about a crazy party he held out there, likely one of the reasons he got kicked out of school. His mother's family goes way back in Greenleigh. His parents met in college. Princeton, Grace said."

"Do you know where his Greenleigh home is?"

"It's lakefront. There aren't too many grand old lakefront homes in Greenleigh. It would be easy to find if you had a mind to look for it. But Shawn, I just want to know that Beth is all right."

"She's fine. She's at my house, actually."

"Oh?" Angela's voice rose. She sounded surprised.

"Yeah. Her plans to go to Seattle fell through. And she isn't sure if she'll stick to the plan to sell the house." At this point, Shawn was lying through his teeth. Beth hadn't said anything about not selling the house, but he crossed his fingers and told Angela the story he wanted to believe. "She'll stay with us until she knows what she wants to do. She could use a vacation from work, too. But listen, is it all right if I tell her that Bob can help her to figure out the house?"

"Of course! Please do! I don't want her to leave Greenleigh, but I understand if she needs to. I just don't want her to be hasty and to make rash decisions. We're here to help. She's helped so many people, it's sad that she didn't turn to us for help herself."

"Thanks for calling, Angela. You've already helped a lot." Shawn was eager to get off the phone. He glanced at the dashboard clock and calculated. He had at least two hours, maybe three, before his dad would want to be picked up. Enough time to try to figure this thing out.

"I'm so glad I decided to call. Bob was a little worried that maybe I was interfering in something that wasn't our business. But I want to make sure Beth is happy. Please tell her that we're going to help her figure out the house situation, just as soon as we get back. We want to do this with her." Angela's voice became thick with emotion. "We owe it to her."

Shawn said that he would, and she hung up. He picked up his phone. He didn't go onto social media very often because he didn't like being reminded of what his New York life had been like. More than once he had been astonished to discover a two- or three-year-old photo of himself in a tuxedo, holding a glass of champagne, a glamorous socialite on his arm. But now he opened up the apps and began to search.

He was going to find Gunnar.

38

Elisabeth was sitting on the couch watching television when Shawn walked into the room. He'd been avoiding her, and she'd been fine with that. She loved his dad and didn't mind his clumsy attempts at conversation, but she wasn't quite ready for more.

Thanksgiving dinner had been spent with a crew of Sam's friends, none of whom knew her all that well, and the average age of the crowd had been about seventy-five, so she'd felt entirely comfortable helping out in the kitchen with a bunch of ladies who rivaled Mrs. Miller in caustic wit and blunt humor. She disliked football and hadn't joined the loud party around the large-screen television in the family room, but had been content to stay in the background, eating pie and listening quietly to conversation about grandchildren. When they'd returned to the Waterstone home late that evening, they were all tired, and went directly to bed.

On Friday, it had been cold and sleeting, so she'd sat next to the fireplace reading a book. Shawn had gone out somewhere, and Sam was banging around in the cellar, working on some project or other. She'd kept her phone switched off and in her purse, so she wasn't tempted to look at it. She knew Gunnar wouldn't be trying to reach her anyway. When he was done with something, or someone, he was done.

On Saturday, she'd awoken to find the house empty. She'd made some toast and coffee, then sat in the kitchen flipping through a woodworking magazine. At some point, she'd been daydreaming, staring into space, before suddenly wondering where the dog had gone. For a weird moment, she didn't know what year it was, before remembering that the dog in question must have died a long, long time ago.

"This house needs a dog," she thought. They had a somewhat unfriendly cat who occasionally made an appearance and didn't seem to want affection. But of course they didn't have a dog. Shawn hadn't lived in this house for years, and Sam was still at the factory at all hours. It had been Shawn's mother who'd been the dog's friend. Misty? Mickey? She couldn't remember its name.

Unsettled, she went into the living room to switch on the television, hoping that the noise would keep her grounded in the present day. She didn't enjoy the sense that she had lost track of time. Would she return to Greenleigh to find her angry mother waiting to yell at her? Would she have to relive that moment when she'd heard her father had been killed in that car accident? When she saw Shawn approach, she was surprised that she felt so relieved, and patted the sofa next to her.

"Hi," she said. "I'm such a slug. Where have you been?"

"Out," he said. His expression was odd, between curious and distressed, as if he had something terrible to tell her and wasn't sure if he should. She reflected for about the millionth time that she could always see Shawn's emotions on his face.

"What's wrong?" she said. "Don't tell me I've screwed up something else. I can't believe I've made more messes with my life when I haven't left this house in two days." She tried to laugh.

"No, no," he said. He sat down next to her, but did not meet her gaze. He was staring blankly at the television, where cooking shows were running nonstop. She reached for the remote.

"I'll turn it off," she said.

Shawn didn't reply, but sat motionless while she clicked off the set.

"I was wondering what I should do with myself," Elisabeth began, but Shawn interrupted her.

"I'd like to take you somewhere."

"Oh? Like—on a date?" She tried to keep her tone light, funny, but knew she wasn't succeeding.

"Not really."

"What, then?"

"On a drive."

"A drive? All right. But why?"

"It's hard to explain. It's better if you just see for yourself."

Elisabeth shrugged, then nodded. "Okay."

They retrieved their coats and headed out to the car.

The Waterstone home was on the edge of Greenleigh, nearly in the next town, but close to the Mountain View Wool operations headquarters. It was convenient to the factory, but pretty much nothing and nowhere else. Elisabeth, who had never owned a car, had gotten a driver's license once upon a time, but was skittish about her driving and was also skittish about Shawn's driving. Today, the roads were wet and glazed with a layer of wet leaves coated with last night's ice. It was November at its finest, brown and drab, and the thinly traveled roads on the way out of town had a thin coating of slush.

"Is it all right if I ask where we're going?"

"You can ask, but I'm not sure how to answer. I don't exactly know."

"What is that supposed to mean? I thought you wanted to—" Elisabeth gazed out the passenger-side window, but did not recognize the area. They were in Greenleigh, but had taken a sharp turn to the west. "At this rate, we'll end up in Albany. Isn't this due west?"

Shawn slowed the car as he picked up his phone from the cupholder to check on directions, but Elisabeth protested, so he put the phone back.

"Okay, I won't look at my phone, but I only have a general idea of where this place is. I guess I'll just wing it." They were driving round a bend, the narrow road not quite comfortable enough for two cars speeding in opposite directions. Fortunately, there was no traffic.

"It's so beautiful out here," Elisabeth said. "I can't believe this is still Greenleigh."

"It's barely Greenleigh," Shawn agreed. "Not many people I know live out this way. There's that big lake, or pond, or whatever it is. It's mostly vacationers, people from the city, out here for swimming in the summer and skiing in the winter."

"Kind of weird. But just look at those houses on the point!" Elisabeth exclaimed. "They're so grand! Have I been here before?"

"Maybe not. I've been out here once or twice." They pulled off the road at what appeared to be a lookout point or a rest stop. There were no facilities, but there were a couple of picnic tables and a wooded view with a gray, gloomy lake beyond.

"Damn it, I have no signal," Shawn muttered. "We'll just have to keep moving."

"Can you tell me where we're going yet?"

"I'm not sure I know how to get there," Shawn admitted. "It's that lake, it's kind of in my way. I'll know when I get there, if I get there."

For a few minutes, they drove quietly, Shawn slowing down to peer at the mailboxes on the side of the road. Finally, he turned down a road that was nearly hidden from view, no sign of habitation but a mailbox camouflaged into the woodland background. It was an unpaved dirt track, heading sharply down toward the lake shore, down and down and down with two precarious hairpin turns. Shawn maneuvered the car slowly as Elisabeth sat with white knuckles braced against her seat, until the woods parted to reveal a spectacular turn-of-the-century mansion sitting grandly at the top of a wide expanse of lawn, turrets soaring into the air. An old-fashioned boathouse sat next to a sweep of sandy beach below.

"Wow," Elisabeth breathed. Shawn pulled the car into a gravel lot. They were still a considerable distance away from the main entrance of the house, but they could see that the house was closed up for the winter.

Shawn put the car into park and sighed. "There. I didn't know if I could figure this out. But here we are. Looks like no one is home."

"Do you know the owner?" Elisabeth asked. "Are we here to visit someone? I'm still confused. This almost feels like a state park, or a museum. But it's obviously closed."

Shawn paused. Then he turned to Elisabeth. "Beth. This is where Gunnar lives."

"Gunnar?" For a moment, she was speechless. She turned swiftly to look at the house. It was brown, shingled, and featured several brick and stone towers, prominent gables, and a wraparound porch. Tennis courts and formal gardens were visible in the distance. All told, the mansion and gardens occupied perhaps ten acres, not including the wooded hill they had just descended in the car.

"A bit Gilded Age, methinks," Shawn said, trying to joke, but Elisabeth's stricken expression prevented him from continuing.

"Is this still Greenleigh?" Elisabeth asked.

"Barely," Shawn said. "But yeah. If you lived here, you would go to school in Greenleigh. Unless, of course, your parents sent you to a posh prep school. Like the one Gunnar went to."

"He said he was kicked out of school. He hated school."

"Actually he was kicked out of Greenleigh public school. He did graduate from school—barely—but it was a preppy boarding school in Worcester. The kind of school where ninety-nine per cent of all the graduates go to a fancy college. He was the one per cent."

He let her take in the view in silence. Finally, she turned to him.

"How did you find out?"

"Completely by accident." He told her about Angela's call.

She turned again to look at the house. "He didn't lie, exactly," she said, as if to herself. "It kind of makes sense."

"I'm sure at a basic level, he 'got' you, Beth. He understood exactly where you were coming from. And he thought he knew what you needed. I think the problem is that he fell in love with you. And you weren't convinced that anyone could love you. Even me."

"But my family hasn't got this kind of money."

"Yes, he knew that. But it isn't about money. It's about ties. Ties that bind. I'm sure Gunnar has some stories about that. He had some kind of noose around his neck, and he was trying to break free." He hesitated, then added quietly, "It's subjective, you know. Whether a noose is a noose or just a tie that binds."

For a silent moment, Elisabeth let the thought roll about in her mind. Shawn had ties, not nooses. She had nooses, not ties. It was all a matter of perspective.

"Did you try to find him?" she asked. "Do you know where he is?"

Shawn shook his head. "No. This is where I bow out. I needed to tell you what I knew, what I found out by accident. But what you do with this is up to you."

"I need to see him," she said. "I want to tell him that I was going to take that flight. I didn't break my promise, and I was ready to join him. And that now that I know what he was trying to escape, I'm pissed, but I understand."

"How are you going to do that?"

Elisabeth took one last, long look at the house and its grounds beyond. "I'll ask Gina. She'll know where to find him." She turned back to Shawn. "Thank you for doing this."

"Yeah." Shawn put his hand on the gear shift to put the car into reverse, but Elisabeth stopped him.

"I've had time to think," she said.

Shawn took his hand off the gear shift. He turned to her, his face grim.

"Don't look like that," she begged.

"I can't help how I look. I can't help how I feel."

"You've changed, Shawn."

"Have I?"

"Yes. When I first went in to Lawson & Lawson, I think you thought it was up to you whether we ever re-started anything. I think all the way up to that night in New York—you thought it was up to you."

"Well, that was stupid," Shawn said shortly.

"No—it was just the old way that you used to love me," Elisabeth said gently. "You took care of me. You wanted to help me to fix everything that was making me miserable in my life. And I want to thank you for that. But I don't want that kind of help anymore. I'm a grownup, and I can handle my life. Maybe badly, maybe stupidly—but I can do this. Gunnar told me I could do it, and he was right."

"You're welcome. I think."

"New York was a good idea," Elisabeth said. "It was like we rewound everything back to the beginning. That was the plan, wasn't it."

"That was the plan," Shawn echoed. "But it didn't work."

"It worked, Shawn. It worked. Because even if I had run away with you all those years ago, we don't know that I could have stuck it out. You had a difficult job. My mother ended up getting really sick. So many things happened. I wanted to keep going to school. Maybe I wouldn't have been able to survive in New York. Maybe we would have broken up then anyway. When we were in New York this time, I realized how hard it is to leave Greenleigh, and how tough it would have been to cope with New York when I was younger." She reached for his hand and grasped it tightly.

"Maybe," Shawn muttered. He turned to look at her now. "Beth, I just can't take any more uncertainty."

"Life is full of uncertainty, though." Elisabeth leaned over to put her arms around him. For a moment, he seemed resistant, before yielding to her embrace. She lifted her face to kiss him, a long, slow kiss.

"I want us to get to know each other again," she said at last. "I know I'm not the girl you used to know. I don't want to disappoint you. But I love you —you're a part of my life. And I want to be with you. All I ask is that you love me where I am today. Not the person I used to be, but the person I am, and the person I want to be."

"You're so complicated, Beth," Shawn said. "Can't you just tell me we'll be together forever? Can't you take a risk on us? Nothing's guaranteed in life anyway." He lifted her right hand in his left, squeezing it, and Elisabeth felt the pressure of the big opal stone against her finger.

"I don't know if we'll be together forever," she

said honestly. "My parents were together until the end, and I wouldn't say that was the best thing for them. And look at Angela and Bob. Those are two people who should be together, but their love was on a razor's edge for awhile."

"I will never stop loving you, Elisabeth Burnham." Shawn leaned in to kiss her once more. "Even if you need to be painfully honest and ridiculously complicated, I'll just live with my delusions. I like my delusions. They involve you loving me forever, in whatever style you want."

"Then here's what I want. I want to go back to my house. I want to draw up a plan to make it a house worth living in, or a house worth selling to a family who will do it justice—either way, I don't want it to just fall down around me. And I want to restart my legal career so that it's a sustainable career, not a part-time charity project."

"That's all very doable," Shawn said. "Will you let me help?"

"Maybe. Let's see how much I can get done on my own. My first task, though, is to find Gunnar."

Shawn broke away from her embrace and grimaced. "His name always comes up, doesn't it."

"I owe it to him, Shawn. He was good to me at a really bad time. And needs some tough love right now. I need to find him."

Shawn put the car into reverse and turned it

around in the driveway. As they made their way back up the steeply wooded drive, Elisabeth turned around, catching glimpses of the turreted mansion through the trees. That house was Gunnar's noose, just as the Church Street house was her own. She couldn't solve Gunnar's problems, whatever they were, but she sure as hell could make a start on solving her own.

39

"Are you going to be all right?

"You've asked me that three times. Yes. I am fine. Thank you for driving me. I've made you late." Elisabeth stepped out of the car. It was a brilliantly sunny day, despite the dead brown leaves blowing about on the sidewalk and the yellowed tufts of grass on Mrs. Miller's bare lawn. She walked around to the trunk, where Shawn was hauling out her suitcases.

"I'll carry them up the stairs for you."

"Thanks. Be careful, the steps look icy. Although it actually looks like someone has been taking care of them." Elisabeth was chagrined. She hadn't thought to mention her departure to the boys down the street who normally took care of her snow removal. That was pretty terrible of her, she knew.

Well, there was time enough to fix everything that was broken about her life. Lots and lots of time. One thing at a time.

She struggled with the key in the door for a moment, then managed to engage it with the old trick of lifting the door with all of her might so that the latch glided smoothly. The door swung open, and she entered the house, looking about herself as if for the first time.

She paused. "I feel like I've never really seen this place before," she said over her shoulder to Shawn.

The storm door banged shut behind him. She heard him put the bags down, then pull the front door closed.

"This damned doorknob," he said. "It was broken twenty years ago. Why didn't you ever fix this thing? It wouldn't have been difficult."

"Gunnar fixed a bunch of things around here," Elisabeth said. "He said the same thing, that there were so many little things wrong that didn't have to be. I think I was just angry. I went years just willing this place to fall down around me. And then every time something finally broke down for good, I could point a finger of blame. At the stupid house. But it wasn't the house, really. It was me."

"That's a bit harsh," Shawn said. He looked around. "Are you sure you even want to live here? It's too big for one person. This house is meant for a family."

Elisabeth turned around in time to see him realize his mistake, and to see him duck his head in embarrassment. She smiled, putting her arms around him, slipping her hands into the open front of his long wool coat, under his suit jacket, feeling his warmth through his shirt. She leaned her head against his chest, closed her eyes.

"You're right," she said. "And if I finally let it go, I want it to be something I know will make a family happy. It needs TLC."

They stood quietly for a moment before he pulled back.

"I'm really late," he muttered. "You're okay?"

"Yes. I'm more than okay. I'm great. I have a lot of work ahead of me, but it's good work."

"Promise you'll call me if you need something."

"I promise I'll call you if I need something," Elisabeth repeated. She smiled up at him, tiptoed to receive his kiss. It was longer than she had anticipated, and for a moment, her grasp around him tightened before she reluctantly stepped back out of his warmth.

"Bob is coming over this week. He'll help me to make a plan."

"You know, Beth—" Shawn had been turning to leave, but he paused. He looked back at her, then around the front hall, at the kitchen behind her. "You know," he said again. "We could live here."

"Oh? What happened to New York?" Elisabeth teased. "I kind of liked that restaurant."

Shawn laughed. "Yeah. I know. I like that restaurant, too. But I didn't like who I was in New York. I would have left Greenleigh for you. But I feel like Greenleigh is maybe a kind of work in progress. Like this house. And if you can work on this house, I can work on my relationship to this town. Maybe one day we'll leave, I don't know. But at least it won't be with unfinished business."

"I honestly don't know if I can work on this house," Elisabeth said, "because it's going to suck while I'm working on it. You know?"

"Yeah. I do know."

"I'll see how much I can stand it. But at least I'll have a plan." She gave him a gentle shove in the direction of the door. "Okay, now you're *really* late."

As the sound of the car faded gently into the distance, Elisabeth went into the kitchen, where she spotted the two cold cups of cappuccino on the table. Gunnar's morning gift to her on the day of their departure. She felt a momentary pang of sadness before she resolutely picked them up and dumped them out into the sink.

She surveyed the kitchen dispassionately. All of the old pots and pans, her mother's worn-out utensils from the seventies, the ancient coffeemaker—it was all gone. It had all been swept up into a box and carted away, she hardly knew where. At the time she hadn't cared, she'd been so desperate to flee. But now that she was back, she realized with a painful ache in her chest that she missed home. Not the home of her mother's angry resentment and cold nights when the boiler had gone on the blink, but the home that smelled like old wood and rag rugs and brewing coffee. When she wasn't worried about money, it was a solid, reassuring roof over her head.

She hung up her coat, dragged her suitcases upstairs, and set about putting the house to rights. There were still towels and linens in a box, and she managed to locate the family china set. She decided with ruthless determination that she would no longer save anything for a rainy day, and there would be no "good china" in her house. Anything fit for use would be used. Anything not fit for use would be dumped.

Elisabeth was unpacking the dishes, wiping the dust off the individual pieces and stashing them in the dining room cabinet, when she heard her phone go off. Her heart began to hammer in her chest.

The number was unfamiliar, but she knew who it was.

"Gina."

"Yeah."

"Where is he?"

"He's here."

Elisabeth sat down. Her head swam. Head rush —she'd stood up too fast.

"I'm coming over," she managed to say.

"He says he's leaving."

"Don't let him leave," Elisabeth said, rising. "I need to see him."

She heard a low murmur in the background, accompanied by the clang of a spoon in a cup.

"All right," Gina said finally. "But you have to hurry."

When Elisabeth burst into the coffee shop, she saw Gunnar at a corner table, his coffee cup empty. He was rising, but as his eyes met hers, he sat down again. His gaze was expressionless. She didn't know if she'd ever seen him look that way before, with no emotion, no humor, no feeling of any kind on his face. He wore his familiar old leather jacket and white tee shirt and a pair of worn jeans. Nothing seemed to have changed, except for his expression.

Well, why would anything have changed, she thought. *It's been less than a week. Nothing has changed—although it feels like everything has changed.*

"Hey," Elisabeth said. She gestured at Gina, who had not moved from her perch behind the register. "Can I get a coffee, Gina? Thanks. Gunnar. You jerk." She sat down across from him.

"Gina said you were looking for me."

"You knew I was looking for you. I texted you. A million times. Actually, here." Elisabeth took the phone out of her pocket and pushed it across the table. "I don't want this. It's a useless device if you won't even answer my texts."

Gunnar picked it up, turned it over in his hand once, then slid it across the table again. He looked at her. His eyes were shadowed.

"Sorry about that," he said. "And I don't want it. Keep it."

"Sorry? What the hell do you mean by sorry?" Elisabeth took a deep breath. She counted to ten. She had promised herself that she wouldn't get angry. It was over, the whole episode was over. There was no point to getting upset, and she didn't want Gunnar to take off. She wouldn't be able to button-hole him again, she knew.

To distract herself, she took the phone and put it in her pocket again.

"I just mean sorry. Nothing else."

Elisabeth finished counting to ten, and wondered if she should make it twenty. Gina came over to slam her mug of coffee on the table and stalked off. She reappeared with a cloth, wiped up the spillage, and marched away again, glaring into the distance.

Gunnar started to slide the sugar across the

table to her but Elisabeth stopped him. "Black is fine."

"Since when?"

"Since now. Since I don't have a spoon. Since I'm not here for the cup of coffee. Gunnar, you know I went to the airport? I was getting on that plane. I was ready to leave. And then you cancelled everything without telling me."

Gunnar looked at her now. He tilted his head in that old familiar habit, a gleam in his eyes. He nodded. "Keep going."

"What do you mean, keep going? There's nothing else to say!" Elisabeth had been raising her cup to her lips but at this she put it down again. "I told you I would be ready for the car at ten. I was ready at ten. And yes, I was with Shawn the night before. And it wasn't your place to judge me for it. If I was screwing up, then I was screwing up. But it was my decision."

"You don't love him."

Elisabeth flinched. "Gunnar. That's just the biggest crock of shit. You know I do. That's the whole problem. I do love him, and that's why you were so angry. You knew it all along. I kept turning you down and you wouldn't let it go."

Gunnar's gaze hardened. "Then why were you leaving town with me?" he demanded. "If you love that guy, then why aren't you staying here to try to make it work? Why are you selling your house? Why are you leaving Greenleigh, then?"

"You're right," Elisabeth said. "You're absolutely right. I should have stayed and I should have fought. But remember—remember when I asked you why you were here?"

For a moment, Gunnar was caught off guard. He looked confused, his black flop of hair falling over his brow and hanging half over his eyes. Elisabeth fought the temptation to brush it away.

"No," he said slowly. "No, I don't remember you asking me anything like that."

"It was back when we first met. We were right here, at Pierre's. I asked you what you were doing here in Greenleigh, why you had left Worcester. You said that you were telling everyone goodbye before heading out west." Elisabeth leaned forward. "You lied to me. You never told me who you were—that you were a poor little rich boy. That house out by the lake—you never told me what kind of family you came from. You never told me what it was you were trying to ditch here in Greenleigh. You made it sound like you were some punk from the wrong side of town. You—"

"All right then," Gunnar snapped. "So I didn't exactly tell you my entire life story. Big fucking deal. It was none of your business anyway. I had my reasons."

"You kept saying I was such a liar!" Elisabeth cried. "You told me to stop lying! And you were right, I was a liar. But so were you! I trusted you, Gunnar. I trusted you! You really let me down!"

"So what happened in New York, then?" Gunnar said, his tone accusing. "Were you just saying goodbye to Shawn? Is that what that was? I felt like a fucking jerk, coming over to your place and finding you gone. I totally assumed that you'd stood me up. You were such a liar whenever it came to that guy. Why are you surprised that I assumed you had lied to me?"

"What happened with Shawn and me was none of your business, is what it was," Elisabeth said. "Shawn and I were always going to be a thing. You knew that. You were the one who kept telling me that, and you were right. You knew all along. Why didn't you trust me when I said I'd be there?"

For a moment, they sat and glared at each other.

Then Gunnar shrugged. "Okay. I shouldn't have flipped out. I'm sorry. Tell your friend that I'm sorry."

"Christine? Well, you ought to tell her yourself, actually. I'm not going to do your dirty work for you."

"I'm leaving. In fact, I should have left already." Gunnar glanced at the wall clock.

"Leaving for where?"

Gunnar smirked. "Do you really want to know? Wanna come along?"

Elisabeth sat back in her seat as if struck. She crossed her arms in front of her and stared down at her rapidly cooling coffee. She'd had it. She wondered if she could just stand up and leave without saying another word. *Sure I can*, she thought. *What a punk. I am done here.*

She pushed her chair back and began to rise, reaching for her gloves and pulling them on in quick, angry movements.

Gunnar said quickly, "Hey. Hey, Elisabeth. I'm sorry. I'm such an asshole. I don't mean anything by it. Really. I'm just going to Boston. And I'm catching a ride with friends. Don't go. I don't want you to stay mad at me."

After a long pause, Elisabeth sat. She removed her gloves. In the background, Gina clattered about. The door opened and shut, people came, ordered coffee and tea, left. The elderly man at the next table, folded his newspaper, leaned his head back, and closed his eyes. He'd removed a hearing aid from one ear and placed it on the table in front of him.

"I'm sorry," Gunnar said finally. "I was just—"

"—posturing," Elisabeth finished curtly. "You were acting like you knew what you were doing, when you didn't."

Gunnar shrugged, turned his head to gaze out the window.

"Will you at least tell me why you didn't explain about your family? I had this completely wrong idea of who you were. I had no idea you lived in that mansion on the lake. And that you went to a posh boarding school. I thought you were a bum dropout. You made it sound that way."

"What makes you think my family has anything to do with who I am?" Gunnar said bitterly. "They shipped me off to boarding school the minute I became an embarrassment. But they don't identify me. They aren't who I am."

"Yes, you're right," Elisabeth said. "And I'm the last person in the world to judge anyone based on their family. But I thought we were friends. I feel like you were misleading me on purpose."

"I've lived my whole life with people either sucking up to me because of my dad's money or giving me dirty looks because I don't look Yankee enough to suit them. I don't wear flannel shirts and I've got a year-round tan. I try not to talk about my parents if I can help it."

"But I'm different, Gunnar. I'm not like those people."

"Yeah, I know." Gunnar shrugged again. "But I could have bought your house with my allowance. It's disgusting. I hate it. And I just didn't want the money subject to come up between us. Just think, if you had seen my house—it would have been weird. With your house the way it was. And there I was with all this money just overflowing out of my trust fund. Gross." He turned his gaze back to her. "I wanted you to like me for myself."

"I do like you," Elisabeth said. "A lot. And I have a lot to thank you for. I'm just sad that in the end you didn't trust me."

"I have a hard time with that. Trusting people."

"Gunnar, I had no idea why you knew what I had to do and how I had to do it. But now I understand. And I wanted to thank you, because I'm in a much better place now. Even without the trip to Seattle." Elisabeth paused, then added, "I'm kind of sorry about not going to Seattle with you, but I was trying to pretend that we could just be friends, too. And that was pretty dumb of me. I'm sorry."

"You're so slow, Elisabeth." Gunnar shook his head at her in mock dismay.

"I'm slow," Elisabeth agreed.

For a long moment, they smiled at each other across the table.

"I want us to be friends."

"That, my dear, will be difficult." Gunnar rose. "I need to go. My ride will leave without me." He reached out to take her hand, and she rose also. She let him hold her hand.

"Why are you going to Boston?"

"Because that's where my parents are in the winter. They close up the big house in Greenleigh and are in town for the holidays. If I'm not going to be in Seattle for Christmas, I'm going to be in Boston. I will be ingratiating myself to my great aunt Sophia so that she lets me use her house in Greece for a big party in the spring."

Elisabeth laughed. "That sounds like trouble."

"It most definitely will be trouble. But she's very deaf, so I'm hoping she won't understand when the neighbors tell her what I've done."

"Can I visit you in Boston?"

Gunnar laughed. "What? Why would you do that?"

"Because I'm guessing your parents' house in Boston is as crazy beautiful as their house in Greenleigh, and I'd like to see it. And I'd like to meet your friends. I want all the things I missed out on because Seattle didn't happen. I'd even go to Greece."

"Seriously?"

"Totally."

"Okay. You got it. On one condition."

"Oh? What's that?"

Gunnar came around to give her a hug. She let him, thinking that the last time she had felt his arms around her, she had almost made a big mistake. But that was okay. It was human, and Gunnar was nothing if not human.

He pulled away. "You've got to let me do a tattoo for you."

"*What*?" Elisabeth began to shake her head. Gunnar was already moving toward the door. Three young guys in heavy-duty canvas jackets and work boots were hollering through the window at him, gesturing for him to join them. A Jeep idled in a no parking zone in front of the shop.

"Otherwise no deal." He was backing away, laughing. "I think Persephone. And Hades. A big one. Maybe on your ribcage. No one will ever see it there and you can pretend to be a big, bad lawyer who would never think of getting a tattoo. But I'll know it's there. I'll know the truth about who you really are, no matter what people think. That's my condition."

"Okay!" Elisabeth called after him as he pulled the door open. A gust of icy November wind blew in, along with a puff of branches and dead leaves. Gina cursed, and went to grab a broom, which she wielded violently in Gunnar's direction as he fled.

"You got it, Gunnar. I promise!"

40

"You know what," Christine complained. "I am just sick of owning that house. I don't want it anymore. Can I sell it to Bob, do you think? Will he take it?"

"You're crazy," Elisabeth said. They were sitting in the parlor, where Christine was painting her toenails and complaining about the fortune she had just spent in window replacements for her house.

"I didn't know that windows needing *replacing* for God's sake. I mean, windows! Who replaces windows! Windows are holes! Why would you need new ones? I had to replace every single freaking window. I was apparently heating the great outdoors with my brand-new heating system."

"But then you don't have to have storm windows," Elisabeth pointed out. "New windows don't need storm windows. Old windows like mine need storm windows. I know it bites, but now you're all set and you don't have to do the crazy thing where you walk around the house shutting storm windows every November and opening them up in May."

"I hate it," Christine whined. "I'm just so done with this adventure."

"You're exaggerating," Elisabeth said. "You just like complaining. And asking for pity."

Christine opened her eyes wide at this. "You're just mean!" She pouted, and bent over her toes again. The shade of her nail polish was bright pink, as bright as her bright pink sweater, as bright as the ribbon holding back the cascade of fine blonde hair. It was a dramatic contrast to the muted reds and browns of the parlor, but a welcome contrast. Christine's energy and attitude masked something a bit dark, something that Elisabeth had never had the courage to ask about, but perhaps one day she would know her well enough to venture down that road with her. Christine could not be the successful divorce lawyer that she was without a clear perspective on the darker side of human nature, she thought. And what's more, Christine never mentioned any ties to any boyfriends or relationships, either in California or on the East Coast. There had to be something there.

"Just because you're so happy," Christine muttered. She grabbed a magazine from the table and waved it over her toes.

"I am happy," Elisabeth admitted. She looked around at the room and remembered a very different scene just a short time ago—when she had been getting ready to dispose of all of the old Burnham furniture, the Burnham clutter she had grown up with, and she had pushed all of it into a corner, waiting for the auctioneer to come and take it away. There had been boxes of dishes, first-edition books, and silverware piled up on top of each other, as well as boxes of photographs and diaries that she hadn't known what to do with. She remembered sobbing with frustration over the impossibility of it all, and letting Gunnar reassure her that she could let other people sever her relationship with Greenleigh for her. She could let the auctioneer cart away the boxes of antiques. She could let Gunnar's pals with the pickup truck take the boxes of junk to the dump.

It turned out that he was wrong about that. She was responsible for her own relationships. No one could do it for her.

So now there was a Christmas tree in the corner, a cast-iron wood stove in the fireplace (Bob Stuart had complained that the open fireplace let all the heat go up the chimney), and a heavy dose of holiday kitsch on the mantelpiece courtesy of Christine, who apparently came from a household that celebrated elves on shelves and other fine traditions. She had talked Christine into coming with her to the Waterstones one day when Shawn was out of town, and heavily over-decorating everything in sight with pine roping and wreaths. At first, when she had seen Shawn's expression upon returning, she had wondered whether she had unknowingly triggered some terrible memory. His face had gone pale, and he'd dropped his coffee mug on the kitchen floor.

She realized much later that the Waterstone men had not seen a wreath on the front door since Juliana Waterstone's passing. But of course—their mom was the gardener in the family. Of course she would have been the one to decorate the house. And of course Shawn would have fled from any memory of it.

Elisabeth was not completely in the clear. She'd had to mortgage the house in order to afford the repairs it needed. She'd insisted on paying Bob something approaching his cost in order to plan the job, but she'd been horrified when she first saw the bills. That reality had caused her to swallow her pride and humbly ask Shawn to help her set up her legal practice properly. She obviously couldn't continue to clerk for Lawson & Lawson, at least not while Shawn was there, so she needed to think about how she could generate cashflow and pay her bills with something other than temporary legal research work.

But it wasn't clear how long Shawn would be at Lawson & Lawson. Shawn spent more time with his dad and at the factory, and less time actually working on cases. Fortunately, Bob and Angela had reconciled, and did not need his services any longer. To the extent that Shawn appeared to be slowly leaving active law practice behind, he suggested that Elisabeth was the logical candidate to help fill the void at the firm, but it was a relief to know that this was not a noose, either. She wasn't sure she would like working at a blue-chip law firm, but she re-membered that her grandfather, Judge Burnham, had been a star litigator for twenty years before he'd been appointed to the bench. He'd hung out a shingle and started his own firm, much as she had, but he'd eventually merged with a larger firm. It was worth considering.

"Can you believe that you're here?" Christine asked for the fifth time. She had had one too many glasses of the dry sparkling wine that she had brought with her, and she was enjoying the warmth of the wood stove and the view of falling snow outside the window. She wiggled her toes, checking repeatedly to see if the nail polish was dry. "Beth, you almost moved to Seattle! Can you believe it? You'd be couch-surfing right now. And it would be raining, not snowing. It would be wet and gray and you'd be alone."

"Not alone," Elisabeth countered. "I would have been with Gunnar."

"That," Christine pronounced, "would have been a mess."

"Maybe," Elisabeth agreed. "Maybe all of that was a dumb decision. But the thought of being able to just sell the house and get out of Greenleigh was like—I don't know, almost like breathing laughing gas or something. Once I had figured out that I could always sell the house and leave, it was like I was on a high. I felt so powerful. It was such an amazing feeling. I've never felt like that before."

"Are you permanently high now?" Christine asked, holding out the bottle to refill Elisabeth's glass.

"It kind of feels like that," Elisabeth laughed. "Maybe not quite. I'm still underemployed and now I've got a scary mortgage."

"Feels like what?" Shawn had wandered into the room, still in his coat and scarf. Snowflakes were melting on his hair and his shoulders. He leaned down to kiss Elisabeth and dropped his briefcase on the floor behind the couch.

"Aack. You're wet," she complained. But she hung onto his neck as he tried to straighten, and forced him down for another kiss.

"Sorry. But it's snowing outside."

"Yes, I know—you're wet! Are you staying? Or just stopping by?"

"Just stopping by. I have to get home to Dad."

"Your dad isn't home," Christine interjected. She grinned. "He's out on a date. Go get a glass." She pointed at the dish cabinet in the corner of the room, and Shawn obligingly went to fetch a glass.

"What! Again?" he said over his shoulder.

"Yeah, another one. I set up this one. He's quite the ladies' man."

"Who with?"

"That nice lady who does the home mortgages at the bank. I can't remember her name. Your dad walked in just as I was done, so I introduced them."

"You're obsessed," Shawn said, chuckling. "So I don't have to go straight home after all."

"No, but I'm not leaving, sorry. So you guys have to be good. No monkey business. Not until I leave, please."

"Aw, darn," Elisabeth joked. She started to rise from the couch, but Shawn plunked himself down next to her so she sat down again. Christine moved over to make room.

"Remember that meeting with Bob Stuart?" Elisabeth said. "In the front room? That was terrible."

"Terrible? But why?" Christine objected. "I didn't think it was terrible. You were awesome. Shawn basically screwed you out of a client, and you fought back. With me. I'm a great ally." She smiled cheekily.

"I know why," Shawn said, his eyes meeting Elisabeth's. "I took you out to dinner afterward."

"Oh," Christine said, nodding. She smiled at Elisabeth. "Right. I remember. But you had nothing to worry about, Beth. There's no way I could have stolen Shawn away from you."

Shawn kissed the side of Elisabeth's head as she snuggled closer.

For a moment, the only sound was of the crackling fire, the occasional rattling of a storm window, and the clink of glasses. Elisabeth watched the snow swirl about under the streetlamp outside, and wondered where Gunnar was. In Boston, presumably, partying hard and working hard and giving his parents grief. Drawing beautiful tattoo designs.

She held up her right hand, admiring the opal ring on her finger. This, right here, was her connection to Greenleigh. Actions, not words. People, not houses. Love was not a noose.

"I think—I think I'd like to get a tattoo," she found herself saying.

Shawn sat upright. "What?"

Christine burst out laughing. "Oh, my God! Beth! Yes! Me, too! Let's do it!"

Together, they clinked glasses, leaving Shawn bewildered.

SPECIAL OFFER

TO READERS OF COMING HOME TO GREENLEIGH

I hope you enjoyed your time in Greenleigh. I live in a town very similar to Greenleigh, and I tried to draw the setting and characters with all the love that I feel for New England.

I'll be working on more Greenleigh novels, and if you enjoyed this one, please sign up for my weekly newsletter. As a thank-you, I'll send you a deleted scene that almost took this book in an entirely different direction! I think you'll enjoy it!

Sign up for my newsletter here: <u>bonus deleted scene from Greenleigh</u> (www.mayarushingwalker.net/greenleigh-list)

ACKNOWLEDGMENTS

To Lisa Manterfield and Teri Case: this book would not exist without you. It took two and a half years, but it's done. Anything is possible with a little help from your (writer) friends.

To Nora K.: there are always new beginnings.

To Sophie: if you hadn't loved Greenleigh, I wouldn't have stuck it out. Thank you for reminding me that New England weather is a thing.

ABOUT THE AUTHOR

Maya Rushing Walker writes slow-burn, often romantic, literary fiction set in both historical and modern times, with a strong sense of place. She lives and writes in a 1780s farmhouse in northern New England, where she homeschooled four amazing young adults and was a dedicated swim and row mom. In a previous life, she was a U.S. diplomat and a Wall Street banker, and holds a B.S. in international economics from Georgetown and an A.M. in East Asian Studies from Harvard.

Her two books, *The Portrait* and *Coming Home to Greenleigh*, were previously published under her pen name, Cassandra Austen.

f facebook.com/mayarushingwalkerbooks

⊙ instagram.com/mayarushingwalker

a amazon.com/author/mayarushingwalker

ALSO BY MAYA RUSHING WALKER

The Portrait

CPSIA information can be obtained
at www.ICGtesting.com
Printed in the USA
LVHW091229240920
666817LV00007B/695

9 781732 515888